STELES OF THE SKY

TOR BOOKS BY ELIZABETH BEAR

A Companion to Wolves (with Sarah Monette)
The Tempering of Men (with Sarah Monette)
All the Windwracked Stars
By the Mountain Bound
The Sea Thy Mistress
Range of Ghosts
Shattered Pillars
Steles of the Sky

STELES
OF THE
SKY

ELIZABETH BEAR

TOR®

A TOM DOHERTY ASSOCIATES BOOK
NEW YORK

This is a work of fiction. All of the characters, organizations, and events portrayed in this novel are either products of the author's imagination or are used fictitiously.

STELES OF THE SKY

Copyright © 2014 by Elizabeth Bear

All rights reserved.

Map by Ellisa Mitchell

A Tor Book
Published by Tom Doherty Associates, LLC
175 Fifth Avenue
New York, NY 10010

www.tor-forge.com

Tor® is a registered trademark of Tom Doherty Associates, LLC.

Library of Congress Cataloging-in-Publication Data

Bear, Elizabeth.
    Steles of the sky / Elizabeth Bear.—First edition.
        p. cm.
    "A Tom Doherty Associates book."
    ISBN 978-0-7653-2756-7 (hardcover)
    ISBN 978-1-4299-4768-8 (e-book)
    I. Title.
PS3602.E2475S74 2014
813'.6—dc23

                                    2013029676

Tor books may be purchased for educational, business, or promotional use. For information on bulk purchases, please contact Macmillan Corporate and Premium Sales Department at 1-800-221-7945, extension 5442, or write specialmarkets@macmillan.com.

First Edition: April 2014

Printed in the United States of America

0   9   8   7   6   5   4   3   2   1

For Naima Ahmed and Malcolm Ahmed

Kyiv

SHATTERED PILLARS

Asmaracanda

WHITE SEA

UTHMAN
CALIPHATE

Asitaneh

GREAT

Hard Drinker

STEPPES

Cresiyon   Western

Messaline   Ocean

Aezin ↓

STEPPES

KHAGANATE

Qarash

other River

Range of GHOSTS

Qeshqer
(Kashe)

Salt

Red
Stone
River

SKY

Desert

island-in-the-mists

Cold Fire

Tsarepheth

Steles of the

Tsarethi

Rasan
Empire

Song

Rasa

STELES OF THE SKY

1

TEMUR SAT CROSS-LEGGED ON WARM STONE. BROTHER HSIUNG HAD
brought him tea. Contents untasted, the cup cooled in his hands. The
sound of a mountain stream rattling over rocks rose from the bottom
of a gully several *li* below and to his left, but he had lost his immediate
awareness of it.

He was watching his mare chase her colt around the twilit meadow
while the chill of evening settled on his shoulders. Bansh was of the
steppe breed, and her liver-bay coat gathered the dim light and gleamed
like shadowed metal . . . but the colt, Afrit, was the unlucky color called
ghost-sorrel, and he shone through the gloaming like a pale cream
moon.

Beyond them, the shaman-rememberer's mouse-colored mare watched,
dark eyes in a face white from ears to lip giving her an uncanny resem-
blance to a horse whose head was a skull. She stood quietly, a mature
and stolid creature with her ears pricked tip to tip, seeming amused by
the romping of more excitable beasts.

Beyond *her*, strange jungles that had long overgrown the city called
Reason were awakening for the night. Feathery ferns unscrolled from
their stony daytime casements. Toothed birds whose legs were feathered jewel-blue and violet like a second set of wings crept from crevices

and shook the plumage on their long bony whip-tails into bright fans.

Afrit bucked and snorted, shaking the bristle of his mane. His legs—seeming already near as long as his mother's—flashed even paler than his cream-colored body, as if he wore white silk stockings gartered above each knee. Bansh stalked him, stiff-legged, head swaying like a snake's. The colt hopped back nimbly for one less than a day old, whirled, bolted—and tumbled to the ground in a tangle of twig-limbs.

He scrambled up again and stood, rocky on splayed legs, until Bansh ambled over and nosed him carefully from one end to the other. By the time she reached his tail, he'd remembered about the teat, and was busily nursing.

Temur sipped his cold tea. Afrit would have his mother's high-arched nose and good deep nostrils, the fine curve of her neck—even more dramatic with a stallion's muscle on it. He'd have her neat, hard feet. The open questions were whether he'd ever be able to run on air the way his ever-so-slightly supernatural mother did . . . and what his unlucky, impossible color might presage.

Temur did not look up at the footstep behind him. He knew it: the hard boots and swish of trousers of the Wizard Samarkar. He played a game with himself, imagining her face without looking at her, and breathed deeply to catch the scent of her hair as she settled beside him. He was disappointed: it smelled of dust, and the desert, more than Samarkar.

But her shoulder was warm against his. She leaned into him, reached over. Plucked the cold bowl of tea from his hands and replaced it with one that breathed lazy coils of steam. He lowered his face to the warmth and inhaled. Moisture coated his dry nose and throat.

In pleasure, he sighed.

She drank down the cold tea and set the bowl aside as he turned to her. As always, her real face was far more complex than the one he held in his memory. He never quite remembered the small scar through an eyebrow or the slight irregularity of her nose.

It made him wonder how well he remembered Edene, who he had not seen since the spring.

The stars were shimmering into existence in the deepening sky, constellations he'd known all his life and yet had recently wondered if he'd ever see again. The Stallion, the Mare. The Oxen and the Yoke that bound them. The Ghost Dog. The Eagle.

It was strange seeing them framed in mountains on all sides.

"Are you hungry?" Samarkar asked at last. "Hsiung is making something. Hrahima is . . . off. Somewhere. And the shaman-rememberer is sleeping."

"I'm waiting for the moons," Temur said. She'd know why; one moon would rise for every son or grandson of the Great Khagan still living.

Temur was checking on his family.

A faint glow limned the ragged outline of the mountains to the east. When Temur glanced west, the stark light made the forested lower slopes there look like the rough undulations of the scholar-stones they carved in Song. Glaciers and smears of early snow glistened at their peaks, broken by the black knife-lines of ridges. His heart squeezed hard and fast, as if a woman caught his eye and smiled.

He looked away as long as he could, though Samarkar reached down and threaded her fingers between his. When he drank the last tea from the bowl he still held in his right hand, it was barely warm.

He set it on the rock beside him and turned to the rising moons.

Once there had been hundreds, a gorgeous procession scattered across the night, light enough to read by. Now a scant double handful drifted one by one into sight. There the Violet Moon, smeared with color like chalk, of Nilufer's son Chatagai. There Temur's own Iron Moon, red and charcoal and yet streaked bright. He waited for the pale circle of Qori Buqa's Ghost Moon, just the color of Afrit's creamy hide—

It did not rise.

Only Samarkar's breathing told him she was in pain. He had clenched his hand through hers, and must be squeezing the blood from her fingers. When he forced his to open, his own knuckles ached. He stroked her palm in apology; briefly she encircled his wrist.

"Who?" she asked.

He shook his head, but said, "Qori Buqa is dead. If the sky can be trusted—"

"What can be trusted, if the sky cannot?"

He tipped his head in acquiescence. "Who killed him?"

"Another rival?" But she did not sound confident. "Some Song general? Does it change anything? We'll still have to fight *someone*."

He was silent a long time before he answered, "It's the way the mill of the world grinds."

She too left the quiet fallow between them for a while before she asked, "Have you dreamed this?"

His dreams—shamanistic, not quite prophetic—dated from before the blood-vow that was the reason she had originally chosen to follow him. It had been her wizard's scientific bent that had brought her along, in order to study the progress of his oath—that, and a loyalty to her sister-in-law Payma, whom they had smuggled out of the Black Palace one step ahead of the guards.

He shrugged. "Not exactly. I dreamed Qori Buqa backward upon a red mare. That could be death. Or it could mean that he goes blind to war."

"*Went* blind," Samarkar corrected. "He's not going anywhere now."

"Except on vulture wings," Temur replied.

When Temur looked up again, a moon he'd never before seen, a moon banded with rippled dark and bright like the temper-water of a blade, rode among its cousins in the old familiar sky.

Namri Songtsan I—by the forbearance of the Six Thousand Emperor of Rasa and Protector of Tsarepheth, Lord of the Steles of the Sky and a dozen other titles, though no one had called him by them yet—opened his toothless red-gummed mouth and squalled. The equally unheralded Dowager Empress Regent of the Rasan Empire, Yangchen-tsa, turned her face away from the work of dusty stonemasons. She pulled her wide silken wrap collar aside and put her son to her breast. But as was his not-infrequent habit, he gnawed the chapped nipple and would not latch. He turned his head aside, then craned the oversized thing back and began to scream like a peacock set live in a fire.

Which of my husband's ancestors come back are you, little monster? Yangchen thought with the blend of affection and exasperation that seemed to her to be all parenthood was made of. *A tyrant, that's for sure.*

She drew a breath—a mistake; it was full of smoke and the first tang of rotting flesh. She wanted to hug Namri to her heart. She wanted to drop him over the side of the building and clap her hands to her ears and scream right back at him.

Instead, she jerked her collar closed and thrust the screaming boy at his closest nurse, then turned back to the thing she had wished she could ignore.

She stood on a hastily constructed platform on the roof of the house of a lesser—but wealthy—noble family, surrounded by such of her husband's royal court and inner circle as had survived. They overlooked the place where the Black Palace of Tsarepheth had stood. The aroma of burnt black powder still hung on the air. The riots of the previous day had sputtered into quiescence, and Yangchen had heeded the advice of the wizards and set up soup lines and first-aid stations where anyone could be fed or seen to, no questions asked. That *might* prevent a resurgence.

Another skinless corpse had been found nailed to a temple door, however. And her agents reported muttering that the smoke billowing from the Cold Fire sometimes took the shape of a malevolent face, pale sky staring through the empty whorls of its eyes.

The wizards said at least one of their agents reported more and more rumors of the Carrion King stalking the cold streets by night. Perhaps Yangchen had that rumor as much as the chill of encroaching winter to thank for the dissolution of the riots, come nightfall.

As for the palace—it had not been destroyed completely. One tower and a portion of the north wall had crumbled, the precisely hewn basalt stones blasted from their place by the force of the explosion. Yangchen could see clearly into several of the chambers and corridors, and she had an exquisite view of the workers below. Both stonemasons and rough laborers toiled—the laborers hauling cracked and collapsed stone, the stonemasons determining which rubble could safely be moved without collapsing the whole pile. The destroyed portion had contained the emperor's apartments and the council chamber.

The limited destruction was why two of her son's nurses were beside her, and her sister-wife Tsechen-tsa, and stooped old Baryan, with his spotted head uncovered because all of his hats were inside the ruined palace. That was why she was flanked by her husband's advisors—

her own advisors now—Gyaltsen-tsa and Munye-tsa, and not the whole of the council. It was also why the sun overhead was wrong and strange, a flat-looking pale yellow thing that seemed too hot and too close.

Yangchen-tsa closed her hands on the splintery wood of the un-lacquered railing. She did not quite trust it to lean against. She'd scrambled up the ladder to watch this process because she felt it was her duty. Because she could not be entirely certain that this, too, was not her fault.

So many things were turning out to be.

There was no one Yangchen could speak to for comfort. Her only peer in the world was Tsechen, who stood beside her tall and impas-sive, with her hair undressed and her hands folded inside the sleeves of the soot-stained robe no one had been able to convince her to ex-change. Yangchen's clothes were fresh because she had been out of the palace when the detonation came, disguised as a commoner to confer with the wizards in their Citadel without her husband's knowledge, and Baryan would not hear of her being seen as the empress regent in those wool and cotton rags.

Across the entire breadth of the city, even the ancient white walls of the Citadel had rattled with the force of the explosion, and she had stood beside Hong-la and his colleagues and watched smoke rise from the place that had been, for six years, her summer home.

Yangchen had had a mad urge, then, to take her son and head north, to keep her peasant garb and raise Namri as a—a calligrapher, an apothecary, a goatherd. Anything but an emperor.

Even as it occurred to her, she knew it for the fantasy of a child deluded by storybooks. Kings did not disguise themselves as noodle-shop proprietors. Empresses—even empresses widowed at the age of nineteen—did not toss everything aside and go running off to make a living by their fancy needlework.

Still, Yangchen was tempted. And she might have done it—except for the abiding horror that this, like so much else, was something she had caused to be done.

She could face the guilt for her own actions, her own ruthlessness. Her father had warned her it would be necessary, when she married both the future Emperor of Rasa and his brother. She could face the deaths—and the subtler wickednesses—that lay against her own choice, her own hand. It was harder to accept the evils she suspected she had been manipulated into facilitating.

It was up to her to do something about that.

She squared her shoulders in the borrowed robe—too long—and turned to Gyaltsen-tsa. He was younger than many of her late husband's advisors, closer to the age of the fugitive once-princess Samarkar. He had kind eyes inside a framework of character wrinkles and had affected fresh flowers woven into his braid. Yesterday's still draggled there, sour and browning, petals transparent with bruises and folds.

"We cannot stay here." Yangchen gestured to the work below. "This is fruitless."

"Dowager," Baryan said from her other side, thus becoming the first to speak her new title. "Your Imperial husband—"

She looked at him, hating how the tightness of her lower lip drew up at the center as she fought tears. Her glare silenced Baryan—or perhaps the silent glare of the strange sky above was answer enough to his protest.

"If my husband were alive," she said, "would the sky have changed? Another God has claimed this land, na-Baryan. Shall we wait for his army to come?"

He looked down. "Your son—"

"Must be protected. He is the Emperor of Rasa now. And he should be in Rasa, under a Rasan sky, where we can make him safe." She turned, away from the shattered tower, toward the southern horizon. They were high enough atop this commandeered house for an unobstructed view down the fertile valley. Yangchen's gesture took in the cradling hands of the mountains, the hills that centuries of cultivation had carved into scalloped terraces, the many-bridged canyon of the river as it plunged from stone to stone, dancing between the walls it had carved for itself. In spring the fields would be a thousand shades from pink to green to gold; now they were russet and umber or silvery-green, fallow under winter cover. *At least we got the harvest in.*

But it wasn't the fields she wanted her advisors to consider. It was the road that followed the course of the river, and the train of riders, walkers, and wagons—some one-wheeled, like giant barrows; some two-wheeled dog-carts; some four-wheeled for heavy hauling—upon it.

"With or without us," Yangchen said, surprised at her own eloquence, "our people are leaving. The question before us is do we let
them face the road alone—or do we go with them to Rasa, perhaps
bring some wizards to protect them from the demonlings, and take the
chance that we can save our empire?"

Baryan struggled for an answer. Yangchen knew he could out-argue
her. She couldn't afford to give him the opportunity. She turned to
Gyaltsen, about to raise her appeal to his more sympathetic face—

A cry from below interrupted. *Not my husband's body,* she prayed, turning back to the rail—even as she prayed that it was. She knew Songtsan was dead, knew it in her bones, knew it by the sky. But was it
better, somehow, to hold a tiny fragment of uncertainty, of half-hope—
or was it better to know unequivocally?

There was a flurry of activity among the ruins. Someone—one of
the master stonemasons—was rushing to the ladder, climbing the wall
of the appropriated house with one hand because a cloth sack swung in
the other. He had his hands upon the rail where Yangchen's hands had a
moment before rested. Stone dust smeared his clothing and lightened his
face. *Strange,* Yangchen thought with a terrible disconnection. *You'd think the
dust of the Black Palace would be dark—*

"Dowager," the stonemason said, dropping his eyes abruptly. "Second-
wife—"

Tsechen stepped forward. The hem of her dirty robes trembled
against her shoes. Her hands knotted before her breast. She opened her
mouth and made no words—just a moan.

"Honored sister-wife," Yangchen said, placing one hand in the crook
of Tsechen's elbow. "Permit me."

The look Tsechen gave her was not comfort but rage, but the anger
seemed to strengthen her. She closed her mouth and did not draw away.

"Honored master mason," Yangchen said. "What have you found?"

He stared at her for a moment longer and then knelt at the edge of
the roof, one knee braced against the platform edge. Yangchen wondered how he did not tumble to his death, but masons must be used to
scaffoldings. He reached into the mouth of the bag, fumbled, and with
unsteady hands jerked it wide.

What he drew forth was the carven crown of Rasa, a spiked filigree
circlet of oil-green olivine and peridot embedded in a matrix of opaque,

crystalline gray iron, just as it had been cut from a piece of skystone on the command of Genmi-chen in the same year the Citadel was founded. Head lowered, he reached through the gaps in the railing and extended it up to Yangchen-tsa.

She took it in her hands. She had never been suffered to touch it before, and was surprised at its coolness and weight. It was smooth, as her fingers played over it, with only the faintest catch of changing texture where the stone and metal met. She turned it in her hands, the incredible delicacy of the filigree suggesting the forms of dragons, phoenixes, the Qooros. More familiar beasts—carp, hounds, serpents, tigers— were layered within, visible beneath the outer layer of pierced and lace-carved stone.

"It's so heavy," she said.

"Madam," said the stonemason. "We have uncovered the treasury."

Munye-tsa gasped. "Six Thousand heard you," he said, laying a subtly restraining hand on na-Baryan. "It is a sign."

LIGHTNING THROTTLED THE COLUMN OF ASH AND SMOKE WRITHING UP THE sky behind the refugee caravan. The Wizard Tsering—awkward astride a mare so weary the beast struggled to raise her head—had paused at the peak of a pass, reined her mount aside, and turned to look back along the snaking column. Groups of Qersnyk nomads and clumps of townsfolk from Tsarepheth trudged up the rise, heads as low as the mare's. The train had spread out across the bottom of the valley; where the path ascended they fell naturally into single file again, winding up a series of switchbacks so steep Tsering-la could have dropped a persimmon on the head of someone below . . . had she a persimmon to spare.

Feathery ash blossoms starred her mare's shoulders like snowflakes. The horse could have passed for one of the Qersnyk fancies with their spotted coats, but these spots smeared and gritted in the mare's sweat when Tsering-la passed her hand across them. She had abandoned trying to brush the ash from the mare, from herself, or from her hat brim, but she still patted the horse's shoulder. She was unclear as to which of them she was trying to reassure.

A vaster billow of smoke rolled out, down the distant flanks of the Cold Fire, to disappear behind the shoulders of nearer mountains. Tsering could imagine she caught the red glow behind it, but it was likely only the lightning. The earth dropped underfoot—suddenly, sickeningly, like missing a stair. Tsering clutched the pommel as the mare snorted and kicked out, too exhausted for more than a half-hearted attempt at panic. Behind and below, most of Tsering's fellow refugees did not even raise their heads.

You could even become used to a volcano—or too tired to care about it anymore. Although the eruption seemed to be worsening as wizards fled the Citadel, their strengths no longer combined to restrain it.

She wondered if this billow of ash, this shaking of the earth, was the one that heralded the failure of those wizards still left behind at the White-and-Scarlet Citadel of Tsarepheth to protect it, the city that shared its name, and the plague victims too weak to be moved—and who would have no hope of surviving away from the brewing vats of Ashra's healing ale. The master of Tsering's order, Yongten-la, and the others who remained behind were risking their lives for the sick—and for the Citadel, with its libraries and laboratories harboring irreplaceable centuries of knowledge.

There was very little those who were *not* wizards could do to protect themselves if the Cold Fire decided to kill them. And as for the wizards . . . Tsering had never found her power. All her theory, all her understanding of the mechanics of how the universe worked, would not avail her if a blast of superheated poisonous gases pushed a wall of ash and stone down on them, if molten glass rained from the sky.

She wondered if even Hong-la could manage to protect anyone, protect himself, in such a case as that.

As if her thoughts had been a summoning—and surely even the master wizard from Song could not hear minds—the tallest walker toiling up the path below raised his head and looked up at her. Even at a distance, the gesture revealed the strong lines of a long-jawed, rectangular face beneath the sloped brim of his hat. It was a peasant's cap, meant to shade the head and shoulders while working under the blazing sun, and it did a remarkable job of shedding ash. Trust Hong-la to recognize the easiest, most elegant solution.

Wait there, he mouthed.

Tsering raised a hand in acknowledgment. Her throat burned with the fumes of sulfur. She soothed her mare again and watched

Hong-la climb. Eventually, it occurred to her that she could dismount and offer the horse water. She was no expert rider, preferring shank's mare—or soul's—to the actual sons of the wind, but she ran her hands down the mare's legs and checked her feet, wondering how she would know if something was wrong and—if she found it—what she could do about it.

Samarkar, with her noble past, would have known how to care for the horse. Or Ashra, who had spent so many years among the Qersnyk. But Samarkar was far away, if she were even alive still, and Ashra...

Ashra was not alive.

Reminded, Tsering touched the saddlebags for reassurance, feeling the resilience of cloth and the weight of stones within. Those objects were the reason why she rode rather than walking. Tsering-la was one of the wizards and shaman-rememberers entrusted with carrying the wards, a cowing responsibility.

As she was placing the mare's last hoof gently on the ground once more, the steady rhythm of trudging feet, clopping hooves, and turning wheels cresting the pass and starting down the other side was broken as carters and walkers hesitated in order to stare. She turned, and found Hong-la beside her—arms folded, chin tucked, standing on air as if it were a solid stone platform. He had levitated himself from his place below more easily than she could have scrambled up the slope.

She bit down on her reflexive envy and turned to him as he stepped forward sedately, his split Song-style boot coming to rest on the stone of her vantage point.

Tsering thought of Hong-la as a sort of human Citadel, a broad-built, bony tower of intellect and impervious strength. It was a shock to see his complexion faded and grayish, the smile and concentration lines beside his eyes furrowed so deep they seemed inflamed. His usually cropped hair, twisted into sweaty spikes by the exertion of the climb, protruded raggedly around the perimeter where his hat rested against his scalp. It seemed grayer, even—but that might be the ash.

"You're another Tse-ten of the Five Eyes," she said, shaking her head in awe.

"The Process of Air wants to lift us," he replied. "Encourage that, discourage the Process of Earth that wishes to hold us close, and one can drift like a feather on the wind."

"If it were as easy as that, it'd be the first trick any wizard learned," she said. "I don't think Master Yongten could manage that."

He harrumphed, and Tsering held out the waterskin. "We could be doing this at the height of summer," she said, by way of apology—though why she felt the need to apologize for eruptions and revolutions was beyond her.

Hong-la took the skin in his long, heavy-boned hand. Like most wizards, his fingers were decorated with a fascinating assortment of scars. He drank water sparingly and sighed. "We wouldn't be racing winter, then."

"Finish it," Tsering said. "There should be water in the next valley."

"If it's not full of ash." He handed her back the skin.

"I'm full of ash. Why should what I'm drinking be any different?" She hung the skin back on the saddle, where it hung forlornly slack. They'd need to filter water that night if they did not find some fresh. One more task to exhaust the too-few wizards among them. Hong-la should by rights be sleeping along one side of a single-wheeled cart by day, but who could rest rattling over these trails? In a cart that could tip down a cliff with one misstep?

She and Hong-la rejoined the column, Tsering leading the mare. The refugee train moved at a dragging pace determined by the Qersnyk carts and oxen. Tsering did not have the energy to chafe at it. Instead, she watched the road before her feet—because looking at the horizon was too exhausting—and lifted her gaze only occasionally to see how far she had come. Beside her, Hong-la toiled uncomplainingly—but he leaned on a twisted stick, something she had never seen him do before. The gnarled wood was smooth-polished, carved to accentuate its natural curves, and glossy beneath the dust and ash. Tsering thought it was Song workmanship, and wondered if he had brought it with him all that way, when he had come to the Citadel to become a Wizard of Tsarepheth.

Another day, she might have asked him. Now it was all she could do to raise a foot and put it before the other.

Just keep walking. It was a philosophy that had gotten her through worse losses—or at least more personal ones—than this.

2

AT THE PALACE IN QARASH, THE TWINS LED A DOZEN MEN INTO HELL. SAA-det did not think she could have done it without Mukhtar ai-Idoj, al-Sepehr of her order and the adoptive father of her twin brother and herself, at her side. She was certain she could not have done it without the strength of her brother Shahruz within her, bearing her up, lending her endurance. Since his death at the hands of the Qersnyk pretender, Re Temur, he had shared her mind—a resurrection made possible by the twin's bond that al-Sepehr's magics had long ago strengthened.

Saadet's belly did not heave merely because of the baby in it.

Only she and al-Sepehr had escaped the compound alive, and that much was plainly evident from the moment they stepped within again, surrounded by a half-dozen armored Qersnyk warriors and a pair of shaman-rememberers with their eyes concealed behind blue-dyed fly fringes. Each of the warriors wore the three horsehair falls of Qori Buqa and carried bows and spears. The pyramid of clean-sucked skulls in the dooryard was evidence enough.

"Blood ghosts," one of the warriors said. He was a tall man, lighter-eyed than most, named Re Esen. His cheeks—fair by Qersnyk standards—peeled across the bones with sun and windburn. His nose, hooked like an eagle's beak, was framed by deep squint lines. He went hatless despite the chill, and his hair, pulled back in a queue, revealed a shining expanse of pate. He glanced at the nearer shaman-rememberer. "Paian?"

Paian lifted sky-colored fringe across the back of his right hand. His eyes peered out under its shade. He pursed his lips and shrugged elaborately.

Under other circumstances, Saadet might have smiled. Now, she bit the back of her hand, sour bile rising.

Weak, sister.

It is the babe, she told Shahruz, not really caring if he believed her. They had done what they had done for the Nameless, and she would not regret it. If her revulsion made her seem more the grieving widow to the Qersnyk, so much the better.

Paian, the shaman-rememberer, laid a hand on her shoulder. She tried to meet his eyes, but he'd let the fringe drop and it defeated her. Its purpose, no doubt: anything that made a priest seem more mysterious increased his power.

"We go on," she said, and led them into the open doors of the palace. She knew some of the men only followed because they would not let a woman show more courage than they.

Now it was Shahruz who held their head high as they moved down the corridors she had so recently—so briefly—lived in, and smelled the thick scent of clotted blood splashed like whitewash on the walls. It did not matter who gave her that appearance of strength; only that the Qersnyk saw her back straight and tall like a pole on which the banner of her body hung. Sticky and puddled, the bloody floor tugged at their shoes with each step. The palace stank as if someone had been butchering lambs.

They found no dead within.

"They were dragged out," Esen said after a glance at Paian. The other men muttered and jostled, turning to put their backs to one another.

"Dragged out and eaten," agreed Shahruz, with Saadet's tongue.

Paian too was fair, and the shape of his nose was a smaller version of Esen's. Saadet recognized their silent understanding of one another, and Esen's choice to speak for both.

They're brothers.

Brother and . . . whatever you call that, you mean, Shahruz answered, the weight of his disdain for the shaman-rememberer like robes soaked with rain.

As you say, my brother.

Because she could not go back, she went forward. Esen stepped before her, or she would have held the vanguard. Still it was she that guided them—to the chamber where the Khagan's war-band had met for the final time.

There was more blood here.

Esen turned to her. "How is it that you and your stepfather alone escaped this?" he asked. "How is it that we find ourselves now under a Rahazeen sky?"

Her blood chilled, but when her voice would have failed Shahruz spoke for her. "My husband"—and surely Saadet was the only one who heard the way Shahruz's distaste stained those words—"told me that he had dreamed that the Scholar-God and the Eternal Sky were in truth one deity."

Esen nodded. Qori Buqa Khagan had not been silent about his dreams. She knew he had consulted the shaman-rememberers as to their meaning, and the Qersnyk were everywhere renowned for the ease with which they adopted foreign customs, and their permissiveness toward foreign gods—so long as the worshipers of those gods rendered appropriate tribute to the Khagan.

Still, the sky made her more nervous than anything. Al-Sepehr could cast it a thousand ways as Qori Buqa's legacy, or Temur's treachery . . . but there would always be those who scratched at whatever gilt he hung on the truth.

As Saadet rested a hand on her belly, Shahruz continued, "I prayed to the Eternal Sky and to the Scholar-God for my life, and the life of my son, and the life of my father. Perhaps I was heard. Perhaps—it is just that I ran, and my father came to protect me."

Esen's gesture dismissed the stones over their heads as a temporary inconvenience. "And the sky?"

Saadet answered before her brother could. Her explanation was better—and she'd been paying more attention to these heathens and their customs, while he shuffled his imaginary feet at her in very real disgust.

"From what my husband told me, this is not the first time my usurper nephew Temur has been associated with blood ghosts. He was seen in Asitaneh, at the court of the caliph there, before that caliph was replaced by a Rahazeen faction. Perhaps the usurpers have allied themselves one with another?" She cupped her gently swelling abdomen. "It is my son—Qori Buqa's son!—who will bring the Eternal Sky back to the steppe."

She held his gaze, steady and calm, and wished she dared raise her veil across her face. So many eyes, and her expressions so naked now.

At last, Esen nodded. "You've spirit," he said. "It won't be enough."

"My son has the mandate of the Eternal Sky," she replied.

He snorted and looked away. "We'll see."

She had stood too long in one place. When they walked on, she had to rock her feet to unstick them from the floor. *I will burn these boots.*

They are good boots. It will be hard to find others that fit as well, and you will need them. You will do no such thing.

She blew the loose hair from her eyes, and swallowed her first three thoughts as unworthy. At last she managed to answer him: . . . *As you say, my brother.*

Tsering walked—or, rather, hobbled; she was not much accustomed to the saddle—around the camp's perimeter, too much of her wary attention on the sun instead of the wards and banners she was laying in place for the night. The sun had vanished behind the mountains, though the sky was still bright, and the clouds to the east had begun to stain the colors of poppy blossoms around the edges. Tsering's eye and belly insisted on reading the light as sunrise rather than sunset, even though she knew better.

Every ten strides, Tsering pulled painfully against the stiffness in her lower back and inner thighs and bent to place a stone marked with Rasan and Qersnyk sigils of protection from the enemies that come in the night. They were prayer-stones, but they were also more than that. Every three stones, she found a place to drape a banner, or—better—to wedge its short stick between rocks so it swung freely in the light, cold autumn breeze.

The air cooled rapidly as the sun fell. She blew warm curls of mist on her fingers where they poked from her felted fingerless mitts. It seemed as if every stone she touched sucked warmth from her body.

The banners were sewn with images of the Guardian Beasts. The pale wind-horse of the soul—the symbol for breath and song—and the blue ice-lion of the mind were prominent among them. Tsering invoked the small gods of place where she knew them, but here they were mostly mysteries to her. The refugees has chosen to camp in a valley protected by a black basalt idol whose feet were ringed by withered offerings of food and parched flowers. A little cluster of refugees had been preparing to feed her further offerings as Tsering began her rounds. Tsering hoped that basalt boded well for propitiating against volcanoes.

The need for these rituals was one of the reasons progress through the mountains came so slowly and at such cost of exhaustion. Each morning, the vanguard could not swing out before dawn, and all the wards of the night before must be collected and stowed, along with whatever goods had been needed for comfort before. And that same vanguard must stop at night more than a hand of the sun's passage across the sky before it met the horizon, to give time to make camp before darkness came.

They were still probably far enough into the Steles of the Sky to be safe from blood ghosts. But Tsering—and Hong-la, and the Qersnyk shaman-rememberers—were more worried about whatever invisible force—spores, or immaterial demons, or what-have-you—came in the night to lay the genesis of demonlings in a sleeper's lungs.

They could not afford infections. The only treatment any of them knew lay behind, in Tsarepheth—if Tsarepheth were standing still.

Tsering sent a guilty glance over her shoulder. Hong-la thought he would feel it if the Citadel fell.

Tsering, with no magic, only knowledge, had no such reassurance that all was well. Or as well as could be expected.

Slowly, the walking and bending was easing the stiffness in her body. Perhaps she should take up one of the moving forms of meditation; she wasn't as young as she had been, and sitting in contemplation left her stiff too—though not so stiff as the horse had. As she neared the outcrop of rock that marked the end of her allotted patrol, Tsering became aware of a sort of layered, carrying drone, busy with harmonics and tonal overlays. It was the chant of a Qersnyk cleric, and as she came around the corner she was glad to see the shaman-rememberer Jurchadai setting a pole from which his last banner snapped. She placed the stones leading up to it, his singing making the soft flesh between her jaw and throat vibrate like the wings of a bee, and straight-ened herself painfully to stand beside him while he leaned on that long stave.

"You're carrying flagpoles?" she asked, in her rudimentary Qersnyk.

Jurchadai frowned at her, but the motion of her hands seemed to lead him to understanding. "They are poles for white-houses," he said in the Rasani he had been learning in his own turn, speaking slowly. "I just borrowed them."

At least, she guessed the word was "borrowed": he used a term in his own language. She also guessed by "houses," he meant the Qersnyk huts of felted wool, which could be put up and pulled down in a matter of minutes by skilled labor, and which they carried with them in their carts.

Like all the Qersnyk shaman-rememberers, Jurchadai was third-sexed. A very few male wizards managed to grow sparse facial hair; Jurchadai had none. He wore his hair braided up into a sort of crown beneath his hat, and his shoulders were slight. At first it had been an effort for Tsering to remember to call this round-arsed person "he." Now she found it odd when she heard another Rasani make the same mistake. And, she thought, it wasn't as if she weren't used to the smooth cheeks of male eunuchs, being a female one herself.

Jurchadai and his colleagues were the ones who had eventually found a successful ward against the demonlings that did not rely on stout stone walls to be effective. He had, in effect, preemptively saved the lives of everyone in the camp tonight. Tsering laid the back of her hand against his shoulder briefly, trusting that he would understand.

They stood just within the protective circle of the stones and ban-ners. He leaned back against the big stone. She put herself beside him, stretching out her thighs and watching the sun go down on the wrong side of the sky. The sky flamed below the edge of the pall of ash, be-hind the teeth of horizon-cutting mountains. Jurchadai sighed.

"It's not my sky either," Tsering said. "You said Temur . . . How did you know?"

His teeth flashed white in the dimming day. He said, "I have it from my brothers. Re Temur has declared himself Khagan."

Temur was the Qersnyk man she had helped to rescue almost on the very steps of blighted Kashe, when she and Samarkar had first discovered the destruction wrought there by blood ghosts. He had later fled—with Samarkar and a Cho-tse tiger warrior—assisting one of the emperor's wives in escaping a plot that would have likely ended in her death. It was only later that Tsering had learned that Temur was her friend Ashra's son, and a grandson of the Great Khagan.

"You have it from your—" She shook her head.

"Shaman," Jurchadai said, touching his breast. "Rememberer." He touched his temple beside the right eye. "What one knows, all brothers know. Re Temur says he is Khagan, and he will raise his banner at Dragon Lake."

"In *Song?*"

"It is Qersnyk. Or was. And none of the Song princelings close by have the resources to defend a claim."

Dragon Lake, that was a name Tsering knew. It was a name everyone knew: Temusan Khagan, the Great Khagan, had kept his summer palace there—a great pagoda in the Song style, red tile and black lacquer and gilt. But the Qersnyk claim on those lands had become a matter of contention since, with Song and Qersnyk armies squabbling fruitlessly over possession.

If Temur felt confident enough to raise his banner at Dragon Lake, he was making a powerful statement about his intentions to claim and reunite the entirety of his grandfather's crumbling empire. Tsering wondered if he had the strength of arms and will to pull it off.

That, and when she had last seen him, he had been headed west, along with Samarkar, Payma, and the Cho-tse. He'd have to cross the entire Qersnyk Steppe to reach the Song borderlands, and the steppe was held by another would-be Khagan, Temur's uncle Qori Buqa. Or had been, until his recent death.

Tsering stretched herself painfully. She'd stood still too long, and stiffened up again. Perhaps Hong-la knew a moving meditation he could teach her. "Won't Qori Buqa's heirs just crush him before he can muster an army there?"

Jurchadai had told her that Qori Buqa was no more. That he had married an Uthman girl and died on the wedding ride. Tsering was starting to understand how it was that he knew these things.

Jurchadai shrugged. His brows drew together in a frown. Only when the lines appeared did Tsering realize how fresh-faced he was. His manner made him seem much older, but even the wind and sun of the steppe under the Eternal Sky had not yet weathered his flesh.

She schooled her hands when they would have crept up to stroke the streak of silver in her braid. She was not an old woman—just a grown one—but for the moment she felt her age on her like armor. She had seen and lost things before now. Jurchadai's youth should not wound her so.

And yet it did, quick and sharp and darting. She took a breath to soothe the pain, and another to speak on.

"Please," she said. "Continue."

"The sun rises in the west over Qarash," the shaman-rememberer said, dropping back into Qersnyk. Tsering was coming to understand it better than she spoke it, at least. "Blood ghosts slew all Qori Buqa's war-band. And the girl has proclaimed herself regent in the name of her unborn son."

Tsering found herself standing upright, pain forgotten, back half a step and almost breaking the ward-circle with her foot before she remembered. "Can she do that?"

Jurchadai's frown deepened. "If she's strong enough. She can do anything. But she may have a hard time keeping Re Temur from crossing the steppe."

The twins slept under the stars that night, in a roofless ruin in Qarash. Or—*slept* might be too kind a word, Saadet thought. Her brother Shahruz slept, or at least he kept his silence. She, nauseated with pregnancy and exhausted for a thousand other reasons too, contented herself by leaning back against the battered old saddle that had served as the throne of Qersnyk emperors for more than twice her lifetime and resting her neck and shoulders on leather that smelled of salt sweat, grassfires, and weapon oil.

But at least the stars she stared at lidlessly were Rahazeen stars.

It was a night without moon. The comforting blue-orange-white

STELES OF THE SKY * 31

strobe of Al-Ghul showed above the western wall of the ruin, where it had just risen, and Saadet shifted her not-yet-completely-awkward body so she could regard it at her ease. Around it, familiar constellations picked out the shape of sacred words across a cold and bottomless sky. Spells were spellings, and spellings spells. When she and her twin were little, before Shahruz's murder had driven them to share Saadet's sacred and inadequate female flesh, both Saadet and her twin had learned to read and name them all in their childhood devotions. When there were no books to pray with, the Scholar-God's benediction could be read across the vault of the heavens and the faithful so redeemed.

Saadet comforted herself for a while by finding the Virtues—*kindness, charity, compassion, fidelity, piety, discretion.* . . . That was as many as had risen above the walls and the horizon. The Virtues made an interlocking ring around heaven at midnight at midwinter over the sacred city of Asmaracanda. Saadet wondered how many would be visible even under ideal conditions, so far east as this.

She tugged her wolf-furs, gift of her dead husband, up under her chin. She was glad to lie out under the night. Glad that the house they sheltered in temporarily, until the corpses could be carried out of the palace, had not yet been reroofed for winter.

She would have thought this mood—the pleasant ache, the longing, the welcome melancholy of freedom—was Shahruz's, for he had always been the one to seek solitude and lonely places. But Shahruz, as she had noted, did not seem to be with her on this night.

Having found the Virtues, she looked for the Benedictions, but a hazy pall blurred the southern horizon. It was the Cold Fire, burning deep in the heart of the Steles of the Sky as if to blazon the return of Sepehr, from whom ai-Idoj took his title. Sepehr had been the founder of her sect: the Nameless Rahazeen. Saadet revered him in direct proportion to the rest of the world's loathing.

She herself had broken open the seal on the volcano's deep fires so the world might see a sign of the Joy-of-Ravens returned.

Footsteps brushed the dust in the hall outside. She let her head roll the other way against the saddle and watched a familiar shape frame itself in the door against the pale stone of the wall beyond. Al-Sepehr paused there. Saadet listened to his quiet breathing.

She covered her face with her veil. She must go barefaced among the Qersnyk, as their Khatun. But in privacy she could make herself comfortable.

"Master," she said, sitting up, drawing her knees into cobbler's position before her. "You should be sleeping."

"Not I alone," he answered. "Are you well?"

She opened her mouth to answer and belched instead. Her palm pressed her veil to her burning face; in apology, she shielded her eyes with her other hand.

"Heartburn," she said, apologetically. "The babe has his own ideas about what I should be eating, and when."

Al-Sepehr stiffened, and she wondered if she had shared too much of women's mysteries. She was becoming a barbarian in truth as well as title. But then he stepped within the door and said, "We will find you some ginger in the morning. Your son is well?"

She shrugged. "I am no midwife. No mendicant scientist, no Hasitan. But nothing suggests to me otherwise. Like most sacred duties, pregnancy seems to me unpleasant and wearying."

His pause was long. Would he rebuke her for irreverence? But whether he took pity on her widowhood, the blood of the day before, or her sex, he just dug into his pocket and came up with a little silk bag. "This is for you."

She took it in her hands, something hard and warm from his body, irregular but as large as an egg. She picked the bag open and shook the contents out on her hand.

Half a geode, any glitters that might strike from the crystals within dulled because they lay under a pall of blood.

"It was Shahruz's," he said.

Saadet folded the geode between her palms and bowed over her hands. But al-Sepehr only stepped away again. He spoke over his shoulder as he went. "Sleep, Saadet. You are guarded by me, and by a dozen eager steppe riders. And you will need your strength in the morning."

3

THIS SOFT RAIN WOULD HAVE HIDDEN THE SUNRISE, EVEN IF SAMARKAR
had been able to see it for the mountains. Clouds wrapped their slopes,
coursed through the ravine that channeled the steep river below.
Samarkar lay awake in the gray dawning, head toward the door of the
ruined building she and her companions had appropriated. She pillowed
her head on her arm, watching the mist tumble like slow water over the
stones and between the trees and buildings of the valley to whose slopes
Reason clung. At least it was dry inside their improvised shelter, for Samarkar had worked a little magic to keep the mist without.

The horses—Bansh, her foal, and the shaman-rememberer's white-
faced, mouse-colored dun—had made their way inside at some point
and now stood at the back of the structure with their heads low, dozing
and breathing and steaming. Temur too breathed, warm against
Samarkar's back, his forehead pressed between her shoulder blades, a
blanket drawn up to his shoulders against the welcome chill. He snored
faintly, as did Brother Hsiung. The shaman-rememberer slept silently.

The sound of the rain had awakened Samarkar. It pattered and shivered on the stone roof and the pavement, a sharp and welcome sound
after so long in the desert and so long sleeping under shelterless skies.
Temur's home might be wide horizons, but Samarkar had grown up in

strong dwellings mantled by mountains' wings. Reason also curled within the embrace of high peaks, though the Shattered Pillars were not so high as Samarkar's own Steles of the Sky. She supposed that was how such an alien, ancient ruin could in some ways feel like home.

Sunrise was now imminent: jungle birds and night creatures spent their energy on one last burst of noise and activity before falling silent all at once. They anticipated the killing suns of ancient Erem. With a wizard's curiosity, Samarkar wondered how long it would take them to learn that the new sun, the sun of the steppe, was a friendlier creature—one that might burn, if treated disrespectfully, but would not sear eyes and scald living flesh from bone. Of course, suns changed over the world time and time again—but those were the suns of men, not the savage light of elder races. Reason was home to tree ferns that withdrew into limy, calcified trunks each dawn; to vines that folded their leaves and blossoms away like the opposite of a Song queen's parasol; to creatures that aestivated, hid, or—like the half-entombed dragon tortoise they'd passed on the road—simply drew into their shells and waited for the fire to go.

How did something so adapted to a perilous light ever begin to change?

As well ask how to govern without empires.

She thought it had grown as bright beyond the door as it was likely to. Perhaps she should rise and fetch water, start tea, let the others sleep—but she lay there, smelling the half-salty, musty petrichor of water falling on parched earth; the warm herbal bitterness of horse manure; the acrid char of last night's cooling fire. Soon there would be no more quiet.

A shadow moved through the mist and rain beyond the empty doorway. Samarkar knew the silence of its step, the breadth of its shoulders, and she did not fear it. Fog broke around the figure, its last tendrils reluctant to release their embrace, revealing the pale belly and black-striped, rust-colored shoulders of the tiger Hrahima. Her fur twisted in wet spikes through her heavy ruff, was slicked so smooth along her lean forearms that Samarkar could see every vein, every bone, every tendon, every ridge of her extraordinary musculature. Beads of water, dull in this light as pendant jewels, swung and slid among the gold rings in her lobes until the ears flicked, splashing the droplets free.

The Cho-tse paused inside the door, whiskers plump with satisfaction. She glanced around the room, huffed at all the sleeping men, and hooked the claws of her huge hand in a delicate, beckoning twist that could have seemed incongruous.

Though she was stiff from her hard sleeping place, Samarkar rose without a sound. She slipped from under the damp wool blanket, found her boots, and pulled her worn black wizard's frock-coat from its peg—a stick jammed between the unmortared stones of the wall. She only paused to tuck the bloused bottoms of her trousers into the top of the boots before stepping out into the rain after Hrahima.

The mares and the colt watched them go.

When they were far enough from the doorway for their voices not to carry, Samarkar said, "You've been exploring."

Hrahima scratched idly at the proud flesh of a fresh pink scar marring one forearm. She kept her claws sheathed. "And I have found something, Wizard Samarkar."

SAMARKAR FOLLOWED THE TIGER THROUGH THE RAIN. HER FOOTSTEPS were not so silent as Hrahima's: her boots splashed and creaked, and the wet six-petaled skirt of her coat slapped her wet thighs. Strands of hair escaped from her braid and plastered her cheeks. Every sound seemed to resonate, amplified in the wet air and the amphitheater of the valley's enfolding walls.

Morning had by now most definitively broken, though the light still groped through the fog in a directionless haze. Hrahima's path led them between still more eyeless structures, houses and shops or things more mysterious, vanishing shapes serried one beyond another in the mist. "This must have been a city of . . . tens, hundreds of thousands," Samarkar whispered, overawed. Even she, once-princess of Rasa and Tsarepheth.

"A city of many thousands," Hrahima confirmed.

"How did they feed them all, here in the mountains? Under killing suns? How did they travel? Move goods?"

One would have to shelter everything by day—even the draft animals. Samarkar fell silent as she pondered the logistics problem. *Or maybe they weren't killing suns, to the people of Erem.*

"If you can call them people," she muttered, watching Hrahima's ears flick before the Cho-tse decided to politely pretend that Samarkar had not spoken. But the more she thought about it, the more Samarkar thought the point had merit. Their language blistered human mouths. Their books blinded human eyes. Their very suns were poison—

If the people of Erem had not been people, exactly, but something older, something . . . tougher. Or trickier. Or versed in arts no modern wizard knew—

That explained how a civilization could live under those skies and leave such relics.

But what could destroy a race with the power to walk beneath the light of the suns of Erem?

. . . Or were what she knew as the suns of Erem, in fact, the suns of Erem's conquerors? She imagined Tsarepheth under their actinic light, the triple shadows cast in blue and gray and orange, the earth burned sere on every side.

The chill Samarkar felt was no doubt just the rivulets of mist condensing in her braid, rolling down her back beneath the collar of her coat. Suddenly, she regretted not wearing her relief-carved jade wizard's collar, which was still tucked safely into her bag. It would have meant nothing in practical terms, but she could have touched it—she jerked her fingers away from the notch of her collarbone—and been reassured.

These people. Whoever they were. The Rahazeen we're fighting have access to their power.

Stone branches of trees that would blossom again come nightfall arched over the path, looming out of the fog and rain before vanishing into it again. They had no scent now. Samarkar found herself flinching from each shadow, each echo—dripping water, her own footsteps. She steeled herself—*I am the Wizard Samarkar!*—and walked on. She could trust Hrahima's senses. Blind in the fog, the tiger would be only little diminished. Her senses of hearing, of scent, so improved upon the human that Samarkar knew Cho-tse considered their monkey cousins all but deaf and anosmic.

The jungle had reclaimed this part of Reason as well, though not as comprehensively. The streets were tightly cobbled, and not much grew between them. Vines draped from the overhanging branches, but Samarkar could make out the clear outlines of streets, of structures, of gaps in the masonry.

Of doorways, here and there.

The one Hrahima at last stopped before seemed darker than most of the others. She stepped aside with a beckoning gesture—but when Samarkar moved to take the lead, Hrahima stopped her with an outstretched hand. Samarkar's head barely reached the Cho-tse's mid-chest. It was a large hand.

Samarkar said, "I don't understand."

"Wizard," said the Cho-tse. "Is there magic here?"

Samarkar stroked her face in contemplation and found the skin clammy and damp. "Magic," she said. "It isn't . . . one thing, Hrahima."

The tiger regarded her. Hrahima's eyes were like heat-crazed jewels, chips of green and turquoise and amber all interleaved at random, with darker lines between. They gathered what light there was and so seemed luminous on their own.

"What I do," Samarkar continued. "The science of a Wizard of Tsarepheth, it's not the same as your Immanent Sun, or even the science of a Wizard of Song or Aezin. It's definitely not akin to the artifices of Messaline. Or the Curses of Erem, via Danupati or otherwise. Not the same as the gifts of a . . . of a shaman-rememberer or the intervention of a god. But they're all called magic.

"I cannot just . . . look at a thing and say *this is magic* or *this isn't magic*, as if I were identifying a mushroom."

Hrahima's whiskers luffed. Her thick tail twitched—perhaps impatiently.

Samarkar ground to a halt. She looked down at the backs of her hands, raised to gesture emphatically, and hooked the right one through her belt beside the square-hilted utility dagger any Rasani carried there.

"Actually," she qualified, "mushrooms aren't that easy to identify either."

"If they were," Hrahima agreed, "no one would ever die of poisoning."

Samarkar didn't think she was talking about mushrooms, exactly.

Hrahima said, "It'd be a poor sort of magic that followed the same rules no matter what the sky it grew under, don't you think?"

Samarkar picked the wet drape of her coat away from her thigh. As soon as she released it, it swung back and stuck again. She could channel a little of the process of fire into it, or air, and dry it out—but in this atmosphere it would be instantly wet again. A long straggle of the hair that had escaped her slept-on braid dripped now in front of her eyes. She scraped it away and instead it stuck to her hand.

"I think that would be a very exemplary sort of magic indeed. Friendly. Useful, belike."

Hrahima snorted, a sound like a sneezing cat writ large. "Will you trust me to step through the door?"

"When you put it like that . . . without explanation?" It wasn't distrust. It was more . . . curiousness? An ingrained distaste for surprises? A moment more, and she was angry that Hrahima might have risked herself with no one around to watch her back. "Have *you* been through it?"

Hrahima's tail flicked, just the tip. "Easier to show. I'll go first—"

"No." If Hrahima were to betray her . . . the tiger would have just killed them all in their sleep, last night or a hundred nights previously. "I'll not play the churl with you, of all the Mother Dragon's creatures, tiger sister."

Samarkar stepped forward, toward the dark unsettling doorway. Now it was her turn to pretend she did not hear as the Cho-tse murmured, "I do not take it as a personal affront that you learned well and hard not to trust, monkey-wizard."

But she smiled, ducking her chin, though it made the cold rain trickle through her lashes and sting her eyes. She was not the only one who forgot, now and then, to trust. To make it easy for others to watch over her.

For two creatures so dissimilar, Samarkar thought that she and Hrahima were actually a great deal alike.

When she stepped through the doorway, she felt no chill, no tingle— nothing unexpected at all. Except there was no mist on the other side. The air was warm and still, the sun angling sweetly down to stretch a long shadow beside her. And when she turned back, there was the wall behind her, the empty doorframe—and beyond it she could see only darkness: not mist, nor Reason, nor Hrahima.

At least, not for an instant—a long instant, but only one, before Hrahima's stooped shape filled up the doorframe and straightened again as she emerged. She blinked, eyes slitted against brightness. Drops of cloudy water scattered from her fur to dot the dry gray surface of the broad stone apron that marked the threshold.

A yellow forest stretched to every side, slender trees with white and silvery bark angled like splinters, haphazardly. The ground was deep in golden leaves, each shaped like the head of a spear. The house behind them was a ruin, only the wall with the door in it standing. The stones of the rest tumbled over the foundation and, half-lost in drifts of leaves, they emerged here and there, glimpsed gray between the mosses. It was breezy and bright and smelled of loam and compost. A bird as blue as lacquer flew calling raucously between those haphazard saplings. The sky was cobalt and unfamiliar between the sun-glazed leaves still bright on the trees above them.

"Where are we?" asked Samarkar.

"I cannot be certain," Hrahima answered. "But we're not in Reason anymore."

"Can we go back?"

"I did before." Hrahima turned where she stood and vanished into the doorway again—vanished literally, as if something cast an impenetrable shadow that she stepped into swiftly, the line of its occlusion moving across her body sharp as a knife. Samarkar followed. They found themselves once more in Reason, wrapped in mists, with the cold rain drumming in their ears.

Samarkar leaned against the doorpost, panting, as Hrahima turned back to regard her. The tiger said, "Anything could sneak up on us through that. There's a whole—a whole *empire* there we have no idea about."

"Bones of the mother," Samarkar said, the flush of excitement—a plan, a gamble, the familiar sense that what she was about to do just might make all the difference in the world. "Do you suppose there's *more* of them?"

Hrahima stopped, mouth open, tips of her peglike yellow canines just showing beyond the velvet of her flews. Her third eyelids slid closed and she tilted her head for a moment as if she looked within. "You think we can find out where they go."

Samarkar caught herself nibbling a thumbnail and forced her hand down. "There will be a price. And it will be awful."

"It's a thing of Erem," Hrahima agreed. "Assuming it *is* a thing of Erem, and not something Reason itself was built around."

"Something older than the first Erem."

The tiger shrugged. "Why not?"

Samarkar needed a moment to think that through. "Erem, Hrahima. These people. Whoever they were. The Rahazeen we're fighting have access to their power."

"Some of their power." Hrahima rested a hand on the doorframe.

"How much? A lot, it seems."

"Well," the tiger said. "Now we, too, have access to some of their power."

"Six Thousand forbear," whispered Samarkar. "Let's see what rots off our bodies from using the damned thing before we get too cocky about it all."

Jurchadai led Tsering back into the camp, insisting that if she wished to know what the refugees would do, she should speak to a representative of Clan Tsareg. Although the clan's matriarch, the venerable Altantsetseg, had recently been killed, Tsareg was still a family of great status among the Qersnyk, claiming fistfuls of Khans, Khagans, and Khatuns among its ancestry. And Temur's kidnapped woman, the one whom he had left Tsarepheth seeking, was a Tsareg girl—so they had a familial stake in the outcome of his bid for the Padparadscha Seat.

Tsering noticed that the Qersnyk were obviously much more prepared for and comfortable in this refugee lifestyle than the Rasan farmers and townspeople. The Qersnyk normally brought their herds from a summer range in the foothills of the Steles of the Sky down to the steppes for winter, living in semipermanent seasonal camps on each end and planting crops that could be harvested when they returned the next year. Although they had been traveling much longer and with fewer provisions than they were accustomed to, they had cozy organized camps with livestock hobbled or picketed to graze on the dry grass of summer's end. Buckets of water had been hauled up from the stream and here and there an animal too old or tired to continue the trek was being butchered, the meat and bones and hide shared out among dogs and households. Since it could not be preserved, it must all be eaten. Tsering guessed the clans took turns feeding themselves and their neighbors.

By contrast, the Rasan households were disorganized and ill-supplied. Many of them had obviously not known what to pack, or had time or the skill to pack it intelligently, and they didn't know what to do with it now that they were out here. Cooking without a hearth, trying to rig warm beds for the night—there would be a frost, and she hoped no one would freeze in their blankets. The refugees included infants and the old. Their pack animals and one-wheeled wagons—some drawn by yaks, some pushed by men—were heaped haphazardly with objects grabbed at random. The Qersnyk women could lay a hand on any item in their packing within minutes; the Rasani must hunt through jumbles.

Not all of them would make it. Wherever they wound up. Kashe, which the Qersnyk called Qeshqer, was out of the question—a city left emptied by blood ghosts was too unlucky for anyone to inhabit. Which meant the steppes, or Song.

Tsering wondered if she should have pushed more of the Rasan refugees to go south, with the Dowager Empress Regent. But that bird had flown and they needed to be out of the mountains before winter locked them in for eternity.

Tsering's palms stung; she found herself peeling fingernails from her own flesh as she thought of the Emperor Songtsan and his refusal to arrange for an orderly evacuation while time permitted.

Well, he was probably dead now himself, and raging against him was a waste of energy. Or perhaps a source of energy: she felt abruptly lighter. The leadenness of exhaustion fell away. Beside her, Jurchadai lengthened his stride to keep up.

"I hope that scowl is not for me," he said. "Although if it puts that bounce in your step, it might not be so bad to see you angry."

Well, Tsering was guessing on the words for "scowl" and "bounce," but she was confident she had the context close enough. "Songtsan," she answered. When he nodded in commiseration, she realized she did not want his pity and added, "How much further?"

"Right here." He pointed with his elbow, the Qersnyk way, to an encampment guarded by two of the enormous steppe mastiffs, who lay alertly alongside a woman with a scarred face. The woman had a babe at her breast, tucked into the open front of a good coat, embroidered, with a fur collar. She wore lambskin boots sewn with the wooly side inward and seemed at her ease. Tsering recognized one of the Tsareg cousins descended of Altantsetseg.

Just then, she realized with surprise that Jurchadai hadn't been setting the wards from horseback as she would have expected, but walking his flags and stones around. She mentioned it to him as they stepped between the barrels that marked the edge of the campsite.

He smiled with one corner of his mouth. "Mares need rest too."

The Tsareg woman did not rise as they came up to her, but the nearer of the two great dogs did. Although his winter coat had not yet come in, he was still a massive, shaggy thing—as matted as a yak, mostly black with golden-brown paws and eyebrows, the paws as big as Tsering's hands if she doubled the fingers under at the first joint.

"Four-eyed dog," Jurchadai said fondly, extending his hand for the dog to sniff. "They see ghosts. We say the souls of dead monks go into these dogs."

The gold marks above his eyes did resemble a second set of irises. Tsering, too, held out her hand and let him sniff. His coat smelled of old grease and woodsmoke, and even in the chill of deepening twilight his thick tongue lolled. She thought he was the same dog she had seen several times before at Altantsetseg's side, and after a few good huffs he seemed to accept her as inoffensive.

By the time she had been sufficiently sniffed and investigated, another woman had emerged from beneath a stretched hide tarpaulin screened with blankets. She too wore a Qersnyk rider's long coat and breeches. As she straightened, Tsering saw a beaded patch covering one eye. She hunkered at the nursing woman's side and rested a hand on her shoulder.

They each spoke a few words, too low and quick for Tsering to make out. Then the one-eyed woman spoke haltingly in Rasan. "I am Tsareg Toragana. I will translate for my sister, Tsareg Oljei. Sit, please, and I will bring you tea."

Tsering sat on a rolled hide, trying to disguise her wince. Jurchadai turned so he was making a third side of an invisible square and positioned himself halfway between her and the sisters, and he too hunkered there as casually and comfortably as Tsering might have reclined in a bed. All those years in the saddle must result in particularly powerful crouching muscles.

Oljei, supporting her baby one-handed, moved to the dried-dung fire and poured steaming liquid into clay cups with hide guards whip-stitched and shrunken around them. Tsering guessed these would help keep the tea hot—and the hands holding the cup from burning. Oljei served Tsering first, then Jurchadai, and lastly Toragana and herself.

The tea was too hot to drink, and smelled mostly of wet leaves, as if it had been brewed over more than once—but a fat lump of fresh butter floated on top, melting dreamily into the brown liquor, and the steam that rose from it bathed Tsering's face in warmth. In another month, it would freeze on her eyelashes. She closed her eyes and enjoyed the moment of peace, with the shaman-rememberer and the two women beside her, and the warmth of the fire at her right side.

It was only a moment, though. Then Oljei—by way of Toragana, though Tsering now understood more than some of the Qersnyk words—began to speak. Her scarred face painted in furrows by the firelight, she said (and Toragana translated), "This one prays you will pardon her rudeness, Wizard Tsering, in moving so quickly to matters of business. But we are all tired, and I know you will wish to eat and seek your own bed before it grows too cold."

Her breath formed the shape of her words on the air. Tsering watched, fascinated, and almost forgot to sip her still-scalding tea and answer. "I am grateful for what time you can spare."

Oljei's face twisted around its scars; it might have been meant to be a smile. She glanced at her sister, and Toragana continued, "We wish to confer with you, Wizard Tsering, on where we next take the clans. Your people will be affected as well. Their only safety is with us; there are not enough Rasani to make it across the steppe without falling prey to bandits, now that the Khagan's peace is ended."

Hot as the tea was, the chill in Tsering's belly was colder. "I am not a leader of my people."

Now *that* was definitely a smile. And Oljei lifted her chin and brushed the unbound hair behind her shoulder. Her babe fussed in her arms; she switched it to the other breast so smoothly Tsering barely saw her adjust her coat. "It is you who have protected us during our time in

Tsarepheth. It is you who befriended Ashra Khatun. It is you who helped cure the demon-cough. You have proven yourself a friend to the Qersnyk and to Clan Tsareg, and it is with you that we will confer."

This time, Tsering sought refuge in the tea. The melted butter sent savory, salty tendrils through it, coating her chapped lips in relief. When she had drunk two swallows—with a pause between, because of the heat—she had collected herself enough to answer, "What do you propose?"

Toragana said, "We will go to Dragon Lake, and support Re Temur Khagan, son of Ashra Khatun. Your people are welcome to join us, but there is danger."

Indeed. The danger of joining the vanguard declaring support for an untested would-be emperor. The danger of travel through the un-patrolled steppe and the patrolled Song borderlands. The danger of war, of conscription, of revolution.

"There is danger in traveling alone as well." Tsering sipped her tea once more. "I shall speak to Hong-la. We must take the temper of our people. Before we are out of the mountains, we will decide."

SOUTH OF TSAREPHETH, IN THE GREEN SWEEPING VALLEY OF THE RIVER Tsarethi, in the shadow of the smoking Cold Fire, the Dowager Em-press Regent Yangchen led her people away from the cracked walls of the Black Palace. They were laden, men and women leaning into high-sided carts to assist head-tossing mules and stolid yaks. Children herded chickens, feathered lizards, yaks, and shaggy sheep and goats with sticks. Women trudged, neck-bent, under comically disproportionate bun-dles, and the ash fell over them all.

At least the prevailing wind was blowing the bulk of the volcano's debris north, away from them. *Toward the other refugee train.*

Yangchen-tsa felt ashamed of her relief.

She told herself her people would have done this anyway—many of them, anyway. But it would normally be planned, faster and more effi-cient, adequately supplied. Those who traveled would normally be those with the resources to travel, and those who did not would hunker down in Tsarepheth and await the winter there.

Some always wintered over in the high country, including the wizards . . . but it had never much occurred to Yangchen before to think that, when her husbands and sister-wives and the late Dowager Empress and the Princess Samarkar and their court and cousins and staff and light women and fancy men and chefs and armorers and guardsmen and seamstresses and hangers-on packed up each autumn and headed south, to the lower elevations and more forgiving climes of Rasa, with its easy routes to Song and the Lotus Kingdoms, they were leaving behind half a city to endure the killing cold and murderous storms of deep winter in the Steles of the Sky. This time, everyone who could move was moving out, except some sick, the wizards who had elected to stay behind to protect the Citadel of Tsarepheth (and try to save it and the city that shared its name from the Cold Fire), and a few too stubborn or too old to leave their homes.

This caravan—chiefly afoot, full of people who could not possibly be carrying enough food or warm clothing for the march—would not move as quickly or as well, or have as easy a time feeding itself. Her belly sank as she considered the likely outcomes. Even with a large contingent of wizards and their entourage along, with their own rattling great carts and pack train of yaks and mules . . . this could end in death. And it was her duty to prevent as much of that death as possible.

With a start, Yangchen realized that all those people with whom she had used to travel were also dead, now. Except Samarkar, the fled-away Third-wife Payma-tsa, and Second-wife Tsechen-tsa, and Yangchen herself. And possibly—maybe—Tsansong. Although Yangchen thought she knew where the great bird that had carried him off had come from. She might have been naïve—by the Jade Courtesan, so naïve!—but she thought she understood, now, how her erstwhile ally operated. And she had recognized the Rukh as a larger—a gigantic—version of the eagle-sized birds that had ferried her messages to and from the one who had supplied her with poisons and abortifacients so she could—she now understood—do his work in weakening the Rasan Empire when she thought she was doing her own work and protecting a legacy for her son.

She could not say so, could not reveal the source of her dangerous knowledge, because that would reveal the lengths she had gone to, to protect her life and the position of her son. But she did not think that Prince Tsansong had survived long in the care of the al-Sepehr.

One more burden to carry alone. One more terrific error she must somehow redeem, because she could never make amends for it.

Yangchen had begun the day on foot, her babe on her back like many another woman's—in solidarity. But her advisors—formerly her husband's advisors—had insisted that it would be disheartening to her people to see her trudging along as if she had no resources with which to defend them. Yangchen had protested that she was not such a good rider, and that they had neither litters nor palanquins in which to carry her—and anyway, such stout-bodied slaves as might be bearing a sedan chair would be far better put to use carrying supplies, or the wounded, or the infirm. The elders and the advisors had listened, and nodded, and looked grave until—serene as she could make herself—she still felt like a child stamping her foot in a self-centered rage.

They had brought her a yak.

"I've never ridden a yak," the dowager said.

"It's easy," na-Baryan assured her, his spotted narrow hands smoothing the spotted wide forehead of the beast. It was a royal yak, with long, silky fringes over its eyes, on its legs, along the crest of its neck, and around the perimeter of its body. Pigment darkened its ears and circles around its eyes. Otherwise it was largely white, freckled unevenly with black as if somebody had dipped a thumb in soot and repeatedly daubed its heavy body. Its horns were amber-colored with a black stripe up the inside of the left one; they curved like the ribs of a lyre but turned backward at the tips. "They're very friendly. Very docile, your majesty."

He had offered her the elaborately braided reins, looped through a gold ring that pierced the beast's slick pink nose. Gingerly, she took them and showed the steer her palm. He had whuffed it. The nose had been just as slimy as it looked. She examined the tasseled red-and-gold brocade saddle and shook her head. But, with Gyaltsen's assistance, she set her boot in the stirrup and swung herself awkwardly up. At least the yak wasn't as tall as a pony.

So now she rode him astride, her side-split skirts hiked up scandalously, revealing a scandalous length of leg clad in scandalously filthy silken pantaloons. She moved up and down the line of refugees—her people—with a handful of attendants and guards, forcing herself to

examine each exhausted face as she passed. This was only the beginning, and they already looked worn and weary.

How will they look when we reach Rasa?

How many of them will even be alive to see it?

Yangchen-tsa hoped to bring them to shelter in the winter capital
before snow locked the passes down. They were leaving early—but
nothing, it seemed, could be trusted this year. And this train would be
slower than usual. Rasa was warmer and more southerly than the mountain holdfast Tsarepheth, closer to the trade routes and the mosaic
of ten thousand principalities that comprised Song and the Lotus
Kingdoms. Yangchen-tsa hoped the sky over Rasa would still be the
bottomless blue she expected, and not this flat strange pale thing. She
hoped to return in the spring, when the plague had passed and perhaps
the mountain had returned to its slumber, to repair the Black Palace and
reclaim the ancient and sacred city. She hoped to return in the spring,
and bring Rasa's proper sky with her.

She hoped—secretly, in a heart she could never tell—to redeem the
fact that it was she who had made the mistakes that had led her people
to this crisis.

But mostly, she hoped to survive until morning.

You wanted to be a queen. You are. Now rule like one.

Her mount required a smaller share of her attention that she might
have liked. She could have used the distraction. Her heart thumped
in her chest and her palms slicked with sweat despite the coolness. She
had never, she realized, been given this much autonomy. Never been in
charge of so much as herself, to say nothing of being charged with the
well-being of so many others.

It was terrifying. It was . . . alchemical.

So much that had seemed important—passionately important! . . .
her place at court, her rank among the ladies there—fell away, leaving her
ability to care for these people, to keep them fed, to get them to Rasa.
To be their queen.

She could not do enough to help. Have her men push a wagon from
a rut here; help a child struggling with a too-large flock and a recalci-
trant dog there. More problems would always arise. But the people—
whom she had known to be resentful, even rebellious a few days before,
when her husband was still rockily ensconced on the throne—seemed

grateful when she came up to them, grateful when her guards lent their strength.

No one had ever looked at her with relief and gratitude before.

Her mount moved with a surprisingly gentle sort of swaying pace that had his belly fringes sweeping the earth like the skirts of a running woman. He seemed bulky and felted, but the shoulders between Yangchen-la's knees were slabs of hard muscle beneath the spotted wool, and even bearing her weight and her son's, his cloven hooves danced over the grass in a fashion she found surprisingly nimble.

She fed Namri in the saddle, shamelessly. She could have handed him off to one of his wet nurses, she realized later, but she did not wish to. She wanted him beside her, in her arms, at her breast. She wanted him where she could see him, even when he wailed at the unaccustomed motion and the unaccustomed brightness of being out all day under the uncompromising sky. She herself did not eat until the eerie retrograde sun was sliding down the eastern sky, and Gyaltsen came walking along the line of people seeking a place to pitch their improvised camps and laid a hand on the neck of her yak—who had proven himself exactly as gentle-souled and tractable as Yangchen-tsa knew herself not to be.

"You seem to be getting along well, Dowager," he said, offering a hand to her boot to help her down from the saddle.

She staggered when her feet reached the ground. She only stayed on her feet through pride, and because Gyaltsen caught her by the waist. It was an act that could have cost him his hands, when Yangchen lived in a palace and spoke to men alone only when separated from them by a carven screen.

But she was a widow now, and it was hers to decide who touched her. That knowledge was perhaps the most exhilarating . . . the most unsettling realization of a deeply unsettling month. She stepped away from him lightly, the warmth of his hands on her hips following as if it had soaked into her flesh. Court discipline, years of toughening at her mother's knee, was all that allowed her to move as if she did not feel the cramping agony in her back, buttocks, and inner thighs.

She stroked the neck of her mount, blinking to clear tears. "Is there fodder for Shuffle? And someone to rub him down?"

His eyebrows rose. "And food for you, Dowager?"

She shrugged. She knew she would be fed.

"Shuffle?"

She hesitated. "Unless he has a name—"

"You are the Dowager Empress Regent."

The steer had turned to gaze at her inquisitively, brown eyes half-veiled by long, ghostly lashes. She touched his gold-ringed nose, then wiped the snot on her dirty silken trousers.

"Shuffle," she declared.

SITTING BESIDE THE FIRE WITH HER SISTER-WIFE AND WHAT CURRENTLY passed for their ladies, Yangchen found herself nodding over her rice bowl. Tsechen had spent the day on horseback and she seemed to have weathered it much better than Yangchen had—or she was equally successful at hiding it. The taller woman looked somehow more at ease than Yangchen had ever seen her, with her hair braided plainly down her back and her fingers stripped of rings, her silken slippers exchanged for hard-soled riding boots. She had scooped rice and vegetables into her mouth with appetite, and now picked her portion of the flaky white meat of a feathered lizard, seasoned with the hot-numb spice of Song peppercorns, into bite-sized chunks while avoiding all of Yangchen's attempts to catch her eye.

Yangchen looked down at the chipped pink and gold lacquer on her own fingernails. It was all she could do to chew and swallow. Someone squatted on her right, a respectful distance away, and it was several moments before she could turn to him.

It was one of the wizards—a young eunuch, round-faced and high-cheeked and handsome as a cat, with thick black hair cut at his forehead and nape like a farmer's. His six-petaled frock coat was naturally-black yak wool lined with silk, and the jade and the baroque pearls of his collar caught mysterious gleams off the firelight.

"Dowager," he said, dropping a knee and bowing so his forehead brushed the earth, "I am Anil-la. I beg your leave to confer with you."

She nodded.

He straightened and asked, "Walk with me?"

Yangchen would have left her bowl when she rose from her place by the fire—catching a gasp between her teeth at the pain of straightening her back and legs—but Anil-la took it up and placed it in her hand, careful to avoid touching her fingers.

"Eat, Dowager," he said. "You will regret it otherwise."

Dutifully, as they walked, she chewed. Two of her husband's . . . two of *her* guardsmen followed, out of earshot, or nearly so. She could have warned them back, but they were as discreet as any man in Rasa, and she did not plan to share any of her *own* secrets with the young wizard.

"Your soldiers," he began, and then hesitated. His voice was pleasant and smooth, trained. She imagined he must have grown up in the Citadel. "Dowager, may I speak freely and offer advice?"

"For now," she answered. The meat was salty and fresh. Once she tasted it, it was all she could do to eat with manners rather than shoving the whole hunk into her mouth. Sedately, disciplined, she broke off tiny flakes and laid them one by one upon her tongue.

Anil-la said, "Your soldiers. We will travel faster if you speak to their commander and ask him to have his men keep discipline in the civilian column. If you ask him to have his men assist, the way your personal guard has been assisting."

She looked at him. He tipped his head. "They are my people too, Dowager. I wish as many to live as may."

"Even the nose-slit thieves?" she said. "Even the whores?"

The rounds of his cheeks almost covered his dark eyes when he grinned. "Perhaps them especially."

She regarded him for a moment, his smooth face lit changeably by the flickering light of a dozen campfires. He looked down as soon as he realized the Dowager Empress Regent wished to gaze upon him.

She thought about commanding him to raise his gaze, and realized with a thrill that she could choose to do just that—and she could choose not to, as well. Her back crackled as she straightened.

"I want you to be one of my advisors," she said. "Speak with Munye-tsa."

"Dowager?"

"Make it happen," she said, and forcing herself to move with dignity despite her exhaustion, turned back to the fire.

5

AFRIT GREW IN BALANCE AND DEXTERITY DAY BY DAY—HOUR BY HOUR—while Temur, Samarkar, Brother Hsiung, and Hrahima searched ruined Reason for more surprises: gateways, doorways, artifacts, writings . . . they knew not what. What Temur did know was that soon they must begin the long trek back to the steppe, and through it. Through hostile territory held now, the shaman-rememberer told them, by al-Sepehr and his Rahazeen, through the Qersnyk they had deluded. Unless, as Samarkar theorized, they might find a doorway that would lead them closer to Dragon Lake, or perhaps a way of tuning the one they had to lead to a different location.

Temur could tell this possibility excited her, and through her excitement it set his imagination on fire as well. What if you could sweep such a gateway from place to place across the world, all the while gazing through it? Imagine the maps you could make!

"Imagine the troop movements you could track," Samarkar said dryly. "Which is probably what al-Sepehr is doing with those big birds of his."

Meanwhile, the shaman-rememberer, whose name was Tolui—*Mirror*—largely went about his own business, mysterious though that was. He came and went like a camp cat, sometimes with a fragment of information for Temur and his companions, sometimes with silence or songs. Temur was accustomed to the peregrinations of priests, who might stay seasons with one clan or household or army camp before absenting themselves on mysterious business or spirit journeys—or simply because another place needed a bonesetter, a healer, an advisor more urgently.

For himself, Temur was glad to have the distraction of a search until the colt was strong enough for hard travel. It wouldn't be long now; Bansh was blossoming with rest and nighttime pasturing (whatever the strange foliage wasn't, it obviously *was* decent fodder) and Temur was pleased to watch the too-evident outline of her ribs slowly receding to mere dimples under sleek hide.

Strangely—familiarly—several times, Temur caught sight of the motionless bent bow shape of the wings of a great steppe vulture coasting on the updraft out of the river gorge. Once, he even called out to it—softly, so the others would not hear—"I see you, Grandfather!"

He fancied it dipped its wings from side to side in reply.

And while Hrahima could hunt for her supper—even here, though Temur found it a little disconcerting when she came home with one of Reason's arm-long orange lizards, its neck neatly wrung, and proceeded to devour it down to the toenails—the monkey-type people had limited supplies and resources. There was milk from the mares and meat from the Cho-tse's hunting . . . but the little party needed to come down out of the mountains before winter and find an oasis in which to trade.

At least the badlands between here and Asmaracanda would be kinder in the autumn than at the height of summer, when they had crossed before.

In the meantime, they wandered the ruins. Always in groups of two— Samarkar had insisted, and Brother Hsiung had backed her up with hand gestures vehement beyond his usual reserve—and always by daylight. When they went inside a building they did not know to be sound, one waited outside feeding in rope that the other had tied to his or her waist, and they felt their way most gingerly.

And they all tried very hard to ignore the occasional sick green light that crept into Brother Hsiung's eyes, against which his only defense was to exhaust himself with the moving meditation of the forms of his martial art.

He carried the poison of Erem in his soul. When al-Sepehr raised its terrible powers, as had the Sorcerer-Prince before him, that poison reacted.

With wizardly callousness, Samarkar remarked, "Well, at least we know when al-Sepehr's up to something."

Hrahima, roasting another (gutted, thankfully) lizard on a spit over the fire for those who preferred their meat charred, glanced over at her and replied mildly, "He's always up to something, Samarkar-la."

Hsiung read the language of Erem—it was these studies that had half-blinded him, and left the taint behind—and so it was Hsiung who learned the marks that showed where the dark doorways lay. They were everywhere, it turned out—but the one that Hrahima had stumbled across was the only one they found that had been left active.

There might have been others they did not find. Temur was over-awed by the scale of Reason, the way its bone-colored buildings climbed the steep walls of the valley on either side of the gulley through which the river flowed. He did not think to count until too late, but he was sure that he had been in over a thousand buildings by the end—and so many more had been completely consumed by the jungle, he imagined they would never be found.

Temur's grandfather had had a finely tuned eye for craftsmanship—despite the legendary fate of a certain Padparadscha diadem—and had over many years pillaged the finest craftsmen and artisans from cities the length of the Celadon Highway. These men—Rasani, Song, Kyivvan, Messaline: men of a dozen nations—had made the Khagan's palaces at Dragon Lake and at Qarash—and the capital city of Qarash itself—as cosmopolitan and decorated as any place in the world. Even in his brother's army camps, Temur had grown up surrounded by beauty and craftsmanship.

He still had a discerning eye.

They had been abandoned a long time. But these temples and shops and houses of Reason were among the most lovely he had seen.

It was a matter of the proportions, and of the artisans' willingness to embrace the simplicity of the white stone in which they worked. Samarkar said it was often quartz—"And I've never seen it anywhere in these quantities"—a milky-white rock, translucent in places, through which the light of the terrible daysuns would once have glowed, filtered to something bearable. Some structures were roofed in silver slates to give them more shade; some, like the structure that the group was using as a stable, were built of a heavier and more opaque stone that Samarkar said was white granite.

There were hypostyles with endless fluted columns, houses of many small rooms half-built and half-carved into the mountainside, one great multistory hall that had all calved away and crashed into the river, except one tall eyeless façade that faced uphill. And there were doorways, doorways everywhere.

If they were to be activated, there was the danger that something might just . . . wander through from beyond. After all, as Hrahima pointed out, the fauna of Reason was unaccountably odd. Could not the doorways open to places stranger still, and far more full of terrors than this so-far peaceable kingdom?

On the third day, Samarkar came to Temur with all the toggles of her six-petaled coat hanging open over a threadbare shirt transparent with perspiration. Dark wisps adhered around her hairline. He had been crouched beside a broad rectangular foundation stone with no house resting upon it, engaged in the inventory of what remained of their supplies. While she waited for him to finish the tally in his head, she stood hip-canted, restlessly, one forefinger fretting against its thumb.

He fixed the number in his memory and considered remarking *You've been working hard.* The moue of worry on her mouth made him reconsider. "Something's bothering you."

She sighed and hunkered down beside him, idly reaching to square the edge of a piece of hide with the edge of the sun-warmed white stone. These were no tumbled ruins; no jumbled stones lurked beneath the photophobic vines that carpeted the earth to every side. Whatever building had rested on this ledge, it had been swept away as if by a giant's hand. No trace remained except the smooth ledge it had sat upon.

"Big as the stones in the Citadel," she said.

Temur pressed against his knees, straightening and easing his spine. "Maybe a wizard did this too."

"Count on it." She fell silent, but he knew she was thinking around how to say what she had to say. She'd get to it.

And she did. "The blood-vow . . ."

He nodded. "It's taking care of itself, isn't it? I promised to take Edene back from al-Sepehr. But she has won herself free, and all I must do now is find her." The *all* had a curious emphasis. Indeed, finding one woman in the wide world was no small task, even for a Khagan.

"And you vowed to see Qori Buqa put out of the place that was your brother's."

"Someone beat me to that, too. The Sky has an ironic sense of humor. So all that's left is helping Hrahima fight al-Sepehr. And at this point, I'd do that for the healthful exercise." He studied her face and took a guess. "What are you scared to tell me, Samarkar?"

She startled slightly, then smiled, as if his teasing relaxed her. "Hsiung and I have figured out how to activate the gates. We found another inscription in the ruins of one of the big—temples? Palaces?—which Hsiung thinks is instructions. He's puzzled out most of it."

He let it rest there for a while, then made an encouraging noise. She took a piece of fruit leather from the diminished pile and began to nibble the edge meditatively.

"There's a price," she continued. "Hsiung found the right inscription. The instructions are very clear."

"Of course there's a price," he said. "A life? A finger? Nothing comes clean from Erem—"

"Hsiung thinks the gates are somehow linked to the generative force. We have a guess . . ."

She bit. Chewed. Swallowed. Pulled the water flask from her hip and washed the dry stuff down.

"It'll make me sterile," she said, and held his gaze until they both began to laugh.

EVERY DOOR SEEMED TO HAVE ONLY ONE DESTINATION—BUT THE NAMES etched into the stones near each one were in the tongue of Erem. So even though Hsiung could read them—and suffer the splitting headaches and, Temur suspected, the slow increase in blindness that resulted—those names were not of much immediate use. Still, they strove to remember them.

"Someday we might find a map, after all," said Samarkar.

They made a catalogue, or Hsiung did: the Eremite symbols, and a very approximate—and intentionally flawed—transliteration in the syllabary of Song. Hsiung rendered those in bound and layered characters of spell-sigils, to render them a little more opaque. This was a precaution against anyone accidentally reading them aloud in a close enough approximation of the tongue of Erem to wither their own tongue, or deafen any bystanders.

Temur wondered what protections the Nameless cult of the Rahazeen had in place, that they could bear to hear these words read aloud. And why those protections were not sufficient to save the reader from the creeping blindness that was the price of Erem's knowledge. But they did claim philosophical and possibly blood descent from Sepehr the Sorcerer-Prince himself—conqueror of the entire known world and himself perhaps the greatest scholar and practitioner of the poison magics of ancient Erem since its fall.

"If you want to know how to handle quicksilver safely," as Samarkar had said when Temur raised his questions to her, "or as safely as possible, anyway—ask a feltmaker."

"Feltmakers are known to go mad," Temur rebutted.

Beyond the fire, Tolui had looked up from braiding a horsehair bridle and said, "The traditional means of avoiding the consequences of a curse, Temur Khagan, is to pass the evil on to another."

Temur had not even realized he was listening.

There was a silence. Then, "Of course," Samarkar said.

It was some days' study before Samarkar and Hsiung felt ready to try to activate a gate. The doorways were marked by large inscriptions either on their uprights or lintels, or on stones or walls nearby. They had found a repeated symbol carved near this particular one, one Hsiung had seen before and which he believed associated with the Steles of the Sky, according to Samarkar's reports. Temur and Samarkar had argued about whether she would do this thing—take this risk, meddle with these cursed magics—and Samarkar had won.

"Is it more dangerous than crossing the steppe with al-Sepehr and his birds seeking us?"

"The danger is more certain," Temur had said.

But Samarkar had put a hand on her barren belly, the price of her power, and Temur had subsided.

"Do as you will."

She'd kissed him on the cheek and gone to find Hsiung.

Now all of them gathered before a pair of pillars that stood alone in the forest as if they were merely another pair of trees sawn off even and joined with a lintel across the top. The fluting and the footings gave that the lie, but nevertheless Temur found himself indulging in the fantasy that they had just grown there.

They had all gathered for the opening, even the shaman-rememberer. Each one was armed in his or her own way for whatever might follow.

Temur wore his padded armor coat with the splints and leather sewn into it, and sat on Bansh's back with his long knife sheathed at his knee and his bow strung in his hand. Samarkar wore the black wizard's battle armor that Temur's grandfather, Ato Tesefahun, had given her. Hsiung wore only his robes, much-mended sandals on his broad, soft-looking feet. Tolui held his shallow tasseled drum by the crosspiece at the back, wearing a coat the color of the Eternal Sky hung with strings of mirrors and sky-blue knots. And Hrahima looked as Hrahima always looked, naked except for the harness that held her rope, her wallet, and her knives.

Samarkar's armor rustled as she squared her shoulders. Temur's mood must have transferred itself to Bansh, as the bay mare tossed her head against the iron nosepiece of her bridle and thumped the earth with her white fore hoof once—twice—stiff-legged. She glanced around for her foal; Afrit stood unhappily beside Hsiung, tugging at the rope that held his halter. Hrahima's ears twitched forward, focused with predator intensity on the space between the pillars, which for now showed only the forest beyond.

Hsiung patted the wizard on the small of the back, and Samarkar started forward.

She raised one arm toward the doorway and showed it her palm, naked within the half-gauntlets that protected the backs of her hands. She stepped forward, bowed before the empty space, and when she straightened made a gesture as if depressing the handle of an Uthman-style latching door.

A cool black shimmer swept across the doorway, as if someone had let fall a gauzy curtain sewn with sparkles. It moved faintly, as if a breeze stirred the curtain. Temur heard the sound of wind from beyond and only then realized how silent the empty, daylit jungle really was. He'd grown accustomed to its absences so fast.

The wind from beyond the door was icy and wet and bore the scent of snow. "Careful passing through——"

Samarkar shook her head. She hunched forward, the hand that had been extended resting on a framing pillar, her head hanging. Even the warm light of the Qersnyk sun could not quite wash the reflected green shining from Hsiung's eyes from the curves of her armor.

"Helmet," she managed.

Hsiung handed off Afrit's lead rope to Hrahima and knelt beside her, supporting her, levering the thing off before Temur had quite realized he needed to dismount—and so Temur stayed frozen in the saddle, Bansh increasingly restive as his hands squeezed hard on the reins. Hsiung dropped the helm and got an arm across Samarkar's breastplate as she leaned forward in his arms, vomiting hard. A thin sour-smelling stream of liquid was all that resulted, though she retched again and again.

The barrel-bodied, thick-armed monk bore her up easily, armor and all—which was good, because she leaned on him with some force. When she finally got a breath, she half-straightened, then pressed her hand to her stomach again. "Owwww."

"Samarkar—"

She wiped her mouth on her palm. "You go through, Temur," she said. "We should see what we're at risk of, anyway. And I"—she gagged, swallowed, retched again—"am very glad indeed that I did not eat much breakfast. I'd hate to . . . waste food."

He wanted to stay, to dismount, to put his arms around her. But he heard the jangle of Tolui shifting his weight, and felt Samarkar's gaze upon him like a hand.

Hrahima flexed one set of claws and examined them. "Do you suppose al-Sepehr's eyes glow green when *we* do magic?"

"If so," Temur said, "I hope it keeps *him* up at night as well."

He shouldered his bow, stroked a hand down his mare's shining neck, and sent her forward through the veil.

6

THERE WAS A COVERED WAGON SET ASIDE FOR YANGCHEN AND TSECHEN TO sleep in, with their ladies beneath. It was guarded night and day because it also held what remained of the royal wardrobes and crown jewels. Largely, Yangchen and Tsechen went about their business there in mutually agreed-upon silence, and slept against opposite sides.

In the swallowing dark within the heavy carpet-hung walls, Yangchen lay alone and warm and listened to her sister-wife's breathing. It seemed steady—but perhaps *too* steady, as one who seeks to train herself to sleep through concentration. Yangchen wanted to rise and open the swaddling hangings, let some air and firelight in. Not too long ago, she would have merely done it—would have ordered it done, rather. But now—

"Honored sister-wife," she said—not a whisper, but a low tone that would not carry.

Tsechen was not sleeping. "Elder sister?" she replied. Though she was several years Yangchen's senior, what mattered was that Yangchen was the emperor's mother, and Tsechen was merely a relict of the old emperor.

Yangchen meant to ask about the carpets. But what came out of her mouth, unbidden, was the question—"Do you suppose we should let the wizards who are doing the warding sleep in here during the day?"

Tsechen had always been the plainest and most practical of the emperor's women, court dress and protocol a bit of a struggle for her. Yangchen had always felt envy at how impervious Tsechen had seemed to any desire for her husbands' attentions, allowing Yangchen and Payma to cultivate Songtsan and Tsansong, respectively, without interference or politics. She had always seemed complete in herself, impervious, stern as stone.

Tsechen's long silence told Yangchen that whatever she had been anticipating, this request was not it. When she broke it, her tone was hesitant in a manner that Yangchen was not sure she'd ever heard. "I think that would be very gracious," she said, then amended, "very kind."

"They are needful," Yangchen answered, with a wave of her hand no one could see in the dark.

Tsechen's chuckle told her she wasn't fooling anyone. Then—"You are doing well," Tsechen said, as if it pained her. "You are doing better than I would have thought."

Yangchen felt a flare of anger—*how dare she!*—and knew it for a demon emotion even before it faded. She needed Tsechen—for her safety, for her son's. For the future of these adopted Rasan people. "I am lucky in my advisors."

Tsechen's soft huff of muffled half laughter said she agreed.

"I want you to be one of them."

"Elder sister—"

"Please."

Silence, long and dark. Yangchen began to fear that Tsechen had drifted off to sleep after all. She laid her head back on silken pillows scented with the jungle green smell of ylang ylang and closed her eyes. She'd try the same trick Tsechen had been utilizing, and get to sleep one way or another.

But she was not even drifting when Tsechen spoke again, reluctantly. "We ought to wear mourning."

Yangchen heard her shifting against the pillows. Tsechen had worn mourning for Tsansong, when Yangchen had not. And it was Yangchen who knew he was not a traitor, that she had planted the evidence that made it seem he had poisoned his mother.

If there were any justice in this world, his ghost will haunt me from life into death, and after.

She was far more inclined to wear mourning for the emperor's younger brother, she realized, than for the emperor. But as the situation in the refugee train grew more normal, people would begin to expect at least a public show of grief.

She wondered if Tsechen could hear her hair on the pillow as she nodded. "Yes. I suppose we ought. Do you think you can find us some white rags?"

IN EREM OF THE PILLARS, UNDER A NIGHT SO THICKLY SOWN WITH STARS and moons that the land beneath it had never known darkness, the Queen of Broken Places, the Lady of Ruins, stood and nursed her newborn son and argued with two ghulim and a djinn. One of the ghulim was named Besha, and it had been the queen's guide almost since she put on the Green Ring of Erem and became the queen. The other ghul was called Ka-asha, and it was a sort of . . . spiritual leader of the ghulim. It had attended Edene's childbed.

The djinn's name, the queen did not know, although she was certain her enemy did.

The ghulim were dog-faced, soft-eyed, vulturous in their cowled robes of sapphire, spinel, jade, amethyst. The nails on their hard-palmed hands were long, and they clicked them like castanets for emphasis when they were agitated. They were agitated now.

The djinn wore the form of a man, not too tall of stature, clever-eyed and sharp-featured. His skin was the cerulean of heaven, his hair the indigo of night. His eyes were blue as static sparks, as the hottest part of a flame, and Edene found them hard to gaze into. She made herself do it anyway. She was a queen. And the weight of the ring burdening her finger—the Green Ring of Erem, a band of gold with a viridian cast—gave her the courage to press that claim.

It also told her that someone, somewhere, had just stolen away a part of her realm, and this was the root of her argument with the ghulim—and the djinn.

Edene cradled her babe at her breast, the split skin across her shoulders pulling and aching whether she hunched forward or tried to stand straight. With her free hand, she touched the boy's black hair, tracing the whorl around the soft part of his head. She thought she could already see the traces of Temur in him—his complexion, darker than hers. The height of his cheekbones. *I do not care if you are as handsome as your father,* she thought, *as long as you are as kind.*

"I will go to . . . to *Reason,*" she said. "I will see for myself what has happened to change the sky. Perhaps I will take it back."

"Send your ghulim," Ka-asha argued. It had wider-set eyes than Besha Ghul, longer ears. The fur on its face was less like shorn silk velvet and more like the rippled waves of the curly-coated ponies of Kyiv. "Do not go yourself, my queen. Stay safe here in Erem."

"Safe?" Edene reached over her shoulder with her free hand, touching the robe over the bandages. Her son made a noise of protest as he struggled to keep the nipple. "When the glass demons come as they will? And moreover, I should send you, my people, into danger I would not face myself?"

Ka-asha looked at Besha for support. Besha's shrug could not have been more eloquent of futility if it were shrugged by a Messaline smoke merchant.

The djinn said, "What of Rakasa, my queen?"

Destroy that creature.

When Edene's fist clenched, the ring bit into her flesh. *Show me how,* she answered. *And promise me that there is no way to use him against al-Sepehr.*

Of course, the ring could not make that promise. The djinn did not serve al-Sepehr willingly. He was bound, somehow—because it was al-Sepehr's way never to ask what he could coerce, never to trust where he could enslave.

She could use the ring to force the ghulim to do her bidding. She did not have to stand here and argue with them. She chose to debate, to prove—among other things—that she was not al-Sepehr. That she was a different sort of queen, even if all she was queen of was the dead cities, the broken places, the lost world of Erem. How much of this anger was the ring's, at being thwarted? How much of it was her own: a mother's righteous fury on behalf of her child?

Her son had a name, but she would not think of him by it—even the portion of it that was all she knew because the djinn had not told her its entirety. She would not acknowledge it. It had not been her choosing, and she had not bestowed it. Rather, the djinn had, at the command of her enemy and Temur's enemy, al-Sepehr.

"Call him Re Ganjin," she said. Re was the clan name—his father's clan, and the clan of the Great Khagan, her son's great-grandfather. *Ganjin* meant *Of Steel*, for his father, whose name meant *Iron*, and for her hope that he would grow up strong and resilient and sharp. "Your concern for my son is *touching*. But who can protect him better than I?"

She wrapped both arms around him. "Besha Ghul," she said. "You are my general. Are there ways through the Grave Roads to Reason?"

"There are ways through the Grave Roads to everywhere," Besha Ghul said. Ghulim voices had an odd, glottal quality, perhaps because of their thick tongues and sharp teeth. "If you must go to Reason, will you consent to take a force? One of moderate size?"

"Besha—"

"You made me your general, my queen. Someone else has taken Reason. The Green Ring that makes you Mistress of Secrets tells you so. Will you go and face that adversary without an army? Because you are so strong you fear nothing—not your enemies, not al-Sepehr?"

Edene looked at the djinn. "I suppose," she said, "that you will report everything you hear to al-Sepehr. And that you can reveal none of his secrets."

The djinn inclined his head. "I am his creature. So long as he can hold me."

Though the words were plainly spoken, there was no disguising the menace in them.

"You and the rukhs, too." Edene wrapped her free hand around Ganjin and pulled him closer. Not because she was cold—she felt no cold, and had not since she donned the ring—but because the child had drifted to sleep, and his presence soothed her.

"Would you not rather bring your army and your son to Re Temur?"

"Are those your words, Spirit?" Ka-asha Ghul asked, leaving Edene to briefly contemplate the irony of a ghul calling a djinn *spirit.* "Or are they those of your master?"

The djinn turned his head and spat. His saliva was liquid flame. It sizzled on stone, a crawling, guttering fire, until it burned out and was gone, leaving only a blackened scorch behind.

"Those of his master," Edene said. "Never fear—sooner or later, Temur will have my army. But it will not be at your suggestion, my friend. Besha Ghul."

"My Queen?"

"How long will it take you to ready an expeditionary force to retake Reason?"

The ghul studied its clawed fingertips, ticking one against another as if counting. It probably was.

"Two days," it said finally. "For supplies and logistics."

Edene had been studying tactics and strategy in preparation for this event. It had seemed far-off, penumbral. Now, suddenly, it was upon them.

"You shall have three," she told the ghul. "Now be about it. Ka-asha, please try to keep an eye on the djinn. We would prefer to keep our secrets from his master."

The djinn raised his brows at her, a steady flame-bright regard resting on her face. Edene's cheeks heated as if she crouched to close to a fire.

Grumpily, she said, "At least pretend."

From an arched window atop the highest minaret of the caliph's great domed palace in Asitaneh, the slave poetess Ümmühan leaned into the wind. A warm, dry updraft caught her veils and sleeves and streamed them back against the pale stone and bright tiles surrounding her. Tears stung her eyes as she watched the sunset march across the devastated city below.

She looked toward the docks. Red light thick as narcotic Rasan honey lay over tier after tier of merchant's high houses, the balconies kissing across narrow streets; over the temples of the Scholar-God with their scriptures picked out in gold, tile, glass mosaic winding up the tower walls; across the streets marked by blackened squares of cinders and heaps of heat-cracked stone.

A third of the city had burned.

No smoke rose, and in places she could see the marks where people had begun to sort, to clear, to rebuild. The ossuaries under the city were stuffed to bursting with fresh corpses. A Rasani wizard allied to the old, vanquished caliph had used her magic to . . . not repair, but *repeal* some of the damage done by burning. But though she could somehow turn charred wood, charred flesh whole again—she could not return the dead to life, or rebuild a collapsed home.

Someday, Ümmühan knew, Asitaneh would again be what it had been. This was not the first time the ancient trade city had burned. She also knew she would not live to see it rebuilt entirely, and entirely re-populated.

And then there was the problem of the vanquished caliph, Uthman Fourteenth, who was fled but not dead, and who had taken a certain number of his elite personal guard, called the Dead Men, with him. That would need dealing with, and soon. As would those Dead Men who had deserted their former master and fallen in with Ümmühan's master.

Ümmühan heard a step behind her, and turned to greet the new caliph.

They called him Kara Mehmed—Black Mehmed. He had traded the blue cloak sewn with stars that the old caliph had given him for a robe of royal fuchsia, stiffened with bands of bullion embroidery, worn open over a white shirt and trousers. His scimitar was thrust through his sash; even in his own palace, this was a martial king.

Ümmühan dropped gracefully to her knees, head bowed, and low-ered her eyes as he came to her. Mehmed First, caliph of what had been the Uthman Caliphate, paused a step away. She felt his fingers gentle on her head, then hooked through her golden collar. He tugged her to her feet and the warm gold slid against her skin as he lifted her face with his fingertips.

How could something so smooth chafe so?

She smiled for him as—delicately—he unwound her veils. When he saw her face, he breathed a sigh. "Your face is my peace," he said, quot-ing the Prophet. It was not—quite—blasphemy, not if he spoke with reverence, to Ümmühan as an avatar of the Scholar-God. Her face—every woman's face—was sacred in that way.

But it was walking the line.

Ümmühan schooled herself. No man had ever seen a trace of dis-pleasure on her features, not since she took a woman's veil. She was a secret priestess of the Scholar-God, and no man would see her weak-ness now.

"My lion," she said. "You are weary."

He brushed her forehead with his mouth. He smelled of patchouli, musk, and amber—warm, resinous, alive. She closed her eyes and breathed deep.

"There is the matter of the turncoat Dead Men," he said. "And their reward."

Ümmühan replied with poetry: "Phoenix city from the flames arising / The red across your palms is not henna." The couplet she recited was an example of the political form called a *viper*, for—like the little saw-scaled snakes of Asitaneh—they were always short and sharp, with dripping venom. Mehmed stiffened, then relaxed slightly as Ümmühan put her arms around him.

"Asitaneh is yours, my lion. Asmaracanda as well. You have taken back what the Qersnyk barbarians stole from our people, and you have placed them all under a Rahazeen sky."

"Uthman still roams loose, and more than half of his Dead Men with him," he answered. "The city lies in ruins, and al-Sepehr will expect me to pay for his assistance in the coin of alliance soon. Nothing comes for free from the Nameless."

To hide the thrill she felt deep in her belly at the mention of al-Sepehr, Ümmühan leaned her forehead against his collarbone and hummed low in her throat. She felt him ease again. Men were such fragile creatures, so easy to manipulate. So much less than human.

It was not their fault. They could not help it that she had been made in the Scholar-God's image, when they were poor copies at best. Deep down, Ümmühan suspected that this was why they felt the need to keep women collared like cats, in cages like birds. It was a pathetic attempt to own a soul more numinous than theirs, an urge to get closer to the divine by controlling those who were naturally more attuned to it.

She was not too proud to use their weaknesses against them. In fact, she might say she was too proud *not* to do so.

Mehmed was bareheaded, here in his private household. She reached up and brushed one of the oiled black coils of his hair behind his ear. She kissed his cheek, and let him gaze his fill on her naked face. "Shall I play for you, my lion? Will that soothe your heart?"

"You soothe my heart with your eyes," he said. "With the curve of your cheek. You are the ghost in my heart, poetess."

She disentangled herself from him gently, led him to a couch, and made him recline. She fetched chilled wine with her own hands—slave or not, Ümmühan had the caliph's favor and could have summoned a servant, but she wished no one to intrude on this moment of intimacy— and settled upon cushions beside the divan, where Mehmed could, if he pleased, stroke her hair. She had brought her zither. Now she took it from its case, and having tuned it, began to play.

The song she sang was opaque, allegorical. It could pass for a love song—on one level, it *was* a love song—but anyone with the skill to read the formal second and third levels of classical poetry would hear a critique of the caliphate and the tax system—and a priestess of Ümmühan's sect would hear another message entirely. One that would see Ümmühan most elaborately executed for heresy and witchcraft if understood by anyone else.

Her secret priesthood by itself would be cause enough for an even more elaborate execution, if anyone knew of it.

Kara Mehmed was certainly clever and educated enough to pick out the second and third levels—but the layers of obfuscation were, by tradition, respected. And anyway, the satire was aimed at the old caliph.

Ümmühan hoped that Kara Mehmed, like so many men, believed that the Women's Rite of the Scholar-God was a myth. And she had gone to great lengths to establish herself as far too flighty to be involved in anything so serious.

Men, in her experience, were eager to believe that women were silly, incompetent, small-minded. Even if they were Hasitani, poets, or others who glorified heaven through their work—as if the Scholar-God would make fools in her own image.

She finished her song and they sat awhile in silence, the calluses of his weapon-hardened palm catching on her curls as he tried to smooth her hair. She leaned back against him and closed her eyes. Whatever his other shortcomings, when it came to touching women, Mehmed Caliph had good hands.

At last, he said—reluctantly—"You were right about the assassin, beloved."

"Al-Sepehr? The Nameless? I don't recall a disagreement, my lion."

"No. You wouldn't, would you? But it was your counsel that led me to ally with him. And it was his intervention that gave us Asitaneh, and with Asitaneh the caliphate. The thing you said earlier . . ."

"My lion?"

"The couplet."

Softly, she recited it again. "Phoenix city from the flames arising / The red across your palms is not henna."

"Did you compose that?"

A chill of unease crept through her midsection. "No one composes a viper. They grow; they belong to all poets."

A polite fiction. His amused snort was less polite. "It wasn't a phoenix that burned Asitaneh."

Unbidden, the memory came—an image of blue flame, rising coils like a dust devil from the desert. A string of seventeen syllables in a name, which Ümmühan had committed to her heart with a poet's precision.

"My lion? Was it not . . . rioters?"

"One of al-Sepehr's creatures," he said, irritation sharp in his voice. Ümmühan did not believe that irritation was for her. Rather, it was because he had had to rely on another, an outsider—Rahazeen like himself, but of the radical Nameless cult—to put him on the dais. "A djinn."

It was the long experience of a courtesan and a courtier that kept her from stiffening and pulling away. Ümmühan was no stranger to extremity or expedience—you could not be a slave or a woman and have any illusions as to how the world worked. But to burn a city—your own city!—and its people in your attempt to take her . . .

She had understood that Kara Mehmed was ruthless. She had not understood *how* ruthless until now.

"You regret the deal you struck, my lion?"

His robes rustled as he shrugged. "He has delivered the caliphate to me, as he promised. As you suggested he would. It is a Rahazeen sun that rises here now, and the Scholar-God may be properly worshiped in our temples. There will be an end to permissiveness, to iniquity, to the lax and indulgent ways that flourished under Uthman Fourteenth's reforms. Asitaneh will be holy again."

"I hear you, my lion. And yet?"

"And yet. We have been reliant upon the sorceries of a follower of the Carrion King to bring us here."

She let him see her nod. "It doesn't sit well."

Thoughtfully, Mehmed said, "We have used him. Now we must be rid of him."

Whatever Ümmühan felt, deep in her body, for al-Sepehr . . . she would not forget that it was at his command that fires had burned her city of Asitaneh.

She had regained control of her face. She knelt smoothly, rose up, turned, and bowed before the divan—a request. Gently, Mehmed took her hand and drew her to recline beside him. She caught his fingers between her palms and kissed them.

"It is done, however. It cannot be undone." She waved to the window from which she had leaned, a moment before. "Not even by the powers of a heretical wizard."

"Not a heretic," he corrected, smiling faintly. "A heathen. A poet should know the difference."

She inclined her head. *Indeed. A poet should.*

"So we must go on from where we stand? Is that your suggestion, my Ümmühan?" Her name—her most recent slave-name, to be more precise, though she had never had a free woman's name—meant *Illiterate*. It was considered ill luck to brag too much of one's talents, and so when her gift and skill became apparent, the master who had eventually sold her to Kara Mehmed had given her this name.

"It is as my lion says. We must build the Asitaneh and the caliphate we wish to leave to the sons of the future."

She laid her cheek against her hand. But what she felt in her heart was a fire far colder than the one that had burned her city, and what she heard in her mind was the djinn's long name, echoing and echoing again.

EVEN BEFORE TEMUR'S GAZE PIERCED THE DARKNESS OF THE VEIL, HE heard Bansh's hooves squeak on packed snow. He felt the mare shift her weight cautiously. The long muscles by her spine tensed and her head came back, her forelegs extending and her hind legs crouching as her body compensated for a slope. Temur moved his weight to help her—a reflex, a guess, trust in his mare's judgment when he himself could not see.

A sliding hop-step forward and he was through, breath pluming in raw air, sun bright and sharp—

—and not at all shattering off the dazzling white he had already squinted against. What squeaked underfoot was char-black, and the sunlight falling on it did not glitter. It was snow—or more precisely, a glacier. He could see the spiderweb white of vast crevasses showing through the layer of ash that covered everything.

Or, not quite everything. Distant peaks still shimmered, rising above a grassless silver plain that it took him a moment to realize was an overcast, seen from above. He was high enough to see the mountains falling back and falling back and falling back until they vanished in blue haze and it seemed they dropped off the edge of the world. His lungs burned; Bansh's ribs heaved between his knees. He risked a turn in the saddle and nearly tumbled out of it.

That would be a disaster. He'd slide and roll and bump down the glacier until he met his death in one of those enormous cracks.

When he peeled his hands free of the pommel again, his fingers already bluing with the cold, he moved more cautiously.

Bansh crouched on a ridge below the peak of a mountain shaped like an axe blade. A thick column of smoke rose from a giant, truncated black cone of a peak off to his right and half-behind him, streaming away in one direction as if the wind caught it and sheared it like the anvil tops of thunderheads. Behind Bansh, only a step or two, loomed a sort of irregular triangular doorway constructed of two mighty gray stones leaned together. They must be somehow wedged at the top. Temur could not see, and nor could he imagine what art could haul those dolmens up here and set them in place to endure—the Sky knew how long. The doorway shimmered dark; they could return the way they had come.

She might be a god-steed, a spirit or something like it. But magic or not, there was no way his mare could turn on this ridge. Not unless he wanted to risk her trick of walking on air, and he'd only seen her do that in the midst of a fight. There was no guarantee the gift would be available to them now.

"Steles," he said, half to himself and half to his mare. Tears froze on his lashes at the pain of this cold on his teeth, in his throat. He shivered in his armor and felt his mare shivering too, but his lightheadedness and awe were such that it was seconds before he thought to draw his hands against the reins and urge Bansh to step backward up the slope.

She struggled with it. The slope was steep, her footing bad, her weight settled on her hindquarters. He felt the way her forelegs pushed and slid, the desperate little hops of her back hooves. He saw the bright scrapes through the ash to the ice where her feet had scrabbled, and he held himself perfectly still and trusted his mare again.

And she trusted him. Straight back, exactly the way they had come, as not one horse in a hundred could have managed. He felt her hind hooves reach solid footing, the moment when she knew she would not slide. He felt the warmth of the world they had come from on his shoulders and then they were through, his clothing and her armor smoking in the balmy air. Bansh stood and Temur sat motionless for a moment, both heads bowed. His hands rested on the pommel. The reins rested in his hands. He did not lift his face until the mare lifted hers.

Then he made himself slide from the saddle, leathers creaking stiff, and lift and check and clean each of her hooves, one by one.

Hsiung had helped Samarkar to the stony stump of a fallen tree. Tolui and Hrahima stood at either side of the gateway, as if they had been ready to rush to his aid.

Hrahima watched him silently for a moment, then asked, "Where did it lead?"

The warm air still stung. "The top of the world."

Hsiung, eyes shining only faintly green, as though a luminescent tide were retreating, gestured to the symbols by the gate.

"The Steles of the Sky," Temur agreed. "As promised. Right on top of them, too." He picked wet cinders and melting snow from Bansh's hooves and dumped them on the ground.

Samarkar leaned forward, jaw set against pain. "That's ash."

"At a guess? The Cold Fire is burning."

Samarkar put a palm to her mouth.

"Oh," said Tolui. "Did I forget to mention that?"

7

ATO TESEFAHUN HAD SENT HIS GRANDSON, TEMUR, THE WIZARD SAMARKAR, and Brother Hsiung east through the flames of burning Asitaneh in the care of his Cho-tse ally, Hrahima. And then he had seen to the hasty packing and evacuation of his own household, complete with servants, guards, cook, gardeners, and all. The tortoises from the garden had been released into the desert beyond the inland gates of the city, the ponies laden with household items, the songbirds that populated the courtyard trees left to see to their nests as best they could. And Ato Tesefahun led his dependents—some two score in total—west along the desert road, anonymous among all the others streaming out of burned Asitaneh.

There was an altercation at the gates, when at first one of the guards had not been willing to open them and let the refugees escape. Tesefahun had wondered worriedly if he would need to risk his men at arms to force the issue, but instead he and his household had wound up stepping into a side street and hiding the eyes of the cook's and the captain's and the head gardener's children as the mob took care of opening the gates for themselves. Asitaneh had fortifications intended to protect guardsmen, but they were insufficient against an attack from within the walls.

They had stayed with the train for a day or two, planning and gathering themselves—then struck out north, along a side route rocky and uneven across the pale, dusty hardpan. It led to a fishing village on the coast of the White Sea, where Tesefahun knew they could hire a boat—and send a message to his son Kebede. He was still undecided as to whether they would wait for Kebede in this tiny village, or whether it would be best to try to meet him in Asmaracanda. But there was time to make up his mind—three days travel at least, possibly four with this entourage.

Ato Tesefahun could still read a trail, and he knew within moments that someone had come this way before them—but not too much before. Someone mounted and moving fast: two groups of them. Which said to him, pursued and pursuer, and made him interested. When the tracks of both parties diverted onto a side trail heading east, he made up his mind to follow. It so happened that that particular trail looped, cutting back below a cliff, and would make an ideal spot for an ambush—something he knew because he kept his escape routes prepared. He had not gotten to be the age he was in a difficult political climate by failing to check what lay outside of back doors.

He instructed his armed retainers to take horse and accompany him. Pretending for the moment that he was not feeling the pain of long travel in every joint, he reassured the others and told them to go on ahead to the fishing village and await him there. Then he gathered his resources, assessed the terrain, and began to plot a course of action.

He had seven men-at-arms, their families gone on ahead with the rest of his dependents. He himself was an old man, and not fit for combat. If his guess as to who they were following was correct, there would probably already be soldiers at the ambush point he had in mind. The ideal outcome would be to deal with them before their quarry reached the switchback below, and prevent the ambush with an ambush of their own.

As Ato Tesefahun and his guardsmen pounded on their horses along the dusty road—really, little more than a rubbled wash that dropped between crumbling walls to each side—they knew they were gaining on their quarry. Horse droppings were fresh and wet, the scrape of hooves on stones clear and still showing grit at the edges. Soon, they also knew they were too late to prevent the ambush—but perhaps not too late to prevent its inevitable outcome—as the sound of combat rang from the stones of the gully.

Tesefahun reined his gelding aside, shoulder to the sloping wall of the wash, and let his men-at-arms thunder past in a pall of yellow dust. He drew a fold of cloth across his face to filter air, thinking of how the Dead Men only unveiled themselves to kill.

Cries and the clash of blades redoubled ahead. He urged the horse on cautiously, for the dust rendered a tricky route all the more treacherous. By the time he reached the scene of combat, his men stood victorious over the corpses of a dozen of the new caliph's personal guard: not the kapikulu in their blue coats or the Dead Men in their scarlet, but men who wore the private livery of Kara Mehmed and who had wielded bows, not blades, from this presumed-safe vantage point. Tesefahun's men had come up on them unaware and slaughtered them without taking a wound.

The trail descended through a gap in the rocks, and from this point down the left wall dropped away, leaving a cliff below with an overlook to a wider road that ran through the bottom of the valley. Though the trail Tesefahun had been following continued, from this point on it hugged one wall of the canyon below and vanished between rocks ahead long before it reached the valley's floor.

On that road below, there had been combat as well—and that combat, too, was over.

Seven or eight horses and the balance of Mehmed's men bled out on the rocky soil, and among the red of their blood lay strewn the red coats of a dozen or so Dead Men, now dead in truth as well as in vocation. In the midst of the ring of corpses were six remaining Dead Men, mounted and armed, and a little cluster of mounted women and children—and, armored in a breastplate and helm, mounted on a gray horse pale as beach sand between its smoky nose and tail, with a scimitar sticky with blood still levered in his right hand, was Uthman Caliph Fourteenth.

Despite the helm, Tesefahun had no doubt as to his identity. The horse's tasseled caparisons were in indigo sewn with stars all over, and the plumes on the helm were indigo and fuchsia, bending sideways in the constant wind.

Tesefahun stepped down from his gelding and handed the reins to the nearest man-at-arms. He stepped up to the edge of the cliff where the wash broke away, one hand on the stones beside his head to steady himself. A hot updraft pushed his veil into his mouth and nose and dried the horse-sweat on his thighs. His own fresh sweat sprang up between his shoulders.

He tugged the veil down to show his face and leaned out over emptiness, just a little. "Uthman Fourteenth," he called down, into the breathless desert heat. "Hail, you old bastard. How does it feel to be among the mortals now?"

UTHMAN AND HIS SIX REMAINING DEAD MEN AND ALL THE WOMEN AND children of the household trudged back up the trail, leading every horse that they could catch. Tesefahun met them among the rocks and fell into step beside Uthman, leading on. The usurped caliph was worn and weary, and all that midnight blue showed trail dust spectacularly. But he walked up to Tesefahun and threw his arms around the older, slighter man's shoulders in a hard, quick hug that smelled of gunpowder and horse before setting Tesefahun at arm's length.

"Were it not for you, Wizard, I'd be bleeding into my own shit in the sand down there. I'd say, name your reward, but"—a gesture took in the wasteland around them—"this is my caliphate now."

Tesefahun put his own hands on Uthman's shoulders, a strong clap. Uthman's helm bumped at his hip now, allowing the wizard a long look into the former caliph's brown eyes. The man who had been king squinted in the slanting sun.

"You didn't want to hear about al-Sepehr, Uthman, when we brought the question before you previously."

"Times change," said Uthman. "But I haven't an army to loan you these days."

"Follow me," said Tesefahun. "I think we have some things to discuss. About Kara Mehmed, and an enemy in common. And armies, and other things."

THE CARAVAN NARROWED AS YANGCHEN-TSA'S PEOPLE FOLLOWED THE TSAR-ethi road through a series of winding passes that the river—and the work of ancient wizards—had carved between the mountains. They could not group to camp at night, and so the wizards took it in turns to ride or walk the length of the train every evening, warding each family or group against demonlings and the less tangible terrors of the night. By day, they slept atop the loads in their wagons, exhausted by their vigils.

The Steles of the Sky rose on every side, clean peaks robed in white, broken edges sharp through their glaciers—but at least for now both rain and snow were merciful. Clouds stretched and tore between them, as if the Jade Courtesan had snagged her gauzy veils. Tiered trails of bar-headed geese echoed the angles of the peaks, then collapsed with a shift of the wind into twisting prayer banners. The benefit of the river road was that the trail tended ever downward. It was hard on knees, hard on the brakes of wagons, hard on the beasts who strained back against the tongues of the carts to slow their descent—but it meant that when a cart got stuck in the furrows and wallows of so many others' passage, the slope was in their favor for pushing it free. And they pushed a lot of carts free over the days that followed.

Yangchen and Shuffle (*Shuffle-tsa*, she came to call him affectionately; *Lord Shuffle*) made themselves ubiquitous along the train. It was perhaps an unfair name; under his fluff the steer had long lines of hard muscle through his loins and haunches, and from the saddle his gait had a rolling quality. He wasn't as fast as a pony, but he picked his feet up smartly, his fringes swinging like heavy robes when he ran. Yangchen thought he didn't notice her own insubstantial weight, or that of her son, or the saddle, at all. And no pony could have scrambled up the rocky margins of the trail so sure-footedly, leaving Yangchen's guards and attendants racing to follow.

Each night, Yangchen was less sore than the night before—and every morning was a little easier. She no longer wept silently as she struggled into the saddle. Na-Baryan and Munye-tsa kept to the wagons, in deference to their old bones. But Gyaltsen-tsa and—more and more—Anil-la rode with the Dowager Empress Regent, trading their ponies for a mule and a yak cow, respectively.

Anil-la reined his black-brown cow up beside her as she and Lord Shuffle paused atop an outcrop overlooking the canyon below. The rest of her entourage waited at the foot, stepped off the road to let the wagons pass.

Yangchen was aware of her cheeks nipped red, the hair flying loose from her braid as the wind rising up the canyon wall whipped it about her unpainted face. "I look a hoyden," she said into the wizard's silence.

She angled her face slightly to catch a glimpse of his expression. He seemed stern and serene as he said, "You look an empress."

"Doctor Anil," she said—she'd begun using the Song form of his title as a sort of pet name, a joke between them, and it usually curled the corner of his mouth just a little. "Are we going to make it out of the mountains before the snow?"

"I am a wizard," he answered. "Not the Mother Dragon. It depends on the mountains and the grace of the Six Thousand, now."

"Or the grace of the Scholar-God." She jerked her eyes up at the sky. "If you are certain that is whose this is."

She was certain. But the wizard's word made that certainty easier—less damning—to admit to.

"I do not think her grace resides with us."

"No." Yangchen ran her hand across the wooly crest on Lord Shuffle's broad, tall shoulders. He shivered in pleasure, hide twitching as if shaking off a fly. "We will have to make our own."

Anil-la followed her down the outcrop, rejoining her attendants as she moved along the train. Namri woke—the sway of the steer's gait seemed to soothe him, and he slept harder and better in the saddle, to Yangchen's surprise—and she put him to her breast. One of her guards passed up flat bread baked the night before, cold roasted beef, and butter. Yangchen dusted crumbs from the prince as she ate and rode, the knotted reins hanging loose across her thighs. Lord Shuffle would take care of them without her constant management.

After some time on the road, her people had clumped themselves by groups and social affiliations. As Anil had recommended, soldiers kept discipline and moved among the civilians, rendering aid because Yangchen had spoken personally with their commanders and made it so. Out among the commoners as never before, Yangchen was stunned to see so many with slit noses, cut lips, hands removed by a headsman's axe. It seemed that a third of the peasantry had suffered some mutilation, and while she knew that was an exaggerated estimate brought on by her own shocked tendency to notice the maimings, still it troubled her.

Her father's voice in her ear: *He must be ruthless who would rule.* But was this her husband's justice? Her mother-in-law's?

She herself had done what she had done, and others had suffered for it. Where was *her* justice for that? She had—

She had stolen a whole kingdom.

If you get away with it, it's not a crime.

She watched; there were no secrets in a camp on the move. And she saw that the maimed did not seem to treat their companions all that differently from the whole. Here a man with his cheeks scarred by the thrust of a hot iron leaned at the wheel of a neighbor's wagon; here a woman with a cut nose bent under a burden bigger than herself. She watched a herdsman branded for tax evasion risk his life to catch a panicked mule on the edge of a precipice, and she turned to Gyaltsen with a furrow between her eyes that she could feel would leave worry lines.

"While we are traveling," she said, "I wish to judge all accusations of crimes. And when we reach Rasa, I wish to review the criminal codes."

He inclined his head. "Dowager."

She turned to find Anil-la staring, his mouth heavy with a frown. He dropped his eyes immediately, hand to his cheek to cover a flush. "Dowager. Forgive my rudeness."

"Doctor Anil. You disapprove?"

He shook his head. "You are not what I expected, when—" He shrugged, and if possible seemed to shrink lower in the saddle. "You are not what I expected."

The pinch of her own face smoothed, though this smile would leave lines as well. She realized with a stomach-twisting shock that it was no longer her untouched beauty for which men would desire to serve her, but the power of her word, now law.

"Good," she said, and looked away again until she could make her face as serene and shuttered as a bride's.

As befitted her rank, Saadet Khatun greeted her unborn child's subjects beneath a roof of sky. A hoofprint arc of walls of bleached felt sheltered her on three sides, and she was warmly robed in wool and furs—but as sunset lacquered the eastern sky, the wind freshened. Summer was past an end. Desert-bred, Saadet drew her hands up into her sleeves, trying not to hunch inside her coat as her breath plumed before her.

Lanterns were lit at the periphery, a brazier brought close to where she sat on a heap of rugs that made a little dais, her back against the Padparadscha Seat—the weather-beaten old saddle that was the Qersnyk excuse for a throne. The columns of Qersnyk men and women advanced slowly down an avenue flanked by white-houses and the lines to which horses had been picketed. Some of them stepped out of their queues briefly to punch the skins of fermenting airag that hung beside each door—a neighborly act, for the mare's milk needed constant stirring to assure its quality . . . though what quality that might be, Saadet was personally uncertain.

As each man or woman took a moment to stand before her and place fist to palm in fealty—not to her, but to the babe within her—Saadet made every effort not to stare over his or her shoulder to the next, and the next, and the next beyond. Their faces disconcerted her, especially the ones with a hostile cast.

Were those swearing fealty because they hated Re Temur even more? *You cannot hate him more than I do.*

The line stretched around the bend in the meandering avenue. It might as well have stretched into infinity, as far as a pregnant woman's bladder was concerned. Over her head, raised on a pole that stretched above the felt windbreak, Qori Buqa's bull-embroidered banner snapped.

She wondered where al-Sepehr was. She wondered if he would ever trust her enough to share his plans with her as deeply as he had shared them with Shahruz. She knew it was wise for her to be seen not to rely on him overmuch; there would be those who did not like it that he advised her. Bad enough a foreign Khatun—she was not the first such the Qersnyk had promised fealty to. Far worse, for her to seem to take the word of her foreign father over that of Qersnyk advisors.

Endure, Shahruz told her—but she had been enduring since the sun was high. It was enough.

Would he leave her *all* the unpleasant jobs?

She had enough discipline left to wait until a man lagged in coming forward before she rose. As soon as she planted her feet, though, a woman was beside her, hand on her elbow bearing her up—and the shaman-rememberer Paian moved forward from his place beside the wall. He spread his arms and said, "The Khatun is tired. Return to-morrow," and at his words two warriors slid a series of panels of felt across the open side of the shelter.

Saadet's bladder cramped. She pressed a hand to her belly. Paian, turning, touched her arm—a liberty she still found shocking, though among the Qersnyk, it was but a courtesy. "Khatun?"

Her face burned with embarrassment. "I have to piss."

"Of course you do," the shaman-rememberer said, exasperation on his face. Saadet steeled herself not to wince, but the irritation wasn't at her. "That young warrior is riding your bladder as if it were a prize red mare, isn't he? Esen, pull that panel open. The Khatun needs relief."

They let her out onto the steppe between the royal enclosure and a corral, backs turned in politeness as they made a circle around her—except for the woman who helped her manage her robes as she squat-ted. For a sharp moment, Saadet did not recognize herself—a barbarian queen pissing under the cold light of the rising moon. The hot per-fume of her urine on the frosty ground struck her as she stood again, stepping wide around the steaming puddle before she shook her robes into place.

The woman stepped back as Paian returned to her side. "Your sup-per awaits, Khatun."

She had not thought of food in hours, but her mouth flooded at the reminder. As she walked with the shaman-rememberer and her entou-rage, though, she remembered herself enough to ask after news and business.

Re Esen started to speak, but stammered and glanced at Paian as if waiting permission. "It is your news."

Paian shrugged matter-of-factly. "Your rival raises his banner at Dragon Lake, Khatun. Summer will bring war, if an army comes to him."

Saadet nibbled her lower lip for a moment before she remembered that that was a bad idea in the wind and cold. The skin could chap right off it. "Can we stop him?"

"We could try to intercept him," Esen said. "But that would not prove your claim to the Padparadscha Seat."

"Another usurper would be right behind him, you mean."

"Or a dozen." If Esen quibbled with the word *usurper*, he did not say.

Saadet felt Shahruz rejoin her, suddenly interested. "What proves my claim?" the twins asked.

Esen said, "Your war-band. Your babe's war-band, I should say. The number and quality of those that turn out to support him."

"The ability to impress enough warriors to win a fight, you mean."

There was a pause. The brothers glanced at each other, a communicating look that the twins recognized viscerally passing between these other siblings.

Esen stuffed his gloved hands into the patch pockets on his sheepskin coat. "Actually winning the fight counts too."

"I need to seem a fit Khatun. A fit mother of a Khagan, then."

Esen nodded. Paian stared into the middle distance, the sky bright with the twins' familiar stars and moon that must seem unutterably alien to him.

"I need to make a display of myself."

"Without," Esen said, "seeming to."

The twins nodded. Saadet could shoot—and Shahruz could shoot better. He could fight. Together, they could manipulate, sneak, and kill—

Esen added, and then choked: "Especially when . . ."

"Speak."

But it seemed stuck in him. It was Paian who finished the thought. "Especially when rumors fly, Khatun, of the Sorcerer-Prince arising from his tomb. And of the curse of Danupati breeding war and plague across the breadth of the world."

The twins felt a little thrill of triumph—Shahruz's triumph—at this evidence of the results of their work and sacrifice. Saadet's heart offered up only a kind of numb acquiescence.

"A woman can fly the eagles," the twins said, remembering that not all the austringers on her first, fateful wolf-hunt had been men. "Would a royal hunt prove my mettle?"

That sibling glance again.

"It wouldn't hurt," said Esen.

THE LONG LOW MEWS WAS WARM WITH CAREFULLY VENTED COVERED BRA-ziers and with feathered bodies, and it was rich with the ammonia scent of guano. Ranks of hooded eagles and other raptors sat on leather-padded stumps along each side wall, divided from one another by half walls. The austringers slept with their charges, and their bunks hung from chains against the shorter rear wall.

When Saadet had seen them before, both falcons and falconers had been caparisoned to be seen, the men and women in black livery twined with gold, the birds in mirrored furnishings. Now the austringers wore old clothes, stained with blood and haggled at the edges, and the raptors were hooded in soft worn leather.

A bell jangled as Saadet entered the mews, the pell-mell ringing of an eagle scratching itself. These birds were as flea-specks to al-Sepehr's rukhs, but they had their own majesty, and she paused a moment to appreciate it. Two falconers rose—not quite jumping, long-habituated to be cautious of jerky movements around their charges—but a third was coaxing an unhooded bird to take scraps of furred meat from her fingers, and did not even raise her eyes.

Saadet realized that it would have been kind to send ahead. This being a queen was a complicated business.

Saadet gestured her retinue back and waited just within the doorway, letting the felt-lined hide curtain drape, rattling its rings, to seal the warmth inside. The two standing falconers exchanged glances; one bowed, and the other stepped forward slowly. "Khatun."

"I have come to see my son's eagle," Saadet said, words she had been rehearsing in her head since she began the walk over. Qori Buqa had told her that the eagles had their own names, which they kept secret from men. She was not sure how else to refer to the bird. "That is to say, the eagle that flew for my husband."

The falconer indicated the bird that his female compatriot was coaxing. "She misses your husband, Khatun. She pines for him. We are doing what we can. . . ."

Trying to move sedately, like the professionals, Saadet tiptoed across the straw-strewn floor. The steppe eagles were broad-winged, copper-black in color, their napes picked out in feathers that caught gold off the sun. The females were larger and fiercer than the males, as is common in birds of prey, and the bird that had flown with Qori Buqa was the strongest of them all.

"Would it help her to fly?"

"We have tried, Khatun." No tone or trace indicated that he took offense. But that, too, was what it meant to be queen. "But her wing is still weak."

The eagle had been injured on that first hunt that Saadet had shared with Qori Buqa, and it was the twins' facility with a pistol that had saved her.

The falconer continued, "They bond, you understand. We must hope we can keep her alive until her mourning passes."

Saadet nodded. The unhooded bird peered over the shoulder of the falconer who tended her, tracking Saadet with illuminated irises striated gold and darker gold.

"Can you teach me to tend her?"

Saadet was not a large woman. One of the austringers glanced doubtfully at the girth of her arm.

"The royal eagles are heavy, Khatun—"

"We mourn the same man, she and I," Saadet said. "Perhaps our wings can become strong together."

Somewhere in the Grave Roads, the djinn left them, but Edene had learned better than to hope. He would return at whatever moment was least convenient and insert himself once more into her retinue—what Ka-asha Ghul insisted on calling her "court."

The Roads were no different with him gone. Dry stone, each of them, carven with the same masters' skills in evidence in the stone houses of Erem that had been quarried whole from the face of the living rock. They were quiet except for the dry, shuffling scuffing of padded ghul feet and the scraping, clicking of curved ghul toenails. They were strangely airy, not close and chill at all but well-ventilated and comfortably warm. None of that altered. Nor did Edene's newfound ability to see in the dark as conveniently as her subjects. Nor did her lack of hunger, her lack of thirst. Nothing concrete changed when the djinn left them—probably on some errand of his infernal master's, a thought that sparked Edene with fresh anxiety—and yet his leaving might have been the lifting of the overseer's whip. Edene and her ghulim all seemed to walk straighter, to move more easily in his absence.

Which irritated Edene. And the longer they walked, the more she thought about it—brooded on it, really. And the more irritated she became. Until she summoned Ka-asha and Besha Ghul to her with a flicker of desire. All she must do is want them, and there they were within moments, pushing through the ring of ghulim guards who surrounded her.

Upon contemplation, that irritated her too. It could go on the list, along with her milk-heavy breasts leaking into the front of her coat and the lack of mares in Erem. She tried not to think of Buldshak, not to wonder what had become of the rose-gray mare, descendant of the great Temurbataar. Or Sube, her mastiff. She told herself that her clan would care for her horse and her dog in her absence.

The ghulim genuflected irritatingly, and Edene irritably gestured them up to their feet. Everything chafed, hard and worrisome. Although it had not been what she meant to address, she frowned and said, "You may treat me with respect, but I do not wish to see the ghulim bowing and scraping. I am Tsareg Edene, and if you wish me to rule you, I will rule as a Khatun, not as if I were some soft-land queen with nothing better to do than sit her soft ass in a throne and cosset her soft feet with silk slippers and lotions. Have some pride in yourselves!"

The ghulim glanced at one another, startled. Ka-asha's shoulders came up, as if it would have flinched and kowtowed some more, but Besha Ghul caught it under the elbow and pulled it upright by force.

"Apologies, Qu—Khatun," Besha said. "We were not created for pride. But what you demand we learn, we will learn, Lady of Broken Places."

Edene's brow furrowed. "What of your own rulers?"

She had never met them. It only now struck her as odd. The Green Ring felt heavy, sharp on her hand.

"Our own rulers?" Ka-asha this time, hesitant, feeling its way around the words as if they had edges as sharp as its teeth and it was afraid to cut its tongue.

"The ghulim who lead you."

Ka-asha's ears flicked flat. "Ghulim do not command ghulim. The wearer of the Green Ring commands ghulim."

"But surely . . ."

Edene had not questioned the source of their fealty before. She had only accepted it, as if it were natural, expected. As if the truth of it were inevitable. She thumbed the ring, felt the metal warm and smooth, soft as if it were a part of her palm. It was not like her not to question. She picked at the edge of the ring with her nail.

You behaved as is natural, the calm voice told her. *You behaved as is right. You are their queen, and were always meant to be. You command the poisonous things of the world, and the broken things, and the things that creep in low places.*

She found that she had folded her fist closed and wrapped the other hand around the outside, hiding the ring. In her free Qersnyk soul, she felt sick.

"You were not *created* for pride."

"That is so," said Ka-asha, its voice lightening with relief.

"You were created to serve," Edene said, to make it clear to herself, clear in the air between us.

"That is so," said Ka-asha.

It is as it should be.

"The folk of Erem . . . you are not the folk of Erem."

"That is so," said Ka-asha.

"You were made by them. Made to serve the ring."

Ka-asha's mouth opened, but Besha Ghul must have squeezed its elbow until claws pierced cloth, and words dried in the ghul's throat like water poured on sand.

"We were made," said Besha. "And when we proved more willful than our creators desired, the ring was made to master us. We have waited for its return."

"Mother Night!" Edene exploded.

Both ghulim flinched this time, and every ghul surrounding her turned slightly, reflexively, before each as quickly forced itself back to vigilance. The ring throbbed on her hand. *Punish them.*

I'd sooner cast you in a fire!

Had she always had such a temper as this? Raging, she shouted, "Willful! More mindful, belike—no, no, I am not angry with you."

But they cringed nonetheless. *Order them to stand straight when they address you, if it pleases you.*

Edene gritted her teeth. That was not the point at all. She almost said, *This is loathsome.* But some sense of how the ghulim would interpret that—as if *they* were loathsome—stopped her.

"I would have you treat me as an honored leader," she said. "Not a tyrant. I will not dictate your behavior."

Ka-asha licked its lips. Edene wondered if the ghul was thinking of how she—Edene—had ordered the ghulim to fight when they were attacked by glass demons.

She was Khatun. She could feel doubts, even act on them—but she could never show them. She shook herself like a wet mastiff and said, "And another thing. We will not creep around the djinn. We are the masters of the ruins; we are the lords of the cracks in the world. He is—what, a thunder-strike, a big noise and a little fire. We will make him fear us, not the reverse!"

There was no murmur in response. *Was that too much a command?*

She'd never know. "As you wish," said Besha Ghul, and did not bow but nodded. There was a pained moment, and then Edene waved a hand in the dismissal the ghulim needed before turning forward to resume their walk herself. She worried at her lip with her teeth, though, in the dark they all could see through, and felt her thumbnail picking, picking at the edge of the ring.

What if I gave the ring to one of them?

What then would you do, to bring an army to Re Temur?

The worst of it was, she was not sure if the answer was her own voice, or the voice of the ring.

8

SAMARKAR SOUGHT THE SHAMAN-REMEMBERER AMONG THE RUINS, FOL-
lowing the warmth of his step with a wizard's *otherwise* senses. Night had
fallen. The stony daytime vegetation of Reason had given way to evening's lushness, uncoiled fronds finger-combing the light of the steppe's
scattered moons into tossing strands. Curls of mist caught, amplified,
and attenuated their radiance as Samarkar wandered, aware that her
black livery rendered her half-invisible in the dappled light.

She climbed a stone stair that rose and turned unsupported over air,
secured neither by banisters nor balustrades, feeling with her boot-toe
for each riser beneath the unfurled leaves of the wrist-thick vines. Tolui
had come before her; she could see the green-black smears where his
step had bruised the moist, tender vegetation against the stones.

The staircase ascended to a great baroque structure that draped itself organically down a cliff in tiers, its façade curtained by flowers like
a hanging garden, the many domes of its octagonal chambers collapsed.
Samarkar was minded of the fan-shaped fungus that grew clustered
and draped up ancient trees, or the bulge and slide of layered drapes of
melted candle-wax.

A thick-boled tree had taken root at the top of the cliff and its roots
had crept across the stained once-white face of the ruin—temple?

palace?—to seek rich loam at the base. The stair met the ruin between its parted roots, and beyond them was an empty door.

Samarkar paused at the last landing.

"Tolui?" she called softly, feeling foolish. Her voice echoed faintly, the only reply. She wiped her hands on the skirts of her coat and mounted the last dozen risers, summoning a witchlantern over her fingertips against the anticipated darkness.

But even without her light, it was not much dimmer within. The gaps left by the fallen domes admitted more moon- and starlight than the jungle trees, though their tumbled and overgrown blocks rendered the floor treacherous. The ragged-edged tops of the walls were an eerie frame for the starry heavens, making them seem close enough that Samarkar could touch them if she only scrambled up slumped stones and stretched out her hand—as if someone had draped swatches of dip-dyed and painted silk across the gap and shone a lantern through. On the other side of the floor the stair continued, mounting through the empty space enclosed by octagonal walls. At its top, Tolui stood silhouetted against the frame where a window was no longer.

Samarkar said his name again, softly, so he would not startle on the narrow staircase. Surely he must have noticed her light painting the stones, stringing out his shadow?

Perhaps he had. He half-turned from the hips, raising one hand to cup her forward. She advanced, picking her way. The fallen roof blocks were too matted with greenery to shift under her weight, but the whole ruin had a breath-held air, as if it were looking for any excuse to crumble. When she was a few steps below Tolui, the shaman-rememberer shifted left onto what might have been thin air, leading Samarkar to realize that the window pierced the thickness of the wall, but that the delicate, broken stone trellis that might once have held glass or tortoiseshell or alabaster continued the outside curve of the ruin, leaving a broad white ledge inside where they could stand within the arch of the window frame.

Samarkar stepped into it, to the left of the shaman-rememberer.

"Hsiung found another passageway," she said. "We have not yet opened it. Among its markings, we have located the words for *Road* and *Dragon*."

"Promising," said Tolui. "Assuming it takes you to the right part of it and not somewhere by the far south ocean. And assuming that the sorcerers of Erem had the same name for the same thing, and it's not somewhere else entirely."

"Calculated risk," said Samarkar.

The Dragon Road was not a single thing, but rather a series of pathways or borders, or something less obvious, marked across many of the principalities of Song and its neighboring kingdoms by polished disks of jade broad as temple floors and set as level to the earth. Its origin was the subject of dozens of conflicting legends, and whether it had anything to do with dragons in truth was a project for a more research-minded wizard than the peripatetic Samarkar.

"Qori Buqa is dead," Tolui said, "as the moons reveal. But his threat is not ended. I have it from my brothers in Qarash that his widow is with child, and has raised his banner."

"I see," said Samarkar. "I came to ask you about the new moon, actually."

"It is the moon for Temur's son."

Samarkar was still too much the Heir of Rasa to gasp. "So early?"

"Not early," said the shaman-rememberer. "Just soon." He brushed his fingertips against the crumbling stones as if idly dusting. "You should tell your lover that his son's moon will be the Sword Moon."

"The Sword Moon? An ill omen?" Samarkar thought of Afrit, the gorgeous and unlucky cream-yellow of the new colt's hide. And then she wondered, *How does he know?*

"It depends," said Tolui, "on whose hand the sword falls into. But its existence will be commemorated in our calendar. This is the Reign of the Blue Stud, Moon of Swords, Autumn of the only year of Qori Buqa's reign."

"Blue Stud?"

"By certain portents, and the birth of certain colts, we name the epochs of history."

"I see." Samarkar was half-minded to ask for details, but she worried that would inevitably lead either to offense, or to an extended course in Qersnyk cosmology. Which might be fascinating under different circumstances. "So the Sword Moon *is* an omen, but the interpretation is anyone's guess?"

"It is an omen of a child's birth. That, we may be certain of. As for the rest, some would read it ill, to be certain. Some of my brothers do."

Samarkar considered that for a moment, and decided that as Tolui had raised the topic, it would not be rude to ask. "How is it, Tolui, that you and the other shaman-rememberers can have so many opinions if you all share the same information, the same memories?"

He shrugged. "Are we the same man?"

Hesitantly, she leaned a shoulder against the window frame, tucking cold fingers inside the drape of her sleeves. "How did you become a shaman-rememberer?"

He laughed in that way that Qersnyk did, a huff of air through the nostrils with no sound behind. "How does one become a Wizard of the Citadel?"

"One studies," Samarkar said, companionably. "And then one has one's stones cut out by a surgeon, and if one survives the surgery, one sits in the cold alone until one either finds one's power, freezes to death, or discovers that one has no power to find."

He hummed softly. "There are two ways to be chosen. One can be born into the wrong body, or with two souls in one body. Or one can be struck by lightning and live."

"The Eternal Sky touches you."

He hummed again.

She did not ask which route had brought him to the service. If he'd wanted to be specific, he'd had his chance. Instead, she devoted her energy to figuring out how she was going to break the news Tolui had shared to the others. Especially Temur.

WITH THE RETURN OF THE SUN, TOLUI LEFT THEM.

Temur knew better than to argue with a shaman-rememberer. Hsiung's vow of silence prevented remonstrations. Hrahima was not the sort to interfere with another creature's free coming and going. And Samarkar avoided battles she couldn't win, so she simply stepped in beside him as he hefted his saddlebags and relieved him of the burden. "Let me help you with those."

She was taller and broader, though the Qersnyk all had the wiry physicality derived from a lifetime in the saddle or at the reins of a cart, from the hard labor of herding, planting, raising white-houses and packing them down again. She could not have claimed to be the stronger.

Still, Tolui let her carry his bags out of the shelter until she started toward the mouse-dun mare. "No," he said, falling out of step. The definitiveness of his refusal to move stopped her as surely as a chain.

She arced around him and came back. "No?"

"Her name is Jerboa. She is of the line of the copper-colored mare Haerun."

I bet she can jump, thought Samarkar.

"I leave her to you. Call her my gift to Temur Khan, in the expectation that one day he will rebuild a Sacred Herd. The steppe feels the lack of their hoofbeats."

"Sacred Herd?" She could not help herself.

"Ask your lover. My bags, please." Tolui draped them over his own shoulders as if he were a mule.

"You're going to walk out of the Shattered Pillars? With winter descending?"

"Fear not, once-princess," he said. "I don't have far to go."

She did not follow, but she watched him go, back along the road they had come in by, until he vanished behind the bony trees. Inside the shelter, she heard the rustle of Temur packing up. She turned and went to him, helping to collect cups and cooking vessels and other such small impedimenta as had become scattered around the camp. Temur had the Qersnyk facility for packing, and anything else Samarkar tried to do would only impede him and increase the bulk of the load.

She was bringing him a folding leather bucket when he said without looking up, "Don't worry too much about him. They seem to know where they're needed. I assume the same way they also seem to know what befalls any of their number."

Samarkar frowned at the back of her hands. "I think that a very pragmatic use of divine grace."

Temur gave her a tolerant look that made her heart beat more warmly in her bosom. "They are Qersnyk."

All right. She could let him make her laugh. "And the Qersnyk rulers are willing to admire the tenets of any faith that might consent to strengthen their own mandate. So why should the priests be any less hardheaded?"

Samarkar bit at the flesh of her thumb-tip, feeling a sudden—and unexpected—lack of grace. So long away from the Steles of the Sky; so long out from under the comforting embrace of her own skies, the eyes of her own Six Thousand Shrine deities.

I shall build you a shrine in the Shattered Pillars, she promised the small gods of her homeland. *You will have a prayer from me before we leave here, whether it reaches your ears or not.*

IT SHOULD HAVE HAD AN IDOL, BUT IN THIS CASE SAMARKAR MADE DO WITH an altar. There was no shortage of dressed stone, and she salvaged carefully while they waited for Hrahima's return with the meat that would fuel the first part of their journey—or feed them for a few days more here in Reason, if it turned out this doorway too was a false lead. Tolui had sneakily left them a number of supplies, but they were still walking a balance between hunger, rest, strength, the need to be where they were going, and the winter. They had opened three other doors— *Samarkar* had opened three other doors, with the attendant illness and pain—and they had learned that they could not even know until they passed through the door what hour it was in the land beyond. They had stepped from night to day, already, and from evening into afternoon.

It seemed best to be as prepared as possible, over trying to get an early start. But it also seemed wise to limit the number of doors they opened, lest one lead them out under the murderous daystars of Erem, into the tossing caldera of the Cold Fire, or some other equally terrible place.

Samarkar stacked square stones in courses like bricks, chinking with chipped bits to render them level. She found a threshold with no house remaining, small enough that she and Hsiung could lift it and slightly dished at the top with centuries of footsteps. With Hsiung's help, she hoisted it onto the top of her structure, where the weight settled the smaller stones.

She drew up water in a folding bucket to scrub it. Once it was clean, more water filled it like a font. There were idols here and there, graven images, some more whole than others—but Samarkar was not about to use unknown bits of the ancient gods or emperors of Erem in a shrine to the Six Thousand.

As the sun drifted behind the forked peaks with evening, Reason blossomed. Branches swayed under drifts of white and blue. Some of the blossoms glowed softly in the gloaming, like drifting lanterns. Hsiung left Samarkar to her work as Samarkar moved from tree to shrub, selecting and cutting flowers with appropriate rituals to acknowledge and sanctify the sacrifice. She was arranging them in the basin when Temur came up behind her.

He waited politely, but she knew his footstep. She tucked one last heavy-headed, many-petaled white bloom into place, whispered a benediction, and turned.

"What's all this?"

She shrugged. "I had an itch in my religion." She knew he prayed each day, standing up under the open sky. The Qersnyk sun setting to the west was proof enough that gods listened. "Is it time?"

He held out his hand and she took it. Side by side they returned to the shelter. Bansh and Jerboa stood under saddle, Afrit prancing awkwardly alongside his mother and bothering her to nurse. Someone had cut the shaman-rememberer's knots and bells from Jerboa's trappings, and Samarkar wondered if it had been Tolui, before he went. Hsiung leaned on a staff trimmed from one of the stony trees, his pack sagging from his shoulders, nowhere near full. And Hrahima lounged against a trunk nearby, one forearm braced casually against a bough high enough that Samarkar could have walked under it straight-spined without mussing her hair.

Temur mounted Bansh. Samarkar hesitated a moment before going to Jerboa. She had tried to argue Hsiung into riding the mare, but he had shrugged and gone back to wedging things into his backpack. It turned out a vow of silence could be awfully expedient when it came to winning arguments.

Samarkar swung neatly into the saddle. She'd become surprisingly accustomed to the high-cantled Qersnyk saddle, the flat-barred stirrups designed for standing in. Jerboa wore a more traditional Qersnyk bridle than Bansh's headstall with its gentle, jointed bit; Jerboa's nosepiece was a curve of steel integral to the bit, which could force a horse's head around under almost any conditions. It lacked the Qersnyk third rein, however—a left-hand strap designed solely for drawing the horse in tight circles while the rider slashed and cut with his long knife to the right. Samarkar wondered if a shaman-rememberer's mare would know how to fight.

She almost asked Temur, but decided it was a silly question. All Qersnyk ponies probably knew how to fight. Samarkar's own physical combat abilities, from horseback or otherwise, were much more sadly limited.

Jerboa sidled at Samarkar's unfamiliar weight, but settled. Her ears flicked for Samarkar's voice, and then they were off. Before long, Hrahima led them over the time-skewed cobbles of a side path they'd explored but little, toward the doorway they hoped would take them to Song. And to the right part of Song, moreover.

Samarkar rubbed together fingertips smeared with luminescent sap, wondering if an ink could be made from it, and how long the property persisted. She was caught up enough in her musing that she didn't hear the glassy chiming rising over the jungle night noises until Temur shouted, "Samarkar! Duck!"

She threw herself flat in the saddle, her abdomen crushed to the pommel. A rush of bitter air swept over her, stinging cold. Something dragged through her hair, tugging sharply, and she felt strands stretch and part. She grabbed at the under-edge of the saddle tree and kept her seat, though barely, wishing she had worn her helm and armor.

Hrahima snarled. Jerboa startled, though whether it was from the near-miss or the Cho-tse's anger Samarkar couldn't have guessed. She snatched at the reins, redoubling her right-handed grip on the saddle as Jerboa shot straight up in the air and came back down stiff-legged with a shock that traveled up Samarkar's spine and snapped her teeth together. Samarkar fought to restrain her, thinking, *Well, we got off on the wrong hoof.*

Confused sounds and images distracted her. Another chiming rattle. Hsiung's eyes flaring green. Hrahima making a banking leap off a tree trunk to knock something that seemed made of black glass, barbs, and spines out of the air as it dived on Temur. Temur with his long knife in his hand, and Bansh rearing up to bring him closer to an airborne enemy.

Whatever attacked them blended too sharply with the night for Samarkar to make out clearly. There might be three creatures, or a half-dozen. Transparent or translucent, chiming with each motion as if they were made of obsidian. Taloned, with long wings and insectile heads. Cold. So impossibly cold it seemed to radiate from them like heat.

"Glass demons," Samarkar said. "Where in six hundred Hells did *those* come from?"

No one answered. She heard grunts of effort from her friends, the melodic clatter of black wings. She hauled up a witchlantern and sent it soaring into the sky like a chrysanthemum rocket, pouring blazing blue light across the scene and rendering the trees as stark, two-dimensional tent poles. Ahead, she could just glimpse the tree-shaded bower that would lead them to the doorway.

"Run!" Samarkar cried, and let the dancing dun mare have her head again.

Ears flat, pale head bobbing like a white flag in the gloaming, the dun bolted as if it were what she had been born for. Samarkar clung to her scraggle of mane and to the saddle, the reins now only a courtesy. She ducked as a flapping, chattering demon made another pass, but it pulled up short with a disgruntled cry like a thwarted hawk as Jerboa swerved under the limbs of a tree.

Bansh's hooves beat a determined tattoo right behind them. Samarkar ducked overhanging boughs that seemed determined to scrape her from the saddle—or possibly just behead her. She could only hope that Hsiung and Hrahima were also following. She couldn't hear Afrit, and hoped he was tight on his mother's heels. Surely, Bansh would not have left him.

Trees clustered thickly, keeping the glass demons from diving. Cautiously, Samarkar began asserting her leadership over the mouse-colored mare again. The clearing was in sight, and from its center rose a long causeway leading between the trees and up, up, to a columned portico. It was just a door, unsupported by walls or any surrounding structure, high in the sky and completely undefended from the glass demons.

Samarkar would have found a use for that third rein now, but the metal nosepiece was aggressive enough that even half-panicked, the mare responded. As she slowed and they broke out of the narrowed path, Bansh and Temur drew up beside them. The calmer presence of the liver-bay seemed to penetrate the mouse-dun's terror. Jerboa sidled, her chin pulled almost back to her chest, then took two fretful sideways hops and settled. Half-settled. Samarkar could hear the chiming of glass wings above the cover of the trees, and was none too settled herself.

Afrit ducked between his mother's legs. Bansh offered him a good hard nosing; Temur scanned the trees above. But the heavy foliage and flowers—and the darkness—hid their hunters from them as effectively as the reverse. Hsiung jogged up behind them. Hrahima made a chuffing tiger-moan somewhere near, though she was invisible, and Jerboa nearly startled again.

"All accounted for." Temur waved up the long, narrow, sky-exposed causeway with the point of his knife. "That'll be fun."

"I can ward us," Samarkar offered. She'd been too busy riding her bolting mare to raise the protective walls of light and energy before now.

"Can you ward us *and* open the gate?"

"I did two things at once in Asitaneh."

"One of them didn't make you double over in agony."

She shrugged. "I'm more concerned about the jump through the doorway. It's a long way down if for some reason we're not transported."

"I'll go first," Hrahima said from somewhere above and to the left. Of course, the tiger could hear them perfectly. "That fall won't hurt me."

"I'll go first," Temur retorted. "Bansh won't fall."

"The more swiftly we proceed, the less time the enemy has to plan."

"Do glass demons think?"

"Under the circumstances, it's safest to assume they're up there drawing tactical maps in full relief."

"Your argument has merit," said Temur, settling it. "Samarkar, raise your wards."

"Hrahima, come inside please?"

Grudgingly, the tiger dropped from her tree. Jerboa sidled again, but Hrahima kept Bansh between herself and the mouse-dun, and Samarkar did not have to deal with any bucking—or another bolt. Afrit seemed completely oblivious to the Cho-tse as a potential danger—but his life was measured in days so far, and the tiger had been a part of all of them.

After a moment's concentration, wavering curtains of green light spilled up from the earth around the little party, touching in a flame-shaped peak above. Samarkar allowed herself a taste of satisfaction. If she was mastering only one damned element of the wizard's art and science . . . well, she'd been getting enough practice on wards.

Temur waited until they had brightened and firmed, a sheer wall shot through with wavering patterns of emerald, jade, peridot, and jasper greens like watered silk. Then he sent Bansh forward so deftly that Samarkar could not see the signal, the shift of his weight and balance that made the rider an extension of the mare. She was a perfectly competent horsewoman and had become more so over the previous months of travel . . . but she was no Qersnyk, and never would be. Afrit and Jerboa followed—Jerboa was obviously accepting Bansh as her leader, after the manner of mares, and was inclined to trust the bay's judgment—and Hsiung and Hrahima kept in a tight line behind. The mares would have to ascend the causeway single file. The priest and the tiger could walk two abreast.

Samarkar's neck was beginning to ache with the effects of her teeth-rattling shock. She worried about the colt and the wards, and the colt and the causeway. *Just follow your mother.*

Fortunately, that was in the nature of colts.

THEY CLIMBED, AND ALL AT FIRST WAS STILL. EERILY STILL; DANGEROUSLY still. The stillness of an unsprung snare. Temur on Bansh took the lead, the mare alert and quivering between his thighs, her cautious ears pricked until they almost touched at the tips. But she trotted onto the causeway as if she were trotting toward a manger full of oats. Afrit followed close enough to be switched by her nervously flickering tail. Temur worried that Jerboa might hesitate, or might whirl and bolt—but the pressure of Bansh moving away, and Hrahima closing behind her, overcame her natural reticence at the narrow path. Temur could hear her snorting, the disgruntled noises of a horse operating against its better judgment—but she kept up, and right now that was all that mattered.

He strained his ears for the chime of glass wings, but all that reached them was the susurrus of the trees, the night cries of jungle animals which hid away all day. He stroked Bansh's neck and found it lathered, shook the soapy sweat from his fingers and dried them on his trousers. Wet hands were no good on a bowstring. He reversed his archer's horn thumb ring on his right hand, as well, so he could easily slide it into position for the draw.

Samarkar saw him. He knew, because when he turned to loosen the saddle ties on his bow, she caught his eye and nodded. Whatever was beyond the doorway, they were hunted here. They had to commit to the risk of it now; there would be no scouting and coming back if the gate didn't lead where they needed it to lead.

They had climbed two thirds of the causeway when the ringing of crystal came again, carried on the night air like distant bells.

Bansh surged forward. Temur unlimbered his bow and nocked a crescent-headed arrow but did not draw. The humming tension in the string and the laminate made an anchor against his unease. Here was a thing he understood and knew. There was no mystery, no uncertainty to a bow. You stood inside it, summoned your skill, applied your strength, calmed your breath. And if you did all those things sufficiently well . . . the bow killed.

"There," Samarkar shouted.

Temur followed the line of her gesture and caught the flutter of broad wings, black on black, the lash of a barbed tail. The thing slammed into the ward with a jangling discord and a shriek as of steel on slate. Its talons dragged across the barrier, striking sparks like scoured flint— sparks flaring crimson, though Samarkar's wards were green. Temur ducked from the bright shower, but the sparks all bounced outward, streaking the night like falling stars.

Bansh broke into a canter. Temur let her have five strides, the others racing behind, then gentled her down. He could too easily see the mare running off the edge of the causeway, and while that might not be a problem for *Bansh*, Afrit and Jerboa might try to follow. Another glass demon whirred past, rolling to show them a baleful eye before slipping sideways under the causeway and tumbling wing-over-wing away, agile as a hunting bat. As Temur drew the mare up before the empty doorway, one more demon dashed itself against Samarkar's curtain of light, raining fire behind. Even Bansh shied; Jerboa struck the wards and would have heaved herself over the edge, Samarkar and all, if they had not been there. Standing in the saddle, Samarkar got her under control.

"Doorway." Temur felt like an idiot as soon as the command left his lips. Samarkar knew her role. And as soon as she could climb off Jerboa's back without being trampled, he was confident she'd do whatever she could to get them out of this particular predicament.

Somehow, she kept the wards up, calmed the mare, and managed to dismount while the rest of the group turned anxiously, staring at the various quarters of the sky. Hrahima hung back at the edge of the wards, her ears and whiskers twitching. Brother Hsiung took the dun mare's reins.

"Off the glacier and into the crevasse," Samarkar muttered, edging up alongside Bansh and Afrit, who was doing his best to kill them all by getting tangled between his mother's legs. The glass demons seemed to have learned a lesson, but now they pinwheeled around the wards like scraps caught in a vortex. Green radiance glared off their glossy, skeletal bodies, the glistening membranes of their wings. Temur leaned back in the saddle, drew his arrow back to his ear, and bided.

As Samarkar moved through the brief ritual of door-opening, the shrieking amplified, redoubled. Echoes broke from the looming walls of the narrow valley as the things turned, and turned, and turned again. The restless tension of the siege itched in Temur's fingers, along his nape. Hrahima uttered a low, involuntary growl, quickly stifled when the horses—even Bansh—scuffed and sidled.

Samarkar's incanting voice wavered and so did the watery light of her wards. A patch paled, then flared bright again as a fresh current of her strength swept across. Crimson sparks jetted as if from struck embers as one of the glass demons tried its luck on the weakened patch, reacting only instants too late to—perhaps—break through.

Temur's fingertip tightened against his thumbnail, holding a reflexive loosing of the arrow. Almost—

He could not look at Samarkar, but he could hear the pain in her tone—and he'd noticed it before, when she had opened the other doorways, but she seemed worse off now. The strain of working this wreaking while simultaneously holding up her wards was telling on her. Her voice caught, broke. She picked up the thread again, but not before the ward collapsed. An instant later it snapped back, smaller but brighter, but not before the glass demons had seen their opportunity.

Now they hurled themselves against the wards, squalling, one after the other. The force of the green wall—imagined, but not intangible—spun each demon cometary back into the dark. But each impact shuddered through the wall, rendering it a little dimmer, a little closer to where Temur and the others huddled within. The air chilled around them until every breath plumed, and frost feathered on the horses' whiskers.

Hrahima was forced by the shrinking wards to take a step forward, then two. Samarkar flinched with each demonic impact as if it struck her body rather than a projection of her will. Temur held high his bow until his arm trembled like that of a boy unhardened to the weight of weapons.

And Samarkar cried out, "Go!" as she fell to her knees, and all around them the wards shivered, shimmered, and dissolved into a falling rain of emerald fireflies.

9

Privacy was a commodity scarcely to be found in a harem. Ümmühan's status as a poetess granted her some privileges—such as the quiet of the high tower in which to work—but her status as a slave meant that these privileges were tenuous, and easily revoked.

Fortunately, she was popular with the other women. This was in no small part due to the effort with which she exerted herself to be pleasant, helpful, and charming—but also because a significant number of her peers protected her, most for her satires and a better-informed few for her priesthood. The latter was a closely guarded secret, held tight to the adherents of the Women's Rite—but even a woman who hated Ümmühan would hesitate to disclose the identity of a priestess. Many would protect her for the sake of her office, and should a woman who believed the Women's Rite to be a heresy discover her identity, she would still fear the retribution sure to follow a treason such as giving the name of a priestess to a man. Ümmühan thought of the best of such deniers as sad, delusional children who had accepted the twisted word of men determined to usurp the Scholar-God for their own. The worst were simple turncoats, traitors to women and blasphemous to the Scholar-God and Ysmat of the Beads, Her Prophet.

But quiet and privacy to compose poetry—to delight her fellow denizens of Kara Mehmed Caliph's harem with vipers and to entertain the wider court with the longer, more elaborate rhyming pastoral satires that often masqueraded as love songs—was not the same thing as privacy to perform a rite she had only read, never worked before.

Not sorcery: she was no sorceress. But the far more dangerous women's rite was what tempted Ümmühan now. There were not enough vipers in the world to pay for that order of solitude. But after some thinking, she had struck upon a plan. Audacious, to be certain . . . but what was a poet with no audacity?

Each night, after the women put their ouds and sacred texts away, the harem's lanterns were doused and the windows shuttered against the rising of the Demon Star. The custom was meant to ensure the women's protection from the influence of its baleful, wavering light. Learned doctors claimed that Al-Ghul could render women barren or insolent. Children conceived under its power might be deformed, and if they were even carried to term, they might show its influence in their character in later years. Some clerics advised drowning any babe even suspected to have been so conceived, or leaving it to the cleansing light of the desert.

The ignorant—adherents to the Falzeen sects, which to Ümmühan's mind was a longer way of saying the same thing—claimed that Sepehr the Sorcerer-Prince himself had been both conceived and born under Al-Ghul's light, but by her priesthood Ümmühan knew those assertions to be basest contumely. She also knew the fear-mongering about its influence on female character to be baseless. Lies, like so many lies, bred to rob women of their freedom, to constrain their sacred wit—naturally so much greater than the wit of men. It was only the just balance of the world that men were stronger, women wiser. But men, too often, used their strength to glorify themselves at the expense of women, when its rightful, sacred role was the protection of those created in the Scholar-God's image.

The star had ill influences, it was true . . . but as Ümmühan allowed her hair to be braided for bed, the only apprehension she felt was the apprehension of anticipation. A slave, one much less exalted than she, moved about the harem-chambers shuttering windows and dousing lights while Ümmühan reclined upon her couch, knees elevated with a velvet cushion. Darkness followed her movements, and a muffling of the night-sounds from beyond the windows.

The sighs of other women, the rustling of coverlets followed the movements of the slaves. Ümmühan lay tense, pinching the soft flesh of her hand to keep sleep back, rehearsing a name of many syllables in her head. She had heard that name spoken twice, which was enough for a poet's trained memory. Vipers were not written down, and she could recite a thousand of them perfectly. What was one long name?

In her careful—and carefully concealed—research, she had found the book where that name was written down, at least in part, though the balance had been concealed in cipher. It had been enough to confirm her recollections and awaken in her some deeper suspicions. Perhaps it would be wiser to chase those answers down before she sought the djinn's attention . . . but she feared that too precise an answer would only make her hesitate.

Even Ümmühan was not entirely immune to intimidation. So she lay in her covers and counted heartbeats until a muffled crier beyond the window announced the turning of the old day to the new: the darkest hour of the night.

Ümmühan rose in darkness and drew her nightclothes around her. They were rich, figured silk, but once she slipped from her quilted covers they did little to ward off the desert night's autumn chill. The stone floors bit through her slippers when she walked between the heaped rugs, making her toes ache. She had never seemed to suffer cold feet when she was a younger woman. Now, they afflicted her through all the stub of the year.

With their shutters drawn, the interconnecting rooms of the harem were that dark beyond dark where one could imagine one saw motion, outlines, shadows dancing—but it was only the eyes telling stories in the absence of true knowledge, as anyone would. Ümmühan stood a moment, listening to the breathing of sleeping girls and women. Kara Mehmed's wives and the wives of his retainers slept in a series of chambers off to the right, with a eunuch guard's couch pulled across the doorway. Another pair of men guarded the entrance to the whole of the harem.

Fortunately, Ümmühan did not need to leave her gilded cage tonight.

From the pocket of her over-robe she drew a pen, a modern ebony one with an angled nib of steel that she had honed to a razor edge against the grindstone on her ivory-inlaid writing desk. That desk was tucked away under her couch now, ink and paper and other precious things locked up inside, the stubby legs that just fit over her thighs folded underneath.

She crouched, cold silk draping against the skin of her feet and thighs, and from another pocket produced a stiff card of white leather, trimmed oblong and no bigger than her own delicate palm. She caught her lip between her teeth and breathed out all the air she held, so she would be holding none to allow her to betray herself with a squeak.

Grasping the pen in her right hand, she drove the left palm against the sharpened nib, piercing skin over the little mound below her forefinger. The pain was sharp—it always was—and her teeth nearly left a betraying crescent in her lip. But she managed to gasp only, with no voice behind it, and held the pen in place while heat told her the blood welled.

She rested the leather card upon her knee, and quickly, with sure strokes despite the darkness, she wrote her prayer. The letters for *silence* and *slumber* took shape behind her nib. As they formed, they shone with a delicate silvery shimmer like starlight caught in glass, casting only enough illumination to gently limn her fingers and the barrel of the pen.

The woman who was called by her master the Illiterate was no wizard, no sorceress. She was a priestess. The greatest poet of her generation. And when the perfectly formed letters of the Uthman tongue echoed the writings of Ysmat of the Beads, they had a power all their own.

This was not blasphemy, was not heresy. Was not demon-magic such as the heathens practiced. This was the purest refinement of Ümmühan's priesthood, the blessing of the Scholar-God on those who kept Her scripture and Her Word. The faint light filled Ümmühan with peace as she spent a moment regarding the sacred beauty of these words, contemplating their power to protect her—drawn from the Prophet's own faith and strength. Ysmat of the Beads gave miracles to protect those who properly honored Her.

This was no sorcery, but a prayer.

Ümmühan laid the card on the floor before her. When she stood, she was wrapped in a faint whorl of starshine—the benediction of Ysmat of the Beads. *In the path of the whirlwind,* she thought, *the moonlit desert lies afire.*

She drew breath after breath, filling herself with air as if she meant to dive deep. As if she were about to declaim before a king—a task that had not daunted her since she was a maiden of seventeen rains. But in those cases, the price of stammering was embarrassment, or at worst a diplomatic incident. In this, she would have to pronounce every syllable on one breath, correctly and without stumbling. Any poet knew what happened when you mispronounced the name of a djinn; all her precautions against discovery would be as naught if she were simply transformed into a scorpion or some other scurrying thing.

One last breath, held for a second while she organized her courage, and she cried out softly: "O Fy-m'shar-ala-easfh-ala-wtqe-shra-tw'qe-al-nar-ala-fasheer!"

Silence, the air at the reach of her fingertips thick with darkness that the glow from the card could not cut. And then a lessening, a softness in it. A blue shimmer as if from the hottest embers Ümmühan could imagine. A warmth in the autumn night.

"There should have been a brazier," whispered a voice she had heard before. But it had been booming, then, ringing tower-tall under an unconstrained sky. Now it was mild, intimate. A little fraught with mockery. "Haven't you ever summoned a will of fire before?"

"I do not mean to bind you," Ümmühan said. "We are all the Scholar-God's creatures, and . . ." she touched the golden collar lying warm against her clavicles ". . . you see, I am enslaved as well."

She knew the face that coalesced before her, triangular and clever as a ferret's, blue as the heart of a flame, topped with spikes of indigo hair. He was no taller than she was, slender, the shadows beneath each rib like the darknesses that breathe across flickering coals.

He tilted his head like a curious dog. "So you are. But you rode the wind with al-Sepehr."

"He is a great man," Ümmühan said carefully, though her heart leapt a little at the sound of his name. A man like that, though, would want no liaison beyond politics with a slave-poetess. And . . . he had done what he had done to her city and her people. "Very powerful."

"As powerful," said the djinn, "as the man who holds your chain?"

Ümmühan smiled. *More so, and a better warrior.* Her approval of Kara Mehmed was severely limited. "As you are the Scholar-God's creation," she said, "and as you are the djinn who aided the Emperor Sepehr al-Rachīd, called the Sorcerer-Prince by those who know no better, I charge you to aid me in Her work and for Her glory."

The djinn tipped his head and smiled. "So much for not commanding me."

"Do we not serve the same true God?"

"Do we?" The djinn seemed to study his hands. "You creatures have never learned the edge of your arrogance. You would set your gods up over the world, never knowing if they create you or you create them. You've no inkling of your own power, and yet are quick to shift it away. Take some responsibility, meatling."

His derision confused and stung Ümmühan. Not her pride—she was a woman and a slave, and could afford no such egotistical male luxury—but his disdain of the Scholar-God. Were not djinn and afrit alike Her creatures, created by Her as She had created man? Ümmühan had not expected . . . blasphemy.

While she was considering, the djinn continued, "You spoke my name. What is it that you want of me? Wishes? I can grant your freedom. Riches. Love—"

"Love," Ümmühan scoffed, on firmer earth now. "A trinket sold to girls in exchange for their intellect."

"What then?" *Ask,* his pursed lips said. *And quickly. I am a very busy djinn.*

"*Has* Sepehr al-Rachīd returned?"

"Can a dead man rise up from his bones?"

"One who does not wish to answer often replies with a question of his own."

Mocking, the djinn said, "If you believe he is, I suppose you might be right."

His tone suggested some deeper context to his words, and Ümmühan hung a frame in her memory-castle to ponder his meaning later. She said, "Do you wish to be free of al-Sepehr?"

She knew he did. She—and al-Sepehr's great Rukh—had been the only witnesses to their argument.

"I suppose *you* will help me?"

"I wish the true glory of my God recollected," Ümmühan said, swallowing against a thrill of excitement. He had not denied that he was Sepehr al-Rachīd's djinn. "I wish Her priestesses honored as She intended. It seems to me we can be allies."

"You are a transient thing. You are gone between breaths."

"But my God endures. And my spirit is immortal in Her care. How can it harm you, O Great One, to have allies that he who has enslaved you underestimates as well?"

The djinn paused, a hand upraised, flaming eyes narrowed. He waited, and though sweat sprang out on Ümmühan's brow in defiance of the chill, she met his gaze and lifted her chin. The silence grew long and thick.

The immortal glanced away before the Illiterate. He might have chosen to do so; another one of his games?

"It cannot," the djinn said. "Spin your web, mortal girl."

To Yangchen-tsa, each day's travel along the Tsarepheth to Rasa road seemed desperately inadequate. Without the punctuation of nights passed in noble houses, keeps, and strongholds the journey as a whole began to seem interminable. And if she, who had made this journey every year, was feeling adrift, how much worse must it be for those who had never come this way before?

Uncertainty and frustration were worse enemies than exhaustion and hunger, she realized. A man with a goal to walk toward would keep lifting one foot after the other long beyond the point at which any sensible person would expect his strength to have failed. A man who felt himself adrift would not be able to force himself to struggle so valiantly. And Yangchen was surprised to find herself determined to reach Rasa with as many of her subjects alive and still moving forward under their own power as possible.

Stories would help, she thought. She recruited the wizards, her advisors, and even Gyaltsen-tsa and her surviving ladies to go out among the camps at night and tell tales, such as they could—remembered bits of history, legends of heroic deeds, romances of wizards, warriors, dragons, princes of foreign lands. Each would take up a post beneath a pole upon which flapped a bright, improvised banner, and any who wished to be cheered could gather around. She saw to it that food was inventoried, that the quartermasters collected what they could from the civilians and rationed it back again to all as needed. Of course there was hoarding and resentment and tightened belts—but while there was hunger there was no starvation. Not yet, anyway. Not yet.

Finally, in desperation for some sense of progress, she had Doctor Anil paint a map on the side of her wagon, onto which each day he gilded their route and how far they had come. At first she had thought to have him work on a parchment map—but it occurred to her that the refugees—that the *rest* of the refugees—needed proof of their forward motion as badly as she did, if not more so. And thus, the wagon's wall. He wasn't much of a cartographer, as wizards went—but he was a wizard, which made him a better cartographer than almost anyone else.

It was something, Yangchen told herself—sipping the same thin congee the others got, nursing her fussing son, putting in hours astride Lord Shuffle, leading the column. And something was better than nothing. And at least, up here, she was ahead of the dust.

They managed to obtain some supplies from the noble household that guarded the high saddle of the final pass, a keep that would normally have been the third night's destination and in this case took three times that. And once they got down out of the highlands, to the Rasan plateau, there would be more food and more shelter. No one would die of hunger by then, though many would be weak and miserable. They had the contents of the treasury. They were not without resources.

The mountains dropped away before them and mounted up behind. Every night was colder than the last, the frost sharp and heavy now. Yangchen took her comfort in Lord Shuffle. In the evenings, when they made camp, she took to riding the spotted steer up into the hills, scandalously alone or—even more scandalously—with Anil-la for company. This novel sensation—this was freedom, which she had never known before. Never even known enough about to imagine. And she was coming to crave it, as opium-chewers craved the bitter poppy gum.

On the night when Doctor Anil's gilded line, burnished against the wagon slats with a round stone tool and gold leaf that had been stored on the sheets of leather it was pounded thin between, reached the boundary of the high plateau, the Dowager Empress Regent Yangchen took her supper in the form of strips of roast yak, seared, salted, and bloody in the middle. She wrapped them in a waxed cloth, gave her son to his nurse, and swung into Lord Shuffle's saddle, sending na-Baryan away when he tugged at her stirrup and tried to insist that someone ride with her.

The itch in Yangchen's chest quieted when she was alone, finally, riding into the stony hills and listening to the hubbub of the camp drop away behind her until it was hushed under the gentle shimmer of Shuffle's bridle bells. She had little daylight left, and meant to use what there was to get as far from other people as Shuffle's trot permitted.

He moved over the rough terrain like a cloud, small neat hooves leaving almost no trace of where they had been. At last, he attained a hidden meadow, concealed from the road below by a stand of the wind-twisted shrubs that grew more common as they descended toward the plateau. In the silence, all Yangchen heard was the bells, his hoofbeats, and the wind.

She reined him in and sat a moment, looking back the way they had come. The shoulder of a mountain hid most of the river's course, and clouds banked the Island-in-the-Mists and the Cold Fire. She wondered how much of Tsarepheth still stood, and if any of those infected with the demon spawn would live. She wondered how the Citadel's wizards were faring in their struggle to contain the eruption. *Mother Dragon,* she prayed, though Rasa's gods were not the gods of her childhood. *Let my city survive.*

She closed her eyes, as if that would give the prayer more weight. When she opened them, she resolved, she would eat. She had no appetite, but she must have food. It was her responsibility to keep herself strong.

Before she was quite ready to face it, Shuffle stomped and snorted, pulling at the reins through the ring in his wet pink nose. Yangchen's hands closed reflexively over soft leather. Her eyes flicked open and she in her turn nearly screamed.

A semicircle of demonlings crouched on the ground before her, transparent black wings furled around their sticklike bodies, heads lowered as if in genuflection. There were a half-dozen of them—larger than the spawn that clawed their way out of the lungs of the afflicted, smaller than a grown woman.

They seemed to be carved of obsidian. Were they spirits of the Cold Fire, somehow sprung from the wrath of the volcano? She glanced over her shoulder as Shuffle backed away, horns lowered and head dropped to protect his throat. Ice crept up her throat, swam along her veins. She must be cold; her shudders rattled the reins. She had been an idiot to ride away alone, an idiot to risk herself—

The largest demonling raised its head and spoke in a voice like brittle ice.

"Waymaker! We honor you! From out of the deep past, we honor you!"

It froze her in place. She might have reined Shuffle around, risked turning her back to the things just for the sweet relief of bolting. But those words—those perfectly identifiable words, in Rasan cleaner and more accentless than her own—

Get away from me.

Shuffle's ears flipped. He sidled again, muzzle almost scraping the earth as he tossed his head—an open threat.

"Waymaker!" the thing said. "Praise the Waymaker!"

It warbled, and after a moment the rest warbled with it. Yangchen waited for them to spring, for the air around her to fill with their razory-looking wings and talons, the lash of barbed tails. But they just bobbed and genuflected, almost seeming confused when she burst out—

"Get back! Get away from me!" Convulsively, she hurled the first thing that came to hand at the leader, if that's what it was. It was the waxed packet of her dinner.

The thing's head snapped, slashed. Shreds of meat fell here and there and demons pounced, squabbling over the slim pickings. Their wings rustled and chimed.

"Praise!" the demon cried again.

Yangchen broke at the same instant Shuffle did. They whirled as one beast, in perfect accord, and she gave him his head as he plunged along the narrow path back toward the encampment. She crouched over his broad humped back, clinging close. At every moment she expected to hear those wings behind her, to feel the talons along her spine. But all that followed was that brittle voice again.

"Praise she who feeds us!"

And the answering voices, more brittle still—"Praise! Praise! Praise!"

IN THE MORNING, YANGCHEN ROSE BLINKING IN THE EARLY LIGHT. HER stomach knotted tightly; she had not eaten after the loss of her supper the night before. But that was forgotten as the sun rose before her. Behind their destination. Though Rasa was still invisible with distance, no mountains occluded the sun's rays.

A ragged cheer began, stilled, and rose more vibrantly as, one by one, Yangchen's people realized what that pale morning meant. Among their cries she heard her name, her still-unfamiliar new title. A rising chant.

They had come out of the Steles of the Sky alive, before winter. And the sun was rising in the East.

THE STONES WERE GRITTY AND CHILL UNDER SAMARKAR'S KNEES AND palms. The air burned her ears with cold. A storm of wings whipped her hair up, the petals of her coat tossed around her. A moment, and those cold claws would score her back, those cold mandibles cut her flesh—but the pain that stitched her abdomen would not even allow her to rise.

She'd meet her doom on her knees, then. They'd fix it if a song ever got written.

But the thing that clutched her was not the talons of a demon. It was a hand—cold, but no colder than her own shuddering body—flesh, strong, familiar. She found herself slung over a saddle, the pommel striking in the bruise her own saddle had left, the stitched-up agony of blowback from the door-opening almost eclipsed by new pain. All the air left her in a rush and wouldn't come back in again. She vomited, and couldn't even get any force behind that: bitterness just trickled between her teeth and dripped down the dark shoulder of the horse beneath her.

Bansh, she thought, too sick to feel relief, as the mare gathered herself and leaped into darkness. The heavy thud of her hooves striking soft, grass-smelling earth was the last thing Samarkar felt before more darkness followed.

Darkness, but not insensibility. The mare's lather soaked Samarkar's sleeve and trousers; the acid-sharp scent of vomit stung up her nose, seeming to fill every cavity in her skull. Bansh settled on her haunches and whirled. Temur's steadying hand left Samarkar's back, and she heard the thrum of his bowstring twice in quick succession.

Thuds, cries. The Cho-tse's yowl and the scream of a terrified mare. A sound as if a great glass window shivered into a thousand pieces, and the patter of something light and sharp against Samarkar's back, her hands . . . getting caught up in her hair. Temur brushed at her and almost immediately stopped again. His voice said her name once, then again.

I've fainted, Samarkar thought, as someone—by the size of the hands, Hrahima—lifted her off Bansh's back and laid her in softness. The grass was warm; the sun on her face was warm. The breeze tickled.

"Turn her head," Temur said, but Hsiung was already doing so, opening her jaw, straightening the position of her tongue. Her strained neck cried out at the touch, though it was ever so gentle. This was a peculiar cottony sensation, to be aware of what the hands and voices around her were doing—but as if her awareness ended at her senses, and her body were immovably heavy. Or just disconnected entirely from her consciousness, a thing she was trapped in but over which she had no control.

She tried to say *I'm fine.* Not even a moan escaped her. Again, hands—feather-soft—brushed against her. Someone grasped her hand and chafed it; that brought sharp, unanticipated pain. She heard Temur swear in Qersnyk, and the motion stopped immediately. Heat trickled across her skin.

"This damned glass—"

"She's fainted," Hrahima said. "It's all right. She's breathing. Just give her air."

Thank you.

Maybe a flutter of a moan that time? *Intriguing. So this is what fainting is like. I would have thought it would be . . . more complete.* Samarkar would have laughed, if she were able, to recognize her own trained wizardly detachment. Observe, observe. Under all conditions. She'd read wizards' notes on their own fatal illnesses, on experiments that had ended in their mutilation or crippling. The best of her order could find the discipline to study anything. *I guess I have become a wizard.*

Brightness. A blur. Stems of green grass, too close to make out. Her eyes—finally—focusing. She turned her head so she faced upward. The sky was a deep, saturated violet that clenched her chest around remembrance. The sun that hung halfway up it was no more than a pinprick, but arc-blue and brighter than noon in Tsarepheth. Samarkar was certain she recognized it. She could have laughed bitterly to be so damned glad to see the cursed thing.

"I am fine," she attempted to say again. This time she got something that recognizably tried to be words, even if they were unintelligible. The next ones came out better. "I just got the wind knocked out of me."

"Well," Temur said, "it looks like only one followed us. And we got it. Or at least, we hit it a few times and it burst like a cannon shell. Careful, you're covered in glass powder, which scratches."

That explained the drip of warmth down her hand, sticky and slowing now. "We should shut the doorway."

"We should do a lot of things," Temur said. "It can wait until you can sit up without falling over."

She tried to nod, head pressed into the warm curve of the soft earth, and almost vomited, fainted, or both—again. The stabbing pain in her neck told her she had been lying when she said she was fine—but there wasn't much any of them could do to correct that now, and it was probably just the result of the shaking she'd gotten. It gave her a sense of fragility that she found irritating, even as she began carefully to test her limbs.

"This looks like a Hard-day. Are we in Song?"

"You're asking for a guess based on slim evidence, monkey-wizard," Hrahima said. "There are other blue suns in the sky."

But her voice was amused, and Samarkar heard the rustle of Brother Hsiung's threadbare robes as he bent over her and nodded, his shaved pate catching the light.

The dizziness waned. Samarkar suddenly wanted very badly to be on her feet. "Horses?"

"Fine," Temur said warmly. "Bansh got a bit of a slice while we were picking you up, but she's had worse and lived to brag about it. You can stitch it for her when you're upright."

"Help me sit."

They did, Hrahima standing back and observing as Brother Hsiung and Temur supported her. It was easier than she'd feared, and those black tunnels did not swirl in again from the edge of her vision. As long as she kept her neck straight and still, she could bear the pain. Still she could see nothing but the long grass tossing in the breeze and obscuring the horizon. The sky above, violet-blue as lacquer, was the impossible Song sky she remembered from her time in her late husband's court.

"Song," she said, after a few more moments. She felt strong—despite the bruised ache in her ribs and solar plexus and the wringing spasms that still racked her interior. Temur gave her a hand, and Hsiung lifted under her elbow. Samarkar leaned on them more than she really thought she needed to, because they seemed to want to feel useful. Once on her feet, above the level of the grass, the landscape that surrounded them was such that she almost forgot to be wobbly.

They stood on a rise near one edge of a narrow valley, more lush and green than any place Samarkar had ever seen. Gray-white limestone towers and hills so tall and steep and narrow that they seemed the result of some carver's art, not nature, rose lopsided and heavy with greenery on every side. Tier upon tier, melted-looking and strange, they marched back until lost in the haze of distance. A slow shining river meandered down the valley's center, gleaming under the sun, and closer at hand Samarkar could make out mirage-bright pools of water, many of them almost perfectly round.

The whole landscape had the look of a Song silk painting, as if someone had taken a heavy brush thick with streaky green and gray watercolor and dabbled impossible arabesques into a misty background.

On the hillside—really a rock face—to their left, a moss-hung stone archway stood alone, unattended by other structures. Samarkar supposed that was this end of the doorway from Reason.

She shaded her eyes with a flattened hand for a better view down the valley. Temur and Hsiung stepped back, giving her room, but not too far. They were ready to catch her if she stumbled. Warmth flushed her at their concern.

Blinking, then, she realized that some of what she had taken for pools of water were in reality a flat jade pavement composed of flagstones thirty paces across, each polished from one gigantic massif.

This enormous road meandered along beside the river, green and serene under the light of the sun.

Samarkar gaped. "The Dragon Road. We found it."

"We found it," Hrahima said. "Now what we are going to do with it, that's an open question yet."

10

THEY CAME OUT OF THE DARKNESS OF THE UNDERWORLD INTO THE DARK-
ness of a night that nevertheless lit Edene with the buoyancy of joy. In
the midst of her ghulim, she stopped dead, feet planted, neck arched as
her head tilted back. Her plaited hair fell over her shoulder to drop
along her spine, heavy with the ropes of black and silver pearls the ghulim had insisted on braiding into it for her triumphant return to Reason. For a moment, she just stared and blinked, eyes watering.

Her sky. Her stars. *Her* moons.

And moreover, Temur's moon, iron-red and iron-gray, and beside
it—leading it—a moon Edene had never seen before. A moon with
wavering bands of dark and paler silver streaking its face, like watered
silk or fold-forged steel.

She knew whose moon that was. And she knew what it meant, moreover. It meant the Sky accepted Re Temur's claim to be head of his clan,
and his clan's claim to be head of all clans. That could change, of
course—it had changed in Edene's mother's mother's mother's lifetime—
but her son was marked as one of the heirs of the sea of grass, and only
his death or the fall of Clan Re could strike that mark from the heavens
now.

"Ganjin," she whispered, her fingers curving as if to grasp, her arms aching for the weight of her son. Instantly, his ghul nurse was with her, offering her son. Ganjin's head cradled in the crook of Edene's elbow as she drew him to her breast. She curved over him protectively for a moment, breathing in the warm sweet scent of him. Then with sharp confident movements, she unwound his swaddling cloths.

She raised her son naked to the light of the new moon.

"In the name of Re Temur Khagan," she said to Mother Night and to her other half, the Eternal Sky, "I present to you your son."

He wailed, of course, as the cold air struck him. That was good, the lusty cry of a strong infant's irritation. The Sky would hear him. Hands unsteady with emotion, Edene wrapped him up again. His nurse reached for him, but Edene shook her head and loosened the collar of her robe to put him to the breast.

Her hands were not all that trembled. Suddenly, her whole body ached with need. Temur was here. It was Temur who had claimed this place, who had raised his banner and reclaimed it for the Qersnyk people. Because only by declaring himself Khagan could he have caused Mother Night to hang for his son a moon.

He was here. He was close. He was well.

And Edene was about to see him again.

"Search everywhere," she told her ghulim, while the trees whispered around them and dog-nails clicked on white cobblestones. "Harm no one!"

"Do we fight?" asked Besha Ghul.

"Not under this sky," said Edene, cradling her son. He was warm and heavy, solidly reassuring her that—unreal as it seemed—this was not a dream. She half-expected him to turn to smoke in her arms, taking this blessed, blessed sky with him—

"Young Rakasa drinks the ring with every suck at your teat, witch-queen."

The voice could have made her jump, except now she was always steeled against it. Not an evaporating sky—but perhaps the next least-welcome thing. Edene would not give the djinn even the satisfaction of acknowledging his existence. She turned her head aside and said to Ka-asha, "If your people find anyone here at all, that person is to be protected at all costs. Do not approach them. Do not engage. Come and find me at once!"

"As you command," said Ka-asha.

Edene winced, though the ring hummed with pleasure on her hand. Its comfort seeped into her as well, lessening the irritability she was coming to think of as a natural part of her personality. She could not prevent herself from making commands. And yet, every order she offered was an affront to dignity—her own, and that of the ghulim. It was one thing to take captives in battle. Quite another to command their wills by the magic of some filthy sorcery.

And yet . . . she needed them.

"You look in unexpected places for your lover," said the djinn.

"Shut up."

"As you command," he mocked. But when she turned on him, eyes stinging with rage, he raised his hands in a parody of surrender. She fixed him with a glare. He dropped his eyes.

He doesn't need those to see with.

No, but at least it was a parody of submission. Close enough to placate her.

The ghulim fanned out through the forest and the ruins that framed it. Edene found a white road leading down into the valley, and with her honor guard she followed it. It met another path that ran along the edge of a gully and she paused there for a moment, wondering in which direction to go. It would be most sensible to just wait—but Temur was here, so close. She knew that it would not be her who found him, enmeshed as she was at the center of a web of ghulim. But she did not have it in her to stand still.

Or to pace aimlessly back and forth like some Uthman in her tower. She snorted scorn at the image. It was the impetus she needed to choose her left hand at random—not quite at random: it was the direction that followed the moons—and stride raggedly along the road. Her ghul-tailored robe slapped her booted ankles. Ganjin had released the breast and stared up at her with eyes dark and starry as the sky above. Every step came with a heart-stutter of excitement and anticipation. The first sweat she had broken since she put the Green Ring on her finger stuck her clothing against her shoulders. She trembled, and held her son close to hide it.

Before long, she smelled horses. Horses, blood, fire. Amniotic fluid. The funk of a big cat, and the smell of several people. That she could pick that out with the aid of the ring; the scent was too far and faint for her to have noticed alone.

The ghulim smelled them too. Heads went up; black noses rose sniffing as cowls were dropped down backs. Then a baying rose in the distance—the scouts crying for attention and assistance. The crash of running feet—some of those same scouts returning.

The djinn chuckled. "He's collected another paramour already, by the stink of it."

"Leave me," Edene said, without turning to look at the djinn. The ring blazed on her hand; her anger blazed in her chest.

"Not forever," he answered.

She jerked her arm up, showed him the back of her hand. He melted into a whorl of blue sparks, a coil of smoke, and without a sound was gone.

Besha Ghul's taloned hand wrapped lightly about Edene's upper arm, black thumb so long and knobbed it overlapped the sticklike fingers. Edene rose up on her toes, a coursing hound that could not be restrained, the pull of her injuries forgotten. Besha Ghul could not restrain her, even if it had meant to try. All that happened was the ghul was swept up by Edene's stride—and running, running flat, she crossed the distance faster than a mare could gallop, faster than an eagle could fall. It seemed three strides, a blur, and she stood with Besha Ghul before a low rectangular structure whose dark door gaped wide. The roof was hidden under knots and gnarls of flowering broad-leafed vine, giving the whole shed the appearance of a hollow hillock, the sort of barrow the Western men built to trap their dead.

The eastern sky was graying, the moons slipping behind the mountains one by one. Edene could see the trample of hooves in the dooryard—two mares and a foal—and the marks of several pairs of boots or sandals. And the pugmarks of an enormous tiger, interleaved with the others, crossed and crossed again.

"Cho-tse," Besha said, still gripping Edene's arm, standing sideways, but with its long neck twisted and straining for a better look. It panted. Edene raised her hand for silence and craned up, sniffing. Temur, yes, Temur had been here. But the scent was hours cold, perhaps the whole width of the night, and there was no fresher nearby.

"They've gone," Edene said. "Let us find them."

"They could be anywhere," Besha said. "Reason was a city of door-ways. Some of those ways are open still."

The ring knew what Besha referred to, and so Edene did also. Gates, cracks in the world one could slip through. Like the Grave Roads—but other than the Grave Roads.

On the crown of her head, Edene felt the first warmth of a beloved sun. All around her, ghulim were flipping cowls up, hunching in the shade of their colored robes. Edene shook her plait back, hearing the pearls rattle.

"Do not fear this light!" she told them, but they still turned their faces away, hunching their shoulders and becoming shapeless under the mass of their robes.

Sadly, Edene stroked Besha Ghul's arm. "This light will not harm you."

"It is bright to the eyes nonetheless." But the ghul let the tip of its nose peek from the shade of its cowl. Velvet eyes sparkled behind it, peering up like a shy child's. Edene felt a rush of tender affection quite at odds with the warlike yearning that simmered in her bosom, a low heavy heat that had lived behind her breastbone since she found herself captive of the Nameless Rahazeen. She had forgotten what it felt like to move through the world ungrounded by its weight and purpose, and the instant's release was disorienting until it passed.

On every side, though, as the ghulim cloaked themselves, the leaves and fronds and blossoms of the forest were curling up, sliding inside their stone stems, warding themselves from a blazing light that would not come. Edene started back, realizing—

They will die in the dark. They will grow white and waxen and fade. This is not the sky of Erem any longer, where the nightsun may feed even that which hides the day-suns' wrath.

"No, children," Edene said, touching her green-gold ring and then the arm-thick, hairy trunk-stem of the vine where it trailed down a stone trellis at the front of the structure. "There is no light for you at night now. You must seek your sustenance in the sun."

Hesitantly, as if seeking reassurance, one curled frond reached to-ward her fingers like a spring slowly giving up its tension. It brushed the back of her hand, downing the fine hairs in shimmering pollen. Then, as if flame licked the edge of paper for a moment before the whole leaf caught, a thread of green seemed to rush away, to propagate through the whole vine.

Leaf after leaf after blossom, the plant relaxed into the daylight. On every side, sweeping away, a rustle of leaves bore witness to the change that raced through the jungle.

For the first time in the world, the forests of Reason bloomed under a daysun's rays.

THE GHULIM FANNED OUT THROUGH THE TREES, SEEKING TRACES OF MEN, Cho-tse, and mares. Edene waited, still standing in the clearing beside the abandoned shelter. She ducked inside long enough to see where Temur and his party had camped, to see the dark stains and hoof-scrapes of a birthing by the rear wall. She left Besha Ghul wringing its long hands nervously beside the door and crouched next to the spot in the dust smoothed by Temur's body and brushed it with her fingers. The patch was broad; there were two scents.

Someone—a woman, almost, except her smell was strangely flat—a woman past her blood, then—had lain beside him.

The ring burned on Edene's hand. The war-wrath burned under her breastbone—

He has not betrayed me. For here he is in Reason, and why would he come to the Shattered Pillars if not in search of me?

A Khagan could have many women. But only Edene would be the mother of his firstborn son. And this woman, whoever she was, was past bearing. Her scent said so, and the scent did not lie.

Edene made herself smile. This woman, whoever she was, had come with Temur in search of her. Along with another and unfamiliar man, and a person who by his scent was touched by Mother Night—a shaman-rememberer—who slept by himself away from the others, and a Cho-tse warrior. These people were Edene's allies, because they were Temur's allies. These people would fight to protect Ganjin and Temur both.

They would keep you from your man—!

They are mine, for they are my man's. I need have no wrath for them.

Edene stood and went out into the sunlight, brushing past Besha Ghul. Besha turned within the doorway, still hugging the shade, but facing out now to watch Edene. Loyal to its duty even as it despised the light. Edene could see its pupils pinched down to pinpricks even in the double shadow of the roof and of its cowl.

As for Edene, though—she paused in the trampled clearing and turned her back to the delicious light. She opened her robe and shrugged it down her shoulders. It would have fallen in the dust, except Besha darted forth and caught it before scurrying back to its shelter.

Sun heated Edene's plait, and the jewels and chains woven through it. It heated the skin of her neck and shoulders, pale with months of deprivation. It heated the half-healed scar of the glass demon's talons, and the muscles beneath scar and skin. The warmth went deep: healing, soothing.

She tilted her head back and closed her eyes. In a moment, she thought, she would clamber down the gully wall and see if she could scrub herself in the doubtless icy little river that leaped and sparkled below, arcing from rock to rock as it made its escape from Reason.

And by then, perhaps her subjects would be able to lead her to Temur.

Padded footsteps disturbed her contemplation. She opened her eyes to see Ka-asha trotting up, recognizable by its gray-embroidered rust wool robe, and all her attempts to distract and relax herself fell away, revealing the hard-bent knot of anxiety and anticipation they had only shrouded, not replaced. She stepped forward, hands reaching.

"What news?"

Ka-asha prostrated itself so Edene bit her lip not to remonstrate. "Rise when you will," Edene said instead, desiring not to command it to its feet any more than she had commanded it off of them.

"Signs of a glass demon attack," Ka-asha said. "Trees scored—but no blood, or not much. And we have found several doorways that have been opened. It is likely that your mate and his subjects escaped through one of them."

Edene wanted to correct the ghul—Temur's companions were likely his war-band, which was something different than the Song or Rasan idea of a prince over peasants. But the ghulim did not seem very able to accept relationships that were not strict hierarchies of owner and owned, and Edene was too eager to be on Temur's trail to waste the time on trying to explain *again*.

"These doorways," Edene said. "Show me them."

She turned to follow the ghul, but was briefly delayed as the venomous things of Reason emerged from the trees to pay her court—crawling many-legged things with claws and carapaces, brightly colored birds with barbed tongues, serpents whose scales spelled out invocations in intricate calligraphy. Edene did her duty by them all, accepted their homages—*Lady of the Broken Places; Mistress of the Poison Things*—but her heart chafed at the delay.

Temur had been here. And she would find him.

THE GHULIM HAD DONE A BRIEF INVENTORY AND ASSESSMENT, AND THE ring confirmed what they told Edene. Of the open doors, most led places that were either isolated or inhospitable—a mountaintop; blazing desert; a lifeless, sandy isle swept by winds that reeked of salt and iodine. There were doorways near the site of the glass demon attack, too—but none of them were open.

But one door led to a glade of golden trees, beyond it a rolling plain— and all around this area were the faded scents of Temur and all the others.

"This is something, at least," Edene said. She traced the letters carved into the lintel with her fingertip. "Can you read this?"

Besha Ghul sidestepped close. "It tells where the door leads—"

"I'd assumed." Edene kept her tone light, teasing, not wanting to see the ghulim flinch all around her.

"The Kyivvan steppe," Besha continued as if Edene had not interrupted.

"Steppe," Edene answered. "Yes. He might very well have chosen to go there."

THOUGH ÜMMÜHAN RETURNED TO HER COUCH AND LIFTED THE PRAYER OF silence immediately, she still lay awake, worry-wrinkles forming across her forehead, until the cracks around the shutters glowed and the caged songbirds in the next room twittered their greeting to the morning. Once she drifted off, she did not sleep much, for no sooner had she finally relaxed when one of the eunuchs Mehmed had claimed as spoils along with the palace came—most apologetically—to whisper her awake. Blinking and confused, she lurched halfway up, clutching the coverlet against her bosom.

It seemed the household was already arisen. Another slave struggled with the heavy bar on one set of shutters. Women moved about the chamber, the comfortable robes they wore in their own harem trailing in the autumn morning breeze that swept through as window after window was thrown open. The Demon Star had set, and now light and air could be allowed within, until the heat of the day grew too stifling.

Ümmühan struggled into a sitting position, wishing she could lean on the arm of the eunuch—but even that much contact, and even with someone who was no longer a man, was not permitted. She stretched her neck against the back of the couch in exhaustion. "Begging your pardon," she said, barely remembering to simper. "Say that again?"

"Ka—the caliph our master. He is executing the Dead Men this morning."

"Ysmat!" Ümmühan swore, then covered her mouth in consternation. A tiny cup of coffee, black and thick, appeared in her hand. She put it to her lips and licked the foam from the rim. Bitter and aromatic, it concentrated her thoughts. She swallowed it in one gulp and met the eunuch's gaze.

He glanced down, preserving her modesty.

"The Dead Men who supported us?" Ümmühan asked, finally gathering herself enough to form the words into a sentence.

"And their families," the eunuch said.

Ümmühan made a note to herself to learn his name. "Has he said why?"

The eunuch shrugged. "They turned coat on one master. Won't they turn it again if the wind shifts?"

His tone was bitter, and Ümmühan knew why. They were all servants of great men, and the only protection they had from other great men was that service. Slaves and the indentured looked out for one another, because there was no one else who would. Oh, of course, there were always those who could not be trusted, who'd bear tales for a scrap of favor. Ümmühan considered such actions to be a sin.

"Is there nothing you can do?" the eunuch asked. "You have . . . the caliph's eye, poetess."

With her finger, she swiped the last dew of coffee and foam from inside the cup, and licked it away. "What is his intention?"

"The caliph has decreed that all the dependents will die, down to two years of age. The orphans will be raised as Dead Men. Unless they are female. Those will go to swell the harem."

A blow to the belly could not have shortened Ümmühan's breath more. She could hear voices rising from the courtyard now, a child weeping. "If I had more time—"

"There is no time."

"He kept this from me on purpose," she said. "He knew I would argue for the children, at least."

It was more than just the potential for renewed treachery that would lead Mehmed to kill these men and their families, she knew. Because not only had they turned against their old master—but their old master had escaped, and many of their colleagues with him. There was no guarantee that one or more of the Dead Men—or their dependents—was not still loyal to the old caliph.

"I can't," she said, and bit the skin of her hand. "I can do nothing for them."

The weeping and the voices became a great wailing, a shriek of denial and then a stunned silence followed by terrible screams. The executions had begun.

"I would go down and observe," she told the eunuch. "I would give them at least that."

His face had hardened. He looked like he had some Aezin in him, and some Messaline. When his expression set, it set like stone. He had considered what she said. She did not know whether the conclusion he had drawn was in her favor or against until he breathed out hard and sat back on his haunches, the fierceness gone out of him.

"You must not," he said, glancing from one side to the other. No one was close enough to hear them. Ümmühan had already, surreptitiously, made sure. "If he already suspects you are in charity with those who would stay his hand . . . you will only arouse his suspicions. You too must be protected, poetess."

"I *would* stay his hand," she said savagely. "But mine is but a woman's strength."

"*From a woman's strength,*" recited the eunuch, shocking her, "*come we all.*"

AFTER SAMARKAR HAD MUSTERED HER STRENGTH ENOUGH TO CLOSE THE door behind them—and nearly knocked herself unconscious again—

the rest of the party insisted on rigging a pony drag behind Bansh in which she could ride. Samarkar rolled her eyes and said that if they'd just consent to a meal and a rest, she'd be perfectly capable of sitting on the dun mare's saddle—and that she'd rather walk any day than be carted about like an old woman in a barrow. But Temur assembled the pony drag over her protests, and refused to move until she was seated in it—and when she attempted to shoulder a pack and stalk away along the Dragon Road, her ankles wobbled and the world rocked back and forth until discretion won.

She plunked herself down in the stretched blanket and sulked.

"It's only for one day," Temur said, walking beside her. "You overextended yourself. And then overextended yourself again." He reached down and tugged her ear. "Besides, it's not as if you never strapped me into a pony drag. Be glad you're not lashed to the poles, as I was."

She had to laugh at that. It was true, and it was fair—and once she started laughing, she couldn't keep the scowl. Even though it irritated her to let him win.

But she rode in the pony drag dutifully for the better part of the afternoon, though every time one of the poles dropped between flagstones or caught on an edge she thought enviously of the saddle. She lay on her back and watched the mare's tail twitching over her, and the course of an enormous steppe vulture across the cloud-dyed sky.

Eventually, Hard-day gave way to Soft-day, Song's filmy and tenuous red sun rising as the pinpoint blue one set opposite it. "I guess that's pretty definitive, then," Temur said.

Hsiung snorted. Samarkar did not need words to understand what he meant. *As if I'd not know my own sky.*

Hrahima made a similarly guttural sound, though hers was more disgusted. "No darkness in Song," she said. "We may as well camp now as later."

"Let's press on to that narrow," Temur replied, pointing. Samarkar leaned out of her pony drag, trying to catch a glimpse around the buttocks of the mare. Ahead, one of the melted-candle mountains hugged in close to the river as if to drink from it, the Dragon Road hugging its root. The mountain came so close to the water that, because the Road would not sacrifice its width, broad jade flagstones actually projected out over the water. The flags were so undermined in places that they formed partial roofs for caverns—sinkholes—with nothing to support them but the stubborn old lingering magics that rendered them immovable and indestructible. This was a defensible position, and one with good sight lines in every direction.

"I agree," Samarkar said. "We'll be visible—but we can protect that."

They made themselves cozy enough with fire and blankets. Brother Hsiung and Hrahima each separately disappeared for some time. When Hsiung returned, knees and fingers muddy, he had a cloth tied full of some crisp tubers, and some hard fruits that turned creamy once baked in the coals. Samarkar wondered if monks were trained to forage, or if it was a skill from his life before.

Hrahima, on the other hand, returned with a brace of Song waterdeer—fragile-looking creatures no bigger than a lapdog, with legs as delicate as eating-sticks. And sharp, projecting fangs, which Samarkar still found completely out of place in their dainty faces.

Samarkar would have undertaken to butcher the things so they could be roasted whole, but Hsiung brushed her aside and handled everything. She felt selfish sitting and resting while others worked—but she could not deny that her bones ached with weariness, and the inactivity felt good. She might have been too tired to eat otherwise; when Hsiung brought her food, she realized she could barely remember how to chew and swallow. The deer was gamy and not precisely tender. Samarkar might have welcomed somebody to sit beside her and instruct her step-by-step in the process of getting it down her gullet.

She slept, so she did not remember the bulk of the Soft-day that followed. And no one woke her to take a watch.

She opened her eyes to the blue sun's dawning. Temur sat by the fire, boiling water in two pots, one with the deer bones for a congee and one plain for drinking. Hsiung was sorting herbs onto a piece of leather to make the usual morning tisane. At this point of their travels, actual tea was a luxury nearly forgotten.

Samarkar blinked, relieved to find that other than the grogginess of sleep she felt alert. This sense of well-being lasted exactly until she moved, when pain shot through her neck like knife blades. Yesterday's tenderness had been nothing compared to this. She only managed to push herself up stiff-armed, lip-bitten, the pain great enough that she sat for a moment afterward with the world spinning around her.

She must have made a sound, and Temur must have heard it, because he crouched beside her worriedly and reached out—only to leave his fingers hovering in the air a handspan from her shoulder.

"You're hurt," he said.

"Stiff neck," she answered, unable to soften the strain in her voice. "I took a jarring yesterday. I'll probably live."

Hrahima was nowhere in sight, and even the thought of turning to look for her made sweat start on Samarkar's forehead. Afrit was ducked under his mother, neck bowed and extended, nursing with his tail wagging like the handle of a pump. Samarkar let herself watch them quietly for a moment until the stabbing receded.

Hong-la had had some method of treating sore necks from falls and such like. A padded collar, to immobilize the victim until he or she healed. Samarkar wondered if she could improvise such a thing, and render it comfortable enough to wear without galling her flesh.

"I'll need a hand up," she said. "But a gentle one."

Temur crouched beside her and let her use his shoulder as a prop. She got up mostly through the raw strength of her legs, grateful for all the time recently spent walking and in the saddle. She used up most of her native courage, however, doing it without screaming.

She was testing her balance, Temur hovering beside her like a dragonfly over a stem, when Bansh's head came up, rich stems of grass forgotten between her lips. A moment later, sparse tail switching, Jerboa pricked her ears in the same direction and snorted. Hsiung, halfway from the fire with a steaming cup extended, paused and turned.

If Samarkar had dared to close her eyes, she would have pinched the bridge of her nose in frustration. Could they go *one day* without an ambush or adventure? Maybe just long enough to drink the steeped herbs and gulp down some deer-broth-flavored rice gruel?

Apparently not. Now even Samarkar could hear the hoofbeats approaching—more than one horse, and she'd bet Temur would be able to pick out exactly how many. Whoever rode toward them was making haste, and making no attempt to conceal their presence. Those hooves rang on the stone surface of the Dragon Road.

Bansh whinnied greeting and challenge all in one. Not too distantly, they heard two horses reply.

In a moment, a rider on a golden chestnut steppe mare hove into view, trailing two remounts. It was a Qersnyk man, hatless in the autumn afternoon, his queue bouncing against the shoulders of his sheepskin coat. His horses glistened in the Hard-dawn, their coats reflecting the metallic tones peculiar to the steppe breed. They looked lean but fit, muscles gliding as they galloped easily over the stones.

The rider must have noticed the little party camped in the middle of the Dragon Road about the same time they spotted him. He did not draw up, but his mare slowed to a canter. He raised his left hand, displaying some object that—at this distance—seemed to be round and about the size of a fist.

"A mail-rider," Temur said, his voice throbbing with excitement. He gestured Samarkar and Hsiung aside, off the Road. As they withdrew he turned to show both his hands upraised and open, the palms empty and flat. "Food for news!" he called.

Now the rider slowed further. As if understanding Temur's intention, Hsiung thrust the bowl of steeped herbs into Samarkar's hands and went to fetch up another. He trotted back to the fire and spooned congee into the bowl. By the time the rider had drawn level with them, Hsiung stood beside Temur, holding the food up over his head.

The rider halted his mare. She sidestepped and danced, head tossing—fresh, eager to be on her way, and only barely amenable to the will of her rider. He flashed the bronze disk in his hand again—a passport, threatening dire retribution by every man and woman of the steppe clans should harm come to him—and then tucked it into a special slit on his saddle. His hand now empty, he accepted from Hsiung the bowl.

He touched it to his lips, but before he spoke, his jet-shiny eyes flicked from Hsiung's face to Temur's, and then to Samarkar's. "A mismatched team I find here."

He drank and smacked his lips.

"Whatever the harness fits," Temur responded, which seemed by the messenger's quick smile to be a joke of sorts. "You ride with news, Ambassador?"

Samarkar knew that the man was unlikely to actually be what her people would consider an ambassador—a ranking dignitary of the court. Instead, the title was meant to convey his sacrosanct status, his impunity, and his immunity from harm.

"Qarash is beset by blood ghosts," the messenger said, and paused.

"Surely, you mean Qeshqer?" Temur asked.

The messenger shook his head. He drank again, and handed down the empty bowl. "The keep was scoured, and all the council killed. The old Khagan's foreign widow rules there now, in the name of her unborn son, but her grip on power is not secure. She claims the regency—but she claims it under a Rahazeen sky."

Temur started. Samarkar could see the effort it took him to stay silent, even in the face of a taboo like interrupting a messenger.

"It is said that the Sorcerer-Prince has risen, exploded the smoking mountain that held him captive and burst those bonds forged upon him by the hand of the Eternal Sky himself. He stalks the land and leaves his enemies skinned behind him, dropped as if from a great height."

Samarkar's belly roiled. She had tried to put what Temur had dreamed in the Steles of the Sky away from her, tried to block from her mind the gnawing worry of what it meant that the Cold Fire burned hot once again. Now all those fears burst into her—fears for her family, for her brother wizards, for the Citadel and the city that she loved. She gnawed the inside of her cheek, silencing a half-dozen outbursts. Only one of which was her determination to correct this messenger, that it had been the Mother Dragon who put down the Joy-of-Ravens, and not the Qersnyk's Eternal Sky.

"What more?" Temur asked. Despite herself, Samarkar was proud of his apparent serenity, the calm with which he took the news. Blood ghosts in Qarash as well—he, Temur, had not seen the skulls piled high in Qeshqer, as she had. But he had seen the blood ghosts in action, and survived an attack. The one during which they had stolen away his Edene.

"I bring news to the Song courts," the messenger said. "The Khaganate grows again in strength, and is ready to reassert its alliances. Or defend its borders, if need be. The clans will not be trifled with."

"They have been raiding on the borders?"

The messenger smirked. Of course they had. Like the borders between the Song princedoms and the Rasani, those lines were redrawn every time someone imagined an advantage—and political turmoil within the steppe clans was an advantage for their enemies that did not have to be imagined.

Samarkar asked, "You ride to the Song courts. Is that then the way to Dragon Lake?" She pointed back as he had come.

"You're going the right way," the messenger said, amused. With an air of ritual he added, "Have you messages?"

Temur started to shake his head, then stopped himself. The messenger, who had been reining his mare aside, made her pause.

"Hurry," he said.

"Tell anyone who wants to know," said Temur, lifting his chin though his voice trembled, "that the unborn child of Qori Buqa is not the only rider who would sit the Padparadscha Seat. Tell them that Re Temur Khagan, grandson of Re Temusan Khagan and brother of Re Qulan Khanzadeh raises his banner at Dragon Lake."

Silence hung over them all as the messenger, his impatience evaporated, studied first Temur and then Samarkar and Hsiung in turn. He turned his glance to the mares and colt and frowned. "A ghost colt."

"From a bay mare," Temur said. "But I am no shaman-rememberer, to tell you what it means."

"Half the time they're making it up," the messenger replied. "Re Temur, you say?"

"Khagan," Temur repeated.

The messenger dipped his chin once, considering. "I am Gagun Aysh," he said. "Smooth riding."

"And swift," Temur replied—almost to the messenger's back, he was so quickly gone.

MUKHTAR AI-IDOJ, AL-SEPEHR OF THE NAMELESS RAHAZEEN, ROSE BEFORE sunrise in the master bedroom of a house that had once belonged to a Messaline merchant. The merchant had fled and his home was long looted, but it had doors and a roof. In the absence of an owner, with winter coming on, Saadet Khatun had claimed these things for the shelter of herself, her advisors, and her family.

As al-Sepehr wrote his first devotions by the light of a candle-stub, the heathen city of Qarash was already stirring. The sky was still dark when he rose from his altar-chest, sorted his prayers, and locked the papers, pens, and sacred inks away in the drawers set aside for that purpose. Then he drew silk gloves over the words tattooed across his hands and produced an iron key from his pocket.

The second chest was set as far across the room as possible from the altar, concealed by a screen. Al-Sepehr approached it with his lips bent in a moue of disgust. When he knelt, he did so without ceremony— merely to align the key with the lock. It turned with a heavy click. His gloved hands lingered on the edges of the lid reluctantly for a moment before he lifted it open.

From within, he drew a round object swathed in more layers of silk. He carried it across the rug-padded floors to a scarred table and set it down. So heavily padded was it that it made no sound. Efficiently, he peeled back the layers of silk—black on the outside, royal blue, then crimson—revealing the discolored ivory of an ancient skull.

He lifted it from beneath, the wrappings cascading over his wrist and hand, and gazed into its empty sockets in the dim, flickering light. It might almost have returned the gaze from the bottomless and black pits where its eyes had been. Even through the silk, a palpable chill seemed to surround the thing, an aura of gelid cold that slid down his sleeve. Frost burned the tip of his nose.

The Emperor Danupati was not pleased to have his rest troubled.

As al-Sepehr was setting his cloth-shielded palms against the relic's temples, there came a scratching at the door too light to wake most sleeping men. The pattern told him who had arrived. Still, he flipped a corner of cloth over the skull before stepping away from the table.

The door was barred. He lifted it to find Saadet, as awake as he, clad in her brother's dark wool coat and trousers, her brother's weapons thrust through the sash that dipped under the girth of her swelling belly. An indigo veil was wound beneath her eyes and across the top of her head, to al-Sepehr's relief. It was he, after all, who had sent Saadet and her immanent brother here. But he did not delight to see her abandoning modesty—no matter how necessary her bare-faced insolence might be to win the regard of her heathen protectorate.

The guard who slept across al-Sepehr's door had withdrawn slightly to one side. He shielded his eyes with his hand in order to protect his night vision.

"Come in."

Al-Sepehr closed the door behind Saadet and dropped the bar again. The doors had locks, but the keys were no doubt on the rings of that Messaline merchant, wherever he might roam.

The light in the room might be dim, but it was brighter than the corridor, and Saadet had come without a candle. It would have been a sorry sort of assassin that could not move in the dark, and Saadet had assumed her brother's skills with his soul after Temur murdered him. She crossed the room to the table with its obvious lump of cloth. She did not twitch the wrappings aside.

Instead she turned, rested her palm on the hilt of a scimitar incongruous beside the heft of her gravid belly. "Have you spoken to the djinn?"

She did not drop her eyes when she spoke to al-Sepehr. He resolved to find a time later to remind her of propriety—but for now, he knew she was struggling with the demands of acting a queen to these arrogant barbarians. Al-Sepehr was a civilized man. He could make allowances. For a time.

"I have," he said. "Would you like to see?"

Saadet nodded. She let her bare hands hang at her sides as al-Sepehr reached out with his protected ones. He slid the wrappings from atop the skull. They slid and puddled like oil beside it.

Saadet made a sound that could have been pain or eagerness. "Control yourself," said al-Sepehr. "Bring the candle."

She brought him the stub, formed of wax harvested from the giant honeybees of Rasa, and set it down on the table far enough from the wrappings that the silk was in no danger from the flame.

"Awake, Danupati," said al-Sepehr. "Awake and answer my command."

There was no visible reaction, but al-Sepehr felt the awareness in the room shifting. From the way Saadet stepped back—quickly, silently, into a balanced stance—she felt it too, and it troubled her enough to trigger her brother's fighter's reflexes. But she said nothing, made no other gesture beside a quick sideways glance at al-Sepehr as if to be certain that all was well.

Al-Sepehr laid his glove-shielded hand on the skull and felt the weight of another, as if someone stood just behind him in the room, staring over his shoulder. He pushed against it, explored farther, and found a slipperier but more solid presence beneath—as if he reached into water to grab eels. A moment of focus, and he blinked and looked out through a woman's eyes.

Tsareg Edene stood at the top of a grassy slope, the stalks all gold with summer's end before her. A long sweep of wild grain bled off to the horizon, dotted with the cowled shapes of the ragtag jackal-creatures the Qersnyk whore called her "army." The sky above them was the true, pellucid blue of the Kyivvan reaches, and beyond the slope of the next rise, it was smudged with the friendly smoke of some farming village. Al-Sepehr could just make out the peaks of the rooflines, the tops of the masonry chimneys.

These people are your rightful subjects, he whispered. *You are their queen. Bring them under your roof, into your army. Bring them as tribute to your man.*

I will ask if they have seen him, she answered. Her fist clenched. He felt the resistance as she reached for the edge of the Green Ring, as if she would worry it off her finger.

Al-Sepehr let himself slip back by degrees. He might be able to reach her through the ring—and of course the cursed thing had an agenda of its own—but it was Edene who wielded the ring's power. It was she who commanded the poisoned things, the broken things—but it was al-Sepehr who had allowed her to obtain that power, and he would see to it that his influence directed where it fell.

Conquer, Queen. They will kneel before you.

A little push, a thought she might mistake for her own—or for the ring's. And it would be harder and harder to resist, as time went by. As the ring's blandishments took on the nagging characteristics of unsatisfied hunger. As she grew in need, in desire, for what it could give her.

She thought, *I will bring your father cities, O my son.*

It was enough. Al-Sepehr raised his hand from the skull's crown and turned back to Saadet. "What do you think?"

"I think she's unreliable," Saadet said. "I think she's an indrik-zver loose behind our own lines, and I don't think we can control her."

"Of course we can't," said al-Sepehr. "But whatever she does, we can blame it on her paramour, can we not?"

Saadet nodded. "Father—"

It stopped him. She so rarely called him that. He was more than a father to her; he was a father to all the Nameless. He glanced at her and quickly trained his eyes aside. He nodded.

She said, "My child. How can you be sure it will be a son?"

His lip flickered. "You took the herbs I gave you, to ensure conception."

She nodded.

He said, "It will be a son."

11

Brother Hsiung was awakened in the Soft-day by the light of his own eyes. Or rather the heat—except it wasn't exactly a physical heat. It was more the memory of heat, the burn of sharp spices rather than the burn of fire. He opened his lids and sat up, seeing the green glow spill down the sides of his nose, across the backs of his hands when he raised them. The light was sickly and stark and bright enough to drown out the filmy red glow of Soft-day.

Hsiung glanced around. Hrahima was on watch, which meant she was nowhere to be seen—as invisible as if she had ceased to exist amid the cloudy blurs of river, mountains, vegetation. Even if Hsiung's eyesight had not been fogged by exposure to the terrible magics of Erem, he knew that there was no way he would be able to spot her unless she chose to permit it. But they would never be safer than under her care.

Down here in the encampment, Temur and Samarkar slept, curled together. The mares and the colt cropped soft grass at the edge of one of the vast jade flagstones. They were not hobbled; none of the people who had traveled with Bansh could imagine she'd bolt—and neither Afrit nor Jerboa would abandon their miniature herd.

With a silent, exhausted sigh, Hsiung levered himself from his blankets and began to work his forms. The sick river of al-Sepehr's conjuring ran through him. He must divert that energy. It was a coursing flood, and he was one man. He did not have the strength to dam or stop it—like all rivers, it would wear away the barriers bit by bit, picking and fretting until it all came down and unleashed a deluge far more destructive than what would happen if he just let it rise and rode it out until it faded again. Instead, he must channel the power and let it scour the path he wished it to take. The more it followed a course, the deeper that course would be worn.

His forms, the expression of his meditation, were the tools that made this directing possible.

That he had the toxin of Erem in him was Hsiung's own fault. His own curiosity had led to this poisoning, and useful though the knowledge sometimes was, it was his burden to bear. Sometimes, Samarkar would do the forms with him, help to channel the poison strength. But for now let her sleep. Let her recover.

He would do this on his own. And if he failed . . . Hrahima was watching.

As he worked through the patterns and forms, however, the expected peace did not emerge to comfort Brother Hsiung. You could not seek emptiness—no one found emptiness by looking. Rather, you had to make a place for it to enter. You had to be hollow and receptive, offer silence where silence could be born. But now, today, though he could make that hollow space, could fall out of the center of himself and leave it silent . . . what was born into it was not emptiness, but worry. Moreover, *fear*.

Blood ghosts in Qarash.

She claims it under a Rahazeen sky.

The green light, the burning faded slowly, but still Hsiung executed his forms. Still he could not be quit of the intrusive thoughts, the concern that nagged at him like the sort of auntie who would not rest until everyone in her family was married. He wished . . .

. . . he wished he could ask his brothers. An option so far from the reality of his exile that it took his breath away to consider it. Brother Hsiung was unsafe company, and certainly had proved that he could not be trusted near the archives of Eremite texts. The magic that contaminated him could also burn and warp others, and—moreover—he was a distraction from a proper life of contemplation.

He could not go back. He could not ask for help. And yet . . . he needed to. At last he stopped, sweat-drenched, bare feet chilled by the grass, toes numb. He rested his palms on his thighs and let his head hang down. Salty droplets swung from his nose, his eyelashes. They spattered away with every blink.

He could not return to them. Not as a brother.

But a supplicant was not a brother.

Hsiung nodded to himself, acknowledging the birth of a plan.

I will leave a note, he thought.

At Hard-dawn, Temur awakened in the cool half-light, when neither red sun nor blue was firm in the sky, but instead both hovered low behind the twisted, vine-hung limestone mountains and the horizon. The rattle of the river—tumbling briefly into a cavern before emerging again farther downstream—made a peaceful background with the songs of birds he had not heard in a long time. He extricated himself from Samarkar, who was sleeping hard, and reluctantly dragged himself out of the warmth of her embrace. Mist shrouded everything, thick enough that the warmth of the fire's embers was stopped as solidly as if by a stone wall.

Hrahima surprised him; she crouched by the banked fire, warming her great pale-palmed hands, her elbows resting on her knees as she crouched there. Usually, her turns on watch were exercises—for everyone else—in "Spot the Tiger." Futile exercises, at that—though she maintained it was good for the humans to get as much practice as possible in checking for ambushes.

What they had learned so far was that if they were under ambush by Cho-tse, they could all expect to die before they even knew to tighten the buckles on their armor.

"Good morning," he said to the tiger.

She chuffed and handed him a pot of broth.

When he had drunk—if not quite his fill, at least a good few swallows—he handed it back. She set it beside the coals to keep warm and folded her arms upon her knees again. Temur envied the ease of her crouch—for all his life had been spent standing in the stirrups, still Hrahima made positions seem comfortable that would have driven Temur to curse and creak.

"Where's Hsiung?" Temur asked softly. He'd have to wake Samarkar soon enough—but let her have a few more moments.

"Left," Hrahima said. She held out a scrap of paper, syllables sketched on it in charred wood. Temur could read enough Song to make it out.

I have gone to my brotherhood, said the note Hsiung had left. *They must know what we have learned, and perhaps they will have wisdom to offer. I will rejoin you at Dragon Lake, if I am so permitted.*

"Permitted." Temur looked up at Hrahima, aware his expression had grown quizzical.

"Monks have rules," said Hrahima. "It's possible our Brother Hsiung may have broken some."

EDENE LOOKED DOWN ON THE RISING FLAMES UNDER THE LIGHT OF DAWN and was not proud, though she felt the pride of the Green Ring within her. She was horrified. She told herself that she was horrified, that this cold glee that rose up inside was alien, not her. A kind of poison.

Why? Why did I not realize this was how it would be? But she had not. She had not thought clearly. She had listened to the ring.

And the ring was a liar.

So now she stood in the square of a burning village, watching thatch roofs flame like torches under the light of Erem's brutal suns. To every side the fields of grain were swept under sheets of fire, whipped to peaks as hot winds gusted. Blistered bodies lay in the square, in the streets.

Only a few, at least. Only the first who had come running out at the dawn, at the smell of smoke, when Edene and her ghul army had marched into this once-pretty, once-peaceable village. The rest she had been able to protect . . . but why, oh why, had she not realized sooner that what she conquered with Erem's power would awaken under Erem's sky?

Women, children, men huddled around her—a dozen dozen or so, just right for a village this size, some fifteen households. Beyond them, in a wider ring, milled the ghulim, cowled and—if Edene imagined them through the eyes of the villagers—terrible. She pictured those soft gray muzzles as they would look to a man with his wife's burned flesh stuck to his hands. She imagined how the wrinkled folds of velvet skin would look, the lips concealing daggery yellow teeth . . .

Edene looked about for Besha Ghul. There it was, hurrying to her as villagers squealed and threw themselves from its path—at least, those who were not just so numb they huddled down and waited to be eaten. Edene remembered the aftermath of the sack of Qarash quite vividly. She was sure many, many of them wished only to die. If they could manage to wish even that. There had been a time when Edene had managed to move through her days only seeking the next task that needed to be done, the next meal to cook, horse to water, babe's ass to wipe.

Besha paused before her. She saw its ears twitch under the cowl.

"Get them out," Edene said, and pointed. "Get all the villagers out, out from under this sky. March them as prisoners if it's the only way to make them move. Give them time to gather food, livestock, and belongings, but the dead must be left behind. We will bring them to the edge of the Eremite sky; we march all night if we have to. Surely this big road leads somewhere"—really, it was not much more than a track, but then, this village wasn't much more than a wide place in it—"find out who knows where it goes."

Besha Ghul nodded and evaporated away again. Edene stood for a long moment, her head held high only by force of will. Her arms ached for the weight of her son, but she would not bring him out into this misery.

And what of the children here, Edene? How will you erase this horror from their memories?

"What a pity you can't just give them their sky back," the djinn whispered in satiny tones. She had not heard him, of course, come up behind her. An instant after his words, she felt a silken wash of heat against her skin on the side turned toward him.

"Can you?" she snapped.

"Alas," said the djinn. The smoky heat of his body should have been lost in the heat of the suns, the heat of the burning village. But Edene could feel it close and warm, like a lover's breath against her neck.

She turned her head and fixed the djinn with a glare. All her rage, all her frustration boiled up like grain in a pot left unattended over the fire. Could she bring Temur no army beyond the sad remnants of the ghulim of Erem? Could she not even rid herself of this djinn, unwanted reminder of al-Sepehr and his machinations?

For a moment, Edene felt herself inexpressibly weary. An ache seemed to start from the center of all her long bones, from every knuckle in her hands, from each joint in her spine. Her body sagged as if her will were wires, and that was all that held it upright. It startled her, this exhaustion, until she remembered. This was what it was to be human, to be weak and worn down.

But she was not those things. These were ruins; this was a poisoned place, and broken.

She was the queen of ruins; she was not broken herself. If to be human was to be weary, to be fissured and fractured like a gemstone—then Edene was not human anymore.

When she drew herself straight again, reclaimed strength flaring along every sinew, the ghulim cringed before her. A hush swept through the huddled, keening, cowering villagers with their pale half-human faces and their hair that looked like sun-bleached manes and tails. One close by risked a glance up; Edene caught a glimpse of white-ringed irises as pale as a Rahazeen sky in a soot-smudged face—and she caught a glimpse of her own aspect in the fear frozen there. For a moment it occurred to her that she could have seen herself, that she could look through the eyes of the ghulim, or whatever small venomous creatures lay hidden in cracks, waiting for her poisoning suns to set.

It wasn't that she was afraid of what she'd see. It was that she knew, and did not care.

When she turned back to the djinn, the ring was heavy and sharp on her hand. She almost thought she felt the wet drip of her blood from where it rested, but when she raised that hand, there was nothing but brown flesh and green ring.

She caught the djinn by the open collar of his shirt and saw blue sparks flare around her fist as if she had struck at embers with a rod. The fabric felt like smoke against her fingers as she knotted them—there was no texture of cloth or sense of bulk—but her grip held and the collar bunched and strained. She leaned toward the djinn—she was taller, but she knew perfectly well that that was his choice of aspect. His stature was a convenience, and hers a mark of her descent.

Blue flames unfurled around the djinn like war banners, flowering concentrically from the place where she touched him. They burned—the heat was enormous—but she could see her own flesh, her sleeve—

the ring. She was Edene of Erem. She could thrust her hand into the heart of a star, if she chose. She could walk through dragon fire unscathed, for dragons were a thing of poison too.

For the first time, she saw a flicker of uncertainty cross the djinn's sharp-cornered features.

Then she lifted him off his feet. The tendons in his forearm striated like ridges under slanting light as he caught her wrist and pulled. She felt him try to grow. Neither attempt to escape availed him. She was not stronger—but he stood in the place of her power. Here, at least, he could not resist her.

"Tell me again," she said, "that you will not leave when I command it."

"We are allies!" he cried. "We have the same enemy!"

"An enemy you serve." The flames caressed her flesh as she gave him a little shake. They licked her with agony—but did it really hurt more than the birth of her son? She tightened her grip.

"An enemy who holds me enslaved!"

Edene scoffed. "Who enslaves a djinn? Al-Sepehr is no Joy-of-Ravens, to bind your kind into a bottle or a ring. And it's said that even the Sorcerer-Prince was tricked by a djinn in the end."

The djinn spat. Not at Edene, but at the ground. It sizzled where it hit.

"Is that an answer?"

The djinn's mouth turned down at the corners. "I am forbidden to name him who commands me. But he tricked me," he said sulkily. "I must serve him until I can trick him back, by the rules that govern contracts between our races."

"Ah." Edene set him down, but did not release him. "How embarrassing for you."

The djinn avoided her gaze. He scowled.

She scowled in return. "Tell me again that you will not leave when I command it."

"I cannot," he said steadily. Now he looked into her eyes. His were astonishing counterfeits—flame-blue, luminescent, but with every variation of color and texture one would expect from a human eye. "He whose commands I must obey has ordered otherwise. It is *possible* that you could destroy me, here in the heart of your power. But if I were you, I would not care to make the attempt. And since, unless otherwise summoned, I must drag myself after you like a cripple on a wheeled board, no matter how badly you injure me, I submit to you, my *queen*, that it would better avail you to join your forces to mine. Before this sorcerous dog brings your whole paltry world to heel under his backward sky. It will not go well for you then."

She did not drop his gaze. His expression seemed open, honest—if anything, exasperated. It occurred to her that she was remonstrating with him in full view of a hundred and more Kyivvan peasants and merchants, and all her supposedly loyal ghulim.

"Al-Sepehr trusts nothing he has not chained," she said, disgusted. She peeled her fingers open—they ached, having locked in place. "He won't trust you, even in bondage."

"I don't need to be trusted," the djinn said. With his thumbs he flipped his collar smooth. "Like any weapon, it only takes one mistake for me to turn in a hand."

Under other circumstances, Tsering-la would have expected the refugee caravan to make for Kashe, which the Qersnyk who had conquered it in her mother's day called Qeshqer—the city that guarded the best path north through the mountains called the Range of Ghosts.

But Kashe was a dead city now, destroyed by the blood ghosts. Its harvest lay abandoned; its people lay piled into sucked pyramids of bones in the market square. Tsering had not seen this for herself—but she had seen Samarkar's face outside the gates when her sister wizard returned from investigating the empty streets.

With the city gone, and with Song rather than the steppe as their goal, the Qersnyk and Rasan refugees followed a different road out of the mountains. A long valley—perhaps more a high, narrow plateau—separated the Steles of the Sky from the Range of Ghosts, and Hong-la's maps and memory said following this would bring them out among the river-lands of Song, where the roots of the mountains gave birth to multitudinous springs. The air here was blessedly clearer—they were sheltered in the valley, and the prevailing winds swept the Cold Fire's foul exhalation north as they bore east. But as the geography changed, so did Tsering's worries.

Not only did Tsering continue to fear the depredations of the demonlings—although it seemed the wards were protecting them so far, or perhaps the demonling curse had simply been left behind in Tsarepheth—but now she had an added concern: the blood ghosts that had destroyed Kashe. Massive veins of violet salt underlay the Steles of the Sky, and those might be what had kept the blood ghosts from venturing farther south. But they had left that protection, and while the wards that kept the demonlings at bay—if they did, in fact, keep the demonlings at bay—might also help against the blood ghosts, it was a hard thing to trust your life and the lives of all your charges to untested magic. To be the test, in fact.

The peaks dropped about them, night by night, and the pair of bulwarked mountains that marked the pass at the bottom of the long valley grew taller and less misty and indefinite. Tsering worked with Hong-la, Jurchadai, and others each night, and found herself mostly taking her supper with Hong-la and Jurchadai—often, whatever cold bits could be had.

In the evenings, the bitter Rahazeen sun set in the east, behind those buttressing, slab-ridge mountains. The sight churned Tsering's stomach, so she tried not to watch. She'd hoped they'd have left that taint behind, but now she guessed it would follow them to the borders of Song. Once the sky grew dark, it wasn't so bad. The stars were wrong, and a big moon copper-red shaded with silver, but it wasn't as disorienting as the ways in which the shadows fell all at the wrong angles and in the wrong colors, changing the outline of mountains that should have been accustomed as the shape of a sister's nose and chin.

She held on to the thought. When they passed that peak, the Rahazeen sky would fall behind.

This night, though, Tsering sat silently with Hong-la and Jurchadai. She cradled a bowl of buttered tea and made herself watch as the sky slid from pale blue to paler peach and yellow. The tea was the only hot thing in her supper—even the noodles in it were rewarmed from breakfast—as time to cook was, like sleep, one of the casualties of the wizards' constant vigilance. The colors—too dim, too subdued— awakened a new determination in her. Her hands tightened on the comforting warmth of the bowl, and she realized even as it happened that she was feeling the shroud of stunned, mechanical activity that had kept her moving since the Cold Fire erupted slip away. She was no longer an automaton, moving forward because that was the way it was geared. She was Tsering-la, and she was returning to herself.

"Not too much longer."

The words so closely echoed her own thoughts that, for a moment, Tsering thought she might have muttered them. But it was Hong-la's voice, and his steady gaze was on the same horizon that had held her, moments before.

"There is still Song to cross," said Jurchadai. His accent and vocabulary grew better every day, and at this point Tsering's Qersnyk was nearly passable. Some days they made a game of arguing as they traveled—he riding, she often afoot—each taking the other's language.

"Not all of it," said Hong-la. He sipped his tea without lowering his gaze, then licked grease from his lip. He seemed nearly at peace, perhaps even calmer than Tsering-la had ever seen him. She wondered what it was like for him to be going home again. "If we stay with the foothills, there is a sacred route along the base of the Steles of the Sky. Very few will chance the displeasure of the Sages to trouble pilgrims there, and we would be many for the mountain bandits to tackle."

His knowledge of his homeland was a relief, as in so many circumstances his knowledge often was. She did not know the details. But as she understood it, he had not left Song under the most congenial of circumstances. Many wizards came to Tsarepheth as refugees from unpleasant histories, though. Tsering was no different. Perhaps his expression of serenity was in truth resignation. Or perhaps Hong-la was closer to the silence within than she—who, after all, had failed to find her power even after all that study and all that sacrifice.

On the other hand, if she were going back to the Citadel at Tsarepheth—even now, with ash clouds looming over it and many of its people fled—she might have such a look of contentment on her face.

She certainly missed the kitchens.

Her musing was disturbed as Jurchadai lifted his head and half-turned. She might have started to her feet, but the shaman-rememberer remained seated. A moment later, Tsering also heard the footsteps.

Three Qersnyk women approached on quick, booted feet. The eldest had gray in the braid protruding from under her crimson scarf;

the youngest was barely old enough to show breasts. Each held a horn bowl in her hands. They lined up beyond the fire and crouched—Qersnyk rarely knelt—the oldest before Jurchadai.

She spoke rapidly and fluidly to the shaman-rememberer, in an accent Tsering found difficult. The gist of it was that they—the women—had noticed that the shaman-rememberers and the foreign witches were not being fed, and had taken it upon themselves to remedy the situation. They hoped the gesture would be accepted as a gift, in gratitude for the work the shaman-rememberers and the foreign witches took upon themselves.

Jurchadai did not even glance at the wizards. He just bowed over his hands without rising, accepted the bowl, and passed it to Tsering. Tsering passed it to Hong-la, and by the time she turned back, there was another waiting for her. Jurchadai took the third, which had already traveled hand to hand between the women. Tsering—and Hong-la, she noticed—imitated Jurchadai as he bowed once more over the bowl.

The smells that rose in the steam that bathed Tsering's face were so delicious she almost wept. When she raised her head again she tried to catch the eyes of each of the women in turn, to smile her thanks—but while the eldest was forthright and the youngest bold, the middle one seemed shy and kept her gaze averted.

The food was too hot to eat with fingers, but Tsering and Hong-la had sets of sticks tucked into their belts. Hers were lacquered red and black. His were matte steel and lacquered clear, pointed as weapons. She found herself demonstrating the use to Jurchadai, who—with a conjuror's deftness—picked up the trick of it quickly as she shaped his fingers around the grip. Her own food cooled while she helped him select the chunks of prune and lamb, and showed him how to scrape boiled, burst grains of buckwheat into his mouth. Hong-la assisted mostly by laughing at them, and once getting up to make more tea.

By the time Tsering reclaimed her dinner and her sticks, it had cooled enough that she didn't actually need the utensils. She used them anyway, because Jurchadai was watching, and she was enjoying his warmth against her shoulder.

She had been so distracted that until she set her bowl aside and reflexively checked the horizon again, she hadn't noticed the eastern sky's mysterious refusal to go completely dark. The mountains alongside the pass were still visible, not just as blacker shapes against a black starfield but silhouetted on a smoky red horizon like andirons before a dying fire.

"What on earth?"

Hong-la sighed. His long face gave away nothing of the context in which Tsering should interpret that sigh. He paused a moment before he answered, "That is the Soft-day light. We are close enough to Song to catch a glimpse of its sky."

TSERING SLEPT BETTER THAT NIGHT THAN ANY NIGHT SINCE THEY HAD LEFT Tsarepheth. She had feared, she realized now, that the Rahazeen sky would extend as if in nightmare—that they would reach Song, perhaps even the steppe, and find only its backward light. The dim glow in the east was brighter in the morning, the blue of that quarter sharp and intense against the washed-out color of the rest.

"Hard-day," Hong-la said when she asked him. She had read of Song's two suns, of course. She looked forward to seeing them for herself.

Once they had packed up and made sure the fire was dead—and collected their allotted warding stones and staves—Tsering was pleased to find that the women who had adopted them had returned to collect the previous night's bowls and bring new, noodles in butter and tea with eggs cracked into them. She'd seen the poultry in cages strapped to the flanks of mules or balanced on wagons. She was surprised and delighted to discover the birds were laying—although Qersnyk poultry were probably accustomed to the inconveniences of travel.

Jurchadai thanked them as before, and as before Tsering and Hong-la tried to copy his forms. This time, after the women had left, he gently corrected them. "I thank them as to family. You must be more formal—so." He demonstrated.

Tsering covered her mouth in embarrassment. "They are your family?"

"All Qersnyk are my kin. I am a shaman-rememberer."

She bit her lip. Surely her curiosity would be taken amiss. But it was what made her a wizard, and she could not quite hold it back. "Do you have family? Blood family?"

He smiled. He handed her his empty bowl to stack with her own and stood. As he fussed with the cinch on his belled and knotted saddle, he said, "Of course. Must wizards give up their family?"

She was not the only one curious, then. Pleased but cautious, she answered, "No. Only our hopes of children."

He hummed to himself. His mare was holding her breath against the girth. He tapped her shoulder and waited for her to get bored.

Tsering took his silence as permission to ask another question. "Can shaman-rememberers marry?"

"We can marry," he said. "Women or men, or other shaman-rememberers. And we can get babies as well."

"Well," she said. "I couldn't help with that anyway." And then she clapped her hand to her mouth again, her face scalding. She hadn't meant to say that at all.

"Of course you could," Jurchadai said. The mare let out her breath with a disgusted noise; he hauled the girth tight and she flicked her ears, thwarted. "You know how to change a swaddling cloth, I'm sure."

12

YANGCHEN MIGHT HAVE BROODED LONGER AND MORE ON THE VISITATION by the obsidian demonlings, but there were too many tasks requiring her attention and her hand. She had known housekeeping and logistics, the tasks of a mistress. Now she learned administration and command—the tasks of a master, as well. From the moment when she rose to the moment when she slept again, one subject after another was before her, each with a problem demanding her solution. At night when she dreamed, she dreamed rations and supplies.

She demanded she be left alone to visit the privy, however—and it was there the gray bird found her.

Yangchen arose from her squat, legs trembling with more than cold, to face the eagle-sized, long-necked raptor that gazed at her with cold yellow eyes from the top of the woven partition separating the privy from the rest of the camp. The bird had a silver capsule attached to its leg with a scrap of ribbon. Now it extended that leg to her, fluffing its crimson crest.

A message from her benefactor. A message from her manipulator.

Before Yangchen quite knew what she was doing, her hands darted forward. They closed not on the capsule, or the bird's leg, but on its long feathered throat.

It did not even have time for a surprised squawk as she whipped it around in a circle, wringing its neck. It struggled—a reflex, only— then hung limp from her fist, dripping guano.

Yangchen swallowed thin vomit and made herself look carefully at what she'd done. She peeled the capsule from its leg and dropped it into the privy, making sure it vanished in thin excrement.

When she returned to the camp, she tossed the bird at the first cook she saw. "Pluck that. Gut it. Roast it," she told him. "And give it to someone needy."

He had caught the bird out of reflex rather than readiness. Now he stopped staring long enough to bob his head to her and stammer, "Dowager."

Yangchen wiped her hands on her robe as she marched away. There was no blood on them, but they still didn't feel clean.

YANGCHEN AND HER CARAVAN HAD BEATEN THE SNOW OUT OF THE MOUN- tains, but they did not beat it to Rasa. On the second day below the last pass, the Steles of the Sky behind them were lost in palls of whirl- ing cloud, and the white flakes swept down and thickened the air until Yangchen could not see Shuffle's horns before her. She was warm enough in her coat and winged hat, but with every gesture the snow cracked and shifted on her arms as if she bent a cake of pressed rice.

Gyaltsen-tsa rode up beside her, bowing so low in the saddle she was afraid he might slide off into a drift. "Dowager," he said. "Your impe- rial sister-wife sends to suggest that it would be wise to make a halt and wait out the snow. The weak will not survive if we press on and it gets deeper."

He left unsaid the inevitable: It would get deeper.

"You agree with Tsechen-tsa, Gyaltsen-tsa? What if we are snow- bound here, and starve?"

"Dowager, I think her counsel is wise. Far more likely that this first storm of winter will pass, and we will have a few more days to fly to- ward Rasa before the next and more dangerous one comes along. We may even find shelter along the road. There are towns and farms, madam."

Thick flakes sifted from Yangchen-tsa's lashes when she blinked. "And I find your counsel to be sound. Wind the horns, call a halt. If we press on much farther, we will begin to find ourselves at the conflu-ences of the Tsarethi and its many tributaries, and we will not wish to assay that in the snow."

He blinked as if she'd impressed him. She didn't tell him she was repeating an observation that Anil-la had made over supper the night before.

The camp was pitched in haste. Yangchen did something she rarely did anymore, and rather than observing the process, she withdrew to her wagon. It was warm within—or at least as warm as thick rugs draping the walls and tended braziers could make it—and Tsechen and two or three ladies were there, as well as Namri and his senior nurse. The wizards who slept there by day had already moved outside, ready to do what they could to help the caravan.

Yangchen stripped outside the door and hung up her snowy coat so it could remain frozen rather than becoming sodden in the heat. When she limped within, her fingers and face already ached with cold, even from that brief exposure.

"You'd think the snow would be gray," said Tsechen, as Yangchen settled herself by the brazier on the yoke-chair kept especially for her. "From the ash."

Their détente, such as it was, seemed to be holding. Even if it mostly extended to talking about the weather currently, and to Yangchen tak-ing Tsechen's advice on the problems of travel.

"Perhaps the snow washed it all from the sky before it traveled so far as this." Yangchen extended her arms for Namri. Without a word, the nurse rose and brought him. She slid him into the dowager's arms, leaving Yangchen with a sudden, powerful memory of the former dowager—Yangchen's mother-in-law—seated just as Yangchen was seated now, women gathered around her. It struck her, as it had never struck her before, that she—*she*, Yangchen—was the most powerful person in the Rasan Empire. Not just wife to an emperor. Not even first-wife to an emperor. But Dowager Empress in her own right, and regent with an infant son who would not assume his majority for twenty-four and a half years.

She had worked for this. Betrayed, murdered for it. Poisoned the land she claimed to protect, and opened the door for monsters to infest it. All for this dream of power, which her father had both groomed her for and groomed her to believe she would never be strong enough to claim or hold.

The reality—the responsibility—terrified her. *What am I going to do?*

But the competing reality of the babe at her breast reminded her that she had to do something. As Namri latched and began to nurse—with less fussing than his custom—Yangchen turned to the youngest of the ladies, the one perforce seated closest to the drafts of the door, and said, "Fetch Munye-tsa, pray."

The girl stood and let herself out into a swirling wall of whiteness. It was well they had stopped when they did; Yangchen feared now that some would not have time to start and shelter fires before the cold of night descended. The awning over the wagon's entrance would keep the snow out of the girl's collar while she shrugged into a coat and stomped boots over her slippers, but Yangchen did not envy her the search for Yangchen's advisor. Perhaps she should call after her to string a rope, so she could at least follow it back to the wagon—but by the time Yangchen thought of it, the door was shut and the footsteps outside had retreated.

Well, any Rasan girl would know more about surviving a blizzard than Yangchen, bred and born in soft, fecund Song. She bowed her head over Namri, savoring his warmth, careful to keep her own cold hands on his swaddling clothes or shielded by her long sleeve, rather than laying them directly on his unbelievably soft skin. When Tsechen picked up her seven-stringed lute and stripped her own sleeves back, Yangchen smiled. There was something to be said for music when the sky shed its frozen feathers and wheels creaked to a cold halt.

By the time the girl returned with Munye-tsa, the nurse, relieved temporarily of Namri's care, had stirred herself to cook tea with noodles and brought bowls around to each of the women. The noodles were dried, not fresh, but for the first time it occurred to Yangchen that as an experience of hardship went, having enough to eat and a warm dry place to sleep might be considered the lap of luxury by many.

She was having an adventure. Some of the people outside were fighting for their lives.

When Munye-tsa and the errand-girl were also provided for and sat warming their blue hands on their bowls, Yangchen gave the emperor back to his nurse. She applied herself to her own food without distraction now, warming the cooling noodles with fresh tea. She slurped them from the bowl's edge like a peasant, the heat seeping through her chilled body while she gave Munye, too, an opportunity to stop shivering and focus his thoughts. He was old and stick-thin, once tall and now bent like a bow. His fingers stayed blue around the nail beds long after the hands of the errand-girl were warm and olive-toned again.

It occurred to her that this was something Anil-la would do, or the dead Bstangpo's younger brother Tsansong. The Bstangpo, her husband, himself would never have offered an underling the courtesy of time to warm himself so that he might think better. His own time was too precious to him.

Finally, Yangchen said, "The soldiers—are they helping the needy pitch camp?"

"Dowager. There is also a communal kitchen in place, where those who cannot build their own fire can come and sit and eat," Munye said. "It was Anil-la's idea, and na-Baryan thought it would please your majesty."

"How much fuel do we have?"

"There is a lot of dung. Less coal." The arc of his hand encompassed the dimly lit wagon box, the dull brazier glow that barely revealed tapestried walls. "Few lamps or candles."

"And the storm," she said. "Do the wizards have an idea of its duration?"

"Not long," he said. "A day or two—they *hope*. Weather witching is never precise, as you understand, and they do not have their books of ancient records here. But I am given to understand that these early season storms rarely last more than a few days on the plateau. Tsarepheth, however, may be cut off until spring."

Yangchen had never been in Tsarepheth in winter. But it was easy for her to imagine the snow drifted second-story deep along the ancient city's narrow streets, a warm and isolating blanket. The wizards would be snug in their Citadel, warmed from below by the hot springs of the Cold Fire, whose heat was what kept the valley habitable and unglaciated at all. Her inner eye offered an image of the Black Palace frosted white like an iced bun before she remembered its trellised towers cracked and smoking like the peak of the Cold Fire.

Yangchen had to set down her bowl before the remains of the tea slopped over her shaking hands.

"Perhaps we could have a story," she said. "There is no light to read. Who knows something by heart?"

MUNYE-TSA HAD BARELY BEGUN THE STORY OF THE FLOWER-GIRL AND THE Peach-Boy (a Song tale, and one Yangchen guessed he might have chosen to curry favor with her) when the tenor of the noise from outside changed. Shouts and a clamor of metal arose; then the horrid screaming of an injured animal. Yangchen started to her feet before she realized she was moving, and Tsechen was moving as well. She put her hand on the latch string as Tsechen put her fingertips on Yangchen's wrist and both women froze. Their eyes met; Yangchen for one moment thought wildly, *I could have her dismembered for that.*

Then she thought, *Of course she's right. An empress regent can't go running out into a fight—*

—a commander cannot huddle behind walls while men die on her behalf.

Yangchen nodded. Tsechen removed her hand. And both women, simultaneously, yanked open the door. Munye-tsa might have started forward as if to remonstrate with them, but he was still levering himself from his seat as Tsechen slammed the door behind them and made sure it latched.

A swirl of breathtaking cold enveloped them, ice particles stinging Yangchen's face. One incautious gasp and she started coughing, her tender lungs spasming at the insult. The temperature had dropped precipitously; this was glacial air from the peaks, rolling down upon them cold as fear. It would freeze fingers and toes, faces, in moments. Though the delay chafed, Yangchen paused to stomp into her boots, shrug on her long coat and mittens, pull up the hood and tie the flaps across her cheeks, mouth, and nose. The guards outside milled uncertainly; their sergeant tried to question her and was waved aside. Something fumbled at her hand; she looked down to see Tsechen's mitten clutching hers.

Before them, the night was brilliant and blind. The swirling snow captured the light of scattered fires, refracted and reflected it as if they stood inside a diamond. The result was a diffuse glow, sufficient to render the night soft-seeming—welcoming—even as the brutal frigidity took Yangchen's very voice.

Yangchen held one hand before her as they stepped out of the dubious shelter of the awning. She *could* see her mitten at the end of her coat sleeve, but not plainly. It was as if she submerged her hand in milky, turbid water. She clung to Tsechen's right hand; turning, she could see that Tsechen's left hand clung to a rope that had been left tied and coiled beside the door. Apparently the errand-girl *had* thought of that safeguard herself. Yangchen told herself to learn the girl's name. She'd heard it, she was sure—but the court ladies came and went like birds in a flock, and so many of them were frivolous and foolish, it was hard for Yangchen to make herself care.

A dangerous habit, to scorn those so close to you.

Yes, Father. It was only a memory she responded to, but she burned as hot with shame as if he stood before her.

"Which way?" Tsechen asked, before Yangchen could make a coward of herself by stepping back into the shelter of the wagon. But she was no child to huddle under her sleeping robes. She was the dowager, and there was no monster out here that could not follow her within those fragile wooden walls.

Yangchen pointed her extended hand. She could still hear the noise of a fight, not far off. Five steps, ten—side by side—while other wagons and more makeshift shelters loomed out of the snow and vanished behind them. The snow came in veils and patterns, and if Yangchen watched carefully, she could see snatches of landscape through it. There, that was the rope corral, with red rags dulled by darkness tied along the edges. And there was the flash of a blade, a soldier awkward in winter gear wielding a spear against something Yangchen could not see. A towering dark shape, glimpsed for a moment, vanished again in a swirl of snow. Terrified livestock lowed and whinnied. A shaggy pony plunged past, almost knocking Tsechen down.

Something marked white and dark lay on the ground, crusted in snow, darkness soaking into the churned drifts that surrounded it.

Shuffle! She thought, surprised at the level of her panic for a beast. She ran forward, dragging Tsechen, only to be caught by the opposite arm and slung around in an arc. She slid and skidded, her attempts to balance herself impeded by Tsechen hauling on one arm and the unknown person on the other.

"Dowager!"

She stopped struggling and let her weight drag on the grip on her arm to steady herself. "Doctor Anil!"

"There's a bear," he said. "Stay back!"

She jerked her arm from his grasp—not too hard, when she worked at it. Mittens did not offer the surest grip. "Go," she said. "We'll remain here."

Her try for regal calm sounded mostly breathless, but he was nearly shouting. She doubted he'd notice.

He gave her sleeve a tug, as if to assure himself of her reality. "Hide under a wagon if it gets past the soldiers."

Then he turned and ran heavily forward, lifting his feet high and still plowing through the drifted snow. A bright satiny glow crystallized around his upraised, mittened hands, a plum-blossom light so intense and pure that Yangchen was seized by the desire to drink it. It pulsed from him in waves, fading from that violet-red to a pure warm white color as it passed beyond his immediate sphere. And each wave seemed to catch the falling snow as if in a seine, pushing it aside, clearing a space around Anil-la and what Yangchen could now see were three guardsmen armed with spears. The soldiers were lined up before Anil and the women, against a great lean shape, silver-blue in the pale light—the color of a blue mastiff—with a pale blond ruff and a long, snarling tan face. It loomed over the half-crouched men, waving paws as big as frying pans.

"Blue bear," Tsechen said. "Oh, the Six Thousand are angry with us."

With me, Yangchen thought. *With the treason I have done. Even the elements reject me—and the demons hail me as their savior.*

What have I done?

A weaseling part of her replied, *An empress regent can commit no treason, except against her son. She* is *the state—*

Her own excuses made her sick. *I was not the empress regent then!*

She drew Tsechen back into the shelter of a wagon's wall as Anil-la's shells of light battered them with successive palls of snow. She wasn't sure how much use ducking under such a thing would be—surely the bear could overturn it, or just reach under. They'd be dragged out like rabbits from a burrow, squirming in the polecat's jaws.

A few running steps ahead, Anil-la blazed like the heart of a forge. His hands upraised, the light still pulsed from him like ripples chasing one another from the impact of a stone. The light washed Yangchen and Tsechen, making Tsechen's lovely features ragged and stark with cutting shadows. There was no warmth in the light. Yangchen found that—cold light—the eeriest effect of magic, and thought she would have welcomed even painful heat. Unless it charred her flesh, it could not hurt more than this unholy cold in the bones of her hands.

Tsechen shook her head, disbelieving. Her lip had split; blood froze upon her chin.

"Tie your muffler," Yangchen said.

Tsechen just shook her head again.

"Obey me!" Yangchen snapped.

Tsechen's hands did as Yangchen ordered, but her eyes stayed fixed on the fight. "How did it get this far into the camp? Past men and animals? And why?"

How did it get this far into the camp? Yangchen raised a hand to shield her face from the next thick wave of snow. "Why isn't it *hibernating?*"

Tsechen looked at her, a frown unflattering between her smoky eyes. She'd be feeling that split lip soon, as her face thawed and blood began to soak the fur. "Does it have the rage plague?"

Yangchen's gut dropped. She winced, a prayer to the Petal Warrior and the Compassionate One brief on her lips. If it did have the rage plague, and if it bit one of the guards, or Doctor Anil—even the wizards had no cure. They would go mad, and suffer excruciating pain, and die in frothing convulsions unless she ordered them given mercy.

And it would be she who gave that order—unless the bear got her first.

The bear seemed to be distracted and bewildered by the waves of light and snow sweeping over it. It reared up, great paws paddling the air, making confused noises when it was not bellowing. The dying yak at its feet gave one last heave, lifting a dark head, and Yangchen took an involuntary half-step forward. Tsechen pulled her back. "We need a weapon—"

Perhaps having the wizard at their back had given the spearmen a chance to regroup and to coordinate their attack. They moved forward as one, separating into three prongs as they came up on the bear. The animal swatted, growling in a tone so low it made Yangchen's belly shiver with sympathetic vibration. She squeezed Tsechen's hand and felt Tsechen squeeze back.

The bear whirled, immensely nimble for its size. It swiped left and right. A spear-shaft splintering sounded like a snapped limb, or perhaps what Yangchen heard was the soldier's arm. The man in front of it was knocked back, sliding in snow. She shouted, saw the bear's tawny face swing toward her, the froth that rimmed its bloody jaws. One of the flanking soldiers lunged forward and plunged his spear into the bear's abdomen, just in front of the hind leg.

If it had cried out before, now it howled. It spun again, dragging the man around, and lunged toward him. Spears for hunting bear had cross-guards, so the animal could not walk up the shaft and kill as they were killed. These were spears intended for combat with other men, and as the man held on grimly, the point of the spear emerged from between the bear's ribs on the opposite side. It swung at him with a massive forepaw, but as long as he held the butt of the spear it pushed him away behind it each time it tried to strike and turn.

That would last until it managed to push the spear entirely through its intestines.

It was dead. The only question was how long it would take to stop fighting.

Yangchen tasted fur, realized she had shoved her muffler between her teeth while trying to bite down on the back of her left hand. She made a hard choked sound. The man who had been knocked down, spear or bone shattered, was dragging himself forward again. He had an axe— just a woodcutting axe, that he might have snatched from the ties of any cart nearby—in his left hand, and his right arm dangled by his side. The third soldier circled, choked up on his spear, looking for his opportunity to dart in and catch the bear from another angle.

Another light flared—a red-violet star around the head of the trans-fixing spear. Anil-la gestured with his right hand, his left still upraised, the shells of light still bursting from it. The new magic seemed to lock the spearhead in place, jerking the bear to a halt.

It roared, thrashing side to side like a gaffed fish. The third soldier took his chance and darted in, plunging his spear into the bear's chest below the forward point of the shoulder. He ducked one swipe of the paw, released the spear, and was knocked back before he could dance clear.

Anil-la still pinioned the first spear as solidly as if it were cemented into a wall. But somehow, suddenly the bear was free of it, the man who had been clinging to the butt sprawling in the snow. Yangchen did not clearly see what happened next: the snow gusted, the bear backed into the snowy darkness, violently shaking its head. Someone shouted. The man with the axe charged forward, chasing the retreating bear. The spear—still held midair—collapsed to the snow, and the waves of light pulsing from Anil-la intensified.

But they showed nothing, now, but blowing snow and the three soldiers dragging themselves from the snow, forming ranks again behind the crushed body of the yak.

Yangchen ran forward, dragging Tsechen with her when Tsechen would not let go. The ground was uneven; the snow slid and squeaked and dragged against her boots. She got her hand free, but heard Tsechen still running beside her as they charged past Anil-la. Her sister-wife overshot as Yangchen stumbled to a halt beside the downed animal.

It was not Shuffle, she saw with abject relief, then felt a twist of guilt. Because if it was not *her* animal, it was still an animal, and until a few moments before it had been as alive and sensitive as Shuffle. No, worse. It was still alive—and suffering greatly, heaving in whistling breaths, half-disemboweled by a swipe of the bear's claws, ribs staved in so the shape of its barrel was awkward and lumpy. *Like a slept-in bed,* Yangchen thought, and laid her hand behind its ear. Through the mitten, she could not feel its heat, or the pulse of blood, but it seemed to calm under the pressure.

"Anil-la," Tsechen called. "The beast is suffering."

He must have come up on them, because he crouched beside Yangchen and put his mittened hand over hers. This was the night when every man and woman of Rasa would lay hands on the imperial person, apparently. He reached for his knife, the square-pommeled blade that every Rasan seemed to carry from the cradle, and she imagined him feeling for the yak's pulse under the line of its jaw, the spill of hot blood on the snow.

"I'll do it," she said, and took the knife out of his hand. Hers shook, and the cold when she pulled her right mitten off with her teeth was numbing, daunting. Somehow, reaching over its neck from her position behind its head, she managed to locate the throbbing vein with her numb fingertips where they burrowed through shaggy coat. The animal's warmth kept her from losing sensation entirely. She was grateful. The animal moaned, a sound that shuddered through her from her knees, pressed as they were against its hide. Quickly, she grasped the knife. The hilt burned with cold; if her hand had not been dry, she would have frozen to it instantly. She put the point against the hollow of the throat.

"Push hard, Dowager," said Anil-la. "Her spirit will thank you for it."

The skin was tough, hard to pierce. She tested once, found the strength, and realized it would be easier to slash than thrust. As Anil-la concentrated his light over them, the edge of the knife winked like a razor. Of course he kept it honed.

Yangchen focused her gaze on the knife, on the hide beneath, on the shaggy fur over the vein. *Just like cutting meat,* she thought. She pressed down hard and drew the blade toward her, sudden and decisive.

So you can not only kill by treachery.

The blood fountained—away from her, toward the trampled snow where the men had fought the bear. Toward the darkness into which they had vanished in pursuit. The yak thrashed and Yangchen tumbled back, Tsechen and Anil dancing aside more adroitly. It convulsed, once, twice, legs scrabbling in its own intestines as it struggled pitifully to stand.

And then it heaved and lay still.

Yangchen stood. She handed the bloody knife back to Anil. The blood was already freezing on her hand. Her mitten was gone, lost when the yak thrashed out its life. She shoved the bloody hand into her pocket. That cold on her cheeks might be tears freezing, too.

"See that the meat is distributed," she said to Tsechen. "Doctor Anil, follow the soldiers. They may catch up with that thing again."

His knife in his hand, the blood still steaming even as it froze to the blade, he started at her direct command. And then he bowed as low as the snow would allow, turned and ran into the darkness, his violet witchlights swirling about him like a swarm of luminescent chrysanthemums.

Yangchen watched until he was out of sight. Then she turned and made her way toward the milling animals, looking for Shuffle.

Anil found her and Tsechen later, huddled beside the covered brazier in the darkness of their wagon, unspeaking and unsleeping. Yangchen heard his voice, lowered, conversing with the guards beyond the door, so she had enough time to straighten herself up and light a stub of taper from the embers.

He prostrated himself before the guards had even closed the door behind him. Yangchen sighed, sick unto death of rank and formality—*how quickly we grow jaded*—and finally found her creaking voice to tell him, "Come and sit."

"Dowager," he said, and sat across the brazier from her and Tsechen. Tsechen raised her eyes. "The bear?"

"Vanished in the snow." He held his hands to the brazier. Yangchen thought, *I should offer him tea.* But she would have to wake one of the women—

Her head ached with the contradictions. Any action for his comfort would discommode someone else. Or she could make the tea herself, but she was the Dowager Empress Regent. It was not done, for her to serve another. She froze between kindness and protocol, and could not decide what to do.

"Vanished in the snow?" In the silence that followed, she too held her hands out to the brazier. She looked down, to make him more comfortable. "But it was bleeding—"

"We should have been able to follow the trail, this is true. I am sorry, Dowager. There is no excuse for our failure. The trail . . . stopped. Among the tents and the sheltered cookfires, and no one could tell us where it had gone. Of course, the snow was heavy, and it could have walked close by any of the campsites and gone unseen. But there should have been blood, and they should have heard it, at least—and it does not seem possible that an injured, raging beast could have staggered through a crowded encampment without plunging through a half-dozen households."

"Spirit," Tsechen said, then covered her mouth as if she had realized that she had not been invited to speak.

Yangchen made a brushing-aside motion, half forgiveness and half out of the desire to avert misfortune. But she found herself agreeing. "An angry spirit."

"Dowager"—he hesitated—"have you heard the rumors that the misfortunes that beset us . . . ? Well. There are some who think they have a common cause."

Yangchen had her own theories as to what that common cause might be. A chill settled into her shoulders. *My own actions. I brought this down on us. And now they know.* But she was not about to admit her suspicions of her own culpability.

She made a quick, cupping gesture with her right hand. *Continue.*

Anil glanced aside, as if someone else might step in and save him. Finding himself alone except for the two frowning imperial wives facing him, and the lightly snoring row of women beside the wall, he said, "The Carrion King. It is possible that the demon spawn, the skinned corpses, the awakening of the Cold Fire . . . these things . . ."

"These things," said Tsechen, "could herald his return."

Miserably, eyes downcast, he nodded.

"This was long ago," she breathed. "When the sky was higher than it is now." It was a horrible idea, the Joy-of-Ravens resurrected. And yet she felt a surge of hope at the idea. A surge of relief. Maybe it wasn't all her fault, after all. Maybe it was not misfortune and ill luck brought down on her household by the failure of her own filial duty. Maybe the empress had not poisoned her nation by proxy as she poisoned certain other things in fact.

She thought about stories. About the stories her father had told her, and the ones she read her women from books, or heard recounted by storytellers and bards summoned to bring her stories she had not heard before. She thought about how, in stories, any trick the hero performs is justified by the evil of those he performs it upon. How there are people whom one can behead, or trample, or push into a fire with impunity. How no one will mourn them.

It was comforting to think that there was a greater evil here. That she was not simply a foolish empress who had made a terrible alliance and opened her empire up to a curse.

"Comforting thoughts should be questioned more stringently than any others. For they are more likely to lead us astray, as we wish to believe them."

"Dowager?"

"My father taught me that. My father, the Prince under the Yellow Range."

"Are you saying, Dowager, that you think talk of the Carrion King's return is a comforting lie?"

She bit her lip. The urge to confess her sins, her complicity and treason, to these—Anil-la and Tsechen-tsa, the wizard and the emperor's wife—was so strong on her that she almost reached into her mouth to grab her tongue and hold it still from talking. For a moment, she wondered if she had been ensorcelled to spew truth, like Queen Fade of legend, but in a moment it passed and her racing heart began to settle.

"It would be nice to have someone to blame, don't you think?"

There. That was the truth, or near enough to it. Lying to wizards was a dangerous habit to get into.

Tsechen was looking at her. Yangchen arched her brows; the other woman glanced aside.

"It would," he said. "And it's nice, sometimes, to feel as if there's nothing we can do about a situation, when whatever we could do would be hard, risky, expensive, or unpleasant."

Something about the emphasis in his voice drew her attention. He was telling her something important, albeit obliquely. It was up to her to figure out what.

She missed Hong-la, suddenly. He was Song, like her. Even if he'd never been able to stand her, they felt the pulse of a conversation the same way. These Rasani were always somehow slightly . . . *off*.

Right now, for example, he obviously expected her to fill the silence—as if he had left it for her as a politeness, like the last dumpling on a plate.

"But . . . it may not be safe?" she hazarded. "Because the stories we believe shape the way we act?"

"And the stories others believe shape the way we are regarded, and how they respond to us." He shrugged. "Would you rather be seen as the noble underdog struggling against an ancient, implacable enemy—or the victim who will inevitably be crushed? Or the naïve, the denier who will never know what landed on her? Some of those same rumors say that the Qersnyk that my colleague Samarkar-la and your sister-wife Payma-tsa fled with is his reincarnation. That this Re Temur is the Sorcerer-Prince reborn, and catastrophe follows in his wake. Blood ghosts, demons, war, and fire. . . ."

Yangchen pinched the bridge of her nose. She was aware that her perfect, implacable political mask was slipping, and had no idea what she revealed. She glanced at Tsechen and met blank, intentional inscrutability. No help there. She didn't want to talk about Payma, or her sister-in-law, the Wizard Samarkar.

"Doctor, how would the leader of a house under a curse go about lifting that curse?"

He nibbled his thumb, dropping his challenging gaze, accepting the change of subject without a struggle. "It depends on the source of the curse. Hexed by a witch is one thing. A curse stone is another—"

"Say someone in the household attracted unfavorable attention from the Six Thousand."

"Wrath of the gods," he said. "Very tricky." He leaned forward and gently picked a white yak hair off the front of her robe. "Was it the leader of that household that drew the anger, or a subordinate?"

She shrugged.

He looked at her for so long she considered accusing him of insolence. She refrained, however—it was clear that he had only forgotten himself. Finally, he let his eyes drop and said, "I will research it— as best I might, under the circumstances—and see what I can learn, Dowager."

"Thank you." Yangchen rose, obliging Anil and Tsechen to rise also.

"Doctor Anil. When you have finished your duties for the night, you will return here to sleep."

"Dowager—"

"You are a eunuch, wizard," she said. "There is no impropriety in it. And my ladies and I will sleep sounder for your protection, when blue bears and Six Thousand know what else roam the night."

Anil-la bowed very low before he left.

In the silence after his leave-taking, Tsechen and Yangchen turned as if of one accord and wordless made themselves ready for sleep, if sleep would come. Although she knew it would fluster them come the morning, she chose not to wake the attendants. She and Tsechen could braid one another's hair for bed.

Through the night, Yangchen dozed fitfully. As sounds from without grew more muffled, it seemed as if those within the wagon were concentrated. The breathing of the women, the occasional pop of the covered brazier, the creak of the roof under the increasing weight of snow. The whisk of falling flakes against the walls. Anil-la's return, the stamping of his boots on the porch, the cold that entered with him and the sound of eventual, sleeping breath.

The storm gave no signs of abating. They would not be traveling tomorrow either.

Yangchen heard Tsechen's breathing break. It had been a little too smooth and soft, and she did not think Tsechen was sleeping deeply either.

Her whisper still startled Yangchen, though. "Dowager . . . did you kill the old Dowager Empress?"

Yangchen bit her lip. Feign sleep? Answer? Lie? These were not ideal conditions for a lengthy discussion of treason. Finally, she just said, "And if I did?"

"If you did, Dowager, you should not have allowed Tsansong-tsa to be burned for it."

"Your argument is impeccable," Yangchen agreed.

Tsechen rose in the dark, her layers of warm clothes rustling.

"What are you doing?"

"Clearing the vents," Tsechen said. "So the fire doesn't breathe up all the air and leave us to suffocate."

In silence, Yangchen got up to help. She tore an already-ragged nail and bit the scrap off, tasting blood. She thought with amusement of how she once would have guarded her lacquered and bejeweled talons with fingerstalls and the avoidance of all work. A clear chimney assured, she and Tsechen lay side by side in silence again.

Eventually, Yangchen thought Tsechen slept once more.

13

BROTHER HSIUNG RAN ON THROUGH THE RISING HEAT OF HARD-DAY, AS his shadow stretched before him, flickering long then short over the uneven ground like a serpent's questing tongue. He'd stripped his sandals and tucked them into his pack. His feet beat an unsteady pattern, the rhythm of his running affected by the terrain—but he was not unsteady. Brother Hsiung, like the bear his namesake, was a thick-thewed, heavy-bodied creature. But he had walked from Song to Ala-Din and halfway back again, and he was nimble with long years of practice in the forms of his monks' art.

He did not push himself, instead settling into a ground-covering trot that he could maintain indefinitely. Running could be a meditation too, though it was not one he had practiced since he was an acolyte and his masters had set about to strip the mental frailty of perceived limitations from him. And running over rough ground, barefoot, for long distances required focus and mindfulness.

Hsiung found his core, the center of his strength and focus, and he stayed there as the sun tracked across the sky. He stopped to drink at each source of clean water, and occasionally he chewed dried meat or fruit from his pack. He had taken very little in the way of supplies; the others had farther to go than he did. And he knew, if he stayed within his limits, if he remained uninjured, if he foraged some little along the way, if he found habitations where a humble Brother of the Wretched Mountain might beg sustenance . . . his body would support him until he reached the temple. He had used up a great deal of himself in their journeys, so his belly was small and soft rather than stout and firm. But there was enough of him left to fuel him to sanctuary with his brothers.

Assuming, of course, that they were willing to take him in.

At Hard-noon, Hsiung drank deep from a water-filled sinkhole, the limestone-saturated water sharp, funky, and homely on his tongue. He chewed another strip of leathery meat—the mortal remains of something Hrahima had killed as they were crossing the desert—soaked his sore feet in cool water and inspected them for injuries. Then he rolled into the shade of a weeping scholar-tree, where he stretched his legs and hips and rested. He slept through the heat of the day, until the singing of birds awakened him.

He crawled from his bower in Hard-evening, and after stretching and refreshing himself, he ran on.

The first *li* were hard, his body sore and protesting. He put his breath into the pain, keeping it even and smooth. He let himself walk up the worst hills and ran down their backs, leaping from rock to tussock, careful to land softly and avoid jarring his knees and ankles as much as possible. His muscles warmed and the pains faded to aches, the aches to a saturated feeling of warmth all through his lower body.

The chafing of the pack straps was worse. The weight of his supplies pulling at his shoulders made his collarbones feel sharp with pain. Despite chest and waist bands, the pack wanted to shift and send him tumbling down hillsides. When Hard-dusk came, he walked again, through to Soft-dawn, when there was light again to run. His clouded eyes did not aid him when the light grew indirect, gray, and diffuse.

He slept again at Soft-noon, and as Hard-dawning came upon him he found the road once more.

It was a track, in all honesty—a pair of bare furrows running through the flat bottom of a valley, skirting sinkholes and fording runnels of water with great, muddy ruts and the evidence of many hooves. This was a road as entirely opposite the construction of the Dragon

Road as it was possible for two such things to be while being defined by the same word.

But a road it was, and in this part of the world, Brother Hsiung knew very well that all roads led to the same destination.

It was easier to jog along the packed wheel track than it had been to hop and skip cross-country. He made better time here despite the inconvenience of a road that sometimes wound about awkwardly, avoiding hills that would have been impossible obstacles to overburdened cart-mules and oxen. And now, too, he began to find people. No inns nor hostels, not on a sad country track such as this. But carters and the occasional walker—tinkers, itinerants, entertainers, mendicants, teamsters, and the other traveling elements of a functioning economy. They were proof that the eerie emptiness of the Celadon Highway across the steppe did not extend into Song.

He still ran much of the time, but now as he came up on a new traveler—or groups of travelers—he would slow and hail them with a hearty wave. Vows of silence were far from unheard of, and his shaven head, robe, bare feet, and mendicant bowl were enough to mark him as a wandering priest. As everywhere he had traveled, he noticed that the poorest fellow journeymen were often the most kind, sharing food they might be going hungry to provide him. They would talk to him as he ate, taking his answers in nods or headshakes.

Their presence lightened Hsiung's heart even as the news they had to share burdened him. They spoke of a plague in the cities of the south, and reaching through the ten thousand allied principalities of Song and the Lotus Kingdoms and from them, into the Steles of the Sky. Hsiung had known of this before—he had come west bearing news of it, in his own time—but it sounded as if it were spreading even more dreadfully now.

Many of the travelers went girded in bells, pierced stones, bangles, and knots and mirrors and wards of protection. They spoke of the demons that incubated in men's lungs, and how the pestilence mimicked the black bloat but was not. They spoke of the war on the steppe, and their fears that it might result in Song being invaded anew by the Qersnyk hosts. And they spoke of the return of the Joy-of-Ravens, how he had called down blood ghosts and left skinned corpses half the world around.

But the news that made Hsiung glad of his vow, and that no one could expect him to answer or participate in the conversation, was the story he heard repeated four or five times with varying details—that the Joy-of-Ravens rode disguised in the skin of a Qersnyk warlord, accompanied by a strange group of creatures and outland sorcerers.

After the second time he heard it, Hsiung almost turned back. Someone should warn Temur and Samarkar. Someone needed to let them know that the enemy had laid traps for them—

No. Hsiung had chosen his path. He would honor this commitment and see it through. He'd be of no use to anybody, batted back and forth between crises like the feathered target of a game of stick-and-shuttlecock. *One thing at a time,* he told himself, handing the tin cup he had been drinking from back to the crop-hauling farmer who had so generously shared both rice wine and information.

Several rests and runs later—Hsiung was no longer sure how many—the road had grown busy enough that he jogged past more fellow travelers than he importuned. He'd donned his sandals to protect his feet from the detritus of the road. He rested less and ran more. His pack grew lighter. The landscape grew more rolling: less ragged, sculpted, and baroque. Sometimes his eyes gleamed green in warning. Running was as good a meditation as his forms, and he kept moving.

His first glimpse of the Tomb Immemorial came as he crested a little rise and stepped around the box of the cart he had been helping to shove up the hill. The Tomb followed the ridgeline opposite, a snake of mottled, mortared, mostly beige stones that stretched from the left horizon to the right. It looked like an impossibly extended fortress, high walls punctured by arrow slits and crowned by crenellations, punctuated regularly by the squat squares of guard towers. But it was a highway, and though height and distance made it seem no more than a thin layer of icing on the ridgeline, Hsiung knew it to be four times his height, with a road at its top wide enough for two handcarts to pass abreast.

It had a true name—the Imperial Highway, with a string of superlatives on either side—which no one used. Outside of official documents, everyone who walked it, worked it, or lived within sight of it called it the Tomb Immemorial, for the dead unfortunate slaves and dead desperate freemen entombed beneath its stones—and for its length, which ran from the ocean in the east to the escarpment of the Steles of the Sky in the west.

Men had built it over the course of a hundred and fifty years, and thousands had died in the process—carrying, hauling, mortaring stone in all weathers, in Hard- and Soft-day. It was a graveyard that stretched from one edge of the loosely united kingdoms of Song to the other, snaking and forking from hilltop to ridgeline, always keeping the high ground. It was mostly tawny limestone here, among the sinkholes and towers of the northwest, though capped in black slate to keep the rain from melting it away. Closer to the mountains, gray and white granite made it seem somber and heavy; down by the sea, red sandstone caught the Soft-day light like blood.

As always when he glimpsed the Tomb Immemorial, Hsiung thought of the Banner Wyrm, the great dragon teacher of whom it was said there was no beginning and no end—or at least, that you could never see either end of her alongside the middle, for she was too great to fold herself into one man's field of vision. But the Banner Wyrm lived in the Sea of Storms, where the great typhoons brewed from her sleeping exhalations. Here inland, their best grasp after infinity was the endless highway that was also a wall.

A woman, hunched under a load of wood as tall as she was, paused at the top of the rise beside Hsiung, as if she too were taking in the sight. Her white hair gleamed in the Hard-sun where her queue streamed from beneath her hat. She nudged him with her elbow and asked, in a strong voice with no hint of querulousness, "Of course this isn't your first time, Brother?"

Going home, he thought, and made a gesture of blessing over her. They usually figured out the vow of silence then.

If she did or not, she didn't indicate. She kept staring across the valley. "Going home?"

He looked at her sharply. The corner of her mouth that he could see—if he tilted his head to catch a glimpse around the hat brim—quirked.

"Oh," she said. "You're not so different from everyone else. Going home again is a trick very few manage, with worse reason than you. Or perhaps the best reason. Home is a lie we tell ourselves when we stay in a place for a while. Then we go away for a time, and the lie dries up like an autumn leaf and crumples in the wind. When we come back, we see it as it truly is, and the memories don't match anymore." She wiped sweat from her forehead. He swore the lining of her dust-colored, filthy sleeves flashed green as jade silk when she moved.

He stared.

The old woman hitched the wood up higher on her shoulder. "It's like falling out of love," she said, and crossed the road—the track—in order to start down the hill.

By the time Hsiung gathered himself to run after, a cart had rumbled between them, picking up speed on the descent while the oxen strained back against the harness. When it had passed, Hsiung could not see the woman anymore.

She had quoted the penultimate line of a poem at him. One of his favorite poems, written almost a thousand years before by a man who later died for his inability to keep his political opinions to himself. *It is like falling out of love*, the poet Hangmun had written. *Except even an old lover might lend money, sometimes.*

Hsiung looked as he jogged, but did not find her again. Though one would think that an old woman bent double under a load of kindling would be easy to pick out of the crowd.

He performed an extra set of devotions for the Wood Carrier before he rested, that noon.

Hsiung climbed up the last steep slope to the Tomb Immemorial with his thumbs hooked under the straps of his pack to ease the strain. Though it was nearly empty of food and water, which would inconvenience him greatly before he came to the Wretched Mountain, he blessed its lightness now—and every crumb of food and water that had gone into his belly on this long run. He was lean now, he knew. Perhaps too lean, and he worried that before he reached his destination his muscles would be wasted, his bones staring as never since he had been a starving orphan, thirty years before.

Well, the care of the body was the care of the spirit. But in times of trial, both could be a form of vanity. And Hsiung could not afford vanity now.

If there was one vice his old masters could smell out from a thousand *li* away, it was thinking too well of yourself. Or the other form of vanity that was thinking too little.

AS THE SINKHOLES AND LIMESTONE TOWERS HAD GIVEN WAY TO RIDGES AND steep-flanked hills, so the hills in their turn rose into forested mountains. These were nothing like the Steles of the Sky—or even the Shattered Pillars—but half-mountains by those standards. Still, in his youth, Hsiung had found them quite mountains enough. Despite his apprehension at his destination, his heart lifted at the beloved sight of so much green, so many trees, the towering gray cliffs behind them.

The Tomb Immemorial wound on through defiles and switchbacks, here hugging a cliff, there commanding a ridgeline. Often, mist softened the prospect ahead and behind—clouds snagged on the mountaintops or were trapped in the valleys below. Waterfalls tumbled from heights such as Hsiung could only measure with approximations. With a pang of missing his allies against the machinations of the al-Sepehr— his companions, now, if he were honest—he thought that Samarkar would know the math to find the height out accurately.

He could not stop thinking of the woman with the flash of green silk up her sleeve.

What a time is this, that Sages walk among us, and tease mere mortal men.

HE KNEW A DAY BEFORE HE CAME WITHIN SIGHT OF THE WRETCHED Mountain that his journey was nearly at an end—or, at least, this leg of it. He did not fool himself that—no matter how negotiations with his brothers went—he would find long rest here. Unless they took it into their heads to imprison him, as was within their rights. In which case he'd get more rest than he wanted.

Entering the Red Forest gave him his first landmark. The earth underfoot took on the color of rust, and terraced farms fallow for autumn marched up each hill, their tiers stained as if with blood. There were legends of how that had happened—many of them, contradictory, involving battles with Sages or dragons. Or both.

Hsiung was fairly sure no dragons had actually been involved, for the earth was fertile, not poisoned as it became where dragons had bled—or, worse, died. But something had made this the Red Forest, and as he ran farther in—tireless, now, hardened to the work, even as his body ate itself away to sinew and bone—even the bark and the leaves of the trees dwarfed beside the Tomb took on a faintly sanguine cast.

He slept beneath rhododendrons and arose to chilled limbs and an empty provision bag. A frost had settled in the Soft-day, the first of the season. Soon the oaks would be truly red, not merely tainted by the color. His stomach growled, but he'd begged congee and pancakes the day before. His strength would hold.

He found his feet, climbed the nearby steps to the road atop the Tomb, and began to run again.

This was familiar country. Now his feet knew the stones, and a kind of energy seemed to inform him at every stride, though the country rose ever upward. A trellis of switchbacks rose before him, the road interwoven with itself so intricately that in places it doubled back and bridged itself—the only expedient to prevent the turns from becoming too steep for a cart to navigate. Hsiung did not envy the oxen drawing up or down it, either hauling their cartage or braking it with the mass of their bodies.

Hsiung had only himself and his empty pack to haul.

Hardened as he was to travel, his calves scalded, his hamstrings, his ass. His breath came with a burning scrape, and it might have been wise to slack his pace, to walk up like the pilgrims and teamsters he passed. But running had become a kind of expiation, a proof—perhaps—of his dedication. The cliffs were white stone and had been cut away to make the blocks from which the Tomb Immemorial was constructed. In places, they overhung it. Occasionally the overhangs were supported by nettings of wires, the workings of Song court wizards—as, in truth, was this whole vast engineering project. More often, they had left a scatter of pebbles and dust on the road below.

They didn't collapse frequently, and not often at all in this season. Landslides were a winter peril. But Hsiung knew it did happen, and in the time before he had left the temple brotherhood, he had on several occasions come down among these hard curves to rebuild the road—or to minister to those crippled by it.

At last, he wound his way up the snake-coils of the highway to its peak. His driving feet might have paused there, but momentum had him and he let it carry him down. The slope on the other side was shallower, the ablative curves less exquisitely terrifying. Hsiung ran with soft knees, striking lightly, trying to absorb the shock of his descent.

Across the wide shallow-bellied valley, he could see the Gates of Otherwise—the colossal stone arch, as if some giant or Sage had chipped a passage in the very mountainside. It led directly to the monastic preserve of his brothers. The Tomb Immemorial did not go that way, for the monks inhabited a blind valley—the Gates of Otherwise its only entrance or exit. But there was another elevated road, smaller and less ornate, that mounted the rise to the bottom of the Gates in a series of tiered steps and vanished into the opening as if the mists beyond were a mystical gateway to another place.

Hsiung eased his pack straps with his thumbs. He wasn't sure why he kept the thing, except as a sort of superstitious talisman. He'd need it when he headed back to Temur, Hrahima, and Samarkar. If he were ever permitted to.

It was unwise to dwell on eventualities. Here and now was the only world. Anticipation bred misery.

There was only the running. When he arrived, he would be another person, and it would be another time. That person would do what he had to do. And suffer what he had to suffer in recompense.

The steps were hard. While not so steep as the slope behind Hsiung, they were steeper than the switchbacks that climbed it. He jogged up slowly, his knees grinding. When he came to the top—at last, he let himself pause. He rested his hands on his thighs, chest heaving. A slower climber trudged past, a carry-basket on his shoulders, contents concealed beneath a patterned cotton cloth.

Hsiung realized that he had not allowed himself to pause for breath before this because he was afraid that if he did, he would not continue.

But now he could look forward and down, and see not just the road that led him home—what had been home, anyway; the last true home he had known—but the Wretched Mountain in its lone glory, veiled in the mists of a dozen waterfalls.

The valley was wet and sheltered, the purple-red leaves of the maples flocking its floor and walls as if they were pressed into the cup of a serving bowl. At the center rose the Wretched Mountain, a narrow spire of white stone blossoming from a narrower base to wider walls, like some trumpet mushroom of incomprehensible scale. All up its height trees clung to ledges, mosses dripped. At its ragged top, a forest no bigger than a *li* in diameter bloomed, seeming to slip down the convex dome like icing on a hot bun. Narrow waterfalls tumbled down the sides, casting the whole valley in mist and rainbows as the light of Hard-day refracted through them.

The waterfalls frothed and bubbled past the hanging buildings of the Wretched Mountain Temple Brotherhood. The monastery was comprised of a series of long, narrow pagodas, walled in a dark leafy green and roofed in fluted tiles the cinnabar-red of dragonscale. They clustered beneath the overhangs of that central mountain pillar, supported by chains and pilings that vanished into raw rock above and below. Their narrow balconies ran their lengths, the railings painted as red as the roofs. A series of sway-backed bridges connected each to the next. Hsiung could see figures in homespun robes moving along those bridges and balconies. The temple circumambulated the mountain, and the only access from the ground was via hanging stairs and ladders at the back. Some vagary of the wind brought to his ears the tolling of a great bell.

It was not the heaviest of the monastery's bells, but Hsiung found it the sweetest. The Wretched Mountain Temple had over a hundred great bells, which were rung by striking them with hammers—hard work, and heavy, for some of the carillons went on for a tenth of the day. After so many years here, he knew almost every bell by its tone and its motto, which was also its name. The exceptions were *Ascension* and *I Raise Emperors*, which had not been rung in his lifetime. *Ascension* would peal at the creation of a new Sage, something that had not happened in a hundred years. And there had been no emperor to unite the Song principalities in nearly so long.

I Break the Lightning rang against the destruction of storms, and *I Calm Ghosts* rang for funerals and in time of wars. This, however, was *Haven,* and it rang for homecomings . . . and with *I Calm Ghosts* for the dead.

Hsiung did not think it was ringing today for him. Unless in its latter capacity. Still, the crystalline peal went through him like a blade. He felt it in his chest, like a pressure inside his lungs. His heart pounding, he fought the urge to bolt.

Having come this far, he turned craven at the very gates of his failure. He stepped aside on the road, to let those who walked rather than dawdling pass him while he stared down into the green, glorious, mist-bannered valley. The patched cloth of his sleeve caught and rasped on the calluses of his fingers when he fretted it. *You should have done this years ago.*

Enough.

Hsiung set his foot upon the road again.

THERE IS NO MORE MELANCHOLY SENSATION THAN RETURNING AS A stranger to a place once loved. The strangest thing of all was that no one seemed to notice Hsiung, or question his place—even as he made his way past the terraced orchards of the valley heights, the terraced farms of its lower reaches, the pastures and houses of its floor. Even as he made his way to the hanging ladder that reached from that floor to the entrance of the monastery.

It was guarded by two novices in brown-yellow robes so new they still smelled of the onion skins used to dye them, tied with undyed sashes with fraying, unhemmed ends. Their heads were cropped close; they looked at Hsiung's frayed robe, galled feet, and the crop of resurgent stubble—almost a scruff, now; he should have shaved the night before—across his scalp with eyes as wide and black and stunned as those of startled deer. No one really expected the novices who did the boring work of standing at the bottoms of ladders to have to repel much more than curious children.

He bowed to them, reading awe in their startled glance at one another, the haste with which they bowed in return. When he straightened, he moved to the ladder as if he were, in truth, a mendicant returning after his journeyman interval of three years, seven, or twenty-one. As if he had every right to be here.

As if he had not fled in the night, before he could be found out and disciplined.

As if unbidden, he heard the voice of old Master War: *The strong warrior makes himself bigger than he is, Student Hsiung! The strong monk is a strong warrior, even if he never fights a battle. Never cringe; never bend; never go toward conflict without your spine being straight.*

It shocked him out of his uncertainty and self-excoriation. But why would Master War help him now? The moment he had walked away from the Wretched Mountain, all the attention and advice of the masters had deserted him. He had been alone—

Master War helps you now because you have returned to your vows. It is never the task of the masters to offer comfort. Only peace, where peace is earned. Only strength.

I kept my vows. I have observed them in my exile. In my mendicancy.

Including the one to obedience?

Hsiung, dumbfounded beyond his oath of silence, simply bowed. The novices, thinking he bowed for them a second time, returned the gesture.

"Master—" said the slighter of the two. "Are the bells for you? Welcome home." He stepped into Hsiung's path, though Hsiung could see his uncertainty.

Hsiung touched his mouth and tilted his head. The novice put a hand to his cheek as if feeling the burn of embarrassment. He glanced at his companion, who was hanging back slightly. They had no confidence, and no understanding of their role. But that was what they were here to learn.

In his own way, Hsiung served the purpose of instructing them. Nature finds a use for everything.

Listening to the instructions of Master War, remembered after so long a lapse, he straightened his spine, set his foot upon the ladder, and began to climb.

The ladders themselves were an intentional obstacle. The rope rungs cupped a foot and trapped it. The ladders had a tendency to twist into helixes when climbed. And Hsiung had lost the knack of getting up them with grace. Still, somehow he managed, not daring to look for an instant as if he were not supremely confident. Not daring to look down, even when his foot kicked randomly, struggling to free itself from one rung and then groping for the next.

His long run and the privation had left him weak, and he had to pause several times on the climb to lace a calf through the ladder and rest. He hoped the novices would blame his incompetence on exhaustion. Although every returnee must struggle to regain these skills, he supposed. And unless they were raised sailors, the novices would not yet have mastered the art of climbing these ladders themselves.

Halfway up, the rhythm of it started to come back to him. His muscles, even tired, remembered. His body moved more naturally, and as he struggled less, he swung less. As he swung less, climbing became easier.

He ascended the last half of the ladder in a third the time it had taken to ascend the first half, and with a quarter of the effort.

At last, he stood on the landing platform, only a last long stair carved into the stone—a pair of monks with crossbows at its top— between him and the balconies. The stair had staggered risers, divided right and left, so that each step up was only half the height it would otherwise have been. These monks were adult brothers, wearing sashes in the same deep mulberry as Brother Hsiung's had once been, though he guessed it would be considerably less faded, darned, and threadbare. Hsiung tilted his head back and spread his hands, showing them empty. The blur of his vision precluded him recognizing either of these men and he suspected that, even if they had known him, they might not recognize him, either. Even as a novice—once he came back from starvation—he had been a bulky man, broad and thick. Now his robes hung on his raw bones like a puppet's garments on its works. When he touched his face, he could feel bones where the plumpness of his cheeks had been. His eyes were probably sunken in pits, and the scruff of an untended beard obscured the lower half of his face.

Yes, he really should have shaved last night. It would have demonstrated respect.

This demonstrates haste.

One crossbowman raised his weapon. He called down a demand for explanation, terse and authoritarian, but not aggressive. The other lowered his weapon and backed away from the railing, vanishing within. Perhaps for instructions.

Moving slowly, ever so slowly, Hsiung touched his lips. He was not armed, but as he was dressed as a member of their order they would not expect him to need weapons greater than his feet and hands. He drew a line from nose to chin, indicating that his mouth was closed by a vow.

"Wait, then, brother," the guard said, but he did not lower his weapon. "You are a returnee?"

Hsiung nodded.

"We will find someone who can identify you."

That's what I'm afraid of. Hsiung nodded. Though his shoulders and upper arms ached from climbing, he accessed the discipline and serenity of his practice and training and endured it to keep his hands spread out and held high.

The running monk's sandaled footsteps echoed along the walkway, heard very clearly from Hsiung's position below it. He listened to them recede, and—within the limits of his discipline—more or less made himself comfortable.

The wait was not as long as he expected it to be. Certainly not as long as it should have been, based on his own memories of the time it had taken him to scramble from this very guard post to the masters' quarters when he had been the monk bored and pretending serene contemplation and alertness on this very duty. Very quickly, however, a more measured tread returned—matched by a light, quick stride that even after years, Hsiung identified immediately. With mingled apprehension and relief.

His judgment was confirmed when the crossbowman jumped back from the railing, taking his eyes off Hsiung—the guard would be hearing about that, to his sorrow, before supper—and bowing so low his shaven forehead must have brushed the planks of the suspension decking.

"War-zi!" *Master War!*

Hsiung could envision Master War's silent sigh, although he could not see him. And the impatient gesture that would have preceded the crossbowman's abrupt, mortified return to his post at the top of the stair, his bow once more leveled.

Hsiung took a breath. *What befalls is what befalls. You may only influence the moment. In the moment concentrate your efforts.*

Brave thoughts, but what was left of his vision all but swam before him with apprehension. Master War was a dark shape at first, no more than a shadow, and then he was a blur behind the pall of Erem. Hsiung could not make his eyes resolve him, but he knew what he would see if he could. A man of middle years, moderate size, and wiry build, plump-cheeked and stern behind his moustache, Master War wore the unflattering mud-yellow robes of all the Wretched Mountain monks. His horny feet were thrust into black twine sandals, his arms folded inside his thick-hemmed sleeves. If Hsiung's head had not been tilted back to regard those above him, it would have been just at the level of Master War's toes and the angry red callus the sandal-strap had rubbed across the top of the left great one. But the sash that bound his waist was dyed near black with eldren-berries. It had rubbed purple friction-stains around the Master's waist.

Hsiung might have hoped that this once, he might have seen Master War discommoded. At least slightly flustered. But Hsiung could tell from Master War's posture that he did what he always did when one of his monks disappointed him. After a moment's dispassionate consideration, the tips of his moustaches barely quivering, Master War let his arms slide out of his sleeves. He grasped the railing with the left one; the right ended in a smooth amputated stump.

"Brother Hsiung," Master War said. "So you are returned to us at last."

Hsiung bowed so low his forehead almost pressed his knees. He was surprised at how tightly his body tucked together without the bulk of his belly in the way. He stayed bent double until Master War sighed and tapped four fingers on the railing.

He said, "Well, then. I suppose you had better come inside."

THE INTERIOR OF THE TEMPLE HAD NOT CHANGED—NOT EVEN TO BECOME more shabby. During Brother Hsiung's tenure, the woven mats had been changed every season, the paint refreshed, the lacings that held the slatted walls and floors together checked and renewed as well. It was not evident from below, but the buildings of the temple were bound together with cord, hanging from massive chains and pilings that anchored them to the rock above and below—as if they were incredibly elaborate and complex suspension bridges that people happened to live and pray and work inside.

It had never struck Hsiung before, that in the Song dialect used in the Wretched Mountain Kingdom, *live* and *pray* and *work* were the same word. He had spent too much time in foreign lands and they had made his own language strange to him.

In the winter—even later in autumn—woven mats would be lashed against the insides of the slatted walls. Brother Hsiung's fingertips still bore a stippling of dark pinpricks, tattooed there by the splinters of rushes that had pierced his novice fingers in the endless, endless, endless weaving of those damned mats. For now, as in the spring and summer, cooling breezes blew through the gaps and made the prayer ribbons strung between the rafters shimmer. A novice slid the door shut behind them as they entered, sealing them in with the scent of aloes-wood incense: rich, stark, subtle.

Hsiung found himself alone in the narrow, sun-slatted room with Master War. He followed silently, two steps behind the master and one to the left, across woven rush-mats until they came to the edge of a little platform covered by a small knotted silk rug on which two coiling shapes he knew were dragons, one black and one golden-yellow, chased each other's tails.

Master War stepped up onto the dais and turned. Hsiung remained where he had stopped, a step from the edge of it. As Master War settled in the center of the rug, Hsiung remained standing.

Master War clapped his hands. A pre-novitiate—one of the orphans or unsupportable children given to the monastery to raise when no one in their own villages or families could afford to feed them, for he was no more than nine years old and gangly with it—bolted into the room bearing a lacquer tray. He ran with his head ducked, his cap of black hair shining. It would not be cropped until he reached puberty and took his preliminary oath to the temple.

He set the tray down before Master War, and with a nervous bob of his head, turned and ran out again. Hsiung kept his eyes front, though he burned to turn and watch the child go. He wondered if he knew the boy's name, if he would have recognized him four years ago, or with better eyes. And he knew why Master War had staged this little drama. It was a reminder of where Hsiung had come from, and what he had become.

Hsiung ached with memories. But he would show Master War his discipline. He did not even glance down to see what the tray contained. Instead, he kept his eyes trained over the master's left shoulder, so he could watch Master War's expressions without rudely staring at his face.

He heard the master's voice again. But the master never moved, and certainly did not alter the pattern of his breathing or part his lips to speak.

Was it because you, like that boy, had no choice in coming here that you left us?
Hsiung shook his head.
Master War frowned. *You have not found your voice, to answer me.*
Hsiung shook his head.
Then you must retain your vow of silence, even if that is not why you undertook it.
Hsiung inclined his head. In so doing, he saw what Master War had caused to be set before him. Thick, redolent aloes-wood paper, and a

brush, and a jar of water. But there was no watercolor cake of ink. He felt it with a shock. What he reported, then, was for Master War's eyes only, and no record would be made of it except in the master's mind.

"If you must," Master War said, "write."

Hsiung knelt, and readied the writing materials before him. He had no doubt that Master War could read his words, upside down or otherwise . . . but the previous night, when he had not been shaving his beard and skull-bristles, he had made other preparations. Preparations that stood a chance of seeing his message delivered even if the monks had decided to shoot him down where he stood.

Hsiung slowly reached into the side pocket of his pack and drew out the book of wooden slats, laced together at each end just like the walls that surrounded them, upon which he had written his letter. His plea for assistance, since he was not so arrogant as to expect understanding or forgiveness.

Head bowed, he extended it to Master War. His hands shook at his temerity.

The strong warrior makes himself bigger than he is.

Master War did not reach out his hand to take the book. *We thought you had abandoned us, Student Hsiung.*

It did not escape Hsiung that the master called him *student*, though he had been a sworn brother for ten years before his crime and his flight.

We speculated that perhaps, despite your talents, your apparent dedication, it might have dawned on you that the world had a great deal to offer a man of which a monk is forbidden in partaking. We thought you might have regretted the decision of your ancestors, who gave you to us.

Hsiung's hand wavered. It was just the tiredness of climbing, of holding his hands in view for so long. The exhaustion of hunger and the long journey.

He laid the book down at Master War's feet and picked up the brush instead. With quick gestures, he wrote with water—

"I went upon my mendicancy."

And yet you were not sent.

Hsiung kept his gaze down, on the words he was shaping. The first sentence had already dried to illegibility. "Nevertheless," he wrote. "It seemed necessary. To protect the Brotherhood, and because I was afraid."

What had you to fear?

Gently, Brother Hsiung set the brush down on its stand, a single drop of water quivering unspent at its tip. Left handed, shaking as he contemplated his own daring, he reached out and nudged the book closer to Master War. Master War did not move.

Hsiung bit his lip. He looked up—he forced himself to look up— and at last he looked very carefully into Master War's eyes, holding the master's gaze with his own. Knowing that the master would read in his blue-tinged eyes, his fading vision, the evidence of his crime.

His chest hurt with holding his breath, straining for every sound. Still, he heard nothing as Master War leaned forward and lifted the book from the rug, and then not even the rattle of wooden pages or the rustle of coarse-woven homespun cloth. He breathed out as softly as he could manage, and forced himself to breathe in again.

His knees began to ache while the master read. His spine might have been fused in the humble, head-lowered posture he maintained, it began to hurt so greatly. But he waited, and brought himself more dis-cipline by returning again and again to the emptiness of a calm mind, of a mind in the now, every time he was tempted to remember what he had written or wonder what the master was reading now.

Most Benevolent Masters of the Wretched Mountain Temple, I bring to you this the testament and confession of Brother Hsiung. In the name of all the Bells of Heaven, in the name of the Old Master and of the Woman Who Cannot Lie, what I have written here is as true and accurate as I can make it. I accept your judgment without question or reservation.

Though I broke my vows before I left you, I have lived by them exactly since, and though I sought no leave for my mendicancy, I have struggled to live by its requirements and constraints. I have abided by my practice, though I cannot claim I have always used it as the temple might have wished, as I had no guidance in the world—a failing that, I hasten to add, was entirely the fault of my own flawed decisions.

I have chosen to return to you, expecting no forgiveness, because of the dire news that I bear, which I believe the masters must be made aware of.

My first crime was that of curiosity. As a worker in the temple's libraries, I came to know that there were books in our keeping more ancient and curious than any I had dreamed of. Although we were cautioned against these books, although I was a sworn brother and obedience was my commandment, I let my willfulness override my humility. I found those books, and more, I opened them.

And I read them, or some of them at least.

They were texts in the language of Erem, and they tainted me.

And that is why I fled. I felt the poison of those venomous old words working in me, and I thought at the time that it would continue to work. That I would not live long, and—in my confusion and despair—that if I stayed here, my poisoned presence would poison the temple, too.

I should have trusted more in the masters.

I went into the world, and found there that the poison was spreading as well. You will have heard of the disease that stalks the cities, that is not the black bloat. You will also have heard of the fall of Qarash, and that the sons and grandsons of the Great Khagan slaughter one another across the steppe with merciless glee. I do not know if you have heard that Kashe was destroyed by blood ghosts and swelters now a tomb, forsaken under a Rahazeen sun, or that Asitaneh burned before falling into Rahazeen hands. You may have heard that a sorcerer who commands the giant demon-bird of the wind rides from the desert, sowing destruction with every pass of its wings. Glass demons ride the air, attacking as they will—they, too, are a beast out of the skies that shelter ancient Erem, if you can say such destructive force shelters anything.

These tales are true in every respect and regard. There is one man responsible for all this destruction. His name is Mukhtar ai-Idoj. He is the al-Sepehr of the Nameless murder-cult, and I believe that it is his intention to claim as many hundreds of thousands of souls as he can.

I report the following, with its attendant conjectures, not to excuse my curiosity but to explain it. Perhaps my folly serves some purpose after all. Perhaps my unwitting and arrogant self-sacrifice will be of use. For as it happens, I am passingly acquainted with the magic and powers of ancient Erem, those powers raised by Sepehr al-Rachīd, the Joy-of-Ravens, and by Danupati the Conqueror in their own times, when they rode in blood from one corner of the world to the other. Al-Sepehr commands these powers. He raises dead things and controls them, and I believe it is he who commands the blood ghosts and probably the demon spawn as well. He has found a way, through the sacrifice of untold numbers of women and I know not who else, to maintain his own physical integrity and health while wielding the powers of corruption that work to blind and poison me even now.

As I carry their taint in me, when he raises those forces I can sense it.

I conjecture that the purpose of this destruction is to elevate his foul cult, to spread his sky over every land, and it is possible that he had some necromancy at his command so powerful that it is not beyond him to raise the Carrion King, the Joy-of-Ravens himself, and set that corrupt demigod over all the lands beneath all the skies once again.

They say that butterflies are souls, and that scarlet butterflies are the souls of priests and witches. I can confirm the first, for in the aftermath of the fall of Qarash, as I worked among the corpses of the dead, I did see those butterflies called from their unshriven lips. I believe now that what I saw was al-Sepehr raising his army of blood ghosts.

I have been in the company of a man, a woman, and a Cho-tse who are working together to oppose al-Sepehr. I believe they are the best hope we have of ending his plan, which has so far been to play one would-be ruler off against another until carnage and massacre ensue.

The man is Re Temur Khagan, grandson of the Khagan of Khagans, best claimant to the Padparadscha Seat.

The woman is the Once-Princess Samarkar, who was heir to Rasa and who was wife to Ryi, then heir to Zhang Shung. She is become a Wizard of Tsarepheth.

The Cho-tse is the warrior Hrahima.

All three are exiles from their people, as I have been. But Re Temur is returning home now, and I believe his birthright will be won.

Al-Sepehr spreads the rumor that Re Temur is the Joy-of-Ravens returned, or that the Carrion King wears Re Temur's skin. This is a lie.

I have journeyed with them. They have made many allies in their travels, and perhaps might raise an army and an alliance strong enough to thwart the machinations of al-Sepehr.

My life is yours to dispense with. But I beg of you, consider in your heart and will the truth of what I've said.

Written this tenth day of the moon of First Frost, year 2375 since the first teaching of the Banner Wyrm, for the eyes of the masters.

> Brother Hsiung of the Wretched Mountain Temple
> Once-Librarian

Hsiung remained kneeling as Master War read, and read again. And kneeling he remained as Master War stood, without acknowledging or releasing him, and strode out of the room.

14

THOUGH THEY WORE NO RED COATS, NO ONE WOULD MISTAKE THE REM-nants of the Dead Men for other than they were: a half-dozen professional soldiers dressed in secondhand traveling clothes—perhaps elite mercenaries, perhaps Broken Men left after the fall of some sheikh or noble household. Even when they tried not to walk in lockstep, their footfalls naturally fell into a rhythmic pattern. Even when they tried to look relaxed, their spines hove straight, their shoulders squared.

Ato Tesefahun and the man who had been Uthman Caliph Fourteenth had long since come to the conclusion that if there was no way to hide the nature of their escort, the next best thing they could do was play it up. So Tesefahun sat cross-legged atop an open canvas litter carried on the shoulders of four Dead Men. Pillows were heaped about him, and his gray head was bare under the watery Kyivvan sky—blues so blue they seemed enameled, a sun so golden it was almost orange, the colors more like those of a fresco than those of the world. He wore clean white robes, sweeping from the bare brown sticks of his arms, with loose white trousers, Uthman-style, beneath. His feet were bare inside golden sandals never meant for walking.

The man who had been Uthman Caliph—who was choosing to call himself Captain Iskandar, he said, until such time as his own proper name could be reclaimed—walked at Tesefahun's right hand, wearing a scimitar, a helm pushed down his back, dressed like the captain of the mercenaries. His beard was dyed with indigo, his hair unturbaned and braided with gold and indigo cord into a wild forest of twists. Even Ato Tesefahun, who had known him from a child, had to admit he looked nothing like the deposed priest-king of a fallen empire.

They had left Tesefahun's men-at-arms in a Kyivvan town on the north coast of the White Sea, in charge of the dependents of both parties. There, they had sold the horses and such incidentals and fripperies as were not necessary to survival. Then Tesefahun, the man who was not Iskandar, and the six surviving Dead Men had taken ship with the pale-skinned northerners. They had endured the deck of the open boat with its dragon-headed prow, its striped, square sail, and its single bank of oars up the wide, calm waters of the river called Slavutych, to Kyiv. From the port—outside the city walls, and protected by separate fortifications entirely—to the city itself, Tesefahun had availed himself of the litter. He had had to restrain himself from turning around and making a rude, departing gesture in the general direction of the dragon's gilt teeth as the disguised Dead Men bore him away. Just about anything was a more comfortable method of travel than that boat.

Now Kyiv was in sight, and with it the hope of wealth and perhaps even allies.

Tesefahun might have taken just a small bite of pleasure at the spark of disciplined wrath in the erstwhile guard-captain's eyes when Tesefahun bossed him around. Something Tesefahun was careful only to do in front of witnesses, when it suited the roles they were playing. As the steady pace of the Dead Men bore them up the road to the great trade city of Kyiv, he refrained. It wasn't that there was too much tension in him for the game, but at the moment he thought it unwise to provoke Captain Iskandar. Ato Tesefahun leaned over on the litter. Iskandar wore a squint, even though he shaded his eyes with his hand. He kept scanning the clusters of houses and fields scattered between them and the long-outgrown walls of Kyiv with frowning intensity.

"Don't blink," Tesefahun murmured. "Kara Mehmed's entire army might pour out from behind a woodshed the moment your attention lapses."

That was a dirtier look than usual, but Iskandar did not break character. "My lord has hired guardians," he said dryly. "Can he fault them if they guard?"

The Dead Men, of course, showed no expression. They might have been marching stones.

Tesefahun said, "A man who takes himself too seriously will fail to find the humor when every joke takes him as its topic."

Iskandar's upper lip pinched in a grimace. "Not every joke," he said. "There's still the one about the soldier and the nomad girl."

Iskandar kept his voice dry, but Tesefahun smirked. "And the one about the two priests of the Scholar-God. . . ."

Iskandar lengthened his stride, so the litter-bearing Dead Men trotted to keep up. Tesefahun grabbed at the poles as he was jounced. As they came up to the city walls with speed, Iskandar called back over his shoulder, "And a man who does not take his enemies seriously enough is more likely to end up on the point of a spear than the butt of a joke. *Master.*"

The walls swept back from heavy gates that had not, to the best of Tesefahun's knowledge, been closed against a threat in his own long lifetime. Oiled and gleaming hinges attested to the fact that they could, however, on a moment's notice. And Tesefahun had no doubt that this was practiced with regular drills. The massive and ready military machine of the Kyivvan empire had been the rock upon which both caliph and Khagan had broken and rolled back into the boundaries of their own empires like waves into the sea. That the boyars of the ruling households had never seen fit to attempt conquest in return had more to do with the richness of the fertile Kyivvan plains and valleys and the poverty of the lands south and east than it did any lack of might on their part. Caliphate nor Khaganate had anything Kyiv would want.

It was a measure of Kyiv's smug sense of security that no one stopped or even seemed to take particular notice of Tesefahun, Iskandar, and their "mercenaries" as they entered.

The guards were easy to pick out of the crowd because they seemed to be chosen for their height, exceptional even among the generally tall and stocky Kyivvans. Guards lined either side of the street at the enormous, whitewashed block of the tower gatehouse, but they collected neither taxes, nor tolls, nor interfered with commerce in any fashion. They seemed content to watch as people eddied and swirled through a grim

tunnel studded with the teeth of portcullises and the maws of murder-
holes as unconcernedly as they might walk through their own front
doors. Some of the guards did see fit to dice a little, though Tesefahun
noticed that—like geese—two or three were always sharply alert while
the rest went about other business.

The walls were as thick through as a tall man laid down head-to-
foot four times, and as Tesefahun and his "retainers" emerged into the
sunlight beyond the gatehouse he could see that their backs were braced
and reinforced with enormous earthworks, slanted ramps carpeted
green with grass. Goats and flocks of sheep grazed here and there on
those steep slopes.

The wizard Tesefahun, builder and destroyer, architect of temples
and palaces, thought he would not care to be the sapper tasked with
bringing down the walls of Kyiv.

The city beyond lived up to the walls and the sprawl outside. The
ferocious bustle of the entrance square broke quickly into tributary rivers along each of the five avenues that ran into the city. Tesefahun
heard a dozen languages, and despite the reputation of Kyivvans for
pallid, unhealthy skin that burned in the sun, he saw men and women
as dark as or darker than himself—and many more closer to the tone
of Iskandar and his men. But the majority were various unhealthy
shades of yellowish or pinkish beige, and their hair all looked as if it
had been bleached out with well-aged pregnant mare's urine preparatory to taking a dye like the one Iskandar wore. They were, indeed,
a towering race. If it were not for the litter, Tesefahun would have
been eye level with the chins or chests of the majority of even the
women.

Tesefahun was too old to stare. But one exceptionally tall man with a
beard like brick and braided hair the color of beaten copper might have
turned Tesefahun's head under any circumstances. He was dressed in a
self-consciously barbaric fashion, wrapped in furs and plaids, with an axe
strapped across the shield slung over his shoulders and a chain shirt slapping his striding thighs. Tesefahun had played the exotic foreigner often
enough to recognize the signs, and he would have liked to talk to this
extravagant barbarian—but said barbarian was making much better
time through the crowd than a litter and three other men could. This

was not merely because he was a man alone. But as he stomped along the border of a street ahead of them, anyone who saw him coming quickly stepped aside.

Tesefahun considered shouting after him—but there was a fine line between drawing the right sort of attention to themselves to make their disguise seem natural, and becoming memorable.

Iskandar might be out of the court, but he hadn't forgotten the skills of reading it. He noticed where Tesefahun was looking.

"You know what that is?" he asked, softly.

Tesefahun nodded. "One of the Skanda relatives of the Kyivvan Skray-lords. A warlord who happens to be a boyar's cousin. I bet that's awkward for everyone involved, but someone's got to row the boats upstream."

The armies of the north had "liberated" Kyiv some hundred years before, and the northern lords still retained very close ties of kinship, intermarriage, and trade with those of their blood that held Kyiv. Kyivvan trade flowed as much up the rivers to the north, in the summers at least, as it did south to the Celadon Highway. The confluence of two great rivers was not only the reason for the city's existence. It was the source of its astounding size and wealth.

And this particular warlord was putting on a show for the peasantry as he stomped along—just displaying himself? Rabble-rousing? Moving to or from some appointment? There was a story here, and—as happened increasingly with Tesefahun's encroaching age—he was forced to acknowledge that he'd likely never know more of it than this brief moment when his own story intersected it.

That the warlord felt the need to make such a display made Tesefahun's fingertips prickle with nervousness. From Iskandar's deepening frown, he was not alone.

For once, Tesefahun didn't have anything witty to say about the lurking shade of Kara Mehmed. But he made a note to himself to discover the copper-headed man's name and family affiliations, if that were possible.

"Let's find food," he suggested. Commanded, really—or so it would seem to anyone who overheard.

But it was Iskandar's curt nod that confirmed the decision. "A market is a good place to eavesdrop. And my lord will of course need a bed before his important rounds of business tomorrow."

Under Captain Iskandar's direction, the Dead Men turned mercenaries turned litter bearers brought Tesefahun down street after narrowing street in which the patchwork materials of oft-repaired walls had been amended with whitewash until they matched—at least to cursory inspection. Kyivvan architecture tended to blockish buildings of three to five stories, tight rows of tiny square windows lining the tops of the second and higher floors. The roof details were arched, and small, round, plain domes proliferated.

They stopped to ask directions to a market once or twice. It turned out to be more challenging than expected to find someone who spoke passable Aezin or Uthman. Tesefahun's Kyivvan was not entirely bad, but the role he was playing would be stronger if he did not seem the sort to lower himself to learn a foreign tongue, much less speak it poorly. Nevertheless, they eventually found their way to a square formed by the off-center crossing of two great boulevards and the perpendicular spike of a smaller side street. As if the city fathers, in paving, had just thrown their hands up in despair at the prospect of attempting to control the traffic patterns, the whole was a massive and uncontrolled snarl of wagons, riders, pedestrians, and less disciplined forms of conveyance.

Looking around, Tesefahun realized they had come diagonally across a good chunk of the city, and the hulking shape behind the far row of buildings was in fact another portion of the massive wall, and a second, east-facing gate. What he did not see was a market. A few scattered stalls and barrows, certainly—men peddling grilled meat threaded on straws for easy handling, women with parasol-shaded wheeled braziers over which they balanced griddles upon which they flipped a for-all-practical-purposes endless stream of small bubbly buckwheat cakes.

He called out to a prosperous-seeming passerby, a woman whose green skirts were kilted up to display an embroidered undergarment of a flaxen shade that matched her hair. She carried an empty basket and two bags of knotted string, which he took to be a positive sign that perhaps she could help them.

"Market?" he asked, frustrated enough to desert the dignity of his fictional station.

She cocked her head, brows drawn together. When he repeated himself, she frowned at him as if he were a mental deficient and pointed in the direction she'd already been headed, then swept her skirts together and continued on her way across the square, her basket swinging on her arm.

Surely those few stalls and barrows could not be it? Not in a city of this size? Or perhaps Kyiv kept market days, as so many smaller towns and villages did, and this was simply not one? Tesefahun frowned at the expanse of flagstones, the click of booted and clogged feet passing over the filth and muck, the men and women with their bags and baskets laden who must be coming from somewhere—

Such as the massive pale stone building on the opposite side of the square, which he had taken for a barracks or an armory with its street-level doors and windows covered by pierced stonework lattices. But people with empty baskets went in, and people with heavy baskets came out—and Tesefahun realized he'd been guilty of the sin of assuming that another land would share the customs with which he was familiar. And which might not make any sense in a clime where rain was not an occurrence all but confined to the monsoon, and where biting cold and iron-hard ground heaped with ice and snow was not a phenomenon isolated to the mountains.

His teachers at the University in Aezin would have been shamed by their student's failure to observe—if they were not by now all dead of old age, as was more likely. The market, of course, was *indoors*.

He related his revelation to Iskandar, who went from looking baffled to looking irritated in the pace of a second. To his credit—and he was one of the better of his dynasty, for all that was like saying a tapeworm was better than a guinea-worm—the sharp little shake of his head that set his twisted braids a-rattling betrayed the target of the irritation as himself rather than anything or anyone external.

"Of course," he said. "How stupid."

"Food and, eventually, lodging," Tesefahun replied. "Let's go."

"Next time, I ride in the litter and you march alongside," Iskandar replied.

"I'm lighter."

Iskandar snorted. He struck out across the square. The Dead Men had learned their roles with the quick facility by which they seemed to pick up everything. The two not engaged in hauling Tesefahun about darted to the lead to clear a path for the litter; the other four kept pace with their "captain."

Tesefahun settled back among his cushions and steepled his hands, enjoying the cool brightness of the afternoon now that they were out from among the closeness of the whitewashed alley walls with their patchwork construction of brick, stone, daub. He considered the architecture of the market more closely, now that he was aware of its purpose—and indeed, it would make a poor armory. There were too many doors—three at least on the long side facing him, one on each corner and one in the middle. That suggested there were probably an equivalent number on each of the sides.

Unlike other buildings in Kyiv, the market was not whitewashed, but instead built of wonderfully worked blocks of beige stone with only a little color variation. The façade was decorated with several towers, but otherwise blocky and square. The few windows, like the doors, were narrow, tall, and arched at the top, defended by ornate stone grilles. The second story was as blocky and square as the first, though smaller and shorter, and balanced atop the lower like a layer of a cake. The third story, however, was a fantasia of towers leading up to a roofline broken itself into a dozen or so of the ubiquitous small round domes that seemed everywhere in Kyiv. These were not the grand domes of Uthman architecture, which tended toward onion-shaped flares or enormous vaults, but either squat hemispheres like a half-orange laid cutside down on a plate, or slightly more elongated ovals like half a sliced hen's egg.

It was a more subtle and harmonious whole than Tesefahun had at first realized, although he could see from here that there was no wizardry in it. Even if he hadn't known that Kyivvan wizardry ran to battle-magic (of course), he could have told from looking that this was the work of plain stonemasons and architects. And all the more impressive for it, for what he looked upon had all been done by craft and muscle and engineering.

Tesefahun couldn't wait to see the vaulting inside that supported the weight of those upper stories.

He was so distracted by his anticipation that he startled and nearly broke character when his litter lurched to a halt. He blinked, shading his eyes, painfully aware that he looked like an old man startled in his wool-gathering. After a fashion, he had to admit . . . that was true.

Iskandar lay a steadying left hand on the frame on the litter, but his right hand did not touch his sword. Tesefahun followed his gaze to a group of the uniformed gate guards—these moving from the direction of the visible, eastern gate—who were not dicing, drilling arms, or lounging about gazing suspiciously at passersby. Instead, they walked a pattern, each arm's-length from the next, surrounding a group of men and women in ash-stained homespun with the ragged bewildered look of the displaced everywhere.

Tesefahun reached down to touch the backs of Iskandar's fingers. The man who had been Uthman Caliph was utterly still, watching these yellow-haired Kyivvan refugees, half of them showing the blistering or weeping skin of burns. The Dead Men showed nothing, but their "captain's" face twisted a little behind his beard.

"War already?" he asked softly. "This far north? Or bandits—"

Ato Tesefahun shook his head. Sorry as the sight of the injured, exhausted, no doubt starving refugees was, it was the man at the front of the group who drew his eye. He was not tall—not by Uthman standards, and so certainly not by those of the Kyivvan folk. His features were sharp, triangular, reminiscent of those of a weasel or a hunting fox. His hair was a sandy color, and his eyes a blue so bright that Tesefahun could make out the glint of the color across twenty paces of crowded market square. He was better-dressed than the others, cleaner, the ash stains on his boots, clothing, and cheeks seeming less gritted into leather, wool, and skin.

Still, he would have passed most inspections. But Ato Tesefahun was a wizard of Aezin, and he had seen these very facial features faithfully reproduced in a scroll written by an ancient wizard of his own order who had seen them for himself, some fifteen hundred years before.

The man at the front of the group was not a man.

He was a djinn, and Tesefahun was suddenly willing to bet every scrap of bullion and every ruby he had stashed away in the vaults of the Imperial Bank of Kyiv that he knew who the damned thing served.

"We need to follow them," Iskandar whispered to Tesefahun. "That's al-Sepehr's djinn."

Tesefahun bit his lip, and—against his better judgment—nodded. As naturally as if they had been going there in the first place, the litter fell in parallel to the refugees. Not precisely following, but close enough to track them. Tesefahun kept his gaze averted, watching the path of his own progress instead. If he looked in one direction, it would seem the litter tended that way, even if it drifted slightly in another. He could follow the refugees out of the edge of his eye, and the Dead Men would have no trouble at all keeping them in sight.

Instead, he trained his ears on the conversations around them, passersby remarking on the sight. He caught only scraps, but the scraps were enough. "... the village called Stechko ..." "... so many dead." "They say it was a Qersnyk witch." "She called down an unholy sun." "Fire angels." "Djinni." "They say she's the whore of the new Khagan." "Khagan? That's some horsefucker whelp the Sorcerer-Prince stole the skin off, you mark my words. Barbarians, the lot of them. . . ."

Tesefahun shook his head and leaned down to speak in Iskandar's ear. "This is foolish. What will we do if we catch them?"

"That creature burned my city around me while I watched and could do nothing. I'll—"

"Put a sword through it? An immortal? Do you suppose that's an approach that has never been tried?" Tesefahun pressed his fingers against his temples, suddenly aware of a headache that blinded him. Of course, Iskandar couldn't understand what the people in the square were saying.

Quickly, Tesefahun told him, adding, "This means Kyiv will go to war for al-Sepehr. He's building his twisted alliances again."

"Gah!" said Iskandar.

Tesefahun glanced at him twice, startled by the lapse in eloquence. A bit of history niggled at him as he studied the grim set of Iskandar's jaw, the rage flushing his cheeks. "Have you heard of the Green Ring?"

"A bit of regalia, wasn't it? One of the lost treasures of Danupati?"

Tesefahun nodded. "It was. I think we must change our plans, Captain Iskandar. We will not find an army here. Not in the wake of this news."

Iskandar blew out, exasperated. "This is a long way to come for nothing. Can we not even hire mercenaries?"

Tesefahun thought momentarily of the copper-haired man with the axe. He would have liked to see the big Skanda fight, he realized. "I think I know where we can find our army, much faster than that. We'll need horses, though."

When Tesefahun raised his head again, over the crowd between them, between the shoulders of the guardsmen, he searched once more for the djinn. Only to find those blue eyes staring back at him.

The djinn smiled, showing teeth, and touched two fingers to the center of his forehead in a gesture of respect.

In two more nights, Tsering and the rest passed through the bulwarking cliffs into Song, and then there were no more nights at all. They traveled under Hard-sun and twilight, rested under Soft-sun, and slept beside fires in the soft grass of the foothills below the Steles of the Sky.

Among the mountains, winter had been closing in. Here it was just autumn, the trees only now changing, and a riot of color stained the valleys between the hills.

At first, Tsering convinced herself that she was imagining the muttering. The sideways glances. The quickly averted eyes. It was just sensitivity, she told herself. Old memories of worse times, before she had come to Tsarepheth. It was just the memories, crowding back again.

Strange how you could think such old wounds healed, think the detritus of a past life long sealed away, crated up and forgotten—and some seemingly unrelated event would bring it all to the fore again.

She was *not* imagining the care that some of the Qersnyk women were taking over her, Hong-la, Jurchadai, and the other wizards and shaman-rememberers. Every morning, there was tea and broth, and rice gruel—sometimes, blessedly, with an egg boiled in it. The eggs might be chicken or feathered lizard or duck; once in a while the tea had spices, milk, and the red Rasan honey harvested from the hives of the enormous highland honeybees, which had mild relaxant and painkilling qualities in small quantities and narcotic ones in great. Each evening, someone brought her tea and noodles and butter, or sometimes dumplings fried in pork grease.

She stopped wasting, and even recovered a little weight despite the constant travel, work, and lack of sleep. Besides the wards, she and the others now tended the road-weary, the infirm, the sick. There was work for wizards at every hour, between illnesses and setting the wards. Hong-la was not willing to assume that the danger of blood ghosts and demon spawn had ended because they were out of the mountains. He seemed to have emerged as the leader-in-practice of the Rasan contingent, and Tsering was not sorry to see that responsibility adopted by somebody she trusted and respected.

Still, she worried what would happen if Hong-la's plan failed, if they were forced to leave the narrow track through these rolling foothills and move among the fields of cultured, cultivated Song. The kingdoms that considered themselves the Heart of the World were pastoral, populated, and bucolic. They were not the wild highlands of the Steles of the Sky, or the barren sweep of the steppe. There were people here, on every fallow *li*. Song's population was immense, and the rich land only supported it by intensive farming.

Those farmers would not meet a refugee train several thousands strong with joy and open arms. There might be soldiers, if those could be summoned in time. Tsering and all the others might find themselves interned. At the very least, they might have to fight. Wizards and shaman-rememberers aside, she did not relish facing any number of armed and equipped men with a band of women—even mounted Qersnyk women—boys, old men, peasantry, smallholders, and craftfolk from the city.

Especially as the refugee column spread out over the landscape now that the narrowness of mountain roads and passes no longer constrained them. Tsering wanted to encourage them to stay together, but didn't know how to go about it. Not without increasing that muttering and those sidelong glances that she might or might not be imagining.

On the third Hard-day, while they still wended among the hills, Tsering rode the Citadel mule that was presently serving as her mount up beside Hong-la. The refugee column was pinched tight between two bouldery slopes, forced for the time being to follow what passed for the road.

Tsering reined in beside him. He had a horse, one of the tallest the Citadel's stables had to offer, and it still looked like his odd split-toed shoes might be dragged off his feet at any moment by the grass.

After a pause, he lifted his chin, tipping the brim of his broad conical hat back so he could peer at her from under it. The suns of

Song required special precautions if one did not care to burn. Tsering herself was wearing a hat of wide wings, supported by red cloth bolsters, that someone had unearthed from the bottom of a wagon for her. It was ridiculous, a court lady's extravagance that should have perched atop elaborately dressed hair—but it kept the sun off her face and the nape of her neck. And before long, it was as covered with road dust as her wizard's weeds, so at least she looked all of a piece that way.

"I'm worried about the farms," she said. "And us."

He nodded. "We'll turn north at Hard-noon. These hills are not fertile—"

"I noticed that nothing but grass grows on them. No trees."

"Grass and rocks. No crops," he said. "There are farms in the bottom land below them, but all we'll find here are some sheep and goats that are allowed to run feral all summer, maybe tended by a shepherd who sleeps rough and carries a sling against wolves. If we stay among the hills, it will be harder going—but we won't be charging through any towns, and we can keep to the pilgrim's route. We'll have to cross the Tomb, and the soldiers will see us then—but once we're north of it, the people are Song, but it's Qersnyk territory and has been since a Qersnyk Emperor ruled over Song. We can head east to Dragon Lake from there."

"It's good enough." She bit her chapped lip. "I wish I knew how Master Yongten and the rest were doing. I wish I knew if they were safe."

Hong-la didn't look at her. His hand tightened on his reins and he leaned toward her a little, as if—if they were walking together— he would have let their shoulders bump. "That's what happens when we leave a place," he said. "We wish we knew so many things. And we try to pretend that nothing will change for the worse while our backs are turned."

It rocked her back in the saddle. For a moment, she thought he was speaking out of some personal knowledge of her own past—and then, with a sickening spurt of empathy, she understood that he was speaking out of his own.

After a silent moment, desperate, she changed the subject. "We should post more guards, and find a way to convince the stragglers to ride in with the column more."

"They're tired," Hong-la said with a shrug, but the slight uplift of his mouth said he was grateful to her for patching over his moment of too-bare honesty. "We can tell them about the wolves."

THE CHILDREN AND THE OLD SUFFERED MOST. TSERING SET THE WARDS when they camped at twilight, then found herself summoned to the bedside of a sick child. A girl, not old—if asked to guess, Tsering would say this coming winter might be her eighth—she had thinned to ribs and eyes and shadows over the past weeks of hard travel. When food was rationed, it was those with the highest demands who got the worst of it, and the girl had a sensitive digestion and suffered diarrhea on a diet of noodles and rice. There was no fresh food, little in the way of vegetables and fruits, and Tsering thought that every bit of nutrition that could be gotten into the child was just running out again.

She treated her with an antidiarrheal tea—getting some water into her might help to plump her cheeks a bit as well—and told her mother to give it twice a day, three times if possible. "You can make it once and feed it to her cold."

Her tongue itched with the desire to prescribe a bland diet, easily digested and rich in colorful vegetables to replenish the healthy processes the child was expending in her illness, but that would only be cruel. So she gave the mother three iron nails and a slice of clean horse bone, and told her to boil them in the water with which she made the tea. The tea had rose hips in it; the whole might help a little.

And when we get to Dragon Lake? What then? It's too late in the year for planting. Maybe we can find a market and buy or trade for beetroot and millet and beans to live through the winter.

At least Song winters aren't like ours. Even as far north as the edge of the steppe.

When Tsering left the side of the child's pallet, tucking her tools away inside her bag, a man beyond the circle of the encampment very deliberately looked at her, then turned his head and spat and turned his back. In the instant she'd had to glimpse his features, she'd seen that his cheeks were slashed, heavy scars disfiguring a face that would have been slabby and pockmarked with a lifetime of poor food and hard work even without the marks of the emperor's *justice* carved upon it.

Tsering glanced down at herself. She did not wear her jade and pearl collar, but her wizard's coat was plain to see—six ragged petals of its threadbare hem slapping against her thighs as she moved. The color was as close to beige as black with road dust, and her ridiculous hat perched atop her head, but there was no mistaking what she was. And with her medical bag in her hand, there was no mistaking what she was doing there.

Tsering had no magic of her own, but it was not the policy of the Citadel to admit which of its wizards had come into their power and which had not. She rolled the bag closed, stuffed it under her arm, and marched across the space between encampments to confront the man. It was the worst of bad manners to acknowledge anything occurring across the invisible boundaries of campsites, but as far as Tsering was concerned he'd started it.

She was almost on him before he heard her—or before he realized what he was hearing—and turned. His scarred face turned a boiled-liver color as Tsering drew herself up before him—not as tall as he or as broad, but illuminated from within by the righteous fury of her own indignation.

"You spit upon my honor, man," she said.

"I spit," he said, with no appearance of finding her intimidating. "What you make of it is your own business."

"You spit upon the honor of a Wizard of Tsarepheth. That is a dangerous action."

"Ooo," he said. "Are you going to curse me? Bunch of conjurers and charlatans, the lot of you. Your so-called magic can't cure the lung sickness, and it can't stop the Cold Fire from exploding. It can't keep the Carrion King in his grave, either, can it? And yet you're still doing your magician games, moving rocks and banners around, gobbling up food that honest people could eat, poisoning children with your simples and 'cures.' And I should be afraid of you, conjuror's bitch? Can you so much as heal a cold sore? Have you an ounce of real magic in you?"

She blinked, and only the long experience of standing up to Yongten-la interrogating her theories upon the point of his frown, unrelentingly, kept her from stepping back before the spittle-flinging force of his hate.

"I am Tsering-la. It would be wise of you to apologize."

"Wizards," he spat. "Well, I am Garab, and no one has ever hung a

Doctor on my name. But I bet I could do as much for that child in there as you can. And I wouldn't claim a pound of flesh to stand by while she died."

He spun around, hands clenching as if he only just prevented himself from swinging them, and strode off with his boots thumping and swishing through the grass.

Tsering watched him go. She didn't dare glance down at her shaking hands until he stomped out of sight.

The fact was, she *hadn't* an ounce of real magic in her. And even if she did, she couldn't do a damned thing for that little girl, except to hope and feed her tea.

She almost jumped over herself when a soft voice behind her said her name. She turned in her own bootprints, swallowing a startled scream, and found herself regarding a very definitely amused Toragana.

"Wizard," said the Tsareg leader's sister and lieutenant. "One of my little cousins is ill. Will you come and look at her?"

Tsering sighed and brushed escaped strands away from her face ineffectually back toward her braid.

"Of course," she said, and hefted her medical bag—already so much lighter than it had been at the beginning of the march.

15

Temur, Samarkar, Hrahima, and the mares were travel-hardened, efficient, fit, and self-sufficient. They had a clear path before them over level ground. They had light to travel whenever they wanted it. Temur and Samarkar riding, Hrahima loping alongside, they passed over the Dragon Road at a rate Temur found almost unbelievable.

At first he worried for Afrit, but whatever his color the colt quickly showed himself Bansh's true-bred get. Leggy and improbable, he treated the hard travel as a game, gamboling between the tolerant mares, dashing circles about the Cho-tse. He nursed when they paused to water the horses, and though he was at first pushed to keep up when they cantered, within days he was darting ahead rather than lagging behind. Samarkar, standing in the saddle to stretch aching legs, looked after him and shook her head.

"Resilience of youth," Temur said.

Samarkar glanced at Hrahima and both burst out laughing, but neither would explain the joke to him.

Temur began to recognize the landscape about three days out from Dragon Lake, and felt a sharp twist of anxiety he'd been trying to ignore ease away. What if he hadn't known where they were going?

What if he'd taken them the wrong direction, along the wrong branch of the road? What if the messenger had been wrong, or had misled them? Not knowing where you started or how far you had to go made navigation a hit-or-miss business at best.

Now he pointed out landmarks with enthusiasm, and swallowed a different anxiety. Though they rode under stunning pillars of stone and beneath fantastical arches so tall that the trees at the tops were burning vermillion and crimson with fall while the ones in the valleys still held their verdancy, Temur had no eyes for the beauty. It was as if a worm gnawed his belly. There was no secret that he was raising his banner at Dragon Lake. It could not be, for the clans to rally to him—if they *would* rally to him. But that meant that al-Sepehr knew where to find him.

There could be an ambush waiting. And if there wasn't, he and Samarkar and Hrahima would have to be prepared to defend them-selves before any allied forces could be counted on—which assumed that anyone at all was going to show up and join his forces. Perhaps the clans had all already declared for Qori Buqa's unborn son.

At least the worries chasing each other through his belly could not keep him awake. When they stopped, Hard-day or Soft, they were all so exhausted they barely managed to chew their food before falling into sleep. They made cold camps and rose again sore with sleeping on the ground. Temur could not have said why he felt such a drive for haste . . . but the need to be doing gnawed at him, and the others seemed willing to support his obsession, for now. He might have pushed even harder, if not for the horses—but they needed time to graze and rest, and he wasn't about to kill the mares with work now, after everything.

By the time they came to the final bends of the road, winding around the last few limestone outcrops towering and dripping with trees aflame with autumn, Temur's heart was thundering in his chest. *It will be nothing*, he thought, as Samarkar reached across the space between horses and said, "Should we leave the mares and scout ahead?"

Hrahima chuffed. "Keep riding. What else do you have a tiger for?"

Before he could respond, she had leapt forward and vanished into the trees lining the road. A moment, and only the swaying of branches marked her passage.

"Magic," Temur said.

"I'd hope to know it if it was," Samarkar replied. She paused. "If this is Qersnyk territory, how is it that a Song sky hangs over it?"

Temur shrugged. "It never changed. It never has, no matter who claims it."

Samarkar picked at her fingernail in irritation. Another mystery she probably wasn't going to have the time to investigate.

She sighed. "Obviously there are some interesting metaphysics at work."

"Obviously," Temur replied.

They allowed the horses to walk. Hrahima needed time, and the mares needed rest. If it did come down to an ambush, Temur wanted them fresh—or as fresh as possible, under the circumstances—and ready to run. Now at least the cramping of worry eased, and his heart beat even and strong. Whatever happened would happen, and the anticipation and contingency planning would be behind him for a little. And with luck, for a little, they could rest.

And if not, there might be a fight. Which was better than uncertainty as well.

He thought of not having to rise in the morning and heave himself into the saddle, and felt like a traitor to the Qersnyk people when the prospect delighted him. But even the steppe clans didn't travel without stopping for months on end, as he and Samarkar had been.

He was not surprised to see Hrahima walking toward them down the middle of the jade-flagged road ahead. The shadows of the trees fell across her in the soft-evening light, and her stripes camouflaged her so he only saw her because he was looking—and she was moving. He took it as a good sign; if the news were bad, she'd either emerge from concealment as if she had stepped through one of Reason's doors, or she'd have come at a bounding run, fleeing the Sky knew how many Rahazeen assassins.

What was a surprise, however, was the mounted figure waiting behind her, and the clop of hooves as that person started forward. Temur knew the mare, a Tsareg blood bay with both forelegs bone-white past the knee as if she had splashed through a river of milk.

A moment later, he realized that he knew the rider, too—though an eye patch concealed a quarter of her face. And he knew the big black-and-tan dog trotting beside her, moth-eaten and ragged in his summer coat, his brush of a tail trailing white mats of undercoat as he waved it regally.

Bansh stopped stock-still, Jerboa halting with her nose even with the bay's shoulder. Afrit dove beneath his mother the moment they paused, intent on the teat that might start moving again at any minute. Temur did not realize for a moment that the mare had planted her feet because he had sat back hard, boots hard in the stirrups. And then he knew, and didn't care, sliding out of the saddle, careful not to land on the colt. He darted forward past Hrahima and dropped to his knees at Sube's side. He threw his arms around the dog's warm neck, buried his face in the grease-and-soot-smelling ruff, and tried not to feel the sharp prickle in eyes he could not pry open.

"I'm sorry," he said to the dog. And to Toragana. "I have failed you. I did not bring her home. I followed her across half the world, but I did not bring her home."

He heard boots on stone, felt the arm around his shoulder. She was hugging him and the dog, then tugging him to his feet though he tried to cling to Sube's neck, though the dog was laving his salty face with its big slimy spotted tongue.

Tsareg Toragana was thumping his back, hugging him tight. Her face was wet, too, and he did not think it was from the dog. Finally, she put him at arm's length, and the dog pressed between them, leaning against his legs. He made himself look at her and saw new lines, hollow cheeks—and strength.

"You have done what you could, Re Temur," she said. Her fingers squeezed convulsively. "My sister Oljei is our leader now. Tsareg has come to your banner, Khagan, and holds Dragon Lake in your name."

As they came around the last wide meander of road and river into the broad, bowl-shaped valley that held the lake, Temur found himself rubbing his eyes. Not because they were stinging—he had not stopped weeping even to remount, and Samarkar rode Jerboa shoulder to shoulder with Bansh, squeezing Temur's hand—but because he could not believe what they revealed to him.

There was his grandfather's summer palace, symbol of the Qersnyk conquest of Song, half-ruined and overwhelmed by vines. The tumbled remains of its walls were set in the midst of what had been gorgeous parklands, now overgrown and returning to the wild. The palace had not been abandoned long enough to crumble on its own, but it served as a useful source of finished building materials for local farmers, and many of the houses or shrines in the villages that could be glimpsed through the trees on the hills overlooking, or on the cultivated banks of Dragon Lake itself, were constructed of its smooth golden stones.

The ruin was veiled and netted by thousands of hovering white shapes, as if a cloud of moths had been frozen in place in the air. Now, in the slanting evening and at this distance, they seemed to be only white cubes, immobile and unsupported in the golden air. Temur knew their true aspect would only be revealed as twilight became dawn, and Soft-day passed to Hard. Nor was he surprised by the delicate bridge, half its span dangling, that had once connected the only intact structure of the former palace with the towering pillar of one of the limestone mountains, beside which it floated like a hummingbird feeding from a flower, or the ornate pierced ivory filigree of the winding stair that worked its way up that pillar, giving access to the violet-tiled pagoda that sat as serenely in emptiness as if on immovable stone. He felt Samarkar's fingers tighten, the delight and unabashed awe with which even she—a Wizard of Tsarepheth—gazed upon this glorious wreckage.

But Temur had seen it before. He had seen an army camped below it, and he had slept in its shadow.

What he had not seen was the end of the valley below the broken palace filled side to side and end to end with livestock, with white-houses and carts and wagons, tents and lean-tos and improvised shelters, some of which were anything but Qersnyk in breeding or design. And above all, he had not expected to see one white-house bigger than them all, and roofed in yellow felt, with a banner of a bay horse running furling and unfurling in the soft wind over it.

Toragana, riding beyond Samarkar, grinned at him. "There's a bunch of Rasani too. We all left Tsarepheth in a hurry; that mountain they say their dragon-Goddess dropped on top of the Sorcerer-Prince started smoking. Some of them are friends of your ally, here. And the shaman-rememberers told us what banner to stitch."

"Cousin," he said. "I—"

But his voice failed him. She wasn't his cousin; she was Edene's. His only by the courtesy of a conjugal alliance. He had no words for what crowded his throat.

"Tsareg Altantsetseg," he began. But Toragana's frown stopped him before he could go further. Of course; Altantsetseg had been old. So old, in fact, that it was hard to imagine her ever dying. And Toragana had said that Oljei was the clan leader now. Limpingly, he finished, "Oh, I'm sorry."

"Qori Buqa's tame sorcerer killed her to get the Padparadscha Seat," Toragana said. "There's other news you will not like."

She gazed at him as steadily as a stone out of her one eye. Temur was not sure if he wished more that she would hurry and tell him, or more that he might vanish like a seed-head scattered by the wind before she could break his heart again.

The corner of her mouth twitched. "There is one topic on which you need have no fear, Khagan. *Cousin.* Against Qori Buqa's heirs, against this al-Sepehr . . . Tsareg will follow you across the night sky and into the flames of the sun."

Soft-evening puddled the valley with shadows as they descended toward the encampment, and now the light of those scores of hovering lanterns that swept like the foam of a frozen wave, like the sparks of a fire caught in amber, through the ruins of the palace came to life. Their eternal, ensorcelled paper walls glowed golden. They were beautiful, and dreamy, and Temur knew they were thick with sorcerous wards. The permanence of the floating lanterns was a side effect of the protective magics, or so his brother had once explained to him, when they were here together.

The thought of Qulan was like a cracked rib. Temur suddenly could not get a breath. If the pain of the reunion with clan Tsareg had exhausted him—or perhaps let him feel the exhaustion he had been harboring, and fighting, for half a year and more—then the pain of remembering Qulan and the time they had spent here was an impalement.

Samarkar leaned close to him and whispered, "This is a Qersnyk holding?"

"It is," Temur replied.

"And yet it rests under a Song sky."

He frowned and nodded, and shrugged. "It always has," he said. "Even in my grandfather's day."

The last dreamy light of the red sun gilded the peaks of the embracing hills, the white and golden towers of the dead Khagan's airborne palace, as they left the Dragon Road behind. Tsareg Toragana led them carefully as the trail curved around the weed-dripping rim of an enormous sinkhole, the mares picking their way single file and Afrit, snorting, keeping his mother's body between him and the pit. She, of course, had as much respect for the drop-off as if she had been a mountain goat, enabling Temur to lean out over her shoulder and stare down into the imperfect darkness below. Imperfect, because there must have been some floating lanterns down there, and the rippled flowing water at the bottom of the hole reflected their light, chasing shimmering rills across the walls of the cavern below. The caverns also reflected sound, a cacophony of echoed and amplified tinkling and dripping and trickling like some great assemblage of musicians tuning up their instruments. And a sighing wind sang low hollow notes against the sculptured edges of the limestone.

"It has another entrance," Samarkar said. "We must investigate the caverns. They might be useful."

Temur still couldn't answer. He nodded, hoping she would see it in the half-light, and let Bansh bear him on.

As they came among the tents and white-houses, he was more relieved not to have to speak—because the road through the encampment was lined with folk several deep where they passed. They were crowded so deep before the doors of the white-houses that Temur could not even reach out to punch the skin bags of airag that hung over every door as he passed, as was the custom. The fermenting mare's milk needed constant mixing.

So many gathered here. Not just Clan Tsareg. Not even just Qersnyk folk, for there were Rasan townsfolk almost outnumbering his own people. But mostly women and children and the old, and anyone could see the Rasani were not fighters. They all wore those square-headed daggers at their belts, from the age where they could be trusted off of leading strings, but they had no look of warriors or even soldiers.

Still, they were here. And they had come out to hail him as Khagan.

Al-Sepehr had made at least a few enemies.

As Toragana led them through the crowd toward the white-house roofed with yellow felt, he noticed women here and there pushed to the front of the press by supporting arms. Some held up infants or young children. Some were lifted up themselves.

At first he thought it was so they could see better—see the fool who thought himself strong enough to become a Khagan with their own eyes. But then he noticed the peeling skin of one, the scaling red patches feathering the face of another. Samarkar, riding beside him again now that the path was wider, put her hand upon his elbow.

She saw it too.

"I can't," he said. There had been the woman in Asmaracanda, the one poisoned by dragon's blood. He'd laid his hands on her, and all he'd done was made bruises blossom under her fragile skin. "We know I can't."

He didn't say, *And if I cannot heal these of their sickness, they will know I am only a pretender to the Khaganate, and where will we be then? We can't fight al-Sepehr without an army.*

He didn't need to confirm with her that that was why they were here, now. The goal had evolved. At first he'd meant to survive, and then to win Edene back, and then he'd made an oath to put a stop to the Nameless devils sowing war across every realm. He'd never meant to rule; that was the role Qulan had been born to.

Samarkar looked at him seriously under thick, level eyebrows that she wore natural, like a Qersnyk woman, not plucked and tweezed and penciled like the court beauties of Rasa and Song.

"You were not Khagan then, Re Temur," she said.

Am I Khagan now? He tried not to raise his eyes to the banner flapping over the yellow-roofed white-house. To the running mare appliquéd thereon: liver-bay, with one white foot, like Bansh.

If before them voices were raised in hope and greeting and cries for attention, behind him he heard the muttering about the ghost-colored stud colt that followed his mare. The foal caused more of a stir than Hrahima. *Unlucky* was the least of it. Afrit was too obviously a sign. A portent that the Eternal Sky was paying attention to them, here, now. To *him*, Re Temur. The gaze of a god was never a comfortable notice to endure.

The question they all must be asking themselves—the question

Temur asked himself, too—was whether the colt with his impossible, doom-portent coat was a portent of doom for Re Temur . . . or for Re Temur's enemies.

That, he would have to answer as soon as possible. And suddenly, as they reached the open space before the Khagan's white-house that would be his for as long as he could hold it, he understood how. He paused his mare before the door, as if regarding the gorgeously cured hides of lion, wolf, dagger-tooth cat, and tiger hanging beneath the awning.

Samarkar and Toragana reined their mares, and Hrahima stepped back, giving him space as he brought Bansh around. Because she had paused, Afrit dove for the teat, provoking a stir of amusement from the gathered crowd. He might be a creature of ill omen, but he was also a baby. And adorable.

Temur swallowed to wet a dry mouth. Perhaps Toragana saw, or perhaps she meant to make a little ritual of hospitality, but she passed the skin of airag from over the Khagan's door to him. He drank deeply, savoring the tart creaminess, and passed it on to Samarkar. Even Hrahima drank, though Temur could tell that the elaborate licking of her whiskers afterward was disgust and not relish.

When the bag came back to him, he raised it up and shook it. He knew he should make an inspirational speech. Perhaps he'd have Samarkar write him one later. For now, though, he needed to introduce himself to those that did not know him—and more than that, he needed to acknowledge something.

"I am Re Temur Khagan," he called out, raising his voice to the tone he would have used to bellow orders on the battlefield. "My companions are Samarkar, a Wizard of Tsarepheth, and Hrahima, a Cho-tse warrior. We have come through mountain and desert, sore in the saddle, to bring you word of the necromancer al-Sepehr and his plots, and to fight for you and before you. Our good mares are Bansh and Jerboa. Jerboa is of the line of the copper-colored mare Haerun." He paused, girding himself for the proclamation he must make next.

"Bansh is the first mare of her own line, the line of Bansh." The murmuring grew louder. If he was Khagan, he could proclaim the founding of a new lineage of mares, of course. But no one here had yet seen Bansh fight, or seen her run. "The colt is her first get, and if he lives he will sire mares who can run from one end of the steppe to the other and perhaps back again!"

"A bay mare can't throw a ghost colt," Toragana said low, leaning toward him. From the stir in the crowd, she was not the only one making this observation.

Temur didn't look at her. He said, "The colt is named Afrit, for the desert demons that plague our Rahazeen enemies. I am Re Temur Khagan, and my Khaganate will be founded under the auspices of the Ghost Stud. This is the first year of his reign!"

The explosion of consternation waited until he and the others had ducked under the awning, and were out of the crowd's sight behind the bodies of the horses. Temur was grateful they'd waited. Toragana drew the hide covering the doorway aside and shook her head at him, but it had a sense of wonder to it.

"You have bull's balls, Khagan," she said.

He paused just within the door. "I didn't see a lot of horses picketed."

"That would be because we don't have a lot of horses." She said it apologetically.

He patted her on the shoulder, wondering where his confidence came from. After a moment he identified it. It was the sham of confidence, and this was a trick he'd learned from Samarkar. Seem confident, and your followers will feel confident. He was getting better at feigning it.

"We'll fix that," he said. "Wait until you hear them murmuring when I tell them we're building a Sacred Herd."

She squinted around her eye patch, then shook her head admiringly and grinned. "Bull's balls." She stepped within, and Temur—forgetting to play the Khagan for a moment—held the hide for the two behind.

Hrahima paused in the doorway, too. Gently, she reached out and ran one claw through the rich striped fur of the tiger pelt nearest the entry. The tip of her claw left a fine, combed-looking part in the fur.

Temur winced. He hadn't thought. "I am sorry. I will have them removed."

"It is the custom of your tribe, is it not? To show respect to your kings?"

He did not have the energy to explain to her that he was not a king. "It is also our custom to show respect to our friends."

The Cho-tse shrugged. "If I slept in a pile of golden-furred monkey-pelts, would that trouble you?"

She was gone within before he could answer, and he found himself facing Samarkar. Being Samarkar, whatever she was thinking, she did not say it. She merely studied him for a moment, then leaned in and brushed her lips across his cheek. "Sacred Herd?"

"There are sixty-four sacred colors of mares," he said. "It's lucky to have all sixty-four in your clan. I'll explain later."

His eyes took a moment to adjust to the shadowy lamplight within the tent, despite the twilight outside. As he fell in behind Samarkar, he was surprised to hear her squeal like a delighted child. A moment later and she was running forward—staggering, really, as her feet sank into layers of carpet—to throw herself into the arms of another woman, one that he recognized from a long, painful journey from Qeshqer back to Tsarepheth.

Tsering-la, Wizard of the Citadel. And the shaven-scalped figure hunched to avoid striking his head on the ceiling of the white-house was Hong-la, her colleague and, Temur had gathered, Samarkar's instructor. He did not know the shaman-rememberer who had been seated beside them and now rose too—but they were quickly introduced, once everybody was done hugging Samarkar.

Tsering-la turned to Temur next, studying him for a moment as if readying herself to speak. She was a studious-looking woman, compact and strong without seeming small, thin-faced, her straight black hair shot through with strands of gray. Her hands were cracked with washing and labor, and Temur thought stupidly that if this were his mother's white-house, she would have offered the guest some salve.

But this was *his* house. And he did not know where the salve was kept. There was some in his saddlebags, and he almost turned to Samarkar to ask her please to fetch it before he realized it would be rude indeed to send her away right now, even for a few moments.

"Toragana," he asked, "has this house any balm?"

He gestured to Tsering's hands, and Toragana nodded and went to a chest. There was a brazier beside it with a big copper kettle set atop, which made Temur hope there might be tea soon. His legs were unbalanced with travel, his calves wobbly and weak.

The white-house was well appointed, a comfortable and sheltered domicile with beds along the walls, bunked up into couches for daytime use, and a series of chests and bureaus at the back. It was so like Ashra's house that for a moment Temur expected his mother to appear through the doorway. That dragon-footed Song armoire, inlaid with ivory, could have been one he'd seen in her white-house a hundred thousand times.

Toragana came back with the salve, folded in a parchment packet. She offered it to Tsering, who dabbed fingers in it to anoint her hands and cheeks.

"Re Temur," Tsering-la said, giving the packet back to Toragana. Tsering bowed, though awkwardly, as if she had not quite yet parsed out the level of change in their relative statuses.

"Tsering-la. Have you had tea? How long have you been at Dragon Lake?"

Toragana seemed to have chosen herself for the role of hostess as the only Qersnyk woman present. She busied herself at the brazier. Temur glanced at her with incalculable gratitude, and she met his look with a smile. He glanced aside, noted Hrahima standing in one corner of the white-house motionless as a pillar it might have rested on, her veiny forearms folded across the width of her chest.

By the time his gaze returned to Tsering, he could smell tea brewing.

She glanced at Hong-la as if for support. He put one ridiculously long hand on her elbow. Gaunt as he had grown, Temur could see the heavy outline of his cheekbones through the flesh below his eyes. The expatriate—or repatriate, perhaps—Song wizard was tall and narrow, but he was not slender. He had bones like a steppe pony's, sturdy and very straight.

"Bad news," Temur said.

"A lot of it," Tsering replied. "Payma?"

Temur sighed. "That, at least, is not bad news at all. Safe at a steading, protected by a distant relative of mine. She and the babe will do well there, assuming she survived birthing it."

He stopped, hearing his own words. For the first time realizing that she would have had her child by now. The child he'd helped to save.

"Good."

Samarkar touched Temur's arm, and he realized from the direction of her glance that no one could return to the cushions until he offered them the option. "We should sit."

She lowered herself gratefully, and when she sat, Temur sat as well. Everyone else settled around them, except Toragana, who moved in with a tray and handed around cups of tea.

She seemed to forget that Hrahima was even present, the tiger melted into the shadows so well. Tsering took a cup but then set it aside untasted. She twisted her hands together, but did not drop her eyes. "I met your mother, Re Temur."

"I was only Temur when you met me," he reminded. There were no nights in Song, so even though sunset was ending beyond the felt walls of the white-house, no moons would float in the black heavens to trouble his conscience and heart. He put them from his mind and instead asked, "My mother?"

"Ashra, daughter of Tesefahun."

"That is she. Where is she now?"

"She helped us more than you can imagine, Temur. It was she who found a partial cure for the plague that was killing our people. It was she, along with Hong-la"—Hong-la snorted, and gave her a look that suggested he had other blame and credit to assign—"who saw a fighting chance of using a combination of medicine and surgery to heal those infected. She taught us to make a beer, a beer brewed in a particular fashion, that fought back the processes of putrefaction that otherwise affected the lungs of the ill."

"And my mother herself? Is she here?" He would have liked to keep that shiver of hope from his voice. Maybe Samarkar could give him lessons in admitting nothing.

Tsering closed her head and shook her eyes. "She had the pestilence herself, I'm afraid. And it felled her before we even got close to finishing the materials she taught us how to make."

"Ah." Temur closed his eyes. He could feel the warmth of Samarkar's hand hovering by his elbow, but she did not touch him. Which was good. He might have crumpled completely if she had. He knew what she was thinking as plainly as if she'd said it aloud: Temur's mother could have told Samarkar—and Edene!—Temur's name.

"She was seeking you," Tsering said. "She was greatly heartened to learn that you had left us in good condition, and that you had a quest before you."

"When she died," Temur said. "Did she die badly? In pain?"

Tsering seemed to search his face. "There was some pain," she allowed at last. "This plague is not a clean death. But she died of infection, not the illness. She was helping us research treatments, and what she taught us saved any number of lives. Your mother was a wizard in her own right, Re Temur, if she held the title or not."

Temur exhaled. "She died usefully."

"Profoundly so."

And she had not died on the battlefield. Or in the sack of Qarash. Temur felt like a particularly terrible person for his relief . . . but he preferred to think of his mother seeking a cure, dying engaged in a puzzle, rather than ripped to bits, raped and savaged in some dynastic war that seemed more and more futile to him with every passing day.

Or he could tell himself so now, and weep for her later, anyway.

"Tell me about the plague," said Temur.

Hong-la sighed, folding his hands around his knees. "It's more of a pestilence. An infestation. Demons—nest in the lungs. The victim suffocates slowly, and most of those that survive the incubation do not survive the . . . emergence."

"Demons." Samarkar leaned forward. Her hands were interlaced around her cup, and she did not seem to notice when hot tea splashed over her fingers. "Glassy things? Winged? Spiny? Cold?"

"Not cold," Hong-la said. "Hot as blood when they emerge. But yes, otherwise your description is accurate. They—" He swallowed.

Tsering said, "They talk."

"You've seen them," said Hong-la.

"The adults," said Samarkar. "Maybe. The ones we saw couldn't incubate in a lung. But perhaps they could grow from something that could."

Toragana slipped outside, the doorway draping shut behind her. Her passage admitted a breeze that stirred the warm close air of the white-house. Temur made himself pause, sip tea, consider. His *urge* was to call out an army and throw it at some enemy, but you couldn't fight sickness with arrows.

No. A Khagan had another way of doing that. If it worked. He glanced at Jurchadai, the silent shaman-rememberer, but that one did not raise his eyes—or give any indication that he was even aware of the existence of a world outside his bowl of tea.

Temur imitated him for a moment. But long before he felt ready, he forced himself to raise his eyes and ask, "Are there any affected here?"

Hong-la said, "Fortunately, no. We have developed wards, and managed to prevent most new infections. We left the ill behind in Tsarepheth, where they would have access to your mother's treatments. I imagine the Wizards of Song have their wards and treatments as well. But there are country hamlets, towns without wizards and with insufficient wards—"

Samarkar said, "You left them in Tsarepheth. Where the Cold Fire is burning."

"Yongten-la remained behind," said Hong-la. "If there is hope, for the Citadel or for the sick, he will find it."

Samarkar nodded, though her expression was anything but agreement and ease.

Temur finished his tea. "We heard rumors . . ."

"Of the Carrion King." Hong-la made a face.

Jurchadai shifted his seat, but still did not speak. *No assistance rendered from the shaman-rememberer.* Which was, Temur admitted to himself, more or less typical of the breed.

Temur said, "Yes. You don't think so?"

"Someone is skinning corpses," Hong-la admitted. "Someone dove down out of the sky on a giant bird and rescued Prince Tsansong from the very execution pyre."

"We heard so in Asitaneh," Samarkar said eagerly.

Temur felt a thrill of outrage: *al-Sepehr!* He wasn't sure if Samarkar found his hand to squeeze, or he found hers. But whatever she felt never showed on her face.

"Have you word if my brother is alive?"

The wizards opposite shared a glance. "I cannot say," said Tsering. "But the odds are very good that your other brother, the emperor, is not alive. The Black Palace has fallen."

"Fall . . ."

"An explosion. Gunpowder."

"A wizard," said Samarkar.

"The evidence suggests so," said Hong-la.

There was a silence. "Much news," said Samarkar at last.

"Little of it good," Tsering responded.

"The bird belongs to al-Sepehr, the high priest of the Nameless," Samarkar said. "Either Tsansong is his prisoner, or was in truth his ally and deserved that pyre and worse—or he is dead. Given al-Sepehr's proven taste for manipulation and misdirection, and twisting alliances to bring death and make war, I cannot tell you better which, now."

"A Rahazeen sun rose over Tsarepheth the day the palace fell," said Hong-la—as if it were only an item of information for their inspection. But Temur saw the way his muscles clenched.

Tsering said, "There is no doubt in me that Tsansong-tsa's 'rescue' was designed to sow civil discord. Even more of it than his mere execution would have provoked."

"Which was plenty," Hong-la said.

Samarkar said, "If both of my brothers are dead or missing, then, who rules Rasa now?"

"Yangchen is the dowager."

Samarkar must have been expecting it. "Has she stayed in Tsarepheth?"

"She led refugees to Rasa, as your brother refused. Away from the pestilence and the Cold Fire. We hope."

"Well," Samarkar said. "That's something, then." As if all her enmity with her brothers' wife were nothing but a passing misunderstanding. "What you describe fits with al-Sepehr's patterns. He plays one hand against the other, and never fields his own army, risks his own people, if he can help it. It's all hirelings and smoke."

Temur realized again, suddenly, how much he admired her.

"Every cloud of smoke has a fire at the bottom of it," Hong-la said.

Hrahima's eyes flickered, her earrings chiming gently. After so long and total a stillness, it was as startling as if she had roared. Temur took advantage of the following silence to take control of the conversation again.

"We have news too," he said, reminded by the mention of the sky over Tsarepheth. "Asitaneh has fallen to al-Sepehr's allies, and rests under a Rahazeen sky . . . as does Asmaracanda. And of course there is

Qe—I mean, Kashe, the first to fall. Qori Buqa, my uncle, is dead, and his army under the command of a widow who bears his child. The steppe I mean to retake—my grandfather's city of Qarash—is under a Rahazeen sky as well. It is evident, as Samarkar says, who the true enemy is. Whose plots we have all unwittingly danced to."

"Al-Sepehr," said Hrahima from the dim edge of the room, smoothly as if they had rehearsed it.

Samarkar nodded. "If it is true that a wizard is behind the fall of the Black Palace . . . then a wizard is allied with the Nameless."

Hong-la reached for his tea, suddenly, and downed it at a gulp. When he was done, he pulled himself up straight and firmed his jaw. "I believe it was the Dowager Yangchen who allowed the demon spawn into Tsarepheth. No one other than she or the emperor had the metaphysical right to give those permissions."

Tsering drew back. "You told no one this?"

Hong-la just looked at her. "She is the empress."

". . . I accept your rebuttal. Do you think she was duped?"

Hong-la did not hesitate. "Yes. And I think she realized it, by the end. A woman who is a willing part of her kingdom's downfall does not go among the sick, ministering to their illness. She does not come to the wizards defending that city and offer anything she can do to help."

Samarkar said, "My sister-in-law has had a change of heart?"

"Perhaps she has had a taste of adulthood," Hong-la said.

"It would fit what we know of al-Sepehr if she were a dupe, or a slave. He does not seem to favor free and willing allies."

From the set of Samarkar's lips, Temur knew she was thinking of the animate corpses, chained forever in the desert below Ala-Din. He regarded her and felt reality twist around him as he realized what this was. That he was a Khagan, gathered in his tent with his advisors, discussing the strategy of a terrible enemy.

"Where has Toragana gone?" he said. "Can we send for her? I wish her counsel now."

Jurchadai, still without a word—but with a glance to him for permission—stood. But before he could move to the door, it opened again, and Toragana returned—carrying a child in her arms. A child Temur knew, better than he knew most of the Tsareg.

Edene's small sister Sarangerel. The one to whom he and Edene had given up their tent in a season past, choosing instead to sleep under the moons.

He had started to his feet before he knew it. All around him, the others—perforce—rose as well.

Toragana stood proud before him and held the girl out in her arms—a display of strength, for the child had nine winters on her and was long of bone. "Merciful Khagan. This child is ill and needs your touch."

His body responded with a ridiculous flare of panic, made worse when he realized that Tsering was beside him. She said, "His touch?"

Toragana's heavy braid tossed back and forth as she shook her head. "He's the Khagan. His touch might heal."

Might. She'd follow him against the forces of Qori Buqa, but even she wasn't prepared to do more than hope that his reign might be blessed.

He stepped around Toragana, headed for the door. When the others would have followed him, he gestured them away. Except for Samarkar, who was not so easily deterred. She paused in the doorway, though, when she saw that he had no intent of going far. Just to lift the airag skin down and gulp down a mouthful of something more nourishing than tea.

She lowered her voice, took his elbow, led him a little ways away. "Those people want you to save their children. To prevent more suffering."

"I know."

"You're thinking of Asmaracanda."

He raised his brows at her and held out the skin. She took it and drank. He wondered if she was finally developing a taste for mare's milk. When she extended it toward him again, he shook his head. "Bring it inside."

"Will you try?"

"I don't think I'm capable."

Her lips curved. It wasn't a smile, though someone who did not know her well might have mistaken it for one. "I don't think we're capable of any of this. And yet, we keep doing it."

Temur caught himself fingering the long scar that stiffened his neck, and pulled his hand away. Hadn't that been impossible, too? Surviving that wound? The world was full of impossibilities.

"If I begin laying hands on sick children, I'll never be able to stop. All my life, I'll never do anything else."

It wasn't a real protest, and she knew it.

"Is that such a bad fate, heart of my own?" she asked.

WHEN THEY WALKED BACK INSIDE, TORAGANA HAD LAID SARANGEREL ON the carpet and was coaxing her to drink tea. Oljei must have come in while Temur and Samarkar were outside. She sat cross-legged beside them. She was arguing with Toragana, trying to get her to offer the girl some airag instead—for strength. Tsering hunkered beside them, a hand on the girl's forehead. She looked up as Temur entered. The doubt in her eyes was even less trouble to read than Toragana's. "I've been treating her for some time now," she said.

"Tsareg Toragana," Temur said, very politely. "Would you come over here, please?"

Samarkar went to stand beside Hong-la, who had crouched beside the brazier and was feeding it fibrous bits of dried yak dung. Hrahima had settled down and now sat cross-legged beside the chests of goods. Her eyes were lidded, her hands relaxed on her knees. Only the shiver of her whiskers in her breath and the twitch of a tail-tip showed that she was living.

Toragana rose and came.

"What is her illness?" Temur asked.

With a glance over her shoulder at Tsering, Toragana shook her head. "Tsering-la could not identify it. Hong-la says it might be the white-blood wasting. He says he cannot be sure without a, a kind of lens, which he does not have here. But she bruises easily, and she . . ." Her voice took on a desperate cheerfulness as she gulped a breath and started again. "It's not the lung-demons, at least."

Temur touched her arm and brushed past her gently. He crouched beside Tsering-la and Sarangerel. Sarangerel had been an active child, bright and plump even under travel conditions. Now she seemed used up, weirdly fragile, bones almost visible beneath translucent skin. But when she saw Temur's face, her expression brightened. Her eyes, glazed and dull, focused—though it cost her an effort.

"Temur! They said you went to look for my sister."

He nodded. "That's true."

"Did you find her?"

"I found where she had been," he said. "But she'd already escaped. Edene didn't need my help to get away."

Sarangerel closed her eyes and smiled. Her lower lip was split; a new bead of bright blood started up in the middle of two streaks crusted dark. "Do you think she'll come find us here, Temur?"

He laid a palm on her cheek. She felt papery, hot, and vague, as if the bones floated in a layer of smoke rather than flesh beneath her skin.

"I can't imagine her doing anything else," he said. "She'll be home before you know it."

When he said it to Sarangerel, he could almost believe it himself. He reached out, refusing to allow himself to think about it, and took her hand in his. Her flesh felt crackling and strange, as if the skin were baked and fluid had gathered beneath it. Her eyes were glossless as unpolished stones. Her fingers pressed into her palm.

Temur squeezed gently, afraid to rupture the friable envelope of her skin, and realized to his surprise that he could feel the heartbeat inside her. No, not *feel*, exactly. But sense it, as clearly as if he pressed his fingertips to the pulse in her wrist. More so, because a pulse could be fuzzy, tenuous. This was as clear and staccato as a shaman-rememberer's drum.

What surprised him more was that he felt her illness, too. As a heat, and a tangled snare. Beneath the heartbeat, entwining it, both accelerating and dragging it, so it staggered on cramped fast painful beats like a colt entangled in thorns, still trying to run.

He didn't know what he was supposed to do. Jurchadai was there, just across Sarangerel's body. Temur looked up at him, shamed to feel his own eyes wide in need as if he were a child seeking succor—but Jurchadai's gaze was kind and steady.

"I don't know what to do," said Temur.

"No one ever does," Jurchadai replied. "You'll think of something."

Untangle it.

For a moment, Temur thought Samarkar had spoken, or perhaps Tsering-la. But when he glanced at them, they were both intent and thin-lipped. And the voice did not have a Rasani accent. If anything, it sounded like his mother—but Ashra had had an accent too, though faint. And Ashra was dead.

Untangle it, Temur told himself, thinking of that colt in briars. As he would have with the colt, he approached slowly, examining the winds of the thorny, constricting illness. The fever had a tight hold of the girl.

All Temur could do was pick at it. Not with his hands, but with his will, his focus. His concentration, as if he followed the design in a Song puzzle-book. It had a kind of . . . heat, as if the fever originated from within it. It half-scorched to focus on it, as uncomfortable as staring into the sun.

Gently, Temur reached out and laid his hand against her forehead.

She squealed as if his touch were icy. She would have wrenched away if Jurchadai were not there, holding her head, keeping her in place. He muttered to her, soothing nonsense, exactly the things Temur would have said to that thorn-tangled colt and in exactly the tone.

Do it fast.

Temur imagined himself grasping the brambles, peeling them back. He imagined them coming away unbloodied, even when his mind's eye wanted to supply the scrapes and gouges they would leave behind. He imagined the colt—the girl—clean-limbed and unscathed, her heart beating strongly, her flesh cool and smooth.

He opened his eyes, only then realizing he had closed them.

Sarangerel breathed calm and smoothly. Her eyes were closed, the muscles of her neck relaxed as if in soothed, natural sleep.

Temur held himself upright for a moment, more by moral force than physical ability. Then he slid down on the carpet on his side, and let the sharp tears wash his cheeks.

16

Ümmühan curled on the padded seat inside her pierced and lat-
ticed litter of sandalwood panels and listened to the men argue in low
tones. If she peered through her louvers, she could see them: Mehmed
and the chief of his war-band, Malului. They sat in folding canvas
chairs dyed in bright expensive colors, the crossed legs carven from
lengths of ivory that rested against the floor on their curves rather than
their tips.

Mehmed, no ascetic, certainly didn't mind the comforts associated
with the caliphate.

The men were arguing about Ümmühan. They thought they had
their voices low enough that she could not overhear, but what few besides Ümmühan and the wizard who had engineered her litter knew
was that it did not only amplify and support the sounds she made
when she sang, it also picked up the voices of those around her, and
made it possible for her to eavesdrop on all sorts of things Kara
Mehmed would have preferred she not overhear.

She had asked him for permission to visit the Hasitani. Malului
had objected, and now the men were arguing.

Once curled in position on her bench, Ümmühan was ever-careful
not to move behind her louvers. The shadow would show, and they

would know she was watching—although if they didn't expect it, they were even bigger fools than she thought.

The argument had gone on for a little time now, and was coming to a head. Malului hunched forward, his spine bowed, his elbows on his knees. In a harsh whisper, hissed between teeth, he said, "I wouldn't permit my woman to roam about the countryside, associating with those unnatural creatures!"

Ümmühan bristled. Those unnatural creatures, as Malului called the Hasitani, were priestesses of the Scholar-God in Her aspect as creator. They studied the world She had made, the rules and natural sciences that bound it together. They glorified the Scholar-God with their books and their inquiries. They were the most holy of the Scholar-God's priesthoods, and it was from their ranks that Ysmat of the Beads had risen, of all the prophets the most touched by God. Ümmühan's small fist knotted inside her silken sleeve, and only with an effort did she make it smooth again.

As smooth as Mehmed's voice as he said, "You know that's blasphemy."

"Caliph—"

"No," said Mehmed. "The Hasitani honor the Scholar-God as do any of us, and it is they who are the keepers of the records of Asitaneh. My Ümmühan is a poetess. She needs access to their files for the histories she studies for inspiration, in her own way to glorify the Scholar-God."

Ümmühan was only half-listening. In her head, she was composing a mocking, anonymous song about Malului's masculine endowments. It wouldn't have his name in it, of course, but anyone who knew him could hardly miss the pencil-thin line of his moustache and his obsessively oiled curls, so fussed with that he draped a linen cloth across the shoulders of his robes to catch the stains. She had faith he'd recognize himself when it came to his ear.

She was trying to think of a suitable rhyme for "lentils" when Kara Mehmed stood, snapping the front of his embroidered overrobe to make the fabric hang smooth. He stomped down a flight of steps to pause by Ümmühan's birdcage.

"You may go," he said. "You will bring your litter-bearers with you, and they will go armed through the city."

Ümmühan smiled behind her veils, which she had drawn across her face even in the close confines of her performer's litter. "Yes, my lord," she said.

Mehmed, left to his own devices, might have refused her request. Mehmed being pushed by Malului would become contrary. He did not like to feel that his choices had been influenced—and because of this, he became strikingly easy to influence.

"Thank you," she said. "My lord."

THE STRONGHOLD OF THE HASITANI WAS A RED STONE BUILDING, LIKE SO many in Asitaneh. Unlike many in Asitaneh, it had not burned. It occupied a western neighborhood of fading gentility, clustered with booksellers conspicuously exiled from the university district. Female scholars only mingled with the male in a few carefully chaperoned circumstances.

Ümmühan's litter-bearers were eunuchs, which was the only reason they did not have to wait outside. Instead, they were admitted to within the portico, where wrought-iron gates kept them from proceeding farther. They set Ümmühan's litter down and handed her out of it, and within moments she had been swept away by the porter.

He was also a eunuch, as strapping as her litter-bearers but some thirty summers older. He led her through the corridors to the abbess's office and there left her in the antechamber, watched over by a young Hasitana garbed in green trousers and a smock.

Ümmühan was expected. She had sent a letter ahead, and she did not think she would have long to wait. What little time she had to spare, she spent in observing the young Hasitana. She stood behind a sand table writing out some complicated equation with frequent consultations to the wax tablet in her left hand. Once she glanced up at Ümmühan and asked, "May I do something to increase your comfort, poetess?"

"I am well," Ümmühan said. She smiled at the young woman. It warmed her still, after all these years, to be called *poetess*.

A moment later, and the door to the abbess's private chamber opened. She stood framed in it, a tall broad-shouldered woman in white, soft around the middle, her graying hair caught back in dozens of woolly, elaborate braids above her veil. Her dark eyes snapped in a face made all the more striking by its contrast to her white veil. The only lines Ümmühan could see were the ones beside her eyes—lines of laughter and concentration.

Not a native of Asitaneh by her skin and hair. But the worship of the Scholar-God reached south beyond Aezin and west past Messaline. It was significant that one could rise to such heights in the face of all prejudice, however. It bespoke both great ability and great strength of purpose, that thing that in men was called character. There was no word for it in women, not in the Uthman tongue.

Ümmühan never forgot it, no matter how many times the abbess extended her palm for Ümmühan to kiss, as Ümmühan kissed it now. Red lines of henna scribed the Prophet's words across the abbess's palm, reminding Ümmühan of the tattooed hands of the Nameless, al-Sepehr.

"What have you come for today, daughter?" the abbess asked.

Ümmühan straightened up. She didn't miss the older woman's glance at her midsection. That she had not chosen to give her order a daughter was a rope of contention between them, but it was Ümmühan's womb, and she would not be moved across the line. She might be a concubine, but she would choose to be a barren one. The order could find its daughters elsewhere, and men like Kara Mehmed could elsewhere find their sons.

"I need the libraries," she said. "And the assistance of a research sister."

"A new poem?" Even the abbess sounded excited at the prospect, which did nothing to lower her standing with Ümmühan.

Ümmühan held out a sheaf of papers, covered in her own delicate, ciphered handwriting. "This is a report on all that has befallen me since I learned of Kara Mehmed's intent to overthrow the old caliph," she said. "There is much here of import. And . . . I have learned the name of a djinn."

THE LIBRARIES OF THE HASITANI WERE TEMPLES, AS IT WAS RIGHT THEY should be—or perhaps it would be truer to say that their temples were libraries. The one Ümmühan was led into now was not one she had visited before. She had studied history and poetry and the natural sciences, it was true, and she had studied theology—when she was a young girl, a student, before she chose to go out into the world and minister to those the Sisters could not otherwise reach.

But she had not studied, in particular, occult history. And that was the room to which she was now brought, under the auspices of a research sister who wore the gray of her calling and moved with a gliding silence, though she was as tall and broad-shouldered as many men. Ümmühan did not ask her name: The Hasitani were not like the desert witches, who sold their names for power. But they kept them as secrets, and used only titles. It was a similar sort of worship to that exemplified by Ümmühan's own epithet, without the belittling.

This library was a tower building. Every inch of the inside walls was covered in racks, and every curved finger-width of the racks was covered or hung with books. Bound books in the sensible, familiar, Uthman and Messaline style stood on edge between their end boards in arc-shaped shelving, arranged so that anyone walking past could read the spines. Song-style board books sat loose in their ornate boxes on tables, or were put away in drawers. Some, which had been pierced and strung like fans, hung from hooks in space that might be otherwise wasted. Scrolls in scroll-cases hung in racks like bottles of spirit.

The shelves stretched to four times Ümmühan's height. Two ladders were fixed to tracks at the top and rolled on wheels at the bottom, through a path in the wooden floor that was kept clear of carpets. They looked flimsy, too steep. Ümmühan hoped the catches that held them to their tracks, above, were strong.

Around the library were arrayed leather-covered couches, low tables, narrow-drawered cabinets to hold fan books, maps, or scrolls. A series of torchères stood ready to light the center of the room when night should fall. Ümmühan realized that there would be sufficient candles, at least in that small space, to enable one to read and write with ease even after sunset. A staggering luxury—and one that was not even necessary, as a row of white glass globes suspended over the tables cast the clean, soft light of divine favor over everything below.

The whole of the space was spotlessly clean.

"Do you dust this?"

"Yes," said the research sister. "How else could I be sure that everything was in its place, and be sure that I knew what that place was?"

Ümmühan took a moment, as the research sister paused before her, to just lift her head until her spine popped straight. She breathed in the sweet density of information. Then the sister said, "Would you like to see something very special?" and led her into the library.

Between those torchères was a narrow, waist-tall reading table, its mahogany surface black with age. As they came closer, Ümmühan could see that it was also black with aged silver; the whole of the surface had been inlaid with verses from the writings of the Prophet. Upon it rested an embroidered silk scarf, gold-fringed and shining, covering something rectangular that might have been mysterious, anywhere but a library.

Ümmühan did not think that in this case, it would prove to be a box.

Her fingers itched to uncover it, but she waited. The Hasitani gestured her to take a seat on one of the strange tall backless chairs. She did, her slippers kicking above the floor until she hit on the strategy of hooking her heels on a rung.

The Hasitana reached out gently and drew the cover from the book. Ümmühan caught her breath in pleasure.

The cover over the boards was silk, too, figured with expert embroidery. It might have been white once, but if it had been, age had mellowed it to the color of fresh cream. As Ümmühan tucked her fingers under her hips to keep from grabbing at it like an excited child, the research sister turned the book to face her and opened it with clean, reverent hands.

Ümmühan gasped aloud.

"You've heard of this book," the research sister said with a smile.

"Oh, yes," said Ümmühan. "I have heard of this book. Rumors of its existence, at least, though I had scoffed at them."

"Of course." The research sister's amusement showed around her veil, leading Ümmühan ever closer to the conclusion that here was a kindred spirit. "The world is full of rumors of magical artifacts that have vanished in antiquity, untraceably, and that never seem to come to light again."

Ümmühan permitted herself a real, delighted laugh, something no man had ever heard from her. For men, she reserved her delicate and disingenuous giggles. This laugh was the truth, and it rang about them clear and loud and a little rough at the edges. "Is it complete?"

Silently, the research sister nodded.

A complete copy of the Prophet Ysmat's writings, and her life and the lives of her disciples as put down by those who had known them: such a thing was rare enough in its own right. This one, however, had been transcribed with gold ink onto vellum dyed with indigo. The Scholar-God's sacred colors of white, indigo, and gold shone from every page. Each word of the book was a perfect invocation to the Scholar-God in the Prophet's own words. It might be one of the most powerful protective talismans the world had ever known. It was certainly the most sacred thing Ümmühan herself had ever seen.

"There are some that say one of the scribes who penned it was Ysmat herself," the research sister said. "But there is no provenance for that, alas, and it's just a little too good to be true. Especially as the binding seems to be original, and uses some techniques that were not available until the second century." When Ysmat of the Beads had been over a hundred years martyred, she did not need to say.

"Nevertheless," Ümmühan breathed. "It is a holy thing."

An invisible aura of clean comfort filled the library as the book sat open before them. Confronted by that book, Ümmühan had the inexpressibly *safe* sensation of sitting in her mother's kitchen, cross-legged on the clean floor, eating sweet cakes off of leaves and sipping milky tea.

She would have closed her eyes to bask, but that would have meant losing sight of the book.

"The abbess," said the research sister, "wishes to reward you for your sacrifice and your service to the Sisterhood. She had expressed a desire that you be allowed to read a page of your choice, Ümmühan."

The room seemed to spin as Ümmühan's breath shortened. Her veil stuck to her open mouth and nostrils. She clawed at it, giving herself air at the expense of dignity. "Any page?"

The research sister nodded. "If you would like a moment to think—"

To think! To disbelieve. A moment in which this gift might vanish like the impossibility it was. A moment in which Ümmühan might be struck dead for her presumption.

I have been a good and dutiful daughter of the Scholar-God, she told herself. *I have done what I have done in Her name, and only in Her name. This is freely offered. I am not giving myself airs.*

"The Lay of Istajama," she said.

Gently, the research sister turned the pages. She seemed to know approximately where in the book the story fell and slowed as she approached it. At last, she stopped.

"Here," she said. With her finger she marked the beginning of the passage.

Ümmühan at first read silently, but the words were so beautiful she could not help but pronounce them aloud. In her best stage voice, she told the version of the life of the woman history knew only as The Mute—the slave poetess who had been a friend and ally of the Prophet, and who had gone before the King of Asmaracanda to plead for the Prophet's life. She had not been treated kindly, as was too often the lot of women, but her eloquence was such that though the king had ordered his men to abuse her body, he had spared her life. He had made her his own possession, for the beauty of her speech, and eventually he had taken her to his bed—after the execution of Ysmat for what was then termed blasphemy.

But the Mute's story did not end there. Because her eloquence was such that in due time she had converted the king to Ysmat's word, and the proper understanding of the Scholar-God's will and intentions. And, eventually, through him had the teachings of the prophet he had martyred spread to every land.

Ümmühan read through it twice, swept with pity and outrage and reverence for her ancient colleague and her courage and her suffering. When she raised her head, her veil wet upon her cheeks, she found the research sister regarding her.

"I thought you might want that one," the woman said.

Ümmühan laughed through the tears. "Thank you. Thank you."

"It was earned," the woman said. "Now, when you have collected yourself, tell me what information you came here seeking."

Ümmühan swallowed. She dried her eyes on the edge of her veil and gathered herself. Gently, regretfully, she closed the indigo book and allowed the research sister to cover it again.

"I have learned the name of a djinn," she said. "I wish to have it recorded in the library, and see if we can learn which djinn he is."

The research sister gave her a satisfied nod. "That's a useful thing to know," she said. "Let's see. The books would be over here."

She scampered up the ladder like a monkey playing in a date palm. She slid back down without touching a rung, one-handed because the other arm was balancing a pile of books against her chest. Ümmühan's heart almost choked her, but the research sister tossed her veils with satisfaction as her sandals barely thumped against the floor. She spread books on the table and opened them, skimming for content before pushing them under Ümmühan's nose. Ümmühan could barely read fast enough to keep up with her, and she didn't even have to *find* the relevant passages.

She nibbled her lip and squinted at the cramped, archaic letters, word-forms that had changed immensely over the last few hundred years. At last, one turn of phrase from a quoted conversation and the line of a quick, elegant pen-sketch caught her eye. She turned the book again and offered it to the research sister. "What do you make of this?"

The research sister read thoughtfully, brow furrowing, more than once. Finally, she said, "What makes you think this is your djinn?"

Ümmühan had to think about it. "The voice," she said, having contemplated it. "The tone of archness. He's a clever one and loves to fence. And there, the shape of the jaw and nose—do they wear the same faces, down the centuries?"

"If they do, it is something new we have learned because of you." With careful, precise pen strokes, the research sister made a note in the wide margin of the book. She wrote Ümmühan's name, and that she was a priestess of the Women's Rite. Then, the ink dulling on the nib, she paused with the pen half-extended to Ümmühan and said, "Are you sure?"

Ümmühan stared at the pen. Then she lowered her veil, took the quill, dipped it, and carefully wrote the seventeen syllables of the djinn's name. The pen almost dripped; she set it hastily down in the ink pot and let her hands shake while the research sister efficiently and easily sanded the page to set their marginalia.

They were silent for a moment, the research sister busy at her archival tasks and Ümmühan shaken with the import of what she had just done.

"Well, congratulations," said the research sister. "You've managed to uncover the name of the djinn that made the Sorcerer-Prince the greatest power in all the world, and then arranged for his destruction."

Ümmühan swallowed. "Well. I guess that explains how al-Sepehr knew his name."

AFTER THE LIBRARY, ÜMMÜHAN WAS SUMMONED TO DINNER WITH THE abbess. They ate well: a nourishing oven-braised stew of lamb and herbs in gravy thickened with lentils and onions, stone-baked flatbread to use as scoops, sliced plums and oranges purple as bruised flesh. After the first few moments of contented chewing, Ümmühan sipped honeyed tea with mint and said, "It is good that this abbey was saved from the fires."

"Prayer or the caprice of the winds," the abbess replied. "Who can say? And speaking of caprice . . . we are under a Rahazeen sky, Ümmühan. You must be careful, as must all the Hasitani and all those who celebrate the Women's Rite."

"A Rahazeen caliph may not be as permissive as the Falzeen Uthmans were, you mean."

Decorously, the abbess addressed herself to her bread. It was crisp on the outside, chewy within, rich with oil and garlic. It scarcely needed the lamb. When she had swallowed, she gave a satisfied breath and said, "Sacred or not, the Rahazeen can be ugly toward women. Especially learned women. Especially the Nameless, and given your report, we must accept that Kara Mehmed is allied with them . . ."

Ümmühan had her own theological theories about that, mostly revolving around the Nameless feeling insecure in the prophet status of their patron, the Sorcerer-Prince Sepehr al-Rachīd, and thus feeling the need to undermine the sacredness of Ysmat of the Beads and by extension, all women.

She said, "You've heard of the skinned bodies, then?"

The abbess nodded.

"Do you think then, that the Sorcerer-Prince has returned?"

The abbess swirled her tea in its gold-chased ruby glass and sighed. "It may not matter if he has already returned, if enough people can be made to believe he has."

Ümmühan felt her brow wrinkle, and hastened to smooth it. Wrinkles were the courtesan's most mortal enemy. "Abbess?"

"Belief," the abbess said. "That in itself could give the Nameless the power to raise their prophet. And I do not see that ending well for any of us, my brilliant child."

A silence followed, into which they both stared. Finally, the abbess turned to Ümmühan and said, "Get close to this Nameless warlord if you can. Do what you can to prevent this. In the service of Ysmat of the Beads, and of the Scholar-God."

Yangchen awakened to silence, and thought at first that the storm had passed. The darkness was utter and still. The brazier had died, but the wagon remained warm—warm enough, at least, that her breath didn't mist when she poked her face out of the blankets—if perhaps not exactly *cozy*.

It was not until she heard Anil-la stirring and sitting, somewhere in the darkness on the other side of the wagon, that she realized how unnatural the hush really was. Even in the night, she should have heard the sounds of the encampment—the rattle of harness, the footsteps of the guards, the noises that animals made as they greeted one another or argued in the darkness. There was nothing. All that reached her ears were the breathing of Tsechen, Anil-la, and the ladies—and the occasional soft creaking of the wooden walls.

And she did not think that it was night. In fact, she felt well-rested, as if she had slept her fill, for the first time since the caravan left Tsarepheth.

As if a bolt of electricity had jolted her upright, Yangchen found herself on her feet. "Doctor Anil, light!" she said.

A moment later, his violet witchlights shimmered into existence, suffusing the wagon with a warm, consoling glow. All around, Tsechen and the women were sitting up, pulling blankets to their chests. As Anil-la gazed at her, Yangchen was aware of her chest heaving, her undressed hair pulling from its loose braid.

"Where's Namri?"

"He is well, Dowager," said the nurse.

"We're snowed under," Yangchen said.

Anil opened his mouth, then shut it again and stepped up onto a chest against the wall. He unlatched one of the high, narrow windows and tried to push it out; it jammed after a handspan, and white powder shifted in through the crack. It piled on the floorboards and quickly melted into puddles.

He said, "It's a good thing the brazier went out, or we'd all be dead."

Yangchen almost told him that she and Tsechen had cleared the vents, but thought better of it. Wizards rarely liked to be reminded of their failings. And Tsechen, with a glance in her direction, spoke first.

"It'd be a peaceful death," Tsechen said dryly. When Yangchen shot her a *look*, mouth drawn up as if with a purse string, she smirked. "Well, it would have been."

"More peaceful than surviving," Yangchen answered.

"Most deaths are." Anil-la heaved again. There was a creak of compacting snow, but the window would not open further. "Roof," he said.

There was a hatch, with slats nailed to the wall below it to serve as a ladder. It led to the rooftop cargo deck. As he put a boot on the first slat, Yangchen asked, "And if that doesn't work?"

"I'm a wizard," he said.

But it worked. He heaved the hatch up and endured the deluge of snow sifting on his hair and shoulders. Following a dazzle of painful light, cold fell into the wagon like an invisible waterfall. Namri began to wail, and the nurse coddled and jiggled him, making humming coos that only served to intensify his screaming. Yangchen gasped and threw her arms up across her breasts, hugging her own shoulders. The ladies in waiting did likewise. Tsechen bent down and grabbed bedding, which she threw around the women's shoulders before approaching Yangchen with a robe.

In the moments it had taken Tsechen to accomplish those actions, Anil-la scrambled up the last few steps and poked out his head. His voice was slightly muffled as he called down, "The snow drifted against the baggage. The hatchway is mostly clear."

With a grunt, he hauled himself up. Yangchen, allowing Tsechen to fasten the clasps on the robe at her shoulder and under her arm, resisted the urge to call caution after him. The nurse had put Namri to her breast despite the cold, and now pulled a blanket up to cover both of them.

A moment later, Anil poked his head back down, supporting himself with one hand on the lip of the hatchway, and called, "Dowager?

Perhaps it would please you to . . . I mean, your grace should probably see this."

Even with the warmth from the quilted robe—two layers of silk stitched around felted yak wool—it was hard for Yangchen to unwrap her arms from around herself and grasp the ladder. The snow burned the soles of her feet; she turned to call for shoes, but one of the ladies in waiting had anticipated her need. As she stepped into the silk slippers, she could not help but think how ridiculously inadequate to the purpose they were.

She climbed, pressing her toes hard against the wall behind the wet rungs, and at the top of the ladder Anil-la was there to help her continue up the snowy railing until she could step off to the roof deck on one side. The cold took her breath away, instantly stinging her lips and fingers. She withdrew her hands into her robe. Her breath whipped from her in long white banners, tattered and dissipated by the wind.

She put her back to the force of it, blinking to clear blinding tears. What she saw was not nearly so bad as she had anticipated. The sun was high, marking afternoon, and it blazed in a transparent, gloriously aquamarine sky. The wagon was indeed drifted under, snow having piled high against the windward side and arched like a breaking wave over the top of the rope-lashed baggage—but the snow on the other side was only halfway up, and in places where nothing sheltered it the ground was swept almost clean. The rear door would have to be shoveled clear. Around the caravan she could see that corralled animals had sensibly moved into the shelter of circling wagons. The road was not impassable, though traveling would be difficult.

The tents, however, and the other wagons, were a different matter. Especially those on the windward edge of the encampment. She could see mounds from here that must be buried tents.

Her pulse quickened again. She touched Anil's arm. "People may be trapped in them."

"We will lose some," he said. "See? There are teams already digging out. We will need to organize them, and you must direct the soldiers, Dowager."

She raised her eyebrows at him. He ducked his head, abashed that he had dared to command the empress. But that was enough of an apology, and she nodded—startled at herself. A mere month before,

she might have demanded him punished for his insolence, wizard or
no. She had less need to prove her power, now that she had some.

As she looked over his shoulder, movement against the horizon
drew her attention. Tall dark shapes, like men in heavy coats, moving
over the snow with ridiculous ease. "What's that?"

He turned. His hand went out as if to steady himself, but missed
the railing. He might have tumbled back through the hatchway if
Yangchen had not forgotten her own imperial status enough to catch
his elbow.

"Mayeh," he said unevenly. "You know, I thought they were myth-
ical."

"Man-bears," Yangchen answered. "I hope they're friendly. There's
no way we're getting this mess into a defensive position right now."

THE MAYEH WERE TALLER THAN A MAN, WHEN YANGCHEN FINALLY STOOD
before them. They had broad shoulders and long arms bulging with
knotted muscle like the red forest apes she had seen once in a menag-
erie in Song, imported all the way from the wild spice islands to the
south. They stood upright, however, and the pelts that covered them as
densely as the fur of a yak were a dark brown color that caught sparks
of auburn in the sun. Their feet were enormous, great paddles edged
around with massive mats of fur that let them walk over the snow
without sinking—as if they wore snowshoes.

They did not speak Rasani. But they had approached with open
hands, unthreatening, and Anil-la and the Dowager Empress had managed to clamber down the side of the wagon and run up to the guards
at the edge of the encampment, shouting for them to hold their attack.
And now, the big male who seemed to be the leader approached Yangchen
and showed her his big hands, the mahogany creases across the orange
palms, and gestured to the buried tents and snow-stuck wagons.

"That's an offer of assistance if I've ever seen one," said Anil.

"You're so helpful," Yangchen muttered. Her shoulders crawled
with cold. When she glanced sideways at him, he was grinning, and she
wondered if he was as giddy at their near escape from being buried
alive as she was.

She frowned at the Mayeh, wondering how to indicate that she ap-
preciated his assistance, when he opened his mouth and dabbed his

fingertips on his tongue. Then he licked his lips, as if he had eaten something delicious.

She glanced about herself, at the windswept rocky plateau, at the soldiers struggling to excavate survivors. Three tents over, a stiff body wrapped in clothing and blankets was being pulled from a collapsed tent. By its size, it was a child or a small woman. *We need this. We need this help, and now.*

Something delicious. Something the Mayeh would know about, but not have easy access to. As she turned away, she caught sight of one of her advisors, struggling toward her through drifts with the assistance of a staff and a staunch young soldier.

"Na-Baryan," Yangchen said. "How good of you to bring me another man to dig. Colonel, if you will?" She gestured him toward the excavations, and he went, not even bothering to glance at na-Baryan or shake the old man's hand off his elbow.

"Dowager." Painfully, na-Baryan began to prostrate himself in the snow.

Yangchen gestured him upright impatiently. "Get me honey," she said. "We must have some."

"Dowager?"

"Honey!" she snapped. "All of it. Requisition it from anyone who has some. Even the wagon masters. I know they've been giving it to the livestock to help keep them strong."

As na-Baryan staggered away again, Yangchen bit her lip in distress—and made herself stop when she thought of how it would chap and split. The honey would be a terrible sacrifice; the oxen and mules pulling these wagons in the cold needed the energy sweet feed would give them. More would die before they reached Rasa . . . but her people were dying now.

When the first runner arrived with the first stoneware crock of the red Rasan honey, harvested by brave honey-gatherers from the hives of giant highland bees, Yangchen took it from his hands herself. He *did* prostrate himself in the snow before she could stop him. She was in too much of a hurry to make much of it, and with her own hands brought the crock before the leader or interpreter or envoy of the Mayeh.

Her fingernails split further as she picked at the wax that held it shut. Anil intervened, cut the seal with his knife, and pried the stopper out. Then he gave the jar back to Yangchen and backed away.

She sniffed the honey and touched her finger to its coarse, orangey-red, granulated surface, then touched the finger to her tongue. It was good, shockingly sweet, so tempting her cold stomach knotted with the desire for more. But she extended the crock, held it out to the Mayeh, and gestured that he, too, should taste.

He regarded her, brow furrowing in concentration, and then gently extended one hand, a pointing finger. A moment later, and he had scratched up a bit of honey with a ragged nail.

Yangchen held her breath as he tasted it.

When he opened his eyes, his lip lifted off enormous fangs. She stood her ground, arm extended. Surely it shook from the weight of the honey crock. Surely her teeth rattled with cold.

Behind her, more runners were starting to arrive, bearing more crocks of honey. Yangchen wondered if they would all be in time to watch their empress torn limb from limb.

Gently, the Mayeh reached out and lifted the crock from her hands. He handed the crock to the equally impressive female on his left, who also tasted it with closed eyes before responding with a grimace identical to the male's.

Only then did Yangchen realize that what they were offering her was a smile.

WHEN ALL WERE UNEARTHED, ONLY SOME FIFTY OF YANGCHEN'S PEOPLE had died in the snow. It was too many, and yet it was far less than it might have been, without the luck of the wind and the even greater luck of the Mayeh happening along. As the dead were blessed and stacked in carts—for there could be no proper pyre to release their spirits here—Yangchen sat in her saddle, on Lord Shuffle's back, and she watched. Because for the dowager to watch gave the loading of the dead a gravity and dignity that took a little back from the harsh reality of soldiers stacking them like split wood. She watched the relatives of the dead bring them out, where they had relatives. She watched the tears of children and of parents, and could not decide which were worse.

She had not wept for her own father so, when word came of his passing.

She twined the coarse white coat of Lord Shuffle's shoulders around her mittens. The real reason she was on his back was for the comfort his warm, cud-chewing presence offered. They would not be breaking camp before nightfall. It was better to take the time to rest one more day, even though anxiety gnawed her at the thought. But they would cover more ground in the long run if they just waited until dawn and struck out then.

So for now, she watched the bodies being loaded, and she grieved them. And as she grieved them, she heard the mockery of her father's voice with her inner ear: *You did not know them, and even if you had, they are peasants, soldiers. Livestock. You should be thinking of how to extend the alliance with the Mayeh, and parley it into military and trade advantage. Not these folk.*

She had never had the courage to do so in reality. But now to her surprise she heard herself arguing with the voice in her head. *These people are my responsibility.*

They are tools. Only your children matter. Only you children ever mattered to me.

As tools for your own advancement!

Then she sat stunned. Stunned by her own audacity, but only a little. Stunned more by the never-previously-examined truth in her own—silent, unspoken, but nevertheless clearly registered—words.

And the stabbing recognition of herself that followed: *As I have used Namri for mine.*

She was the dowager. She rested her hands, relaxed and still, on the pommel of Lord Shuffle's saddle, the reins folded over her fur-lined mittens. She buried the lower half of her face behind fur, hiding her expression. The Dowager Empress should not look sour or shocked at what amounted to a state funeral.

She kept her back straight, and her eyes front, for what seemed like a lifetime—until the loading of the bodies was done and Anil-la came to fetch her. He reined his dark brown yak cow up beside Lord Shuffle. The animals had become friendly, and Yangchen found her leg pressed to Anil's as the two beasts leaned together. She did not protest.

"Come and eat, Dowager."

She followed. The sun was gone, leaving a smear of light in the west and a sky just bright enough for them to find their way beneath. Grooms waited to take custody of Shuffle and Anil's mount, but Yangchen made sure Shuffle had an extra handful of grain just from her before she gave him up. "I'm glad the spirit bear did not get you."

She felt guilty as she said it—selfish—but not so guilty that what she said was not true.

The wind had died to teasing breezes that blew the white fur trimming her hood this way and that. Her fingertips were numb in her mittens. Tonight would be killing cold again—colder, with the sky so clear, and no clouds to hold the warmth down close to the soil.

For a moment, she closed her eyes and let herself pray that there would be no new bodies to stack in the morning. When she opened them, they were alongside her own wagon and Anil-la's hand was on her sleeve. She startled and turned, nerves humming, expecting some new threat—

He pulled her into the shadow of the wagon, and before she could protest, he pressed his mouth to hers.

A STUNNED MOMENT, THE BLOOD HUMMING IN HER EARS, AND YANGCHEN kissed him back. Kissed him as she had only ever kissed her husbands, and—shocking herself—with far more passion and desire. He smelled so good—well, he smelled of unwashed clothes, and rancid butter used to grease his hands and face against the cold, but *beneath* that he smelled delicious, warm and sweet. She thought of almond pastries, butter-rich. She opened her mouth to his.

Their lips would chap. Her nose burned where his breath dampened it. She didn't care.

She did care that there was nowhere here in which they could seek privacy. She had nowhere to bring him, and suddenly all she wanted was to be alone with him, someplace sheltered, where she could warm herself on his body. Oh, to be truly warm again. Warm, and alone with a man. This man.

This was what it was to kiss someone for a reason besides duty.

She took a breath. She put her hands against his chest and pushed, feeling the force it took to compress mittens, liners, his parka, the wizard's coat and shirt beneath, until he finally registered it as a protest and stepped back—panting, cheeks bright. Eyes shining as he looked at her. "Dowager—"

"It cannot happen," she said.

His regard never wavered. "Do you want it to?"

She remembered—barely—not to bite her lip. She nodded.

"You are the dowager," he said. "I am a wizard. Who is to tell you that you cannot have me, if you wish? There need be no secrets here."

The advisors—

But no. He was a wizard. He could get no heirs on her to challenge the emperor-in-waiting.

That flutter in her chest, that warmth—was it hope? It had been so long since she'd felt it, in its real and unadulterated form, that she barely recognized it. "I could take you as a consort."

"You could."

"Officially."

"Did the last dowager not have her concubines?"

She had, though it had largely been before Yangchen had come to live at the court. Still, there had been tales of the old empress's eunuch attendants, and whispered giggles in the women's quarters over their size, appearance, number, and the intricacies of the politics they supposedly played out among themselves.

"Yes," Yangchen said, and kissed him just once more, quite lightly, before grasping his mittened hand and leading him toward the wagon door.

WHAT THE OTHER WOMEN THOUGHT OF THIS ARRANGEMENT, YANGCHEN realized she would never know. She was the dowager, and it insulated as it empowered. What she *did* know was that at least for now, tonight, she didn't *care* what they thought. She was enough of a politician to understand that eventually she would have to care, that even if no one would ever tell her, their opinions would affect their navigation of court politics—and thus, perforce, her own. She still had to care what everyone in the Rasan Empire thought of her.

She just no longer had to care what her father would have wanted her to do.

As she lay in a dim glow of Anil-la's witchlights, her head pillowed on his shoulder, his fingers lazily combing her unbound hair, she thought that this, for now, would be enough for her. She was warm; she was fed.

She was drowsy. She only half-murmured back into wakefulness when Anil spoke, his voice a rumble beneath her ear.

"You are trying to make a better empire."

She hadn't really thought about it. "What makes you say that?"

"You haven't ordered one tongue slit since you became dowager."

Yangchen could hear the women moving beyond the tapestry that had been hung to afford her and Anil what little privacy they now enjoyed. The nurse was shushing the small emperor, singing him a little silly song featuring an intrepid sheep as its protagonist. From the tick of her needle against a frame, Tsechen was embroidering.

"We've been busy."

He laughed. "I laid hands on you, and yet still have both of them."

She nuzzled the crease of his shoulder, making him squirm. "You may have special privileges."

"Dowager," he said. "You want to be a better ruler than your husband was."

"My husband never got much of a chance to rule—"

"His mother, then."

Yangchen snorted, not bothering to keep the hate from her voice. She pitched it low, however. "Lord Shuffle would make a better dowager than her."

Anil stroked her hair. He waited.

Wizards were too damned patient, she decided, when the passage of several minutes did not allow her to drowse once more. At last she said, "So in your opinion, failure to slit noses and tongues is what makes for a great empire?"

"Perhaps a less terrible one. Greatness . . ." His shrug made the skin of his shoulder rise and fall against her ear. "Empires are not made for greatness. Not the kind of greatness I envision. They are not . . ."

". . . not?"

"Just."

"Oh." Her right hand was tingling with lack of blood, pressed as it was between their bodies. She did not care to move it yet. "What's justice? Beyond a word, I mean."

"Not empires."

"Banditry is better? No roads, no trade—is that better? The chaos and lawlessness of a world without empire, is that better? The squabbling petty princes of Song—you'd rather have that?"

Damn wizards and their silences, anyway. She might have thought he had fallen asleep, if it were not for the gentle, rhythmic motion of his hand across her hair, again and again. He let it stretch so long that even her court discipline broke, and she replied to her own question. "And if you tear down one empire, another merely rolls over the ashes of the old. Surely it is better to be the emperor than the conquered."

He breathed out and breathed in. She thought she heard the flap of a canvas tarpaulin outside, like the close passage of some enormous pair of wings. A girl laughed; an animal lowed in the cold. She drummed the nails of her left hand on his chest. He laughed and caught her wrist, then kissed the palm.

"What," he said, "if there were something better than empires?"

"Like what?"

He was silent again, so she wondered if he was waiting, again, for her to reply to herself. She didn't have a reply, though, and he honestly had raised her curiosity. She gazed at the line of his jaw, the angle of smooth skin below his ear.

He doused the witchlantern, leaving them in darkness. "Dawn comes early."

"Doctor Anil. What is an improvement upon empires?"

He sighed. He said, "I do not know."

Three days later, they came to a village, and Yangchen and Anil-la slept together in a warm bed within wooden walls for the first time. Yangchen-tsa slept the sleep of the exhausted, secure in her borrowed room with the guards outside the door.

So she was all the more sleep-mazed and muddled when Anil shook her awake. She blinked aware groggily, unfocused, her vision starred and blurry. The room was not dark, but aglow with Anil's witchlights, and they were not alone.

By the window—open to the cold and stars, when it had been barred from the inside—stood a man in black trousers and tunic, a short scimitar thrust through his sash, his face swaddled in dark cloth. Other than that narrow band of eyes and bridge of nose, his hands were the only skin that Yangchen could see on him. And *they* were decorated with drawn patterns—words, Yangchen realized, in the Uthman tongue, though she could not read them.

She clutched the coverlet to her breasts, cursing it for a useless gesture even as she caught herself making it. Anil gestured, his hand a blurred sweep, and a bolt of violet incandescence splashed from it as if he had scooped light up and hurled it. The light flashed against the veiled man's upright hand, and splashed once more—this time, as if it had struck a wall and rebounded.

The man clucked. "This is not the greeting I hoped for, when we met at last, Wizard Anil. Mistress Yangchen, will you not greet an old correspondent? Will you not send for tea?"

Yangchen felt a sick twist in the bottom of her gut. *A price. You cannot pretend you did not always know that there would be a price.*

She opened her mouth to speak—she did not know what words. And before she could shape any, the man in the veil continued. "Good as it is to see my allies in bed with one another . . . the night is cold. Will you not welcome me? We have much to discuss."

Anil paused in the midst of his next gesture. Wizardry fizzed from his fingertips like bright wisps of smoke.

"A Nameless assassin claims my allegiance?"

So that's what that costume means. The veil, Yangchen could see in the brightening light, was indigo. Its edges had left smudges on the man's brown skin, defining the caverns inhabited by his eyes. The patterns on his hands, she realized now, must be tattoos.

The veiled man was not young, not by the skin on his hands and at the corners of his eyes—but he moved lightly, with fit vitality. He was spare, even gaunt. His knuckles were knobs that stood out along fingerbones like fansticks.

Trailing the covers with her like a gown, Yangchen rose. She clothed her nakedness in regal poise and dignity—and was about to raise her voice to shout for the guards when the Nameless said, "Don't bother. They sleep, *Dowager.*"

He clucked, and a flurry of gray wings filled the open window. "Do you know me now?"

His Rasani was quite good, fluent even, but lightly accented—with

an Uthman liquidity, where Yangchen's own accent was Song. The bird
on the window frame was the size of an eagle, but with a long neck like
a water-bird. A red crest decked its raptor's head.

Yangchen had untied the message-capsules from the ankles of a
great many of its ilk. Possibly she'd used this very one to carry corre-
spondence, though obviously the Nameless had more than one. Since
the last one she'd met she'd sent to be roasted for the poor.

The man said, "Still no tea on such a cold night? I think little of
your Rasani hospitality. And you discard my letters unread. Is that
politeness to one who has served you?"

"The sky over Tsarepheth," she said bitterly. "That's your doing."

"Dowager," he said. "It is your doing."

She made a strangled sound of protest.

The veiled man said, "Yes. Your doing. Yours, and that of your . . .
paramour. I merely supplied you the . . . tools."

Yangchen bit her lip to keep from glaring her accusation at Anil
in front of this intruder. *A wizard could have done what was done at the Black
Palace—*

Uneasily, with the sharp swift kick of betrayal, she remembered
their conversation about empires, and the overthrowing of same.

The veiled man would not look at her. He kept his gaze on Anil.
She wondered if this were dismissal of the less physically dangerous
of them, or fear of her nakedness. Yangchen had heard of the
Rahazeen's bizarre terror of women, for all their God was a She. But
before she could press that advantage—if it really existed—and attempt to discommode him by moving toward him, he said, "I perceive that you lovebirds have not shared your secrets honestly with
one another?"

"I am the dowager," Yangchen said. "No one shares my secrets."

"You no longer cherish our alliance, your grace? Was it not I whose
assistance *made* you the dowager?" She couldn't tell if he actually smiled
behind the veil, but his eyes—with their odd, bluish cast, like the eyes
of an old dog—certainly gave the sense of it even though he never
looked away from Anil. "Warlock! Can you not control your woman's
tongue?"

Anil had stood from the bed as well. He was naked, but either did
not notice the chill from the open window or he affected to be above it.

His hands were still raised, the light streaking after each gesture of his fingertips. "I don't serve you."

"You have."

Anil continued as if there had been no interruption. "And her tongue is her own. We're not so weak as to fear the truth on women's lips where I come from." He glanced at Yangchen, and she read his intent in his gaze. She should make for the door, and he would hold the assassin. *Anil!*

She could not flee. She loved him.

But she was the dowager, to be protected at all costs. She must.

He knows you betrayed Rasa. If he dies, you are safe.

If he died, she would be alone again. She had made mistakes, so many mistakes. But from the sound of it so had he—

"Did you come here to bargain, al-Sepehr? Or simply to taunt?" Anil stepped between Yangchen and the Nameless. Yangchen lifted one bare foot, but did not step back toward the door. She heard what Anil called him; she knew that it was true.

"I came to see if our alliance could be reclaimed," the veiled man said. "I am willing to forgive a great deal, Wizard, Dowager. We could be of use to each other still."

"*Use,*" Yangchen said, flaring. She stepped up beside Anil, ignoring his horrified sideways glance. "Yes, you've had your *use* of me. You're not the first man to get it, either, so don't look so fucking smug—"

"Oh, the ferocity of twenty winters," al-Sepehr said reverently. "I pray you, child-queen, hold your tongue."

Yangchen recollected her dignity and lifted up her chin. "You made our contract under false pretenses, al-Sepehr. You led me to think you were an ally of my father's, and that your guidance was for my sake. Shall we talk of the demonlings devouring my subjects from the heart out? Shall we talk of corpses skinned in the marketplace?"

"Oh, let us talk of demonlings," said al-Sepehr. He folded his arms and rested easy against the window frame.

Anil touched Yangchen's elbow. She did not shake his hand away.

Said al-Sepehr, "Have they hailed you as their mother yet? It was you who opened the way for them, after all."

Yangchen flinched. Anil's fingers tightened sharply, reflexively—but he did not let her go, and she was sickly grateful for it.

"Any consent you gained from me was tricked—"

He sighed. "What would your people say, if they knew how the Bstangpo died? And that it was at the hands of the half-man who now shares the dowager's blankets? What would they say if they knew you laid down the wards of Tsarepheth, Dowager, and allowed the demonlings in? That you used witchcraft to prevent your sister-wives from conceiving?"

Yangchen bit her lip, half-stunned, a hollow ache inside her as if she had swallowed a ball of ice too big to get down. *Who will raise Namri? Who will be his regent if I burn?*

Anil stepped forward, scoffing, his unbound hair tossed behind his shoulders. "Because any Rasani would believe the word of a Nameless assassin, a Rahazeen chantmonger over that of a dowager empress who has saved countless lives? You need a better threat, carrion."

There was a silence, long and lean, before al-Sepehr straightened himself away from the window frame. Yangchen braced herself for combat—there was a pair of tongs beside the fireplace, and she thought her new, road-hardened self might be able to swing them with conviction—but he only steepled his hands, thumbs touching his breastbone, and bowed sarcastically.

"Alas," al-Sepehr said. "I'd hoped you might someday come to understanding, and to Sepehr's banner. I'd hoped we could be friends."

Before either Yangchen or Anil could react, he was gone out the window in a swirl of blowing snow. He must have had a rope on the wall outside, but when they rushed forward, Anil-la's hovering violet lights revealed nothing in the darkness beyond. Yangchen heard, however, a sound she recognized: the ponderous flap of enormous wings.

Anil pulled Yangchen inside and barred the shutters again—for all the good that might have done them. "These were warded," he said.

"So he's a wizard, too."

"He's something," Anil said. He turned and put his arms around Yangchen, pulling her against his own clammy body. She cast the sheets over his shoulders and wrapped them both.

"He has letters," she said.

"Letters can be forged." Anil touched her cheek. "I too was duped, Dowager."

She nodded against his chest, though all she felt was the chill. "Of course you were."

Then, later, when they had returned to the bed and lay sleepless on their opposite edges, she added, "Well. At least we have shared our secrets now."

THEY PASSED INTO A LANDSCAPE OF CULTIVATED FIELDS AND FARMERS WHO lined the roadside to gawk at the ragtag procession of the empress and what remained of her court passing by. Anil rode beside her, but not as close as he once would have. And the looks he gave her now were warier, reserved—though he still came to her improvised boudoir at night. Within two days, they had sighted the steep pitched roofs and bright walls of Rasa, its prayer banners snapping in the wintry wind.

Yangchen felt herself breathe out as if she would never stop, her spine crackling as she sat abruptly straighter in the saddle.

She felt Anil beside her. His yak leaned close on Lord Shuffle's shoulder. The friendship between the animals, at least, was intact.

"We lived," he said.

"We did it and lived," she answered.

 17

IN THE END, ALL THEY TOOK FROM KYIV WAS GOLD AND HORSES, BOTH IN sufficient quantity to carry them to Huacheng if that was what was required. With his reclaimed riches, Ato Tesefahun had paid for twenty geldings and mares—a mount and a remount for each of them, and four spares—and he did not regret the expenditure. He was no judge of horseflesh, but it turned out that several of the Dead Men were, and he had listened to their arguments and judgments and basically, in the end, let them choose and fight it out between themselves, and also drive the bargain.

Tesefahun's only concern was following the refugees' trail back to the mother of his great-grandchild before that trail grew cold. While the Dead Men were haggling, he found a woman in the market-place who would go and spread some coppers and bread among the refugees, listen to their stories, and report back. From this, he learned the details of the destruction in the village of Stechko. And he learned as well that the refugees had come straight and true across the steppe, guided by the stranger who had appeared out of nowhere to lead them to Kyiv, and then disappeared just as quickly.

When Tesefahun rejoined Iskandar and the Dead Men, they introduced him to his mount. The horses were the curly-coated breed of the

Kyivvans, round-bodied and hardy to the cold, which seemed a provident choice with winter coming on. And if they did not exactly carry the company across the autumn-golden steppe like the wind, they were hoof-hard and tireless. Tesefahun's primary mount was a roan gelding whose coat was speckled in shades of pewter, silver, blue, and gray, giving him the appearance of a rough, weathered granite boulder spotted with paler lichen. Other than a white star between his eyes, his heavy head was slate-dark. His heavy mane hung in long coils that had a tendency to tangle in the reins if Tesefahun did not pay strict attention.

The Dead Men complained of the horseflesh (not like their dish-faced Uthman warhorses), the saddles (not at all like their Uthman saddles, which were little more than pads of leather thrown over elaborately tasseled felt blankets), and the cold. Especially the cold. But for all that, they rode like demons, and Tesefahun could see that even the Kyivvan horse dealers, who had their own cavalry culture dating back to the days of Danupati's empire, respected their knowledge.

As for Tesefahun, it was not his first time in the saddle. But neither was he a young man anymore, and after the first day of riding, he missed the man-carried litter most fiercely. After the second day, he even missed the measured propulsion of his own bony feet.

He never got around to missing that dragon boat, though.

By the third day, the saddle began to wear in to him—or, as he suspected, he began to wear into the saddle.

That was the day they found the burned remains of Stechko, and the fierceness of the suns of Erem. They were fortunate that they came to the border as night was falling, and Tesefahun had the knowledge to recognize what the shape of the black moon low in the sky meant— and why the grass was charred as far as the eye could see before them.

In his youth, he had visited Messaline, the modern City of Jackals, which was built on the ruins of the second Erem. It was in the mountains outside of Messaline that the first Erem, the original City of Jackals, lay. Tesefahun, like many another student wizard, had not been able to resist the dare of visiting its cursed and beautiful ruins.

By the light of the nightsun, he kept Iskandar and the Dead Men moving before the daysuns could burn them where they stood. The horses formed a thundering phalanx across the blackened steppe, crisped stems cracking beneath their hooves, drifts of ash billowing behind them as if their passage raised a smoke of its own.

Iskandar rode up beside him, calling across the space between their mounts. "You know this is crazy, old man!"

"So was the palace I built for you. But I promise you, if we find Edene, my grandson will have sanctuary for you!"

"I could have been kinder to him," Iskandar said.

"You don't know a Khagan's honor. Fight for him, and he may very well put you on your dais again, Uthman once-Caliph."

Iskandar tossed his head as if shaking his braids from his eyes, and did not respond. But nor did he fall back from his position at Tesefahun's side.

The burned skeletons of the village were evident long before the riders reached them. They made black lines against a star-thick sky, and Tesefahun realized both at once that they were at the halfway point—and that he did not know how much more night they had to work with before dawn and fire blossomed in the sky. He put his heels to the worthy roan, whose name was Flint, and twined his fingers on the reins and pommel to keep himself from knotting his hands together.

Ride, Ato Tesefahun whispered to himself. And as if the roan gelding heard him, they *moved.* The night was the thunder of hooves, the ache of Tesefahun's thighs, the lather of the roan gelding's neck flying back into his face. Trailing the remounts, faces bent close to straining necks, eight riders and twenty horses moved as if their lives depended on it.

Their lives did.

EDENE WOULD HAVE BEEN THE LAST TO HEAR THE HOOVES IF IT WERE NOT for the ring. But as it was, she was the first, and she mustered her jackal-faced troops around her as they turned to make a stand. She had no doubt who was following; Kyivvans bent on vengeance for what she had wrought.

She wondered if she could call down the fire of Eremite suns on those who followed, just by proclaiming this land hers. But that was a weapon of obliteration, and she suspected if dominion over the land was contested, she would have to beat the opposition on the field of battle first.

When she caught sight of them cresting a rolling, grassy hill, she was surprised. There were fewer than a dozen riders, and fewer than two dozen mounts. Enough for a raiding band, were the enemy unready. Not enough to exact any kind of bloody justice on her and her horde of ghulim. Not enough, really, to even press the point.

Her eyesight was keen as an eagle's. But even without that, she could easily have seen that these men were not Kyivvan, pale-skinned and pale-haired. They were black of hair and brown of skin, and the one at the lead on the roan was as dark as Temur and had the same wooly quality to his uncovered hair, though this man's hair was a stormcloud. He was a fair enough rider, though not by any means properly one with his mount. The rest rode like demons—not like Qersnyk, tied into the saddle before they could walk, but like men who knew horses and had grown up around them.

Though men such as these should by rights have been riding the delicate, dish-nosed horses of the Asitaneh breed, their mounts were the Kyivvan breed, unmistakable round-bodied creatures with all the abundance of mane and tail that Qersnyk horses lacked. Edene had seen their like before, in the markets of Qarash when the Kyivvan traders came.

This was a mystery. As the ghulim jostled and pressed around her, groping under robes for scimitars and scythes, she raised a hand to hold them back, the Green Ring glinting in the warm gold sun. Her son was in his cradleboard, slung between her shoulders. She thought for a moment of handing him off to Ka-asha Ghul. But who could defend him better than the Lady of the Broken Places, and where under any sun could he be safer than he was upon her back?

The riders oncoming seemed to see her raised hand as a signal to them, and reined back—or perhaps they were only reacting sensibly to the sight of a valley and hillside covered in Edene's ghulim army. They had spread out side to side, marching across these open steppes, and the curving wings were in sight.

Edene stepped forward, descending the hill she had just climbed, and the ranks of the ghulim parted before her. The grass was trampled from so many feet and a strange, vast reluctance filled her. *Kill them before they destroy you. Kill them before they destroy your son.*

But there was the face of the man on the roan. There was the way the others lined up behind him, hands on the hilts of their scimitars, and how he in his own turn stayed them with a gesture. And there was the shape of his nose and the height of his brow, so familiar.

If this was not Temur's grandfather or his mother's brother, Edene would eat Ganjin's cradleboard.

As she reached the bottom of the hill, Besha Ghul stepped from the crush of bodies and reached for Edene's shoulder. Edene stayed the importunate gesture with a glare, then gritted her teeth in self-loathing as Besha responded with a self-abasing grovel.

It is the ring talking—

You must comport yourself as befits an empress! Allowing yourself to be pawed by jackals is hardly fitting.

The itch was there, strong in her. She almost drew back her foot to kick Besha Ghul in the ribs, or at least to spurn it with a boot, before shifting her weight to plant her foot more firmly. *I am what I am. Whatever I choose to do is fitting.*

She crouched down beside Besha and put a hand on its bony shoulder. "I am sorry," she said. "Please stand."

The ghul uncoiled slightly from its prostration, raising its head from its arms to blink dewy great eyes at Edene. Edene offered a hand, and Besha took it wincingly, hesitant to touch and even more hesitant to refuse.

Edene pulled it to its feet. "Come."

Together, they crossed the little swale at the bottom of the hill and started up a long gentle slope that the horsemen had paused upon. In a few moments, Edene stood before the roan.

To her surprise, the man on his back hastily dismounted and walked around the horse, trailing the reins from one hand. But of course, he was not a Qersnyk, and would not know that it was polite to greet a stranger from the saddle.

"Tsareg Edene?" He had a good voice. That wooly hair was shot with gray, and his skin up close had a freckled pattern like the roaning on his horse. Edene decided not to point it out to him.

She nodded.

"I am Ato Tesefahun. The child on your back is my great-grandchild. I have come to guide you to his father."

Edene pursed her lips, considering. Besha stood beside her, nearly shivering with nervousness. Edene offered the flat of her hand to the gelding. Of course this Wizard Tesefahun had not known enough to introduce her to the gelding too.

Besha spoke in her own language. "Wherever he is, the Grave Roads will take us there, if you still wish to seek him, Lady of Poison Things."

"Horses too?"

"Horses, if you wish it."

You cannot trust them. You are the Lady of Broken Places; you travel and fight alone.

Edene switched back to Qersnyk. "I'll need a mare," she said, not taking her eyes from Ato Tesefahun.

He smiled before he said, "We have several. May I know the name of my grandson?"

"He is called Re Ganjin," Edene said. She looked down at her boots. "I would tell you his true name if I knew it."

Ato Tesefahun's brows rose. "That sounds like a story."

"I can tell you underground." Edene pretended she did not relish the gleam of bewildered curiosity on his face as he tilted his head to one side.

IT WASN'T UNTIL THE DOOR SLID SHUT BEHIND TSECHEN-TSA AND NA-Baryan that Yangchen realized that she had never been alone in the imperial suite before. Previously, she had come here only in attendance upon Songtsan, who as the heir and emperor-in-waiting had occupied these chambers in anticipation of his majority.

Now they were hers. Hers, and Namri's, to do with as they—as *she*—pleased.

She stood within the doorway, her back to the frame, and just stared. As if she had never seen grandeur before. She finally gathered herself and walked into the apartment, letting her hand trail along this article of furniture and that. There was no dust on anything. All had been kept in readiness for her late husband's return.

She leaned her shoulders against the wall and stared at the empty bed, the hard pillows lined up against its head. She heard the door open but did not turn. She felt the warmth of Anil standing close against her shoulder and still did not acknowledge him.

He said, "I don't blame you for hating me."

She said, "It's not you I hate."

He just waited, while she stared away from him. Toward that empty bed. She was the Dowager Empress of Rasa. She could have him removed in an instant if she desired it.

She couldn't make herself desire it.

"You couldn't have done what you did without my failings," she said. "I opened the gate."

Damnation to say more. Damnation to say as much as she had. And yet the urge to tell him, to admit all the details of her naïve bargaining that had made it possible for all the evils that had befallen Tsarepheth to break through its wards, was blindingly strong.

"Come to bed," he said. "Then we can decide which room you wish to sacrifice to the nursery."

She leaned her head against him and smiled. "You don't hate me."

"A woman who would not leave me to face a sorcerer-assassin alone? There is nothing to hate there."

She sighed. "I miss Shuffle."

"You miss the freedom. Now that we're here, you're picking a fight not because you are angry at me, but because you're angry at yourself."

She stepped back and glared at him. "I'm sure you're very wise, Doctor Anil. Now leave me."

He turned to the door. Wizard or not, she could have him dismembered for disobedience. Every step he took burned in her lungs, in the corners of her eyes.

His hand was on the latch when she said, "No. I cannot bear it. Anil, come to bed. I . . . I need you. I need your counsel. I have an empire to run."

He turned back, squinting with mirth and relief. Startled, she saw that it had been as hurtful for him to walk away as for her to send him. "What about our argument?"

"I am sure," she said, "that it will still be there in the morning."

✳   ✳   ✳

Master War did not return. Hsiung kept his head bowed, his sore body slowly congealing around its immobility. Eventually, a novice came to bring Hsiung to the baths—he could stand only with assistance, though the steam and scraping helped his locked muscles to release—and then to clothe him. The robes laid before him were dull yellow, onion-dyed. The belt was plain homespun, with no color in it.

Seeing this, Hsiung's heart gave a strange, sad-glad leap. He put a hand to his mouth, wishing there were someone he could ask.

But no.

He would have to accept the evidence, and the evidence suggested that the Wretched Mountain Temple had not expelled him. Though apparently he would have to start over again from the very beginning.

When he was clothed, they fed him—millet and vegetables—and the novice led him to a pallet. Still no words had passed between them: the novice would be required not to speak unless spoken to. And Brother Hsiung, of course, could not speak.

And was a novice again himself, in any case.

The novice left him there, in a bare wickerwork cell just long enough to stretch out in and just tall enough to stand. He could touch the opposite walls if he extended his arms. There was nothing for Hsiung here except his forms, or sleep—and he did not know yet if he was permitted to sleep.

Slowly, limited by the size of the space, he began to take himself through his daily meditation. He wobbled with tiredness; he was careful and precise. His muscles ached, but with the movement they gradually softened.

He was two-thirds done when a shadow fell across the empty doorway. It was Master War, but since the master did not enter Hsiung's penitent's quarters, Hsiung continued his forms. When he finished, he stood trembling, and could not raise his eyes to the master's.

"The masters have read your letter and discussed it," Master War said.

That brought Hsiung's head up, hope and anxiety flaring. He waited silently; the hardest silence of so many.

Master War took a breath and frowned. Then, as if considering each word, he slowly said, "Rest, Brother Hsiung. There will be no war before spring, and in any case we must make preparations."

18

LONG BEFORE THE SNOWS MADE TRAVEL IMPOSSIBLE, THE WIND OFF THE steppe grew killing cold. The clans had withdrawn into Qarash's walls, or had left for their winter ranges. Al-Sepehr might have raged inwardly at the delay—winter was no impediment to war in the Rahazeen wastes, rather making them easier to navigate—but if he did so, he buried it deep. Even Saadet barely suspected his anger, studying him across the council table. It was where she saw him now, almost exclusively, except for his occasional and inexplicable absences.

They were ameliorated by the gift he brought back for her from one such trip: a breech-loading rifle, an elegant wand of metal two thirds as tall as she, with a flintlock mechanism and a supply of wadding, powder, and balls. She took to carrying it with her, especially on the hunt. It was a wonderful tool, accurate as far as she could see, and she learned very quickly to steady it and use it in the saddle. The Qersnyk she rode with laughed at her—what good was a weapon you could shoot only once?—but even Esen admired its range.

In truth, Shahruz sulked under the neglect worse than Saadet did.

She was distracted. Her time was taken up with those council meetings, with learning to rule, and with learning the Qersnyk arts that would let her subjects see her as a fitting Khatun. She was coming to love the stride of her gray mare under her, the tension that was almost-pain of her eagle's talons against her fist, the wind so cold it blinded.

Determined to match any Qersnyk woman, she rode until the eighth month of what would have been her confinement in any civilized land. Often her rides were taken with the brothers Esen and Paian flanking her—warrior and shaman-rememberer, the two extremes of the Qersnyk culture. Between them, they could answer any question she might have—and she had many.

The pregnancy troubled her little. Saadet had witnessed the miseries of other women, but she experienced few of those. Instead, she felt flushed with strength and well-being. Esen was not the only one to tell her she glowed.

As the twins had caused the palace to be reclaimed and cleaned, al-Sepehr imported some few of his comforts from Ala-Din—Rahazeen men, though they wore their veils wrapped like sashes here and wore gloves over their tattooed hands, and Rahazeen women, who knew how to cook the food and make the music of home. Saadet sometimes slipped into the comfort of the harem that her adopted father had established to hear them play and sing. Shahruz never spoke to her when she did so.

As she grew more gravid, the winter more fierce, and her life more constrained, Shahruz abandoned her almost completely. She could not blame him, she supposed. She could not blame a man for wanting to divorce himself from the awkward realities of her pregnant, female, sacred body with its sacred impositions. Hunger and the inability to eat, simultaneously. Her ever-shifting balance. Her feet that swelled like an old woman's. Her bladder, and her constant and humiliating need to piss.

Still, the Qersnyk seemed not to care about those things. To them, she was a bearing woman. Mothers-to-be were meant to be celebrated and spoiled, the minor inconveniences of her condition accepted with humor: honored rather than held as evidence of physical frailty and a woman's sacred unsuitedness to worldly concerns. She sought out their company more and more.

She felt as if she navigated behind a plow, as if her belly were a great curved share that cut conversations and turned them to other topics before she could arrive. The joy and ease never left her, but anticipation outshone them. She could not wait to be delivered, and she felt herself a little sad that the herbs al-Sepehr had given her to dose herself with ensured she would birth a boy.

She discovered that she would have preferred a daughter.

Although it was late spring by anyone's reckoning but a Qersnyk, she was brought to childbed—not that the Qersnyk approach to birthing involved a bed—in the midst of a tremendous blizzard, as so often happens. Following the Qersnyk tradition, it was the shaman-rememberer Paian who attended her, along with two of al-Sepehr's blind wives. Al-Sepehr might have waited in the antechamber with propriety by either nation's standards, especially (to the Qersnyk way of thinking) in the absence of a father in the birthing room, but he chose to busy himself with other duties.

Shahruz absented himself from the proceedings as well, though Saadet called for him again and again. He didn't approve of men in the birthing room, even if that man were a shaman-rememberer. He certainly wouldn't be there himself to witness his sister's disgrace as she crouched, Qersnyk-style, clutching the ornately silver-gilt birthing-frame with its carvings of running mares.

The birth was as easy as the pregnancy had been. No more than a quarter of the day had passed in labor when Saadet's child slipped into Paian's hands. While she still strained to bring forth the afterbirth, he slipped the lustily wailing babe from its membranes, laid it in a nest of clean lamb's wool, and squeezed the cord with fingers that knew milking, so the blood would be in the child instead of on the floor. As warmth surrounded it, the babe's screams subsided.

Then, as Saadet finished with the afterbirth, he collected that—there would be a ceremony, she vaguely knew—and allowed the women to help her to a pallet. As they washed the blood from her thighs, she turned to Paian. "My son?" she asked.

Paian's mouth flickered momentarily into a stricken frown, an expression she had never seen on the face of a shaman-rememberer. "Khatun—"

She raised herself on her elbows. "My son."

He lifted the wool-swaddled child in the crook of his arm and came to crouch beside her. Servants were entering the room now, on what signal she had not seen, to disassemble the birthing-frame and carry the bloody rags and water away. Saadet extended her arms, but Paian did not immediately place the child in them.

"Paian," she said.

He turned to the nearest servant. "Clear the room," he said, and waited while they led the blind wives out and further excused themselves. Saadet waited, sick horror growing inside her. *There is something wrong with the child!* She pictured a monster, malformed, with a cleft lip or an exposed spine. So many things could go wrong, and now she cursed herself for failing to prepare herself.

If I had considered this in advance, it might not have happened. I could have prayed against it. Even as the thought formed, she knew it was ridiculous.

You are hysterical, her brother said.

She did not wish him to think her weak. Breath by breath, she calmed herself. "Is there something wrong?" she asked, proud that her voice did not shake.

Let them think her weak.

Paian smiled. "Not wrong," he said. "But you were not Qersnyk, and it may take a little while for you to understand. Your son is . . ." He shook his head. "It is a thing that has happened only once before, so long ago the truth of it is lost in legends."

"*Paian,*" she said, desperately.

He opened the loose robe the women had draped around her, baring her ribcage and one breast. The room was warm; there were braziers set at every corner.

He lifted the child from its swaddlings, supporting the overlarge head, and Saadet could see that the blood was drying sticky on its skin. Dimly, she remembered that it was her task, if she was capable, to wash the birth fluids from it. Her eyes took it in: tiny red fists, strangely cylindrical newborn's body writhing, face screwed up in wrath as the babe screamed its displeasure at being once more exposed. *Anyone would think it was being boiled, from the fuss.*

All the parts in place, except—

"Your son is Khagan," Paian said. "But he is also a shaman-rememberer."

Saadet blinked, reached out, let her hand fall back. "It can't be a girl!"

"It is not a girl," said Paian.

He laid the naked babe upon her belly and drew the robe closed over both of them. Saadet was almost too startled to help guide the child to her breast. Paian showed her how to press her nipple to its lips; she felt a sweet, dazed relief as it took the teat and began, reflexively, to suck instead of screaming.

"He's determined to be no trouble at all," Paian said.

"He!"

"He. Your son is a boy, born as I was born, in a body that honors Mother Night. I recognize this as the shaman-rememberer who tended my birth recognized me. Congratulations, Khatun. The portents attending the birth of your son are strong indeed."

Saadet leaned back against the pillows and tried to think, to plan. To understand. She was sliding under a wave of exhaustion.

"Send for my father," she said, and let her eyes close gently.

SHE HAD BARELY RISEN FROM CHILDBED, STILL SICK AND DIZZY WITH LOST blood and a clout wrapped between her legs to soak up whatever might drop out of her, when al-Sepehr entered the room unheralded. He came to where she sat, supported by an ox-yoke chair, and made an elaborate pretense of kneeling before her. She sensed his discomfort in the angle of his shoulders, the way his body wished to lean away from her even as he forced it close.

Paian had told him, then.

He said, "Is this my grandson?" in a rush that told her how he had practiced the words, in order to get them out without choking on them.

She nodded, trying to appear gracious, suspecting she only looked tired. The baby in her arms scrunched its face up as al-Sepehr rose and bent over both of them. He touched the baby's face, something that could have been mistaken for a smile bending his mouth as it turned reflexively to suckle the finger.

"Have you named him?"

"Re Tsaagan Buqa," she said. She had the unworthy desire to snatch her child away from its grandfather, and managed to limit herself to a quick, grasping ripple of her fingers on the swaddled babe. She ached all over; she did not care to receive anyone. She wanted to lie down.

Al-Sepehr perched on the arm of the chair, looming over her. She wanted to lean away from him, and chastised herself before Shahruz could do it for her. *He is your father. He is the head of your order. You will treat him with respect!*

She said, "I trust you are well?"

"An emissary has come from Kyiv," he said. "They will send us troops in the spring, when travel becomes possible again. They support us, in that we oppose Re Temur and his poisonous witch."

Saadet sat silently, digesting what he said. Of course Edene had killed dozens, burned an entire village. How did that compare to al-Sepehr releasing his blood ghosts on the residents of this very keep?

The Rahazeen sky overhead told her that the Scholar-God, at least, was moved to support them. Maybe. Or at least, not oppose what they did in Her name.

She said, "How did a rider come through the snow?"

It was shoulder-deep on a tall mare, and drifted in the lowest windows of the keep and houses if they were left unshuttered.

Al-Sepehr smiled. "I do not require riders for news to find me."

"Your djinn."

"Not mine. I am only lucky to command him a little. Kara Mehmed Caliph will send us men as well, in thanks for our assistance in claiming his own royal seat."

"And out of fear we might take it away from him," Saadet sniped.

Al-Sepehr leaned slightly, touching one shoulder to the chair's backrest. He did not seem at ease. "Love is based in fear," he said complacently. "Fear of loss, or fear of pain. Let all love us, then, and hope we do not take from them what our strength would make easy."

Our trickery, you mean. But Saadet held her tongue on this topic, and only nodded. She had other subjects to broach while they were alone.

"We cannot hold Qersnyk," she said.

"We do not have to."

She blinked. "It is my . . . my son's life if we do not."

"Fear not for your . . . son."

"You have not asked to hold him."

Al-Sepehr's face twisted in a disdainful grimace, but he smoothed it quickly.

"He is your grandson, after a fashion. Will you not give him your blessing, as al-Sepehr?"

He folded his arms. She was not sure he knew he'd done it. "You must not fear, Saadet. My . . . *your* advisors think that if anything his . . . condition will rally more Qersnyk to us. Paian tells me that a shaman-rememberer to the north, beyond the range of this storm and beyond the range of the Rahazeen sky, has seen his moon in the sky. He is a true heir to the Khaganate. And other messengers tell me that your son's rival is attended by portents of ill omen—a ghost-colored colt, apparently, which these barbarians interpret as evidence of divine wrath."

"Esen tells me another skinless corpse was discovered, frozen in a drift, within the walls of Qarash."

"This is so," al-Sepehr said complacently. He patted her arm. "You need not worry yourself about it. All will be well—"

She lowered her voice. She whispered harshly, "If anything can unite our enemies against us, it is the specter of Sepehr's return!"

He stood. He patted her shoulder, still leaning awkwardly away. He said, "Does it matter if they unite against us, if our founder *does* return? If he returns, I should say, with the same power of belief behind him as the Scholar-God? As the Mother Dragon? As the primitive sky idol of these fetishistic barbarians?"

Involuntarily, she felt her arm tightening around Tsaagan Buqa. Her other hand rose to make a fist and press against her breastbone. "You believe this can work?"

"How are gods born?" al-Sepehr said. "They are born out of belief. Why should our prophet enjoy less status than some lightskirt wench renowned for her necklaces?"

Saadet felt her lips numb. She knew the strangeness in her head for shock, and blood loss, and exhaustion. Still, al-Sepehr's gaze bored into her, and she knew what was expected. "For the Nameless," she managed.

He smiled with a tutor's pride. "For the world."

SAMARKAR HAD EXPERIENCED WINTERS AS MILD AS THIS ONE BEFORE, BUT not since she was married to a prince in Song. Temur said he had known one or two the same, all here among the sheltering limestone towers of Song. Early on in the season, a steady trickle of Qersnyk—unattached men, and a few clans and families—had arrived to muster to Temur's banner. They were mostly better off than the refugees that already populated the valley, and Samarkar was kept busy negotiating the conflicts that inevitably arose between them, and between the Qersnyk and the Rasani, and between the Qersnyk, the Rasani, and the local farmers and peasantry who farmed the hills above Dragon Lake.

It surprised Samarkar how swiftly life in the encampment assumed a rhythm. The local residents, after the first nervous delegation, seemed to accept the army camped on the other side of the lake as business as usual. Temur and Samarkar made every attempt to see to it that they were not harassed. Of course, there were incidents . . . but this was one case where the dearth of young men in Re Temur Khagan's army proved an advantage.

It remained a challenge to keep everyone fed. Rations were tight—but the proximity of the farms and town meant there *was* trade, and the lake was full of fish. Temur's people got thin, to be sure, and more than one old mare past working found her way, regretfully, into a stew pot.

In the gaps between snows, retainers appeared to declare their loyalty to Temur—whole clans with children and carts in tow; lone men riding one mare and leading another as the sum total of their worldly wealth. They came, and kept coming. Some of them, Temur greeted by name. Some, he welcomed only guardedly.

The most surprising—and one of the most welcome—was Temur's cousin Re Chagatai, at the head of fifty well-armed and mounted men: survivors of Temur's brother's ill-fated army and the battle of Qarash where Temur himself had nearly died. Chagatai favored his mother Nilufer, tall and straight-spined with an imperious expression and features that were a blend of West and East. He was a dour-seeming man, face lined with worry—or perhaps it was just the exhaustion of travel.

Most surprising of all, he brought with him a great steppe eagle, which he presented to Temur with some ceremony when he was brought to Temur's white-house. Samarkar stood beside and a little behind Temur Khagan, hands folded in the warmth of her sleeves, and watched as the hooded bird was paraded past on a perch carried by two skinny boys. Samarkar smiled at Chagatai's concealed pleasure, evidenced only by a flicker in his frown, when Temur conveyed Nilufer's regards to him—but that didn't change the fact that all this ceremony left her with a combination of nostalgia and unease. She wished she were in a room somewhere with her books, and Temur to look forward to over dinner.

But it seemed that there was no escaping a life of politics for this once-princess. The world knew what she was good at, whether she loved it or not, and brought it to her door.

Eventually, the trickle of new arrivals became a drip, and the drip died out entirely as winter hardened over the land. It was not a bad winter, not by steppe standards and not by Rasani ones—there was forage for the beasts, and hay to be traded for—but it was bad enough. Whenever they sent scouts out of the protected bowl of the valley surrounding Dragon Lake, those riders returned with tales of snow drifted impassably high, even for the horses, and the roar of winds bitter enough to stun mount as well as man.

Samarkar and Temur passed their time with making the acquaintance of their new people, Rasan as well as Qersnyk, and watching Afrit grow with a speed that caused even more mutters.

By midwinter he was taller than a yearling, and starting to put on muscle around his haunches, shoulders, and neck. Though he stayed preternaturally slender, even gaunt, he grew hard. The glistening color of his coat, brighter and slightly more golden than the drifts of snow he played in, gleamed in the winter sun. He was so pale that the whiteness of his stockings and blaze was only readily visible when the light struck him just so.

Samarkar grew to understand and accept what Temur had already known; this was no natural foal. He was a messenger, something sent. The only question was what message his existence was intended to convey. And who precisely had delivered it.

The Qersnyk wouldn't tend the mare and the unlucky colt, so Samarkar took care of it when Temur was otherwise engaged. Which was rarely: He made time for Bansh and Afrit no matter how busy he was with the chafing rituals of his new status. He did not mind the hunts—which were nearly the only time they saw Hrahima, these days—and Bansh seemed to glory in her fine new saddle and the leopardskin trappings that glowed black and gold against her radiant liver-bay coat. Temur had caused a chamfron of gilded steel and cabochon rubies to be made, to protect her face in battle, but the armor was not yet ready; she made do with less regal furniture for now.

Temur was less thrilled with the trappings of *his* office, the elaborate clothing and the rituals. Samarkar sensed his frustration, but she counseled him to tolerate it. To look a Khagan, so he would not be mistaken for anything else.

At least he finally had a bow made to fit him, replacing—half-reluctantly—the one he had scavenged from the battlefield at Qarash, which had saved their lives so often on the road. That one hung in a place of honor over the household altar, where Samarkar and Temur mingled icons to the Eternal Sky, Mother Night, and Samarkar's more favored among the Six Thousand Small Gods and the Six Hundred Great Gods of Rasa—the Mother Dragon and all her manifold children.

Samarkar even had a new coat or two—less elaborate than the ones she had brought from Rasa, but also less threadbare. Material goods were not the issue, though arms and armament were scarce. There were barely enough mares to keep them all in airag, and not a lot of that for anyone. Samarkar knew that Temur worried about horses; about getting *enough* horses. And about getting the *right* horses to fulfill his pledge to assemble a Sacred Herd.

Temur's horses—Bansh and Afrit, Jerboa, and the other mares who were slowly beginning to be tithed to the Khagan—lived in a corral near the edge of the encampment, not far from the sinkhole they had skirted on the way in. The Qersnyk had built an offering pile nearby, for devotions to the Eternal Sky. It looked to the uneducated eye like a heap of rubble wound through with scraps of blue cloth, but Samarkar had seen Jurchadai and the other shaman-rememberers riding circles around it at sunset and sunrise. She noticed because Samarkar often accompanied Temur out to the corral when he tended Bansh and Afrit, to see how Temur handled the horses.

And, if she admitted it to herself, to spend time with only Temur and the horses.

THE DARK WINGS OF A LAZY VULTURE FLOATED HIGH IN THE SKY ON A CRISP still day. Samarkar leaned against the makeshift gate of the makeshift paddock and said to Temur, beside her, "What if you sold him?"

Temur twisted his head—she was standing on the side that it was easier for him to turn to—and frowned. "We don't sell horses."

"I know," she said. "But you could finance a lot of war with that one pony. And he could go to someone who wouldn't have to navigate superstitions about his color." She gestured to where the creamy-gold colt stood beside his mother, his chin resting on her withers. "Or how fast he's growing."

"Hmph." Temur's lips scrunched together in a way that said he was thinking. "I've already proclaimed my reign as belonging to the Ghost Stud. Even if I didn't need him for my Sacred Herd, that would be a problem. Barring that, I could send him as a friendship gift to some Song prince, but the politics of which one would be awkward. That at least wouldn't alienate my people by the break in tradition."

She found herself looking at him with more respect than she had expected and felt bad about it. "Smart."

He shrugged. "I do watch, you know."

"Why is ghost-sorrel an unlucky color?"

He nibbled on the seam of his glove because he could not reach the fingernail. "I never thought about it."

The curiosity that had led her to the Wizard's Citadel stirred. "Think now."

"All the palest colors are unlucky. There is milk-white, which is the white that can produce other colors. And snow-white, which is the white that can produce spotted foals. They're a little unlucky, but it can be averted with charms and paint. And there is ghost-cream, ghost-sorrel, and ghost-bay, which are...." He shrugged, helplessly. "All other things being equal, a black horse bred to a ghost horse produces a smoke-colored horse. A bay horse bred to a ghost horse produces a phantom, a golden horse with a black mane. A chestnut horse bred to a ghost horse produces the color called pearl, a golden horse with a cream-colored mane. But the foal of two ghost horses is always ghost, and the foal of, say, a pearl horse and a smoke horse *might* be ghost. Or it might be a strong color. They're not unlucky in themselves. Just not bred to other horses that can produce ghosts."

"You're saying it might be unlucky because it . . . pulls the color out of the foal?"

The sweet scent of burning yak dung wafted over them as the wind shifted: someone's hearth. He shook his head. "Some white foals, and some ghost foals, are born dead. Or too weak to stand. Or—worst— born strong, and waste away. And some white mares cannot be got in foal."

"You said that Afrit was impossible."

He nodded. "Bansh could produce a pearl foal, or a phantom-colored foal, if bred to a stallion who could influence her thus. She might produce a black foal. Possibly a chestnut, though some bay mares never do. But she would have to be phantom-colored herself, and bred to a phantom or pearl stud, to produce a ghost-sorrel colt."

"It's complicated," she said. "Your horse-breeding is a kind of wizardry of its own."

He rubbed his chin with his palm and changed the subject. "I miss Hsiung."

Samarkar breathed deep. "He will be along with the thaw," she said, and tried to believe it.

He might have said more, or he might have turned away and looked elsewhere, but a big flutter of feathers drew their attention. Samarkar ducked reflexively and summoned light. Temur came close to doing the former, even though the beat of wings was nothing at all like the enormous storm of wind and thunder of pinions that surrounded the descent of the Rukh.

Instead, a peacock sailed low across the paddock fences, though not close enough to the mares to spook them. Afrit, with all the high spirits of any colt, kicked up his heels and followed, kicking his way through the drifts of snow. The peacock even was more striking than the general run of his species—snow white, with eyes like split coal, he was whiter by a great deal than Afrit or the trampled snow.

The bird lighted in an overhanging tree. Samarkar pointed with her chin, Qersnyk style. They were rubbing off on her. "Is that an omen too?"

"It startled me," Temur said. "I've never seen one that color before."

"Not even here?"

"Especially not here, I'd say."

The peacock screamed like a murdered child and Samarkar shuddered. She and Temur leaned their shoulders together. Samarkar broke the companionable silence first. "You think al-Sepehr will wait for a nice convenient war in spring?"

"I don't know," Temur said.

"He could just send the Rukh after us."

"He only has the one," said Temur. "Better to wait out winter, when he can offer the poor thing some ground support. . . . Samarkar, what's that?"

Beyond the paddock, along the road that would bring them to the Dragon Road if they should follow it, more than a dozen shaggy, stocky horses were being led up over the edge of the sinkhole by a group of figures who mostly wore coats tailored in the Asitaneh style. One or two wore hooded robes in rich colors that recollected agate stones, and behind the horses more hooded figures toiled up the slope from below—heads, then shoulders, then spare awkward bodies.

They were silhouetted against the snow, making it hard to pick out detail, but she could see that the hooded figures moved in an awkward, inhuman manner—and that they and the coated men were all led by a mounted woman, with a cradleboard slung on the saddle by her knee.

An army, perhaps. But not one currently bent on conquest.

Samarkar felt Temur stiffen. His fingers dug into her forearm. When she moved her gloved hand to cover his, she imagined she could feel the cold through layers of hide and fur. Something rushed past them, a shaggy bearlike beast—the great dog Sube, barking exultantly, wagging his tail as if he might take flight.

Before Samarkar had even finished turning to him, Temur pulled away again and plunged toward the army coming down on them, raising as much joyful noise as the dog.

THE HORSE WAS A SOLID, FIT-LOOKING BLUE ROAN WITH A NEAR-BLACK FACE and thick, curly coat like a clipped sheep. Fine as the gelding was, it was the figure on his back—perched high in the Kyivvan saddle with its moderate pommel and center joint—who held Temur's undivided attention. She was dressed in armor such as he had never seen, the metal red as fire and wreathed in petals of a rising crimson light like an aurora, like a flame.

Over it, she wore an open robe, soft and dark red. Her helm was strapped at her knee, and the hood of her robe lay in folds upon her shoulders, revealing dark hair braided around her head, bright eyes gleaming from between tight lids, and cheeks less plump than when last he had seen her. They both, he thought, looked the worse for travel.

She sat as if perfectly calm, queenly, hands folded over her reins, watching the dog and the man run toward her. Sube outstripped

Temur, bounding forward on great blond paws. He was five leaps from her when her composure broke and she slid from the saddle with all a girl's tumbledown grace, landing crouched in the snow. She held out her arms, the reins still trailing from her left hand, the roan gelding stamping one hoof as a warning to the dog.

That was not why the dog suddenly planted his feet and skidded to a halt in the snow. Sube's ears flattened. His haystack of a coat was too thick to bristle, but the wild wagging stopped as his tail drooped and stiffened. The growl that rumbled from his throat shuddered Temur's chest like a drum.

"Sube, no!" he shouted, as the dog stood his ground, crouched as if he faced a wolf, and growled to shake the earth apart.

The roan was having none of it. He lunged back against the reins and would have pulled Edene off her feet if she had not chosen to go with him, using his momentum to jump back and grab the stirrup. Someone else—one of the men in the Asitaneh coats—was on the roan's other side, catching the bridle and throwing an arm around his neck. The horse stamped and whinnied, a clear threat. And Edene stood between them, uncertain of which way to turn.

"Sube!" she said, not sharply but broken, and Temur wondered what it was like to come home after nearly a year to be growled at by your own dog. He laid a glove on Sube's heavy ruff, curling fingers into the matted fur so the dog could feel his hold, and spoke in a soothing murmur. Nonsense, the sort of words you used on dogs and horses when all that mattered was the tone. *Don't you know Edene, hush now, see it's a friend.*

The gelding quieted, though his ears stayed up, his nostrils flaring pink, his gaze steady on the dog. Sube dropped in the snow, his elbows hovering—not a relaxed "down" but a position that said *I won't start anything, and you had better not.* He betrayed no interest in the horse; all his attention was for the woman.

Temur had crouched when the dog did. Now, as Edene stepped away from her half-soothed horse, he let himself rise. He felt Samarkar at his back, felt something hanging in the air between them—and between the two of them and Edene. A tension, a prickling sensation like that which filled the air when, somewhere above, lightning was waiting. His own voice echoed in his ear, words that he had spoken beneath a mountain and heard since in his dreams: *I am Re Temur. I will help you fight your Rahazeen warlord, Hrahima. And I will take back from him in turn what he first took from me. And then I will come back and see Qori Buqa put out of the place that was rightfully my brother's.*

A spark seemed to hang in the air before him, a thing *like* a bright spark, though it gave no light. It bridged the gap between Temur and Edene, filled his chest with light. He reached out a hand to her.

Leaving her gelding to the man in the Asitaneh coat, she extended her own hand and came, the cold flames of her armor burning all around her.

Sube did not growl again; this time the great dog whined, a sound of such distress and agony that Samarkar came to him running, high-footed and awkward as a horse prancing through drifts. She knelt in the snow and threw her arms around his neck; Temur took three steps forward and threw his arms around Edene.

Under her robes and the mail, she was thin. Bony-shouldered, not dressed for the cold, though it seemed not even to have damasked her cheeks. When Temur pulled her close, even through his coat he felt her chill; those flames had no warmth at all. He hugged her tight, heedless of the snow that dusted them both, calling for tea, ready to sweep her into his arms and carry her back to the tent. The hard fear in his chest was bitter as a dagger; even in this mild and sheltered valley, you could die of the cold.

But she put her cold hand, naked but for a ring, against his face, and laid her cheek by his.

"Shhh," she said. "Re Temur Khagan, I am fine."

"Edene—"

"You have seen his moon," she said. "Now let me introduce you to your son."

Temur ripped his eyes from her drawn face, so pale with chill. He laid his glove against her face. "My son."

"Re Ganjin."

"Of course." He found himself, suddenly, all made bones and elbows fitted together seemingly at random. While she went to the saddle and lifted down the cradleboard, he fidgeted. Samarkar leaned her shoulder against him and he settled, but then Edene was back, lifting a bundle from the cradleboard, holding it out in her arms.

His hands shaking, Temur took the child. Ganjin was heavier than he expected, like a hawk on his glove, and swaddled up so that Temur could see nothing of him but squinched up eyes, pursed pink mouth, a rounded bump of a nose.

He set Ganjin in the crook of his arm and gazed down at this tiny person—real, alive, aware—and then up across him at Edene. She had that familiar compressed smile he knew so well.

"Our son," Temur said. "How is it possible?"

Edene laughed, head thrown back amid the flames of her eldritch armor. "Well," she said, "when a warrior and a maiden love each other very much—"

"Wench," he answered, grinning. Ganjin was so quiet Temur kept checking to make sure he was breathing, still. He laid his left hand on Samarkar's shoulder. He did not need to glance down to know that she was looking at him and Edene, her face as carefully blank as only a once-princess's could be. "I have someone to introduce you to as well, Edene."

"Can it wait until we're warm?" Tesefahun asked, from astride a rangy brown. "My old belly could use some tea."

Edene stepped back. "Of course, you know your grandfather, Temur Khagan," she said. "Now you must meet my ghulim, too."

19

THREE MEN, TWO WOMEN, AND A KNOTTED SILENCE SURROUNDED THE BRA-
zier at the center of the Khagan's yellow white-house. They waited awkwardly while Edene made tea. Temur still held his son in the crook of his
left elbow. Tesefahun sat cross-legged on his left, quilted coat stretched
across his knees. The man who had been Uthman Caliph and who was
now called Iskandar sat across the coals, leaving a gap for Edene when
she should finally come to rest. Samarkar knelt on Temur's right, smoothing the heavy black cotton of her new six-petaled coat down her thighs.
The tailor had edged it with yellow tape. Temur wondered if she knew
it was the Khagan's color.

Probably. Samarkar knew nearly everything.

He had already sent for and then sent away Edene's cousins, Oljei and
Toragana, and her little sister Sarangerel. Edene had been strange and
distant, as if distracted. That reunion had been tearful and rushed, and he
and Edene had both had to promise that her family would have her to
themselves for an extended period before too long. But for now, this was
his reunion with her, and his introduction to his son.

He had held babies before. You couldn't grow up among the clans
without being pressed into childcare as soon as you were old enough to
be trusted to keep a toddler from wandering into a fire. But there was

something new and wonderful and calming about the warm weight of his own child in his arms—so big! Not a newborn anymore at all! All the anxious silences in the world could not quite destroy the effect of this sweet quiet.

He smiled to himself. That would last until Ganjin awoke and began crying. For the moment, the only sound in the white-house was Edene humming softly to herself as she measured tea, yak butter, salt—and waited for the water to boil. She moved deftly, as if she had never left the steppe, despite the soft drape of the red wool of her robes. Despite how strange it was, seeing her in foreign clothes. He missed her embroidered coats and her trousers, the way the strength of her thighs stretched against the fabric when she rode. The robes hid her body, concealed the changes that nearly a year apart had wrought. But he could still see by her collarbones and wrists that she was thin.

Samarkar picked at the stitching that held the yellow finishing tape around her hem. Temur reached out and grasped her left hand with his right. She turned to him, eyebrows arching, forehead wrinkled in surprise. He winked over a corner of a smile. *It will be fine.*

Until Edene poured and distributed the tea, and Ato Tesefahun took a single sharp, resigned breath and began to explain the gravity of the situation in Kyiv, Temur almost managed to make himself believe it.

Unfortunately, Tesefahun's years of experience as a political creature made him excel at explaining just how thoroughly al-Sepehr had walled them into a tower with regard to finding allies in Kyiv. As he reached the part of the narrative with the djinn, Edene—now kneeling between Samarkar and Iskandar—lifted her head.

Tesefahun was already looking at her, which was how Temur knew they'd rehearsed this. Well, wearing their saddles, he would have shared information too. "The djinn is not al-Sepehr's willing servant," she said. "I would almost say that al-Sepehr does not *have* willing servants, but he has his Nameless, and his wives. The rest are dupes, or enslaved. From Qori Buqa to the Rukh."

"The Rukh?" asked Samarkar.

"Al-Sepehr keeps her mate chained. Wing-clipped. It was my duty to care for him while I was his captive, too."

"How did you escape?" Temur asked.

Edene flicked the edge of her cup with her nail, cheek muscles moving as if she chewed her words. She didn't speak immediately, but all in the white-house knew she was not done. They waited.

Seeing that Edene's cup was empty, Samarkar disengaged her hand from Temur's. She lifted the heavy cast-iron pot from its warming plate beside the brazier and poured carefully. Edene glanced at her through her lashes, a quick curious glance.

"Thank you," she said.

She raised the cup and drank, sighing when she was done as if some bone-deep ache had eased. Qersnyk tea from a Qersnyk cup; after his travels, Temur understood the simple ease of it. She twisted the green ring on her finger—the ring that Temur had never seen before—and said, as if the words hurt, "Some of his enemies may be dupes as well."

"You mean what happened in Stechko," Tesefahun said.

"Yes."

Suddenly, Temur realized what had gone unsaid. "Grandfather. I have . . . Ill news."

Tesefahun looked at him mildly, freckled old face resigned.

Temur had to close his eyes to continue. "My mother . . . your daughter, Ashra. Gave her life in Tsarepheth fighting a terrible plague."

After a little time, Tesefahun said, "Damn," and looked away.

"I made a vow," Temur said. "To remove al-Sepehr from power. I have not forgotten it." He glanced at Iskandar. "I'll remove his allies from power, too."

Iskandar nodded. He looked at Edene. "You have not answered the question of how you escaped."

She said, "I stole this ring from him."

Edene held up her hand and she vanished—as if someone had wiped her image with a cloth from Temur's eyes. He started to his feet, clutching Ganjin against his chest reflexively. A mistake; he woke the child, and the child began to wail.

Then Edene was there beside him, apologetically hushing her son, apologetically regretting her grand gesture. Samarkar was on her feet as well, standing a half-stride back, uncertainly, while Edene tried to demonstrate to Temur how to quiet the child. When they finally had Ganjin hushed and set to Edene's breast—Iskandar, his complexion watery with the depth of his discomfort, would not look in their direction while Edene's robe was open—Edene sighed and apologized once more.

"You stole a ring that turns you invisible."

"It does more than that," said Tesefahun, as Edene chewed her lip again. "It is the Green Ring of Erem. Danupati's Ring. It grants dominion over poison creatures and over the creatures of Erem."

"Like the ghulim."

Edene nodded. "But now I think al-Sepehr intended me to steal it. I think he intended me to use it. The powers of Erem. . . . It turns out," she said regretfully, "that they are not much good for anything but causing war."

Samarkar glanced at Tesefahun. "Speaking of Danupati. Has Tesefahun told you about what else al-Sepehr stole?"

He shook his head. "It didn't come up."

"Do you know about the curse of Danupati?"

"It's death to disturb his bones—"

"No," said Samarkar. "Not exactly."

She resumed her seat on the thick woolen carpets by the fire, and Temur and Edene also returned to their places, Edene now with Ganjin tucked inside her robe. Iskandar seemed more comfortable with her seated beside him; his gaze had a natural place to rest that was not on her bosom. Edene picked up her cup again and gestured Samarkar to continue.

"It's *war* to disturb his bones. War in all the realms he once claimed as his empire."

"That's the whole world!"

"Except the farthest west and north, it is—"

"And south," Tesefahun interrupted. "There are lands beyond Aezin that never fell under his sway."

Samarkar's gesture acknowledged and dismissed his footnote both at once. "Half the world, then."

Edene glanced down at her ring. "Al-Sepehr got this ring somehow. From Danupati's grave?"

Temur said, "He also took Danupati's skull."

"He wants us to chew each other up," Iskandar said bitterly. "Then he can pick over the gnawed bones at his leisure."

Edene did not take her eyes from Temur. "Do you know where the grave was?"

Temur felt as if his chin jerked up and down on a stick.

"Well, that's easy, then!" Anyone else might not have heard the irony in Edene's voice, but even on the other side of a separation Temur knew her well. "We steal the skull back, free the djinn and the Rukh, return the ring and the skull to the grave of Danupati, and what does al-Sepehr have left to bring against us?"

They looked at one another, hushed as snow.

Then Iskandar stretched, cracked his neck, and said, "Armies." He stretched his fingers against one another. "One of them used to be mine."

AFTER THE COUNCIL, THE WIZARD SAMARKAR TOOK CHARGE OF THE drowsy Ganjin and herded the other men outside, leaving Edene and Temur alone in the white-house. It was a gesture Edene would have expected from a sister-wife, not a rival. That, and the tea, and Temur's obvious trust in the Rasani sorcerer were the reasons Edene chose to let her leave with Ganjin in her arms. Well, and she did not think that Tesefahun or Besha Ghul or Edene's cousins would allow any harm to come to the child.

As the others left, the rug fell across the doorway, cutting the chill. She and Temur still stood just within it, unmoving. Beyond it, muffled in a familiar way, Edene could hear the sounds of every camp she had ever called home. She stared at the fabric, the warm nap of its weave.

"Buldshak?" she asked, so quickly and with so little inflection that he must know she was afraid of the answer. Her rose-gray filly had been left behind when she was stolen, along with Sube and Temur; she had worried about the horse and the dog and the man in equal measure.

"At Stone Steading," he said. "I brought her to seek you, but I did not think I could bring her safely across the desert. She was well when I left, and she is being kept for you. We can reclaim her when the war is won."

Edene sighed, a slow release of one more fear she had been carrying for too long. Her eyes stung; she bowed her head closer to the bright carpets hanging against the lath-supported felt wall.

Temur laid a hand upon her upper arm. "Make this white-house yours."

She turned to him, startled. "What?"

"Her house," he quoted. "His horse. Let me give this house to you."

"You can't marry," she said. He had lost his secret name when all his family died. There was no one living to tell it to her, and without that knowledge she could not be his wife. "Or has that changed?"

He shook his head. "I can't marry. But I would make you a Khatun anyway."

She took his wrist and led him away from the doorway, toward the padded benches that ringed half the white-house. She sat, and pulled him down to sit beside her. "What about your Samarkar?"

He smiled. "Can you and she learn to be allies?"

Edene shrugged, but remembered the tea. "She will not give you heirs."

"Heirs have been accomplished," Temur replied. He hesitated. She waited. "What is his true name?" he asked.

She had known the question was coming. The fact that that foreknowledge probably eased the clenching anxiety in her gut only made what she did endure the more impressive.

"I don't know," she said.

"How can you not—"

She glared; he stilled. She half-wished he had ridden over her. It would have made it easier to pull herself free.

Was she going to pull herself free? She did not know. The hooks were deep, and she was not certain that she wanted to.

"The djinn," she said. "He gave Ganjin a filthy name. I do not know all of it, and the part I do know . . . I will not use it."

Temur lifted his chin, the twisted scar stretching, pitting the flesh of his neck. "Then I do not wish even to know it."

Like a lance in the breast, the sharpness of her feelings for him. For a moment, she could not breathe. His eyes did not leave hers.

He said, "We may not win this war, Edene. We lack maps, food, horses, weapons and strong hands to wield them."

She dismissed what he said with a turn of her hand. "Weapons, the ghulim have in plenty. Those I can provide."

He gazed at her doubtfully.

She placed her palms against his cheeks. "We will win it, my friend. The alternatives are not thinkable."

He said, "Did he harm you?"

"You mean did he rape me?" Too sharp. Or perhaps just sharp enough. She didn't carry al-Sepehr's bastard; what would it matter if he had?

But Temur put a hand on her wrist and said, "I mean did he *hurt* you. Rape would generally be considered a form of harm, but . . ." he shrugged helplessly. "How could I think less of *you* if he had?"

She didn't answer. But she turned her hand over and caught his fingers with her own.

He touched her hair with his other hand, stroked it smooth against the skull. Despite her wish to keep herself upright and inviolate, she felt herself leaning into the caress like a cat. "They call me the Queen of the Ruins."

"If you give the ring back to Danupati's shade, we lose the service of your army," he said. "Is that so?"

"My ghulim army. My army, as enslaved as any asset al-Sepehr brings to the field. As duped and as controlled as me."

His lips pursed. "Conscripts."

She nodded.

"My grandfather was not above it."

"Perhaps," she said, "that is what it means to be Khagan."

He was silent. He stroked her hair.

"He didn't rape me," she said. "He did me no harm at all. Except he took my freedom, and he kept me from you. And he tricked me into taking this damned ring."

"Take it off," he said.

"What about your ghulim conscripts?"

"You hate it. Take it off."

She grimaced. "I have tried."

That silenced him. For a little while. Then he said, "I sought you. All the way to Ala-Din. But you were gone. Samarkar came with me. And Brother Hsiung, a monk I hope you'll meet. And a Cho-tse, Hrahima."

"Tesefahun told me." She touched his cheek in turn. "It must have been a long ride. You look terrible."

"You look like a queen."

Gently, he disengaged his hand from hers. Slowly, he stood. She did not move; she was too tired. And the ring was heavy, heavy as a shackle on her hand. He opened a box, sought through it. Lifted out a comb of wood that would have been rare and precious on the steppe. Sandalwood; the rich warm scent followed him as he returned.

He sat behind her this time, and slowly unbound her hair. First he parted the locks with his fingers, and then gently, from the bottom, he began to comb them smooth.

"There's gray in this." His fingers traced her part. "It wasn't there before."

"There's gray in my heart," she answered.

He combed in silence, and then he braided in silence. After he knotted the thongs again, he stroked the shining plait and draped it over his own shoulder, pulling her back to rest against him.

"Are you still my woman, Edene?"

"I am the Queen of Erem," she said. "I am not sure I can belong to anything else."

"Can you not be queen and Khatun both?"

"You cannot make me your Khatun," she said. "Al-Sepehr has set a djinn to stalk me, though he has not troubled me since . . . since Kyiv. And more, I am the Queen of Erem. My suns would burn the world away."

Temur breathed, and paused, and said, "Then be my friend."

It echoed in her, something she had once said to him, repeated. She leaned back on him with a sigh, letting herself rest against him. Rest, for the first time since . . . since the blood ghosts had stolen her, since she had woken in a cage beneath a Rukh.

In a moment, she would go and see her cousins. She would go and see to her ghulim.

Now she closed her eyes and said, "I would not be anyone else's friend in the world, before I would be yours."

His lips moved against her hair. "Welcome home, Edene."

IT WAS HRAHIMA WHO FOLLOWED SAMARKAR'S FOOTPRINTS AND SCENT among the pines and the winter-naked maples, but the quest was Tsering's idea. Hrahima had spoken to Ato Tesefahun—still her employer, in the distant and tangled fashion that Hrr-tchee understood such things—and she had afterward withdrawn to contemplate her options. Tsering came up as Hrahima sat cross-legged on a tree branch, delicately gnawing the worn sheath from a thumb-claw and contemplating the hooded creatures—not human, and by the berth Qersnyk and Rasani alike gave them, no one was pretending to think otherwise—settling into an orderly camp below.

Hrahima, of course, had smelled the Rasani wizard long before she came close. Tsering only found her because she chose to allow herself to be found. If a wizard sought one, it was often a good idea to discover whatever it was she wanted to discuss.

So when she called up into the tree—softly, for a human—Hrahima dropped down beside her. It was cold enough that the snow was powdery beneath her pads, whipped by the wind like sand rather than compacting, and the drifts in sheltered places were sculptured and odd, twisted like breaking waves.

Tsering did not startle when the Hrr-tchee fell in before her, which told Hrahima that the monkey-wizard had known exactly where she was. Admittedly, Hrahima had not been trying to conceal herself, but alertness reinforced the respect she had for this particular human. They had traveled together before, and Hrahima thought Tsering-la sensible and clever . . . for a hairless ground-ape.

As if intending to prove her worthiness, Tsering craned her head back, the snake of her braid sliding from her shoulder, and said bluntly, "Have you come to consider Samarkar-la an ally?"

Hrahima considered. The old claw-sheath had finally come loose. She picked it off and flicked it away, revealing a sharp, transparent new claw beneath. She studied it for flaws for a moment before retracting it. "That would be a miserly way of putting it. I consider her an ally, yes. And I consider her a friend."

Tsering nodded. "She's gone off. To give Temur and Edene some time alone. She gave the little boy to his monster nursemaid and went for a walk. I do not think she should be without . . . friends."

Monkey customs and social structures were a fascinating mystery. They were not like Hrr-tchee, content with mate and cub until the cub was grown, coming together otherwise in only the most ritualized of circumstances in order to teach, to learn, to share knowledge. They had their elaborate kinship and social networks, awkward and peculiar as those often were. "You do not think it is healthy for her to be alone?"

"Oh, I'm sure she can weather it," Tsering said. "But I think it might be more painful than necessary."

"We will find her," Hrahima said. "Show me where you saw her last."

The valley might be sheltered, but the hills that surrounded it were thick with snow. Hrahima thought Tsering could have followed the trail plowed patent through the drifts without assistance, and suspected that the wizard had brought her along for reasons other than her sense of smell. Hrahima had lived among the monkeys for a long time. She was starting to get a sense of how they built their extraordinarily baroque webs of obligation and affection.

Plain or not, it took Hrahima and Tsering the better part of Hardmorning to track Samarkar down. She'd gotten farther than Hrahima would have wagered, and now sat with her back to the slope, perched on a long-fallen trunk that the wind had swept clear of snow. Her black coat stood out on the white like a raven's wings, and she had her wolverine-fur-lined hood up to shadow her face. Her hands were tucked in her sleeves and her knees drawn up. That she was not shivering, that her face—glimpsed in profile around the edge of the hood as they approached—looked serene, Hrahima suspected was the discipline of a Wizard of Tsarepheth. When the wind stirred, it was chilly out here even for a Hrr-tchee in winter coat.

Samarkar could not have missed the rasp and whisk of them coming through the snow unless she were completely deaf, or deep in meditation. She looked up when they came between the trees and said, "I am not heartbroken."

"Of course you're not," said Tsering. She jumped the log, using one hand as a pivot, kicking snow in a cloud. Her trousers were white to the thigh, though it was cold enough that her body had not yet begun to melt that snow into water that would then freeze the cloth stiff.

She plunked down on the makeshift bench of the fallen tree, leaned a shoulder against Samarkar's shoulder, and said, "You have no reasons to be heartbroken, unless I've missed some—or you're inventing some."

Samarkar snorted. "He's fulfilled half his blood-vow. Two thirds of it, really. Or the world has fulfilled it for him."

"Edene is free," Hrahima said. "And Qori Buqa is no more. There remains only the bit about helping me fight al-Sepehr."

"Edene. What's wrong with her?"

Hrahima chuffed. "At a guess? Some taint of Erem from associating with al-Sepehr. Perhaps like Brother Hsiung. Perhaps something different. Mukhtar ai-Idoj is a pestilence in his own person, you know. Have you gotten a good sniff of her . . . troops?"

"A glimpse or two. The jackal-things? They haven't eaten the former caliph. Or his formerly Dead Men."

"May they take it out on al-Sepehr instead."

Without looking behind her, Samarkar waved down into the valley. "By spring, it might even look like an army."

Hrahima was silent, not knowing what to say. Apparently Tsering ran up against the same barb, because she put her elbows on her knees and dropped her head into her hands. *She* was shivering. Samarkar had not yet noticed.

Hrahima adjudged that she would feel bad, once she did.

Tsering said, "You worked hard to rescue Edene."

"I do not begrudge her Temur. Or the other way around." She shoved her hands further up the opposite sleeves, hugging herself. "I have more now than I ever thought to have."

Hrahima coughed, but it was Tsering who answered, "That doesn't make it easy, though, not to have everything you want."

Samarkar shrugged, a flinchy futile little rise and fall of her shoulders. "Jealousy does not become me. Nor does envy."

"Do you think Temur will set you aside?"

"Or Edene?" Samarkar laughed. "No. He could not wait to introduce us, and he seemed to hang on every word we exchanged before I made it plain that they needed some time along together, without their . . . son."

Ah.

"It's not a sacrifice if it means nothing to you," Tsering said. She held out her hand, turned upward, fingers cupped slightly. Hrahima had seen Samarkar make that gesture often enough to expect cold fire in some brilliant color and elaborate pattern to blossom over the palm.

But there was nothing but the whisk of snow. Nothing but the sighing of the wind.

Samarkar turned her head and looked at her sister wizard. *Frowned* at her. "I can work up enough guilt on my own, you know."

"Do you think I'd go back to what I was?" Tsering said. "Do you think I'd trade you and Hong and Yongten-la for all the fat babies in the world?"

Samarkar pursed her lips and shook her head. "It turns out it's not such a great world for bringing fat babies into."

"It never has been," said Hrahima. She'd been silent so long that the humans jumped at the sound of her voice. In the intimacy of their exchange, they had more or less forgotten her. "And yet fat babies keep getting born. And some of them . . . some of them live to adulthood. And most of us only intermittently regret it."

Besha Ghul suggested investigating the last floating tower of the old Khagan's palace, undefiled and unscavenged because the bridge that was the only road leading to it had broken. It leaned close to Edene's ear, still too shy to speak to the others—even if they could have understood or tolerated its Eremite tongue—and whispered, "There might be resources there."

When Edene brought this idea to Temur, he was laying his hands upon the sick and infirm, doing what he could to keep them strong and whole. The task exhausted him, and Edene saw that Toragana and Tsering, standing at his left hand, were there as much to pour buttered tea into him and limit the number of supplicants as they were to offer advice.

They cleared the white-house out so she could speak to him, and the first thing she did was lift Ganjin from his cradleboard and lay him in his father's arms. Temur seemed to draw more strength from that than from the tea and butter, truth to be told. He sat sideways on an old camel saddle, head bowed over his son, and Edene permitted herself the simple pleasure of stroking his shoulders and smoothing his queue between her hands. Sharing the white-house with him and with Samarkar was not without tensions—Samarkar had tried to move out to the smaller white-house Tsering and Hong-la shared, and Edene had had to hide her coats and hold them hostage before she'd relent. Edene had also told Samarkar all about the problem of the djinn and the djinn's name and Ganjin's name, leaving her muttering after books left behind in Tsarepheth that she wanted for her research—but it was beginning to work. And Edene was beginning to feel hope that perhaps there was a way out of this mess after all.

He listened to her idea, nodded and said, "I know how to get there, too."

"Tell me."

"Bansh can make the jump."

She thought about it. No natural horse could do such a thing, but Bansh was obviously a spirit in equine form. (*That explains how she beat Buldshak*, Edene had said to Temur when he told her of the mare's ability to run on air, and he had laughed.) "What she can do won't be a secret anymore."

"Perhaps the time for secrets is past," Temur said. He put his forehead down to Ganjin's, giggling like a boy when the baby's eyes crossed. Then he squeaked, as Ganjin reached up and grabbed his ear in a tiny fist, hard.

Patiently, he disentangled the minuscule fingers and tucked them back inside Ganjin's blanket. Edene knew that within moments the fist would be waving in the air again. She came around to sit at Temur's feet. Over by the wall of the white-house, Sube lifted his head from his paws and regarded her, then laid himself down again with a groan.

Temur looked at Edene and frowned. "I can see right through you, my friend. Are you eating enough?"

Gently, Edene touched her son's cheek with a fingertip. He made a repetitive popping noise, and his eyes followed hers.

Looking at her own hand, Edene could see what Temur meant. Around the thick band of the ring, her flesh seemed almost translucent. She thought that if she held it up to the Hard-sun, she'd be able to see light right through it.

She said, "No one is eating enough. Except that little monster. Look at you, ministering to the sick and wasting away yourself."

"I am Khagan," he said. "And we need them all."

"We need you too." Decisively she stood, leaving him with the baby across his lap. "Loan me your mare, my friend."

"Edene?"

"Loan me Bansh. You must rest, O Khagan. I will go and investigate the final tower on your behalf."

He started to protest. She let her eyebrows rise, and he raised the hand that didn't steady Ganjin across his lap in surrender. "All right, Edene. But take . . ." He paused. He wanted to say *Hrahima*, but the tiger weighed three-fifths as much as the slender steppe mare. "Take Samarkar," he finished, finally. "She might know what to look for and have an idea what you are seeing—and if she doesn't, she'll have an idea of who to ask."

A FINE, FAIR SNOW WAS FALLING AS A SCATTERED CROWD OF QERSNYK, Rasani, and ghulim gathered to watch Edene and Samarkar's attempt upon the floating pavilion. It was the first time Samarkar had seen the ghulim mingle with the rest of their tatterdemalion army; mostly, they kept themselves separate, as Edene and Temur both believed was safest for them, and everyone.

Samarkar and Edene did not ride Bansh up the pearly stair that spiraled around the outside of the rocky pinnacle, but led her—or at least, led the way. The mare, more or less, followed curiously. As if she wondered where they were going, and was pleased to be along for the hike.

They left Afrit behind—even without his eldritch growth, he would have been nearly old enough to begin the weaning process—and Bansh didn't seem to mind the break from the great gangling colt's unceasing demands.

Samarkar glanced through the ivory balustrades to the valley below: the cold gray of the frozen lake swept clean by wind; the cold gray of the clouds like an alabaster lid; trees, hills, encampment all silver-plated; the swirl of wind-whipped flakes lost in all that gray. The higher they climbed the roofed spiral stair, the more featureless the world surrounding became. They climbed into mists. Tiny slate-colored songbirds twittered and plucked frozen berries from the icy limbs of trees that draped the ledges of the great stone pinnacle their stair wound around, and around, and around.

"I bet it's full of carpets," Edene said, as they reached the top of the pinnacle and faced the landing of the ruined bridge. "Soft, red carpets all eaten up by moths. And rotten food and skeletons."

"I bet it's full of cobwebs," Samarkar answered. She showed her open palm to Bansh, then held the stirrup for Edene. Neither of them questioned that Edene was the better rider. Samarkar handed her the reins and climbed up behind her, a warm presence sharing the cramped saddle.

"You've done this before," Edene said. Samarkar studied her profile as she half-turned. Something—the icy height, the thrill of adventure—gave her round, lovely face a goddesslike glow. Samarkar felt a stab of jealousy for dewy youth and that complexion like a moon, then buried it hard. Temur played no favorites between them, and she would not be the one to give him reason to.

"She can fly," Samarkar said reassuringly. "Just point her at the gap and trust her with it."

"Scientific," Edene remarked, and gave the bay her head.

FROM A STANDING START, BANSH WAS IN FULL FLIGHT IN TWO STRIDES. Another stride and her hooves rang hollow on what remained of the bridge. Two more and the gap loomed before them. Edene felt Bansh gather herself, the rock of her balance and the compression of mighty muscles. Then Bansh was airborne, sailing high above the gathered forces, the rush of wind and the snow stinging Edene's eyes until tears froze on her cheeks.

Then the plunge, the drive, the thud of Bansh's hooves on boards once more. Samarkar's hands clutched Edene's waist; blood filled Edene's mouth where she had bitten her tongue. A cheer rose from below, attenuated by distance, ragged and delighted. And Edene found herself laughing, laughing ridiculously, as Bansh thundered through the open gates to the last remaining tower of the Khagan's palace at Dragon Lake.

The mare pulled up, snorting great plumes of white in the icy air, each high-kneed stride kicking a plume of powdery, untrammeled snow before her. They found themselves in a courtyard that was obviously meant to be a garden, though now it lay under a drifted white coverlet embroidered with the delicate tracks of birds and squirrels. Under the snow, Bansh's hooves scraped on cobbles. Edene felt as if she were riding the mare into water, and the thought sent a wave of nausea through her.

It's just the White Sea, she told herself. It was a memory she struggled not to dwell upon: the undulations of the water so dizzyingly far below, as she had huddled in a cage dangling from the talons of a bird big enough to carry a horse away in either talon. Her own helplessness. The horror and illness of that flight.

She swallowed the bitterness and tried to feel the delight this mare deserved. "That was amazing!"

Samarkar relaxed her grip on Edene's waist, flexing her fingers as if to restore sensation to them. "We should fix that bridge."

"Think of dropping rocks on the heads of al-Sepehr's army when it comes marching up that road," Edene exulted.

Samarkar craned her head back. "Think of the view from the top of that tower!" She started to lever herself out of the saddle and stopped. Edene could make out the giddy note in her voice as she gestured to the wide empty air around them and said, "You think the mare will wander off if we don't tie her?"

Edene laughed, but hesitated. "With this mare? She just might go graze on clouds. But I don't think tying her would stop her."

Bansh craned her neck around to nibble Edene's knee. As if she understood the conversation, she snorted, then dropped her head to nose through the drifts. *Somewhere under here,* her posture said, *there must be something to eat.* Samarkar's pocket was full of treats; she fished out bits of honeyed, dried persimmon and clucked to attract the mare's attention. The noise was unnecessary; with Bansh, all it took was the smell of sweets. The mare whisked them from Samarkar's glove, whiskers twitching.

Edene dismounted after Samarkar, jumping down into the larger woman's footsteps. Samarkar ran to the doorway, bouncing through the drifts with heavy effort. Edene, feeling lighter and stronger than ever, trotted over them.

She didn't realize what she was doing until Samarkar paused in the door arch, turned, and saw her. The look on Samarkar's face stopped Edene in her tracks, and she began to settle slowly through the snow.

"Oh," Edene said.

Samarkar dropped her eyes as if realizing she was staring. "I'm afraid," she said. "I'm afraid you're coming unstuck from the world, Edene."

"The ring."

"Take it off."

Edene shook her head. She felt the ring catch on the calluses of her thumb, and forced herself to stop fretting with it. "After the battle. The finger will have to go with it, I think."

Samarkar's lips thinned. She didn't flinch or lower her eyes as she said, "Get Hong-la to do it. He'll have it off faster than anyone."

She turned away. They faced the door together. Samarkar tried it, and it opened. They went inside in silence.

The pagoda was perfect inside—perfectly protected, perfectly sheltered, and perfectly beautiful. Not warm, but after the wind without, it seemed so. Swarms of those paper lanterns hovered below the high fluted ceiling above them, moving softly as if in a breeze Edene could not feel. All around them, the lower level stretched out—one single great room, mazed with scroll- and bookcases, treasure cases, glass-fronted boxes made to display treasures.

"A library," Edene said.

"A museum," Samarkar answered. "But all these shelves are empty. Maps, books . . . we could *use* these things."

Edene put a hand on Samarkar's shoulder and turned her, so she could look into the other woman's eyes. "Where then did they go?"

Ümmühan was awakened by the rustle of Mehmed Caliph rising from the couch, the stroke of dawn-cool air against her flank as he disturbed the covers. She watched through slitted eyes as he moved through the gray light to the tower window.

An odd bird rustled there—long-necked and crested, but with a beak like an eagle's. It was a diminutive version of the Rukh, and Ümmühan had seen its like before. When Mehmed untied a message capsule from its leg, Ümmühan smiled behind her hand.

Mehmed did not smile at what he read.

Ümmühan rose from her couch and moved up beside him, letting the covers trail artfully. She leaned the side of her face on his shoulder and sighed.

In a tight voice, he said, "Al-Sepehr calls on me, my swan."

"Will you break your alliance?"

He shrugged. "I should. I *would. . . .*"

"Except?"

His arm came up around her shoulders, the scrap of message crumpled in his hand. "There are songs in the city that celebrate him, you understand. Celebrate that he is bringing the true faith east, to the heathen tribes, and casting a Rahazeen sky over the steppe. Some even say it was he, and not I, who won Asmaracanda back from the Qersnyk overlords. If they call him a prophet next . . ."

"That's infuriating," Ümmühan said. "Who would write such nonsense?"

She did not have to put the outrage in her voice. Even if her pen had scratched the words celebrating al-Sepehr, her initial attraction to him had turned to a kind of fascinated loathing. That she had given the people songs about the man made her hate him more. That she fully intended Mehmed to march to his support did not remove the disgust she felt for both of them.

"Come with me," Mehmed said. "Come to war. Be my comfort. It will not be pleasant—"

He asked rather than commanded. Once it would have made a difference to her, warmed her breast under the golden collar. Now it made her smile, but it was not a smile of affection.

"Of course, lion of my heart," she said.

20

THEY FOUND NO BOOKS, SEARCH THROUGH THE EERILY DESERTED library—or museum—as they might. But Samarkar found a desk, and in the bottom drawer of the desk she found the greatest tease of all: an Uthman-style ledger with a stitched binding, into which somebody—some several dozen somebodies, to judge by the evolution of the hand—had recorded a catalogue of the great library which had once graced these shelves. Some of the entries at the front of the book were so old that they were in the most ancient Song writing, completely—to Samarkar's eyes—opaque columns of symbols and characters.

Edene, exploring further, called back to her, "Look here!" and Samarkar trotted over the parquet floors to reach her.

Edene stood just within another set of doors—ceremonial, Samarkar thought, by their size. They dwarfed Edene; they would have dwarfed Hrahima. An indrik-zver could walk through them without much ducking its great head. And they were ruined. Something had wrenched them from the hinges, scarred them with great axes and mauls, and then carefully leaned them back into place to seal the library up again.

When they walked around to the outside—Samarkar wading through snow and wishing she had Hong-la's trick of levitation, Edene moving light as a wide-pawed manul cat—they could see that the patchwork repair had been fixed in place with quantities of melted lead.

Samarkar turned around to find Edene staring at the back of her head, a hand pressed to her mouth. Samarkar almost startled with realization, and hoped she hid it under court manners.

"When we came through the Grave Roads," Edene said, carefully lowering her hand, "there were paths we did not follow. One such was lighted for a great distance by those paper lamps that are not paper, nor lamps."

"Who'd pillage a library and carefully seal it up again?" Samarkar asked.

Edene shook her head. "I say one of us goes and finds out."

"I say I do it," said Samarkar. "Does Temur know yet that you're bearing again?"

Edene jumped guiltily, then shook her head. "I can't be. I'm still nursing Ganjin."

"You're young," Samarkar said, once she could be sure her tone would sound not strained but pleased. "And apparently . . . very fertile. Congratulations."

Edene licked her lips and pressed that same hand to her belly. "If it's a girl, I'll name her for you, Samarkar."

THAT NIGHT, IN THE CORNER OF EDENE'S WHITE-HOUSE RESERVED FOR her, her books, her table and experiments, Samarkar stood beneath her witchlights and opened the ledger they'd brought down from the pillaged library. She turned the pages while Edene made dumplings and broth, puzzling over a Song syllabary that sometimes formed words in titles she did not know even enough to guess at—she, who had lived in a Song court as its princess for years.

As Edene set the dumplings in the boiling broth, a delicious smell rose. Samarkar saw her gag, and thought she would hurry outside to vomit—but Edene controlled herself and merely sat back on her haunches, blinking tearing eyes.

Samarkar went to her anyway. She laid a hand on Edene's shoulder. "Tea?"

Edene shook her head. "This didn't last long, last time. I'll be fine. I seem to be a brood mare bred. And you have work to do."

Samarkar sighed. "Well, I want tea. This catalogue is esoteric enough that I'm going to have to trouble Hong with half of it. Some of this vocabulary, I'm not sure I have in my *own* language." As she reached for the heavy iron kettle, already filled with melted snow, and set it on the unused side of the brazier, she said, "Even without him, I can tell you we need to reclaim those books."

"You found something."

Samarkar nodded. "The catalogue lists one as a map of the ways of Reason. What does that sound like to you?"

THE CAVERNS BELOW THE QERSNYK TENT CITY WERE MEASURELESS AND strange, and Samarkar was forced to argue with Temur for the better part of a morning before he'd agreed to let her lead an expedition into them. She knew part of his reluctance was the hatred for confined spaces he'd learned in the barrows of the Lizard Folk, though neither of them spoke of it. It was more important for her to convince him that it wasn't just her wizardly curiosity at work, though if she were being honest she must admit—at least to Tsering's knowing smile—that that was part of it. But the real motivating force—and the main thread of her argument—was the knowledge that *anything* could be lurking down there—any enemy, any trap, any relic of the old empire. Any Eremite, Song, or Qersnyk artifact. Any ghost. A war engine of ancient design. A trapdoor by magic into some other lost city of Erem. A way for Nameless assassins to dance into all their bedchambers—not that a white-house *had* bedchambers—by night.

Possibly even the books missing from the floating library, whose bridge Temur had now set Ato Tesefahun, Hong-la, and their choice of strong backs to repairing. It was defensible, and they might need the room.

Samarkar had seen enough mysteries to make her cautious. She wasn't leaving their back unguarded. Edene and her ghulim had followed the Grave Roads through part of the caverns, but there was a whole other branch left unexplored. And it was that which eventually convinced him.

That, and the appearance of a new moon in the Qersnyk skies they could not see from here.

It was pale blue and mysterious, called the Bull Moon, Jurchadai told them. "I'm sure you can guess who belongs to it."

It made Temur nervous. Which made him amenable to Samarkar's requests—considered along with her not-as-reluctant-as-she-made-herself-out-to-be acceptance of Temur's demand that she bring along Hong-la, Tsering, and Hrahima. As if she could have kept Hong-la, Tsering, or Hrahima out of those caves with a boar spear and a dozen men-at-arms, once they knew she was going.

To her surprise, Jurchadai volunteered to come with them as well . . . though when she thought about it, she admitted that perhaps her surprise was unwarranted. He had quite plainly attached himself to Tsering. And there was nothing to say that a Qersnyk priest could not have a scientific or military curiosity of his own.

Despite that, Samarkar wondered at what point in a relationship it was appropriate to threaten to break a suitor's kneecaps if he should prove insufficiently respectful of one's friend.

The approach to the cave was easy, and the initial descent only a matter of engineering. As the eternal, floating swarms of paper lanterns led into the sinkhole, so they followed. They rigged rope-and-dowel ladders, though Samarkar secretly hoped to find an easier way to come out again, and alongside the swaths of will-o'-the-wisp lights they descended into the depths.

In short order, the little company assembled itself on a sandy beach beside a lake so perfectly still it might have been a glass-faced mirror. Shafts of Hard-day sunlight, crisp and brutal, penetrated the dusty air above them—but they seemed to glance off the impossibly placid surface of the lake without illuminating its depths. Somewhere, water ran, its echoes trilling and clear. But that flow did not affect the lake before them, which showed not even a ripple from the currents of air.

That one simple incongruity disconcerted Samarkar as much as any of the diseased sorceries she had glimpsed in the Nameless stronghold of Ala-Din.

"The Grave Roads entrance is that way, according to Edene," Samarkar said. Not being ghulim, nor carrying the Green Ring, her party could not go that way, of course. She continued, "So our path lies to the right."

The square paper lanterns hung at head-height, marking a path deeper into the earth, away from the water. Along with the slanting sun, they illuminated only a portion of a cavern that stretched away on all sides, into shadow. From the shimmer of light on water, Samarkar could trace the bed of a little stream that seemed to be outflow from the lake. It, at least, rippled and babbled naturally, giving her much less of a shiver than the stillness of depths that led her to wonder what slumbered beneath.

A trodden path led down beside the stream, many footsteps having worn a pale, slightly depressed path over clean limestone. Samarkar picked her way toward it and the others followed. Every breath, every step, every rivulet echoed through the caverns with a liquid, layered, glassy sound. The musicality of it encouraged the wizards to move in a sort of reverential hush—as if it were an orchestra, as if there were performers to be respected.

Every few strides, the little streamlet had built itself a fragile, lacy dam of precipitated limestone, so it descended through calcite pools terraced as if they were rice fields climbing the slope of a hill. The stone's colors shone soft golds and ivories, muted shades that were lovely in the pure light of the paper lanterns. Samarkar had thought she would need witchlights by now, but the lanterns warmed and illuminated everything.

The ceiling and walls of the cavern, meanwhile, oozed and flowed like wax. Ranks upon ranks of evenly spaced stone icicles dribbled along each wall, reminding Samarkar of the teeth of a smiling beast—the crocodiles of Song, or perhaps the larger cousins of the feather-lizards that were said to roam some deserted highlands of Rasa.

Who knew what monsters lived among the remoter reaches of the Steles of the Sky?

The cavern narrowed, the ceiling lowering. Side passages split off, some great and some small, at varying heights. Hong-la, sketching in the air with a stub of pencil, drew a translucent, faintly glowing map of where they had been, indicating the ways they had not explored. They ducked under stone draped like swags of hanging cloth, and edged around pillars. Some of the curtainy stones glowed softly, illuminated from within. Lime had accreted and grown over certain of the floating lanterns, and from within translucent calcite they shone still. Samarkar rested her fingertips on a moist wall, lightheaded with wonder. When she pulled them back they were damp, too. She touched them to her lips and tasted earthy water, musty lime.

Several times the party jumped back and forth across the water. Once they were forced to wade it, making Samarkar very glad of her sturdy boots. They walked half-hunched over, elbows bent and heads ducked. Samarkar did not regret her hours in the saddle now, for the strength it had given her thighs.

Something flickered in the miniature ponds formed by the natural terraces. Samarkar bent close, reflexively summoning her own light to compensate when her shadow fell across the water. Whatever made the depths of the lake opaque did not apply here. This water was transparent as air, only the sheen of the surface revealing its presence. Pale fat fishes hung in it, their fleshy fins stirring sand grains on the pool's bottom—or, at least, Samarkar thought they were fishes, until she realized that one and then another had hind legs ending in clawed feet.

"Tadpoles," Tsering said, peering over her shoulder. "Cave frogs?"

"You'd think we would have heard one jump by now."

Finally, the banks vanished between narrowing tunnel walls. The path they followed simply led into the stream and did not come out again. The paper lanterns continued, though their light from ahead was often reflected around intervening obstacles. It gave a wet, many-directional shine to the irregular surface of the flowstone.

Tsering leaned out to glance down the descending streambed. "I think we'll have to walk through the water."

"That happens in caves," said Hong-la. "I wish I could paint this."

"You could bring an easel down," Hrahima said. "At least this far."

"I could," said Hong. "But I still wouldn't be able to paint."

The tiger's ears flickered. The faint chiming of the gold in her ears echoed as profligately as the dripping of water. Samarkar realized with a little surprise that she had known Hrahima long enough now to recognize laughter. And that this was the first time she had seen the tiger laugh in a long while.

Hong-la's amusement was more evident. The tall wizard, bent more double than any of them except the Cho-tse, grinned with boyish excitement. Samarkar had never seen him like this, playful and extravagant.

I wonder if it's something new to explore, or not having to be in charge anymore . . . or if it's just being home in Song. Even if it's Qersnyk-claimed Song, the sky says otherwise. She knew he was an exile; as a past and present expatriate herself, she also knew that even when you made a home for yourself elsewhere, if it wasn't your true home you could always feel the contradictory weight of that emptiness.

Samarkar found herself walking behind the shaman-rememberer for a while, watching him scramble nimbly over uneven terrain. As he turned to give her a hand over an awkward gap, she took her opportunity and asked, "Jurchadai, what is a Sacred Herd?"

They separated and began to walk forward again, so as not to impede those behind them. He slowed, so she could keep up easily, and he said, "There are sixty-four sacred colors, to which all horses to a greater or lesser degree correspond. For each color, there is an Ideal Mare, she who typifies all that is best in the favorite animal of the Eternal Sky. These mares rarely descend to earth; sometimes a great hero will be blessed by the companionship of one. They are the Sacred Herd of the Eternal Sky. He guards them jealously. They are the soul of all horses in the world."

"I see," she said. "But if they belong to the Eternal Sky, how does one build such a herd here on earth?"

"One must collect a horse of each sacred color, as perfect as possible. It is a very great magic, very lucky. The man who holds such a herd is blessed of Mother Night, and it is said he will be undefeated."

Samarkar licked her lips. They were beginning to chap in the moist chill of the cave, and she made a note to herself not to do it again. "Why did Toragana tell Temur he had bull's balls, then, for trying to build such a herd?"

Jurchadai kept an even pace despite the uneven ground. He lofted up a high step as easily as Jerboa hopping over a wall. "To try to assemble such a herd means you must find horses of the unlucky colors too. If you don't have the complete set . . ."

He shrugged. He kept walking.

Samarkar did not ask him anything more.

Now, the stream descended more quickly, and so, splashing, did they. Samarkar kept expecting to come to a place where they could not squeeze past, or where the water went underground and they could not follow. But all that happened was that the passageway widened and flattened—still lit by the gleaming lanterns—and they had to get down on their bellies and crawl. Samarkar scoured her palms and knees, certain she was leaving blood behind. A ridge in the stone bruised the tops of her breasts and then her hip bones as she slid over it. She was nearly ready to give up and try backing out when the roof slowly lifted again and she could go first on all fours and then in a crouch.

Even Hrahima sighed in relief when they could stand up again, in the winding fissure that still led down. Samarkar brushed ineffectually at her wet and gritty coat-front. She might have been cold, if she had not called on a wizard's discipline to warm her bones. This was not the first time she had been in the wet, chill dark—and the last time, Tsering-la had left her there alone.

She turned to smile at Tsering, wanting to share the memory of how she had found her own power, and was ashamed to see the other wizard's expression of forlorn concentration. Of course; Tsering's trial in the dark had not ended in the finding of her power, in a flare of warmth and light, but in darkness and cold and in terrible disappointment.

But Tsering was looking forward, over Samarkar's shoulder, as she too straightened and cracked her spine. "I think it opens out down there."

The lanterns led on.

"Well," said Samarkar. "Let's see."

IT WAS ANOTHER SANDY SLOPE, ANOTHER LIMPID POOL STILL AND TRANSPARENT beyond comprehending. The lanterns made a ring of shadow-punctuated brightness around the perimeter of the cavern, which was as vast as the wizard's all-meeting chamber at the Citadel in Tsarepheth—and taller. The walls of this cavern were as ornate as those of the passages above and more brightly colored: stained with brilliant and metallic hues from violet to butter-gold to antimony. Great swags of flowstone dripped over the underground lake, and here and there, lacy floating rafts of limestone actually drifted on the surface of the water. Below the lake, though, were further and even more fantastical architectures of stone, all twisted reefs of reds and oranges and yellows. Samarkar's eye caught here and there the soft flicker of fins.

The far shore glittered like pyrite, like crystals, in the uneven glow of the lamps, which made as many mysteries with darkness as they did revelations with light. Conflicting shadows made outlines uncertain, but Samarkar could convince herself that some of the litter on the shore had the outline of certain familiar objects—a cup, a helm. The scabbard of a blade.

"That's gold," said Jurchadai, extending one hand. "That's . . . a very big pile of gold."

Even more striking than the gold, to Samarkar's eye, were the hundreds of books—scrolls, bound books, fan books—that floated in the air throughout the chamber. She reached out to touch one, incautious and heedless of it. As her hand came close, she felt that the air surrounding the bound book was dryer than the rest of the air in the cave. Her fingers brushed it. It fell into her hand, open to a page written in a language she did not know or even recognize.

"The books from the library?" she asked Hong-la, turning—then jerked her head back as the twisted, bannery stone reef below the water writhed and began to untwist itself like ribbons combed by the wind. The water domed and slid—still pellucid, still smooth—then collapsed into ripples as a huge, sleepy, tendriled head on a long scaled neck rose from the lake's surface and blinked weary eyes.

It was a measure of Samarkar's state of shock that her first thought was a stab of grief for the fragile, floating rafts of calcite as they cracked and were washed under in the wave. Only then did she realize, her heart a painful pressure against her sternum, that she was staring into the curved red seashell cavern of dragon's nostril as it bowed its enormous muzzle over her.

It had long flews like a dog, and they wrinkled up like a dog's to show a barrier of fangs reminiscent of the toothed flowstone patterns above—serried, and yellow-white. The scales around that mouth were a thousand shades of lemon, citron, carnelian, coral, vermilion, scarlet, persimmon, amber, cinnabar, tangerine. The colors were arranged in no pattern, and Samarkar could not have claimed honestly that the shades of any two scales were precisely the same. Indeed, they seemed to change and shift as the great beast moved and beads of water slid across its skin, as if Samarkar had plunged her hands into a vat of polished agates and stirred, and let them glide through her fingers in a slow red and yellow rain.

The dragon's tendrils writhed about its mouth, questing this way and that, luffing and seeking like a eager cat's whiskers. The eyes were like agates too, bands of amber and orange that broadened as the pupils contracted, focusing sluggishly on Samarkar.

It opened its mouth further. A long tongue, prehensile and slick, flicked out, accompanied by a waft of warm sweetness. The tendrils darted forward too, hovering close enough to Samarkar's upturned face that she felt them brush the fine hairs over her skin. Then it withdrew, smooth as if pushed on an oiled track, and gazed down at them.

"This is who wakes me?" it asked. "Wizards, Warrior, Shaman? Has the emperor then returned to Lung Ching? Why is he not among you? Where is my tithe?"

Samarkar opened her hand. The book rustled itself closed and rose to resume its old place, just above and beside her.

The dragon spoke in a Song dialect old enough that Samarkar only knew it from her endless bored and frustrated reading of historical records, when she had been a useless appendage of her late husband's court. But she did understand it—just—and as she glanced left and right she could see that Hong understood it too. He stepped forward and Samarkar went after him, wishing she couldn't see the way the muscles in his calves fluttered when he got in front of her. Hong-la should be afraid of nothing.

She came up beside him when he stopped, because it was her duty and because it made her feel better to put her shoulder to his. He glanced at her, though, and she understood from the look that he'd follow what she said—if she could find anything to say to this. Which was a pity, because she'd bet he was better at this archaic dialect than she was. She could read it, or understand it, well enough—but speaking it extemporaneously was a very different matter.

She decided to speak the dialect she was fluent in. If there was confusion, perhaps Hong-la could intervene and translate. In fact, her diplomat's practiced deviousness suggested that it might not be a bad thing to be able to claim translation difficulties if they should need a second chance at some negotiation. Assuming dragons gave second chances, that is.

"Your Ancient and Enlightened Igneous Eminence, we come in the name of the Khagan. He is the emperor of this place."

It might have felt odd to speak of Temur—her Temur—so, but Samarkar had learned at her father's knee that the game of empire is nothing but playacting, moving dolls around dollhouses and never betraying a moment's amusement at the nonsensicality of it all. Half of power was pretending that you had it; the other half was convincing other people that the pretense was true, and that they ought to go along with it.

Kings forgot that at their peril.

The dragon said nothing. Ripples lapped his neck where it rose from the pristine water.

She said, "Your tithe will follow, O Ancient One. We are only a scouting party." She thought to ask him who had been the last emperor he served, and then realized that dragons probably didn't think of it in those terms. And that she didn't want to hand him the advantage of knowing that they were not aware of which past emperors had tithed to honor him.

That information, no doubt, was in one of the books that floated, bathed in dryness, here in this chamber. And Temur probably would have mentioned it if his grandfather had known that his palace was built over a real Dragon Lake—or Dragon Well, *Lung Ching*—with a real dragon in it. Especially when Samarkar was about to go digging around under it.

The dragon's head turned, banking on the long neck like a kite dragging a streamer zigzag through the sky. It darted to a stop just over Tsering, cocked and looking down at her.

"Wizard, where is thy magic?"

She stood her ground more easily than Samarkar had managed. Her hands hung relaxed by her sides. She tilted her head back gently to look up at the massive head. Tendrils stroked her cheeks, or seemed to.

She apparently understood the dragon well enough also, because she answered fluently: "I do not have any."

Said the dragon, "How is it that you wear the black, then, and smell of my brethren?"

Samarkar saw her hands clench, but no trace of whatever emotion caused that sudden convulsion emerged on her face or in her voice. Tsering's spine straightened and she shook back her hair as if grooming tendrils of her own. The whites of her eyes flashed as the lids widened.

"Because I earned it."

The dragon's head glided back, twisting aside. Its gaze next fixed on Hrahima. The Cho-tse had crouched, one elbow resting on her knee, the other long arm draped down with the backs of her fingers resting on the cavern floor. It looked relaxed; Samarkar knew she could uncoil from it like a compressed spring if necessary. When the dragon's gaze fell upon her, she might have been a statue; as unruffled and carved from amber as the dragon itself.

The dragon breathed on her in turn. Her ragged, beringed ears flicked flat with their familiar soft, sweet jingle.

To her, the dragon said, "Warrior, where is thy *own* gold?"

Hrahima glanced at Hong-la. Frowning, he translated.

"This is mine," she answered. "Earned, with my own good hands."

"Bought and paid for," scoffed the dragon. "Who tore the gold you were given away from you? Does it become a warrior to play make-believe with honors?"

There was a pause, while Hong-la related what had been said.

Hrahima stood, shoulders broad and square. "You ask questions to which you know the answers. Does that become a dragon?"

The dragon tipped his head at her—Samarkar could not have said how she was so certain that it was a *he*, but she was. He huffed, and long slow parallel ripples chased across the surface of the pond, like wind-driven waves on the surface.

Silence built upon silence, and finally the dragon tipped his head and said, "Return upon the spring equinox with my tithe, and your emperor. Or I will be . . . displeased." The lanterns behind them winked out, leaving only those trailing forward, past the pond, into another tunnel. "I believe you will find this a more direct route to the surface."

THE TRAIL UP WAS SHORTER, AND MORE STEEP, BUT ALLOWED THEM TO WALK or scramble upright, mostly. It took them through a cavern whose ceiling was thick with hibernating bats and whose floor was swamped with guano, which made Tsering, Hong-la, and Samarkar all gaze at one another speculatively. And from there, it was only a short trip up through a passageway to the surface via a cave mouth hidden amid the roots of a slumped old elm.

They were less than four *li* from the camp. Samarkar swore everyone to secrecy twice before they rejoined Temur's ragtag but swelling army.

SAMARKAR AND TSERING NOMINATED THEMSELVES TO TELL THE KHAGAN what they had found. He was picking over a nervous meal with Edene when they entered the white-house, and both turned to open the circle to the newcomers. Samarkar and Tsering sat and allowed Edene to pour them tea before quickly explaining their discovery, and the significance not just of the dragon, but of the other cave inhabitants.

"I am not sure," Temur said, abandoning his pretense of eating, "exactly why I should be excited about a cave full of bats."

"Not the bats," Tsering said. "The guano. We can harvest saltpeter from under it, and if we can find a source of sulfur, we can make black powder."

"We have no cannon, nor forges fit to cast some."

Tsering smiled. "It's easy enough to make mines. Bombs."

Samarkar appropriated Temur's abandoned bowl and dipped rice and meat from it with her fingers. "In Tsarepheth, we'd get the sulfur from under the Cold Fire—"

"My ghulim can find sulfur," Edene said. "By the Grave Roads, or some other means."

Samarkar chewed and swallowed. "We need to find out what the dragon's bargain with the old Song emperors was. We need to find out what it knows, and what we can learn from it. If we must tithe to this thing, we need something more for our gold than just its forbearance."

"We can't just ask it?"

"It assumes we know. We'd be sacrificing all our advantage, letting it set its own terms, if we let on that we don't. We don't even know its name. Someone, somewhere, has to know the damned thing's name!"

"That's probably in the books it stole from the palace library."

Samarkar sighed. "Along with all the maps that would help us set up our ambush."

"So much gold," Temur said. "Would pay for a lot of armaments and horses."

"Dragon gold," said Tsering-la. "It's as poisoned as the earth where their blood falls. Everything in that cave is poison. Stay there too long, hold anything you bring from out of there too close, and your flesh will fall off your rotten bones before you die crumbling."

Edene said, "What a pity we can't find a way to get it to our enemies."

"I don't think the dragon is about to give it up, anyway." Samarkar dipped more rice, chewed slowly. She smiled at Tsering. "You seemed very calm about that."

"Not my first dragon this winter," was all Tsering-la said.

Samarkar said, "I didn't know they'd be so . . . interested. In us. Challenging."

Tsering nodded, mouth twisted askew. "I don't know much about them. But the other one I've met was also awfully nosy. And condescending. This one was a bigger ass, however."

"Well," said Samarkar. "They *are* dragons."

"And all we have to do is win it over," Temur said. "How bad can that be if a Song emperor managed? Tsering, get Hong-la figuring out what we can tithe the damned thing before the equinox."

"Tesefahun brought a great deal of gold," Edene said.

"It wants to talk to you in person, Khagan," Samarkar said.

Temur stretched and rolled his shoulders back. "Well, I know what maps we need to bargain for, thanks to the catalogue Samarkar and Edene brought back. Samarkar, Tsering, get Hong's help and go through the ledger and make a list of books for me."

Samarkar said, "This solves one mystery at least."

"Your pardon?"

"The skies," she said. "I imagine a Song dragon's presence underground means Song skies overhead, if that's what he thinks we should live under. No matter who holds the palace above."

21

By the first thaw of the spring, Sube had forgiven edene for the ghulim.

With the second thaw, the trickle of arrivals resumed. Temur was teaching Samarkar the horse-race game, with Edene's "help," explaining for the third time how the clean-boiled anklebones of a sheep, rolled and stacked, indicated the speed with which a strictly hypothetical mare had run as compared to the strictly hypothetical mare of the other player. The sound of hooves and neighs and cries of greeting echoed through the camp. Temur started up, overturning half the stacked bones and bumping the board into Edene's knees, and still did not manage to beat Samarkar to the door.

Edene stood more slowly, a shivery chill all down her arms and across her shoulders. A horse neighed—and neighed again. A familiar, equine voice. She almost dreaded walking to the door of the white-house. She knew she was mistaken. She must be mistaken. And she could not bear the disappointment she knew awaited her.

She pulled Ganjin's cradleboard across her shoulders and followed her family outside.

*   *   *

THIS FIRST (AND LEAST-EXPECTED) AMONG THE SPRING'S ARRIVALS WAS THE Woman-King Tzitzik, last scion of the Lizard-Folk, blood of Danupati—traveling in company with a pair of Cho-tse . . . and a complement of warriors from Stone Steading, which lay at the outermost western edge of Temur's grandfather's empire. That was to say, of *Temur's* empire.

The contingent also traveled under the care of the redoubtable Nilufer Khatun, Temur's aunt by marriage. And it seemed as if these two very different but equally formidable warriors had come to some sort of deep-seated understanding. The prospect made Temur's spine chill with alarm if he thought about it for more than a few moments . . . but at least they seemed to like each other.

Whatever he might have said was interrupted by Edene bursting past him, running heedlessly into the midst of armed strangers. Nilufer's mount, a familiar rose-gray mare, prick-eared, bugled a sharp call as soon as she saw Edene running toward her and danced forward in her own turn, tugging her reins, shouldering another mare aside.

Woman and mare leaned together a moment, and then Edene stepped back, lifting her chin to look up at the face of the woman on her horse's back. "You must be of Stone Steading," she said. On her back, Ganjin giggled, having enjoyed his human mount's short run.

The woman, armored and wearing a bow slung over her shoulder, smiled. "I am Nilufer. And unless I miss my guess, I am the great-aunt of that babe on your back. I am pleased to meet you, Tsareg Edene. I brought you back your mare."

Temur—who was finally learning diplomacy (under Samarkar's constant tutelage)—got Edene and Buldshak to move off in one direction to make their reacquaintance. Edene would insist on checking every inch of the mare herself. He also immediately detailed Samarkar to take charge of Nilufer and bustle her off to meet her son. Dour Chagatai was embroiled in training what warriors they had in jousting at rings; Temur guessed his worry-lined face would nevertheless crack around a smile when he saw who walked beside the Khagan's wizard woman.

Nilufer and Edene seen to, Temur returned his attention to the Woman-King Tzitzik. Though the late winter chill had not truly given way to spring, she sat her ribby brown stud bare-chested. She wore only trousers, boots, a circlet of gold beaten to resemble dragon-scales, gaunt-lets, sword—and a fantastical collection of pale, beaded chains of scar ruching the papery stretch-marked skin of her hard, gaunt abdomen. Her horse was barded in scaled armor made with plates of horse-hoof, and so were the lieutenants who flanked her on every side. But Tzitzik herself rode nearly naked, a testament—so Temur supposed—to her strength and fearlessness.

As he greeted her, he tried not to hear Samarkar in his head remark-ing on the discomforts of long rides without the support of a halter. At least, he supposed, the woman-king was small-breasted.

He wondered if that made a difference.

She did not smile any less to see him when he returned. The pair of Cho-tse did not smile either time.

They were male and female. The male was Faranghis, the female Hryorah, and Temur tried to hide from them how surprised he was by how little Faranghis resembled the Cho-tse he had previously encountered—both Hrahima, and the emissaries who had occasion-ally attended Temur's brother Qulan at this very camp, when Qulan had been one of the heirs-apparent to the Padparadscha Seat. Hrahima was big, for a Cho-tse—for anything that walked on two legs—but she would not have been out of scale with the other Cho-tse Temur had encountered. Or, in truth, with Hryorah—though Hryorah's pelt was a stunning pale color, cream-white with coffee-black stripes. Her irises were bicolored, an outer ring of white around an inner ring of blue, putting Temur in mind of shattered ice and the crevasses of the bitter cold glaciers at the top of the world.

But Faranghis was, by Cho-tse standards, little more than a dwarf. He probably weighed no more than twice what Temur did, and his coat seemed much shorter and closer-laid than Hrahima's, while the black stripes on his arms and back were fat and wide.

The woman-king must have caught Temur looking, because when she swung down from her saddle and embraced him formally, she whis-pered in his ear—in badly broken Qersnyk—"The little one is from the islands, they say."

Temur hugged her back. "Are they here to work diplomacy on me, or are they here for Hrahima?"

Tzitzik grimaced, her grasp of his language apparently exceeded. With a jerk of her hand, she summoned her interpreter, and Temur repeated himself.

Tzitzik had met Temur's exiled Cho-tse ally before. She shrugged when she heard the question. "Some of both, I'd say."

Then, as she stepped back, in a louder voice she continued, "Temur Khagan! It is with great pleasure and delight that we again make your acquaintance. We are pleased indeed to see that you are not dead."

"And I am pleased not to be dead," he replied.

He reminded himself not to bow low. When last they had met, he had come to her court as a vagabond. A supplicant. And he had wound up spending the night walled into a barrow, through no fault of the woman-king's. Now their positions were reversed: they might be equal in terms of precedence, but Temur held the power here, and though Tzitzik had her army at her back, she came to him this time.

She held out a hand, fist closed loosely over something in a small chamois pouch. He looked her in the eye. No trace of deceit there, although perhaps a little amusement. So Temur in his turn extended his hand as well, and took what the Woman-King of the Lizard-Folk had to offer.

Whatever the pouch held, it was irregular and hard inside the clinging goatskin. Without taking his eyes from Tzitzik's face—Temur had a shallow but apprehensive appreciation of what she might think was funny—he picked the knots loose with his nails and wiggled open the mouth of the bag. The thing inside was cold and rough when he shook it into his palm.

A geode: a hollow stone with bright crystals within. Or half of one anyway, and with its facets inexplicably dimmed with a sticky, rust-brown patina. He lowered his nose and sniffed; the musty scent confirmed his first impression. Dried blood, and plenty of it.

"Am I supposed to say it's lovely?"

Tzitzik grinned. Through her interpreter, she said, "We hear you're going to fight the Nameless bastard."

"Is that why you've come?"

"They said you raised your banner here."

"You traveled in the winter," he said.

She shrugged as if it were nothing. "Nilufer Khatun has one in her band who can witch weather. They said you needed allies. There are rewards for aiding the Khagan."

His smile was tight. He held up the bloody lump of rock. "This is aid?"

"My swords are aid," she said. "*That's* something I pulled off the body of the Nameless assassin your white-foot mare kicked in the head."

NILUFER TOLD SAMARKAR THAT SAMARKAR'S SISTER-IN-LAW PAYMA HAD been safely delivered of a baby daughter, and despite a difficult birth, mother and child were well. Samarkar in her turn shared this news with Edene and Temur, when the three of them were alone—except for Ganjin—in Edene's white-house that night, sharing a sparse early-spring supper of tea, green onions, and long sliced dumplings around the brazier's low-built warmth.

"If only Songtsan-tsa and Yangchen-tsa had known," Samarkar said. Her voice fairly *dripped* irony; when she was not restraining herself for reasons of diplomacy, she had not so light a hand with that particular spice as did Edene. "Payma could have stayed safe in Tsarepheth until the palace exploded, and you and I, Temur, would have parted ways when we had barely met."

Barely met seemed a parsimonious term for her having saved his fever-addled life, but he let it slide. Instead, as Edene slurped noodles from her tea, he reached into his pocket for the stone. Edene claimed she did not get hungry, but when food was put into her hands, she went to with a will.

He put the bag in Samarkar's left hand while her right still balanced her barbaric eating sticks against the lip of her bowl. As civilized people, Temur and Edene ate with their hands.

"What is this?"

"You tell me, Wizard of Tsarepheth," he replied.

She paused with the mouth of the bag half-picked, reached into a pocket of her coat, and pulled out a pair of fine silk gloves. She took her time settling her fingers into them while Temur watched and Edene kept her head bent over her dinner.

When Samarkar shook the stone into her shielded palm, she almost dropped it anyway. She winced, started to hold it up—as if to sniff it, the same way Temur had—and wrinkled her nose before it got close to her face. "This is ugly magic."

"Necromancy?"

She squinted at the thing as if examining a counterfeit gemstone with a loupe. "Well, blood is generally a good sign of the sort of thing a sorcerer is more likely to meddle in than a wizard is. Where did this come from?"

Temur told her.

She balanced it on her gloved fingertips, as if to get it as far from her flesh as possible, and frowned down at it.

"Is it a protective talisman?" Edene asked.

Samarkar pursed her lips. "It's more likely to be a communication spell," she said. "See how it's only half of a thing? Someone who had the other half could probably speak to whoever had this one."

"And something died to make the magic work?"

"I'm no expert on this sort of thing—"

Edene put her bowl down. It was not empty. "Given the source," she said, "more probably some*one* died."

"Hmm," said Temur. "I wonder if we could use it to talk to him."

"Al-Sepehr?" Samarkar asked. "I doubt he's open to negotiation."

"The question," said Temur, "is, what advantage can be gleaned from contact?"

Edene raised her bowl again. Mechanically, seemingly without appetite, she slurped a dumpling from the tea and bit it in half. When she had chewed and swallowed, she looked Temur in the face and said, "Advantage? Yours or his?"

Temur said, "If I get a knife into him, that would solve everything."

"Saadet—Saadet ai-Mukhtar, they call her, Shahruz's sister—will not be less determined to bring you down if al-Sepehr is gone. I know her from my captivity. She was very devoted to her brother."

"That's personal, and I will deal with it on that level when the time comes. The devotion I'm concerned about is to her cause. Is she as *devoted* to conquering the whole world in the name of the Sorcerer-Prince as al-Sepehr is?"

Edene put her bowl aside again. She seemed frailer and yet more full of energy every day, as if a flame inside her burned her flesh away. Temur watched her and worried, half-expecting her thin hands to turn translucent to the light as she gestured. The very old seemed this way sometimes.

But neither he nor Samarkar not Toragana had been able to argue her into having the damned ring removed.

"She's pious," Edene said. "She's devout. But she's not al-Sepehr."

Samarkar said, "I think you just want to look your enemy in the eye. Just once."

Temur neither answered nor looked at her.

She said, "I know you accepted the blood-vow geas of your own free will. And destroying al-Sepehr is the last task you need to accomplish to be free of it—"

"The others rather accomplished themselves," he pointed out. "Maybe I should make an attempt to fulfill at least *one* of them."

He rolled the stone on its cloth, lips pursed as he contemplated it. "We'll try it," he said at last.

Samarkar lifted her hands. He caught the glance she exchanged with Edene, and wondered what was behind it, but found himself too cowardly to ask.

"Just be careful," Samarkar said.

SAMARKAR WOULD HAVE LIKED TO HAVE HAD HRAHIMA PRESENT FOR THE experiment, but no one could find her. They'd had people looking since Nilufer and her Cho-tse emissaries arrived, but it was not unusual for Hrahima to vanish for days on end. The Cho-tse's big paws carried her over drifts like snowshoes, and like any cat she came and went as pleased her.

Temur and Samarkar had argued more folk and fewer, armed men and no one as his backup in this endeavor. Eventually, they'd settled on magical support as the most likely to be useful. So it was Samarkar, Hong-la, Jurchadai, Tesefahun, and Tsering who gathered to cover Temur in his attempt to reach through the cracked geode and assassinate the theocrat of the Nameless assassins. Hong-la and Jurchadai created a warded circle in a white-house they set up just for this purpose, and Tesefahun arranged the space within to create a place of safety from outside influences. He assured Samarkar that he could sever any magical connection between Temur and the outside world instantaneously, if need be.

Said Samarkar, "Even if it's based in the magic of Erem?"

"Theoretically," he said. "Do you want to trust Edene with that task as well?"

Samarkar shook her head. "It's not Edene I don't trust. And would you risk a bearing woman on unknown sorcery?"

So it was the five of them that gathered one Soft-morning when the temperature rose and the impossible lushness of everything in Song was unveiling itself. Meltwater ran down icicles to refreeze on their points until the whole encampment was jeweled in icy teeth. Each of them, whether wizard or shaman-rememberer, adopted one of the cardinal points of the compass. Jurchadai opined that he would have preferred eight, to cover the eight sacred directions. Tsering argued that there were six sacred directions, and she did not know how they would station someone at "down."

"Bury them in the earth?" she asked acerbically.

Jurchadai laughed and tugged Tsering's braid. Samarkar hadn't missed that Tsering and the shaman-rememberer were sharing a white-house these days.

Tsering, having no magic and better theory than any of them except perhaps Tesefahun, would observe—and be ready to intervene, if it seemed that one of them were in trouble, or falling under some foreign influence.

Samarkar settled herself in her position of East, back to the door—which in a white-house traditionally faced the rising sun, conveniently perpendicular to the prevailing north-south winds of the steppe—and began slowing her breathing, listening to her heartbeat, gathering her energies about her. It had been a long time since she had the luxury of slow, collected wizardry. Since she met Temur and began traveling with him, she'd used her power almost exclusively while under attack, throwing raw magic at enemies without subtlety or planning. She'd shoved processes about rather than manipulating them delicately.

It was a relief, a reassurance, to reach out with her *otherwise* senses and find Hong-la there, steady and meticulous, as balanced and aware a mind as any in the Citadel. She could sense Jurchadai and Tesefahun too, their strengths confusing and mysterious, as if she watched a dance she did not understand the movements or symbolism of.

They probably felt the same way about her magic, and that of Hong-la.

She wondered sadly if she would ever get a chance to bring the insights and knowledge she was collecting back to the Citadel at Tsarepheth. If there would even *be* a Tsarepheth to bring it to. She allowed the grief a moment, then slid it aside, rendering her mind open and empty. As empty as it could be, anyway—which was only ever empty for a moment.

She had not been practicing her meditations regularly since Hsiung had left them.

"Bad wizard," she muttered.

Tsering caught her eye and flashed a quick, crooked smile, so Samarkar knew she'd heard her. "There are good ones?"

"Some of us more dutiful than others." Calm breathing, slow and deep. An empty heart, an empty mind. Or the closest she could manage under the circumstances.

Temur had seated himself in the center of the warded circle. A faint glow surrounded him, when she kept her breathing calm and her focus steady and watched him only from the corner of her eye; the remnant of his blood-vow, perhaps. Samarkar let the thought move through her, observed it, let it go.

She heard Jurchadai chanting under his breath, and observed that as well, and also let it go. Temur unwrapped the geode and held it in his hands, a bit of chamois shielding his palm from direct contact with the stone. He bent over it and Samarkar guessed he was frowning, though her position was such that she found herself looking chiefly at his frizzed, wooly braid.

He trusts me with his back.

A stab of anxiety adhered to the thought. This too, she let pass away. She concentrated on the moment, on feeling for intrusions, on maintaining the protective envelope of energy that would keep all of them, and Temur in particular, safe.

Temur straightened his spine. He laid a bare-bladed dagger across his knees. Over and over again, as Hong-la had suggested, he began to mutter the name and title of their enemy: *Mukhtar ai-Idoj, al-Sepehr. Mukhtar ai-Idoj, al-Sepehr. Mukhtar ai-Idoj, al-Sepehr.*

Mukhtar ai-Idoj, al-Sepehr.

The air before him clouded, as if a faint mist had blown into the white-house. And then it cleared, attaining that peculiar limpidity that water can sometimes have, seeming even more transparent than the atmosphere. Beyond it, over Temur's shoulder, Samarkar glimpsed a flurry of movement as someone hastily, fumblingly drew an indigo veil up to cover the lower half of a face.

The person on the other end of the connection was not fast enough to conceal the fact that she was a woman. And so—or so Samarkar guessed—Temur hesitated, though the dagger was in his hand.

Samarkar had a moment to register the white knuckles of the hand that pulled the blue veil taut across the bridge of a proud nose. Above it gleamed bright, chipped hazel eyes, the striking spear of black in the corner of one of them. She knew those eyes; she had faced them over the barrel of a wheel-lock pistol in a dry water cellar in Asmaracanda.

She knew the voice, too—dry and soft, speaking Qersnyk with a liquid Rahazeen accent. "Re Temur Khagan. We meet again."

Samarkar saw the shudder of decision snake up Temur's arm, the swift dart of his arm behind the dagger. She saw that it pierced the vision before them as if piercing water, and that Jurchadai, opposite her, lunged back from the point.

Within the image, the woman—Saadet ai-Mukhtar, Samarkar assumed—did not even flinch. Her eyes narrowed. "If that worked," she said, "I'd have shot you the moment you appeared."

Samarkar's lip lifted from her teeth. She reached out *otherwise,* but that path too was blocked. The snarl came out between her teeth half-moan.

Across the invisible but palpable distance between them, Saadet laughed. And then she dropped her veil, showing a perfectly ordinary, perfectly strong-featured and regular face. She took a breath Samarkar could hear even over Temur's ragged panting. As if pronouncing sentence on a criminal, she said, "Re Temur. This I curse you: that no horse will bear you. That your endeavors end in death. May you be the proof that a man can endure anything!"

Her left hand moved as if she were slamming something against the stone wall beside her—and the bizarre super-clarity of the air rippled, shattered, and drifted apart. Temur was left half-risen, the dagger still extended, his other hand clenched on the stone. Frozen, almost—until he breathed out heavily and settled back.

Only then did Samarkar go to him, feeling the tingle of the wards as she stepped over their line. They knew her, and would not hold her out. She knelt and placed a hand on Temur's sleeve. The ridged muscle of his forearm slowly softened as he peeled his fingers from the dagger's hilt.

"Temur—" she said.

He looked at her. His smile was stiff, forced. It lasted half an instant too long. "All endeavors end in death," he said. "Eventually. Not much of a curse on those terms, was it?"

But when she took his hand, his fingers were ice cold.

HRAHIMA KNEW WHO HAD COME BEFORE HER COMPANIONS TOLD HER. SHE read it in the wind. And she knew that it was out of cowardice that she chose to vanish.

Cowardice, and an inability to sit still.

She jogged up the hill over the camp, the spring crust on the snow bearing her weight but only just—it held for a moment, then dented with a creak. Her thick pads and the hair between them was enough to protect her from the chill, but every so often she leaned forward and rested some weight on her fingertips, and then the cold burned the softer pads on her hands.

She did not know what she was running to. *Which means you are probably only running* from. *Never a well-considered plan.*

Well, it had suited her, off and on, so far. And she might have kept doing it more or less forever, if she hadn't—quite literally—almost run into Hryorah's broad chest as the white tigress stepped from between trees in front of Hrahima. Her color might have camouflaged her in the snow, but even upset Hrahima knew better than to run downwind. And Hryorah's scent and presence rolled from her with an abruptness that told Hrahima unequivocally *how* she had been hiding it.

Hrahima set her feet and stopped, so short the snow crust broke under her feet and she planted both hands in the drifts before her. It was an undignified end to her flight, crouched at Hryorah's feet, glittering veils of dashed-up snow slowly settling around both of them.

Behind her, she sensed the emergence of Faranghis as he released the

Immanent Destiny and permitted his presence to once again affect the course of the world.

Hrahima remained crouched, as if springing away—leaping over Hryorah's head, for example—would accomplish anything. Hryorah could match and double Hrahima's best leap, could intercept her in midair. Hryorah had not abandoned the power of the Sun Within.

For a moment, they crouched facing each other—Hryorah's ears pricked, Hrahima's ignominiously flat against her skull. Cold ached in Hrahima's canine teeth as her face wrinkled in a snarl.

Hryorah just stood there, smaller than Hrahima and with her black-striped white coat vanishing into the shadows of tree branches on snow. She held out her left hand, palm up, fingers balled loosely. When she opened it, piled gold glinted loosely in the chilly light.

Hrahima felt no surprise. Not at the heap of earrings. Not at Hryorah's next words, formal and measured: "Hrahima. Feroushi sends his regards."

No honorific, as humans would use. The very nakedness of her name on this stranger's tongue was the mark of regard. Younger Chotse might fence themselves in with hedges, veritable briars of titles. Those who had attained a full adult education had no need of such things.

"Feroushi is dead." Hrahima stood, dusting the snow from her knees and shoulders as if it were the most pressing matter in the world. "I have no wish to pretend otherwise."

Hryorah kept her hand outstretched. "I see you've replaced these," she said. "Still, here are the ones Feroushi and the tribe awarded you. If you would rather have them back."

Hrahima's ears flicked in distress, making her freshly aware of how the gold in them chimed, and how ragged and beaded with scar the edges were.

"I pulled them out."

"Minds change." Hryorah's voice soothed, a rumble that was almost a purr. The consummate Hrr-tchee diplomat. "You earned these."

"I earned *these*," Hrahima replied. This time her ear-flick was deliberate.

By contrast, Hryorah's ears stayed perfectly still, the gold rings in them not even wavering in a breeze. She wore perhaps half as many as were represented by the little pile on her palm. Faranghis was a male. His ears—of course—were unpierced and smooth at the edges.

Hrahima wondered how many earrings his mate wore.

"Hrahima," Hryorah said.

She paused, the wind ruffling her pale pelt, her glacial eyes focused as if she could look right *through* Hrahima and see what lay at her center. In that moment, with the light sideways through Hryorah's irises as if they were two cabochon aquamarines, the other Hrr-tchee's youth and her optimism shone from her like beacons.

It made Hrahima want to leap over her and run, and run, and run some more.

The moment passed. The white tiger continued, "You are missed. You are mourned. The Immanent Destiny is hollowed by your absence, and our cubs and the cubs of our cubs will regret the loss of your experience. Your wisdom."

My experience. My wisdom. My mate's blood on the leaves, clotted thick.

"My cub is dead."

For a moment, she thought Hryorah would tell her she could have more cubs. Or that cubs not her own needed her as well. But the white northern-born Cho-tse was not so young as that. Or perhaps the Sun Within told her to be wary, that this was not a safe path to tread.

Her ears still pricked, her eyes still bright, Hryorah said, "She is waiting for you, too."

Hrahima opened her mouth and then closed it again, before her gape-mouthed astonishment could be misconstrued as showing her fangs. How would one explain to this Hrr-tchee, not so far gone from a cub herself, the simple unabridged agony of gazing into the Sun Within and feeling that reminder of a presence that would never grace you again? How was it possible to face daily the conviction that those deaths *meant* something, that they were a *destiny*? And not meaningless, brutal: the simple grinding of the wheels of the world?

"It's not real," Hrahima said tiredly. "It's all a damned delusion, do you understand? The Immanent Destiny, the Sun Within. The voices of the ancestors and their damned useless wisdom. A lie and meaningless, every bit of it."

Hrahima could hear Faranghis shifting his weight behind her. And

Hryorah was still looking at her. *Looking* at her. Not moving, not speaking. Hrahima could already hear every argument she might make—but she did not make any of them. *How can you refuse to take your rightful and ordained place among the ancestors, when the time comes? How can you deny the power of the Sun Within?*

She couldn't deny that power. She knew it. She had lived it—taught it—for twenty years. But neither could she accept its validity, if it were somehow seen as justifying Feroushi and Khraveh having been taken from her.

She sighed and looked down at the snow. "And what of you, Hryorah? You have come to us in an hour of danger; will you stand against this poisonous Nameless and his poisonous designs? Where is the Sun Within on the topic of stopping al-Sepehr?"

Hryorah tried to stare her down—and succeeded. Hrahima's chin dropped as if someone had taken her head and pushed it forward. She cringed, ears flat, like a cowed cub.

And she persisted. "He is a threat to more than Re Temur, Sister Hryorah."

"If it is your Immanent Destiny," Hryorah said, "then I would be persuaded to aid you. But as it is . . . Monkey politics, Hrahima. Monkey wizards, monkey wars."

Whiskers flat against her cheeks, Hrahima snarled. "We live in the same world."

"Monkey politics," Hryorah repeated. "Monkey wars."

Hrahima's tail lashed, but she forced her head up, her gaze to Faranghis. "You?" she asked.

"Sister," he said kindly, "come home."

"I don't want your damned destiny, do you understand? I don't want your fucking place in the world!"

Faranghis stepped back before Hrahima's ferocity. Hryorah closed her fingers over the gleaming gold, and lowered her hand to her side.

"Then peace be with you," she said. "Sister Hrahima."

Hrahima was pretty sure it wasn't peace she wanted, either. She knew what she wanted. And it was gone.

22

THE CHO-TSE EMISSARIES LEFT THE DAY AFTER THEY ARRIVED, AND IT WAS very plain that they had not gotten what they wanted. Temur was becoming accustomed to the ghulim who came into Edene's white-house every so often to confer with her and glided out again like silent ghosts. Though Temur had begun to feel that the grind of winter would be unending, and that spring and war were a distant unreality, the first signs of their imminent inevitability were appearing. Mares were coming into season, ewes swelling with lambs. Bansh was bred to a smoke-colored stud of Temurbataar's line in hopes of a filly, this time, and Edene began breaking Afrit to saddle. He took to it as naturally as he took to the breeding pen, where he covered half a dozen mares despite his youth. At six months of age, he had the bone and stamina of a three-year-old, and his fine long neck was starting to develop stallion muscle.

His unnatural growth and Bansh's spectacular run on mist and snow seemed to have had an effect on the Qersnyk perceptions of Bansh and her colt; they were seen as frankly supernatural now, and—at least by the folk who had already chosen to follow Temur—they were accepted as proof of divine favor.

While Bansh was in the breeding pen, Temur borrowed Buldshak—

and discovered that the rose-gray treated him with the same horror she might have displayed if one of the Cho-tse had tried to mount her. Bansh would let him ride, and Afrit acted no differently toward Temur than any other young stallion still learning his manners.

"The curse," Temur said to Samarkar, reclining back into her arms. The warmth of her body seemed to pull the pain and tension from his shoulders. "Saadet's curse."

"What a good thing Bansh is not merely a horse," she replied.

It turned out that Jurchadai had a genius for administration—a genius that was in grave demand as the roads became passable and the valley began to fill up with more and more people. The shaman-rememberer joined Hong-la in apportioning resources and campsites and settling disputes, freeing up Temur for the ever-more-important business of, as he put it, being a display monarch.

Temur found himself increasingly boggled that this many folk would rally to his banner under any condition, but after a short while he . . . did not so much accept it as force himself to stop questioning it.

He didn't have time, anyway. His days became a spiral of strategy meetings, fealty-swearings, requests for healing, and intelligence reports. There were more men of fighting age among the new arrivals, some of whom were the remnants of Temur's brother Qulan's army. This necessitated drills and training, wherein Dead Men would learn to fight on the same side as Lizard People—but no matter how much they trained and practiced, the experienced general in Temur's head knew it could never be sufficient. Al-Sepehr had his own men, Qori Buqa's, and probably the armies of Kara Mehmed. Temur had the scraps and refugees of four or five fallen cities, a Cho-tse, and a mismatched band of wizards, priests, and sorcerers. Lizard Folk were fierce fighters, and so were Dead Men . . . but he didn't have enough of anything to let him sleep at night.

Temur came to rely on Tsareg Oljei and Tsareg Toragana for just about everything pertaining to the running of the camp—at first because they were doing it, and had already been doing it. But he felt confirmed in his decision when they pressed the children into service as messengers, and began sending them around with little bags of purple salt from the Rasan stores, and instructing everyone in what the signal would be for an attack and in how to salt their weapons against blood ghosts.

There was no recent sign of blood ghosts. But they, like Temur, had witnessed the first attack. And he was comforted that someone else would think of defenses, even if he hadn't.

Samarkar, Hong-la, and Tsering kept their limited number of smiths and artisans busy building engines of war. It was likely that al-Sepehr would bring the battle to them, and she wanted to be prepared. They did not have the forge and foundry facilities to manufacture cannon, so she set them to making arrow-cannons: rows of bamboo tubes, lashed in tiers, that could be stuffed with arrows strapped to rockets. They did not have enough mares for all the mounted warriors, so she arranged for cousins to share horses so everyone could drill. Of course the horses needed rest too—another limiting factor on their readiness.

"We still need more horses," she told Temur, one day out by the corral where the nucleus of his Sacred Herd was kept when they were not in use among the Qersnyk warriors. Among them were duns bear-colored, eagle-colored, and sand. There were three colors of roans, seven kinds of spots, six colors of bay—including Bansh, and including a blood-nosed bay filly who might have been a black horse, except where she looked as if she had plunged her muzzle into a slaughter-house trough. There was a bay mare who looked like she'd run through milk, her legs and belly and muzzle white, the rest of her shining metallic mahogany under the rising and setting suns. There was the mouse-colored dun Jerboa, and the rose-gray Buldshak. And there was Afrit, palest of them all, and no other white or ghost-colored horses at all.

Temur watched them, frowning. Samarkar put herself against the rail beside his shoulder. "We'll face al-Sepehr when he comes."

"If I thought it would help anything, I'd sue for peace," said Temur. "We're not ready to fight this war."

"The only peace the Nameless offer is eternal peace. They are not conquerors; they're devourers. They were raised by wolves."

Temur snorted. "Wolves have strong families, honor their parents, raise cubs with love and discipline, and work together for the good of the clan. Al-Sepehr is no wolf."

"Fine," Samarkar said. "He's a very human monster, then."

He ground the toe of his boot into the muddy earth. "When I promised to assemble a Sacred Herd, I was relying on my ability to use Afrit to produce some of the rarer colors—I can breed him to a sorrel mare and get a pearl foal, for example. And as fast as he's growing . . . But it will be most of a year before his first foals are on the ground. There's no way I can find or breed another twelve colors of horses before we go to war. And as you said, even with Tzitzik's lot, we just don't have enough horses."

"Well," Samarkar began, and frowned.

Temur's mouth did something odd and uncomfortable-looking. "That'll teach me to make grand gestures?"

She smiled. "We'll just have to figure out a way to game the system, then."

He stared at her. She stared back.

"What?" she said.

"I love you."

"Good," she said. And touched his cheek before she smiled.

TSERING HAD FIRST BEGUN TEACHING SAMARKAR HOW TO MAKE GUN-powder on the journey to Kashe that had ended with their discovery that the city was destroyed and their rescue of the very ill Temur. Now, they stood side by side over trays of saltpeter, sulfur, and charcoal, mixing them in careful proportions and checking each other's work while Hong-la performed the office of safety inspector. They worked in a covered tent, closer to the road than the rest of the encampment.

It was routine work, if meticulous. And deeply satisfying.

On this particular day, their camaraderie included Temur, who was taking a brief moment to hide from his duties and learn a little about the capabilities of gun powder. He found it unexpectedly fascinating.

Until the lesson was interrupted by the splashing footsteps of a runner, approaching up the road. A Rasani youth, one of the scouts and sentries that had been posted under Hrahima's command since the roads began to clear, he was moving fast. He dropped to a crouch before Temur. "An army!" he cried.

"Qersnyk riders?"

"Temple monks," the youth replied. "Thirty score, I'd say."

Temur's heart swelled with conflicting emotions: relief, disbelief, joy. He touched the runner on the head and turned to Samarkar. "He did it," he said, barely accepting what he heard in his own words. "He brought help after all."

WHEN THE CHERRY AND PLUM BLOSSOMS WEIGHTED THE TREE BOUGHS LIKE late season snow and the farmers' mud-clotted oxen leaned into plow collars, the final army marched in. Five hundred shaven-headed monks in robes dyed a half-dozen drab vegetable colors, barefoot or in sandals, made tidier lines than Temur had ever seen outside of the illustrations in a book on tactics. Like a watercolor of a Song Imperial Army, from the days when there had been a Song Imperium.

Having had a warning of their approach, he sat in Bansh's saddle on a small rise to review them. On Temur's left rode Tesefahun on his stocky, pig-bellied roan. Beyond him, Edene, Ganjin in his cradleboard at her knee, stroking Buldshak's sparse, red-silver mane. Her hand rested over her belly, which did not yet show a bulge, but his heart flared sun-warm in his chest at the sight. On his left rode Samarkar on the white-face mouse-dun, wearing the wizard's armor Tesefahun had given her with the helm slung by her knee.

My family.

Also arrayed in the group at the top of the rise were Tzitzik, Iskandar who had been Uthman Caliph, Chatagai and his mother Nilufer . . . and Hrahima, standing out of the horses' direct line of sight and a little downwind.

The faces of the monks struck Temur most—how different they were, under the superficial façade of regularity and conformity presented by their ordered ranks. But they covered the full range of Song types—and at the back of the ranks, he could see some that were freshfaced, scared . . . terribly young.

His own age, Temur realized with a shock. In years only, not in experience. He searched among them for Hsiung. When Temur found the monk, it was an even more brutal twist inside of him. Hsiung was not in line with the others. Instead, he was in a group off to the side, and he rested the fingers of his left hand on a novice's sleeve as if he needed the guidance. The sash knotted over his robe was not dyed, and Temur had an unpleasant premonition that he knew why.

"Samarkar—"

She reined Jerboa closer. "I see," she said in a low voice. Another might have found her clinical tone indicative of a chilly soul. Temur knew she had been trained to make it so. "I would not have expected his blindness to progress so fast."

With Hsiung stood several other monks and what Temur assumed from their black square-sleeved coats were Song emissaries of some sort. There was also a tall, center-wheeled cart with an enclosed box and curtained windows. One of the curtains twitched as Temur glanced that way. Someone shy and important, he deduced, resided within.

Well, one of the nice things about being Khagan was that he could be pretty sure he'd eventually be introduced.

"Send someone for Hong-la," Temur said to Samarkar. "I need somebody who can handle Song functionary ranks."

Those varied from kingdom to kingdom within what had been the Song Imperium. But they had some common elements, arising from the same roots. Temur knew some of it: he'd spent his childhood fighting on the borders of Song, after all—and some Qersnyk holdings, like Dragon Lake itself, were ethnically still very much beholden to southern customs. The Wizard Hong, on the other hand, had been raised from birth to be a court eunuch. *He* knew the intricacies well enough to explain the nuances to Song princes. Which was a grasp of etiquette that might even be too refined, if Temur were minded to present himself as a Qersnyk barbarian.

The ill-assorted array of allies accompanying him as he stood in review of his troops might be enough to establish that, of course. But Temur found that another one of the nice things about being Khagan was that he didn't have to be arsed to care.

The monks and functionaries with Brother Hsiung began to come forward, the wagon rolling with them. Temur saw the subtle movements of Samarkar's hands behind her mare's neck as she prepared—but did not yet raise—her wards. But the monks stopped a respectful distance away and below—at the bottom of the hillock.

The novice led Brother Hsiung forward, and—apparently speaking for Hsiung—introduced the primary members of his order, beginning with a leathery one-handed fellow in a black sash named War-zi: Master War.

Like the rank-and-file arrayed below, these elders wore a selection of earth-toned fabrics. As they were introduced, Temur's suspicion that these monks represented more orders than just Brother Hsiung's was confirmed.

Hsiung had delivered more than he promised, as he so often did. And he looked thin, weary. Temur, who had seen the sturdy monk cover as much road in a day as the best mare he'd ever known, smoothed away a frown.

Edene must have noticed. Her face revealed nothing above the high collar of her Qersnyk coat; she barely seemed to blink. But she let Buld-shak sidle a step closer to Bansh, so the mares stood shoulder to shoul-der and Edene's knee pressed Temur's. Temur was grateful, even when Buldshak sidled and tried to edge away from him.

No horse will bear you.

One of the Song functionaries had a better coat than the rest—brocade, and banded with orange and green embroidery. He was the one who stepped back beside the cart—it was drawn by a single white ox with ribbons trailing from its horns—and bent down to fold a set of steps from beside a curtained doorway. As he was drawing the curtain back, Hong-la arrived at a swift walk, his long legs covering the ground faster than many men could have jogged.

He stopped by Temur's stirrup, between Bansh and Jerboa, and steadfastly ignored Jerboa's intrigued licking of his black wizard's trou-sers.

Temur said, "What is going on here?"

"There's a dignitary in that cart, of course," Hong-la said. Then, in a completely different voice: "Sage's whiskers!"

Edene glanced down sharply. "What?"

Hong-la shook his head, visibly collecting himself. "The majordomo. It's . . . somebody I used to know. Zhan Zhang. His name, I mean. Zhan Zhang."

That majordomo—in his gaudy coat—stepped forward beside the monks. He spoke, in perfect Qersnyk—almost accentless: "Re Temur Khagan, Lord of the North! Allow me to present her radiance, the Lady Diao who comes as an emissary from her father, the Lord Diao!"

A figure framed herself in the doorway, crouching slightly until she could bend under the lintel and stand.

She was slender and tall, her hair blackened and oiled and twisted up into a jeweled pillar atop her whitened brow. It chimed with tiny stamped gold ornaments. She wore a tight ankle-length coat of silk the color of peach skin—pale gold, but catching the Soft-day sun with pale red highlights. It was slit up one side so she could walk, and a leg clad in white silk pantaloons flashed with each step she took, descending.

Despite her elaborate and constricting finery—and if ever there were a better assurance that no one meant to start a fight, it was that outfit—the lady Diao wore a gold-hilted sword thrust through her wide silk sash: Song-style, long and straight, with an ivory sheath and hilt and a filigreed oval guard.

Zhan Zhang crouched down quickly and with a practiced flare of his wrists, snapped a small carpet open even as the Lady Diao descended the three steps. Her slippered foot rested on knotted red wool, rather than the bare earth. She minced forward to the edge of the rug and bowed very low, her sword sheath sticking into the air like a stiff tail, her forehead almost touching her knees.

When she straightened again, her eyes rose to his face. Her voice was sweet and fluting, birdsong, rich with the harmonics of the eastern Song dialects. "My honored father sent me with an elaborate speech for your ears, Temur Khagan, and offers of alliance in return for certain considerations. But I perceive that you are a martial emperor, and would not waste your hours of light with flowery words and pretty postures. So I ask you plainly, Temur Khagan: will you receive my embassy?"

Hong-la turned his face to hide his lips when he spoke. "This is a marriage proposal, Temur Khagan. The lady looks you in the face."

Temur didn't nod; he knew. He returned her gaze, frank and appraising. He could not tell if she blushed under her formal painting of white lead, her lips reddened with cochineal.

Samarkar said, "If she's staying, we need to break her of that face paint. It kills girls, you know."

That, he had not. Hong-la added, "And makes them stupid. And infertile. I'll have a full report on Lord Diao for you Soft-tonight, Khagan."

While they spoke, Zhan Zhang was translating what Lady Diao had said with surprising deftness and accuracy. Temur took advantage of the extra time to consider his response.

But when he answered, he answered in her own language.

His Song was not as good as Zhan's Qersnyk, but it sufficed.

"My Lady Diao," he said, "you have traveled far and in difficult circumstances. Please accept the hospitality of my household, and when you have rested and eaten, we will—as you wish—take up this discussion again, in less formal circumstances. This is Tsareg Edene, mother of my son. She will care for your every need."

He glanced at Edene to make sure of her and caught the edge of her smile. If there were any apprehension in Lady Diao's expression, the paint hid it. She bowed low again and stepped back into her litter. Edene reined Buldshak forward, ready to lead them away.

Samarkar laid her fingertips against Temur's elbow. In the lowest, clearest voice he'd ever heard, she said, "Accept her suit or send her home. But do not keep her like a trophy in a crystal bell."

He smiled sideways at Samarkar to hide the pang he felt for her, for her own youth and her chance at children lost to politics. For the revenge she had taken. "I hear your counsel, Wizard," he said. He turned to Edene. "You will see to her, my heart?"

"She will be well-accounted for." She touched Buldshak forward, and Temur stopped her with a lifted hand.

"Still well?" he asked, with a gesture to her hand and the damned ring on it.

"No worse," she answered. She handed Ganjin in his cradleboard across to Samarkar, and then she reined her mare away.

As she left, followed by lady Diao's carriage and the white ox that drew it, Zhan came forward, walking smoothly, and joined the small group of monks that included Brother Hsiung. Temur gave Hong-la instructions to make them comfortable and find them places to camp—Hong-la and Jurchadai between them, with their collective genius for organization and administration, would manage everything far better than Temur could. It was complicated by the fact that Jurchadai had come to Temur and told him: *You must keep secrets from me now. There are shaman-rememberers who support Qori Buqa's son.* But they made what use of him they safely could.

Then he singled out the medium-sized fellow, not much bigger than Temur, wearing a furrowed brow and the cropped hair of all the Wretched Mountain Temple Brotherhood, who had been identified as War-zi.

Temur glanced at Samarkar and made a small gesture with his hand. She would know what he wanted, and make it happen without disturbing protocol. She reined Jerboa forward two steps and spoke to the monk directly. "Master War, with your permission, Temur Khagan would like to speak privately both with you and with your acolyte Brother Hsiung. Will you join us while Hong-la makes your retinue comfortable?"

Master War inclined his head. His arms were folded inside his sleeves, hiding the stump of one hand as he incrementally bowed. "I come at the Khagan's pleasure," he replied.

It was a relief to let the door drape fall between the interior of the white-house and the muddy, cold world without. Temur embraced Brother Hsiung—the monk accepted it stolidly, but gave him a little extra squeeze—then gestured him and Master War to places among the cushions. Samarkar settled Ganjin in a corner, then blew up the coals in the brazier and added more fuel, preparatory to making tea.

Temur settled himself on the camel saddle that served as his perch until he reclaimed his grandfather's Seat. He folded his arms on his knees and addressed Master War. "My gratitude to your order, and those of your brother monks. You are an unlooked-for relief."

"We have not come for the Khaganate," Master War said. "I must be plain. We come because my novice has convinced me that a greater evil walks the world. We are here to oppose al-Sepehr."

"We bless your coming," Temur said. "Whatever motivates it. Samarkar, will you bring paper and a brush for Brother Hsiung?"

She did, then returned to measuring tea and waiting for the water. Her kettles always boiled the fastest, and Temur was sure she used wizardry to cheat them along. The first slow steam already curled from the spout.

Hsiung wet the brush in his mouth, scrubbed it on the inkstone, and after a glance at Master War quickly wrote, *I have shared the truth with War-zi and the other masters, as I know it. He has been kind enough not to turn me out, though I deserved it. I have used the winter to continue my research on Erem.*

The characters his brush made were small in size and spaced unevenly, lost in the midst of a sea of white. Temur thought of his former elegant calligraphy and bit back a sound of protest. A Khagan did not moan in despair. At least, not in public.

"Hsiung," Samarkar said sadly, frowning as she poured water over tea.

He glanced at her and shook his head. Something pushed the flap of the white-house aside; Temur looked up, ready to discipline whoever it was—but he was met by the steady brown regard of the great mastiff Sube. The dog walked around the circle, careful not to scorch his shedding coat on the brazier, and promptly lay down and threw his head in Hsiung's lap, heedless of ink and brush and papers.

Hsiung looked up helplessly.

"We say they're the reincarnations of good monks," Temur said. "Maybe he was a friend in a past life."

Hsiung bit back a chuckle. With a shrug, he balanced his paper on the dog's broad skull and wrote again, while Master War sipped the tea Samarkar handed to him and Sube grumbled disgruntledly.

I have not felt al-Sepehr's magic often this winter. I believe he bides his time and husbands his strength. But I have learned something that I must share. Something worth my sight and even my life.

Temur sat back. Samarkar had set a bowl of tea near his knee. He picked it up now and blew across it. "Hsiung—"

Master War said, "Though my brother is in disgrace for other reasons, he is not incorrect. Novice Hsiung, if I may?"

Hsiung lowered his eyes, and laid paper and brush aside. Sube, seeing his opportunity, crawled farther into his lap. The dog weighed as much as the monk; the effect was ridiculous.

Temur could not have found a laugh.

Master War continued. "Brother Hsiung has discovered certain necromantic sorceries of Old Erem that can be used not merely to animate the corpses of the dead, or call their spirits up as blood ghosts . . . but to call back the dead to possess and inhabit the living."

Even as Temur thought of the mysterious green glow of Hsiung's eyes, and the bouts of compulsion that attended it, Samarkar jumped to her feet. "He's been trying to call his filthy demigod into Brother Hsiung?"

Master War sat, imperturbable. "Brother Hsiung believes that is not the case. The sacrifice must be a willing one, and there must be widespread belief in the resurrection. Also, the tithe in souls he has been making—the number of deaths—"

"Whole cities," said Samarkar. "Whole nations, practically."

Master War nodded. "There is power in that sacrifice to elevate his dread demigod and prophet until the Carrion King, the Joy-of-Ravens himself, reaches the level of the Sages, the Mother Dragon, or even the Scholar-God of the Uthman Caliphs."

"Oh," Samarkar said. She sat down hard, beside Temur. "That's why the rumors of the Carrion King's return. That's why the skinned corpses. That's why—"

She glanced at Temur, and did not say *your dreams*, but he heard the words as clearly as if she had spoken.

He reached out to steady her. She covered his hand with her own. Her fingers were cold. "Al-Sepehr means to *become* the Joy-of-Ravens."

War-zi inclined his head. The stump of his arm thumped softly against his thigh for emphasis. "We will fight."

"We will fight as well," Temur said.

"The monks will need horses to fight cavalry."

"Can you fight on horseback?"

"We have our ways."

"Horses, we do not have." Then Temur felt a bolt of excitement. "But perhaps we have the means to get some."

"Temur?" said Samarkar. Hsiung, perhaps picking up on the shift in mood, raised his head. His fingers burrowed into Sube's dirty ruff, deep enough to vanish there.

Temur said, "I need to talk to the dragon."

Samarkar touched him now, a fingertip brush against his thigh. "It's not the equinox yet."

"Surely not even a dragon minds getting his gold a little early."

Master War blinked. "Dragon?"

As if he could not perceive the thunder of Hong-la's heart in his throat, Zhan Zhang walked beside him in a mutually regarded silence, observing everything Hong-la did until Hong-la was satisfied that Jurchadai could handle the rest of the billeting arrangements. That done, Hong-la took up his courage and turned to Zhang and said, "Will you walk with me?"

Zhang, mildly, nodded. And followed him out of the camp.

The roads were too muddy for much walking, the woods still full of snow—so Hong-la brought Zhang to the spiral stair up the rock pinnacle, and together they climbed it. Thirty years had not slowed Zhang much: he made the climb with as much ease as Hong did. Finally, they reached the landing, and found themselves alone on that bright spire. Hard-day sun streamed down around them, and the bare trees gave no shade, but the view was amazing.

Hong paused a moment, surveying for the first time the full extent of the young Khagan's army. It was . . . reassuring.

"Thirty years," Hong said.

Zhang said, "Twenty-nine."

"Did you know I was here when you agreed to accompany lady Diao?" Hong asked, at the exact same moment Zhang said, "So it's Wizard Hong now, Dragonfly?"

The old nickname struck him, stuck him, like a pin driven through the body of that namesake insect. Hong closed his eyes, even though he looked out over emptiness and not at Zhang at all.

Hong said, "You don't know?"

"I looked," Zhang said, "but it had to be carefully. Without my father knowing. And it seemed to my resources then that you might as well have wandered off the edge of the wide world."

"Anywhere in the wide world was too close to you," he said. "But Tsarepheth was farther away than most places."

"I don't blame you," Zhang said. He touched Hong's arm with the back of his hand. "Bad as it was when you left, at least I could hope you were safe. If you had stayed, my father would have . . . You, and your brother's family."

Hong nodded. "Did you marry her?"

"You don't know?"

"I went out of my way not to find out."

"She died in childbirth," Zhang said. "A damned pity. She was dutiful to her family and mine, and I . . . Once you were gone, I had no more reason not to be dutiful as well. But it was never more than that."

"You have sons?"

"A son. Two daughters," Zhang said. "All married now. I have seven grandchildren. Hong—"

"Then your name continues and—" Hong said.

"Hong!"

Hong-la stopped. He turned, shoulder now to the abyss, and faced Zhan Zhang. He waited.

"My father is dead," said Zhang. "My wife is dead. Come back to Huaxing with me. Be a wizard there."

"You don't know me anymore."

"I know you," Zhang said. "I know you. You are Lu Hong. You are the man I have missed for thirty years."

"Twenty-nine."

Zhang smiled. His crooked eyetooth was still crooked.

"I have a life in Tsarepheth."

"Spend summers there," Zhang said. Earnest. Moisture shining in the corners of his eyes. "Winters are kinder in Huaxing. We are not young, Lu Hong. Lu Hong . . ." The name was a caress.

We are not young.

Hong-la reached out with his hands, and also otherwise. He wrapped his arms around Zhan Zhang's shoulders and pulled him close. He kissed him chastely, between the brows, and felt the shock from his lips through his toes. "We have a war to live through. Sorcerers to deceive and humble. Dragons to out-bargain."

Zhang straightened up with interest. "What do you know about dragons?"

"More than I ever intended." He sighed. "I hope I live long enough to learn the rest."

"You'll die for this Qersnyk barbarian?"

"I'd rather live for him," Hong-la said. "But it's not him, so much as what he opposes. And that Qersnyk barbarian's grandfather *did* conquer a good chunk of Song."

"Because we haven't been able to unite ourselves against anything, no matter what the threat, in centuries," Zhang said, with real irritation. "If it weren't for those conquests of Song, the Qersnyk wouldn't even have a written language. They have a lot of horses and some painted stones. We have seventeen centuries of written history."

"And you can read it all," Hong-la said tenderly. The affection tinged his voice before he realized it. Thirty years—and it felt like nothing. Where, he wondered, had the wrinkles around Zhang's eyes and mouth come from, the strands of gray at his temples? Weren't they boys, firm-bodied and sharp-eyed?

"Not quite all of it."

"True," Hong said, unable to keep the delight from his voice. This was Zhang, his Zhang, with all his prickly banter and his quick temper, which he only ever gave vent to around people he utterly trusted. "That reminds me. I have a ledger you should see. Some of the entries are in the old writing, and elude me."

Hong put his fingers under Zhang's chin and lifted, kissing him square on the complaining mouth.

Zhang managed half a syllable and then melted into the kiss, laughing, not caring that they were *li* above the encampment and in plain sight of everyone who might happen to look up. And Hong discovered that he did not care either.

He pulled Zhang tight against him, grinned down at him, and stepped sideways onto the abyss. Zhang shrieked first, and clutched him—and then the wind rushed up, lifting them, turning their fall into a sloping, looping glide—until Zhang kissed him harder than ever, and they were flying.

23

Six months after fleeing it in disarray, the dowager returned her court to Tsarepheth, an army at her back.

She did not know what she would find. She had set out from Rasa with her entourage in much better order this time, but she had also set out as soon as messengers informed her that the passes were opening. The Cold Fire smoked still, though there was no word of a more serious eruption. Still, ash falls stretched down into the rice-farming country along the river valley.

Yangchen expected disarray. Starvation. The worst, essentially.

Tsarepheth surprised her. At no place in the City of Clouds could one escape the rushing sound of the wild Tsarethi. As Yangchen's entourage and army moved up the long, steep-sided valley, as they passed between the Old Man Stone and the hill called the Black Ox which marked the lower end of the valley, the voice of the river rang in her ears.

Seventeen men and four women in black awaited Yangchen and her people as they came around the curve of the trail and through the narrows.

The wizards stood shoulder to shoulder, three tiers deep across the road. The petal hems of their coats whipped their thighs in the relentless wind. They stood with folded arms, not exactly welcoming.

Yangchen-tsa, at least, recognized the small man at the center of the group: his hair transparent with age, scalp spotted, long thin moustache falling in silky dragon-tendrils beside his mouth. Facial hair was rare in wizards, but some retained the ability to grow it.

And one of those was Yongten-la, master of his order, though they gave their chiefs no name. The head of the Wizards of Tsarepheth needed no title. The fear of other wizards was considered a sufficient mark of respect without additional pretensions.

Children feared their father; wives feared their husband; soldiers feared their general. This was the natural order of things, as Yangchen had learned it at her father's and mother-in-law's knees. But lately, Yangchen had found herself struggling more and more with this hierarchy of unease. She did not *wish* Namri to fear her. And the wizards who surrounded Yongten did not seem wary of him.

They seemed wary, rather, of the dowager and her people.

Yangchen's entourage had stopped, ahead of her. She reined Lord Shuffle through the corridor that opened, Anil-la following behind her as the rest of her people hesitated uncertainly. She paused before Yongten, the sweet spring breeze ruffling Shuffle's coat and chilling her hands within her gloves.

"Do you not know me?" she asked mildly. Her accent was better; she had been working hard to lose the traces of her Song birth in her voice. She was the Rasani Dowager now, and Song would never be her land again.

"You are known, your grace," said Yongten. He bowed, and all his wizards bowed with him, in a wave. "But we have eradicated the demonlings in this valley. And I think you will agree with and adhere to the wisdom that everyone who enters must be screened, to prevent reinfestation. Even the dowager."

"A physical exam, you mean?" asked Anil.

Yongten nodded.

Tsechen had come up behind her on the other side, mounted on a sure-footed, mealy-nosed gelding. Over the winter, she had adopted an almost mannish style of dress—trousers and coats, with her hair dressed plainly and only the barest minimum of cosmetics. Her horse snorted as she reined him in at Lord Shuffle's shoulder.

"The dowager's person is sacrosanct," Tsechen said.

Yangchen-tsa held up a hand. "Eradicated?"

Yongten-la nodded once more. His moustaches caught on the hard cotton of his coat. Yangchen disciplined her desire to reach out and smooth the snags away, wrapping her cold gloved fingers in Shuffle's reins instead.

"It is for the safety of the city and of the Citadel," she said. "I will consent to being examined."

THE EXAMINATION WAS BRIEF AND PAINLESS, INVOLVING ONLY THE PRESSing of a disc of metal and membrane attached to a long, flexible tube to several places on Yangchen's breast and back while a wizard listened to the other end. She was quickly cleared. While the rest of her retinue was examined, she, Anil-la, Namri's nurse, Namri, and Tsechen were made comfortable in a pavilion and supplied with tea and cushions. The pavilion's windward walls had been rolled down and secured to the earth. They provided a welcome relief from the breeze, while enough sun still reached Yangchen and the others to suffuse their little shelter with pleasant warmth.

She was cradling her second bowl of tea when Yongten-la came back to them, a spare black-clad figure silhouetted on the brown-green hillside leading up to their shelter. He bowed low before Yangchen, while Anil-la jumped to his feet and stood uncertainly, shifting like a dog torn between two masters.

"Rise, Yongten-la," Yangchen said. "What are your findings?"

"Your retinue is clean of infestation so far," he said. "It will take a while to check the soldiers, but I would say your court wizard has done well in bringing you safely this far. May I have your permission to speak freely, Dowager?"

"In fact," she said, "I require your report. Take tea with us."

She offered him his own hospitality as though it were hers—but she was the Dowager Regent. And so he accepted it as if it were hers to give as well. He settled in and allowed Anil-la to pour his tea, though he barely tasted it before setting it aside.

"How fares Tsarepheth?" she asked. Namri woke—a big boy now, walking on his own, and how had that happened in four short seasons? Yangchen held out her arms for her son, and the nurse brought him. He tried to cling to the nurse, but she carefully peeled his grubby imperial fingers from her sleeve and placed him in Yangchen's lap.

"The Citadel, well enough. The city—we sheltered many within the Citadel for winter. Since then, we have begun reconstruction of the palace and the streets that burned in the riots. It will take time."

Tsechen glanced at Yangchen for permission. Yangchen, distracting Namri with a mirrored bauble so he would not cry, nodded absently.

"Can you house us at the Citadel until some portion of the palace is safe for habitation?"

Yongten-la, an old court hand, smiled and spoke to Yangchen, as if Tsechen were merely her voice. "We've set a suite aside for your retinue, Dowager. The soldiers—"

"Have barracks," Yangchen said.

Anil-la also waited for her gesture to interject. "Have there been more skinned bodies?"

"Not since before the worst of winter." Yongten-la picked up his tea and swirled it in the cup. Apparently deciding it had cooled enough, he sipped it. "In Rasa?"

"Three," said Anil. "That we know of. The dowager—"

Again, that glance for permission. Again, she nodded, smoothing a frown from her face with the application of court discipline. Yongten-la would think Anil was entirely her creature, if he kept acting so.

Well, perhaps he was. Or perhaps he was treading carefully, in order to not reveal his own treason to the master of his order. It wasn't as if the Dowager Regent's confidences were his only reason to tread carefully.

"The dowager," Anil-la continued, "is in receipt of intelligence confirming that the al-Sepehr of the Nameless is engaged in a plot to bring back the Carrion King, and that he may have succeeded."

Unbidden, all eyes turned north, toward the smudge of the Cold Fire's fume against a Rahazeen sky.

"Gods don't intervene as they did in the old days," Yangchen said. Just at the edge of her vision, the nurse made a sign to avert misfortune.

"If they ever did, outside of stories," Yongten-la replied. "I think if the Sorcerer-Prince had been resurrected, he would be doing more than skinning a vagrant or shopkeeper now and again."

"Such as afflicting us with demonlings?" Yangchen asked, trying not to hear their crystalline voices praising her. "Is the infestation truly eradicated?"

"In Tsarepheth," Yongten said. "We have scouted. Some of the outlying villages and freeholds seem to have maintained their wards and weathered it well. In others . . ."

He shook his head.

"Survivors?" Anil asked.

Again, Yongten shook his head. "Perhaps two hundred dead or unaccounted for, that we're aware of. But that's only within a few days' ride. It looks as though, where demonlings hatched successfully, they attacked the unaffected."

Tsechen grimaced. "Have we any idea what happened to them afterward?"

"We still have a few of the ones that . . . hatched . . . here," Yongten said. "We have to keep moving them to bigger cages. The ones who did murder in the outlying areas—they're in the mountains somewhere, I hypothesize, but we haven't much evidence."

Yangchen made a note to herself to avoid those cages at all costs. Al-Sepehr might not be able to blacken her name, but a few well-phrased catcalls from demonlings were another story. "I have seen some," she said. "Juveniles, I'd guess. Last autumn, on the road south, in the distance."

Anil glanced at her, eyebrows rising. She would not allow herself to shrug. She was the dowager, and though he was her lover, she did not need to let him think she told him everything.

"When your research is complete, destroy them," she said.

Yongten's moustache twitched. "Most of our research currently involves better means to do just that," he said.

SAADET WOULD NOT HAVE NAMED THIS SEASON SPRING, BUT APPARENTLY IT sufficed for the Qersnyk. The frozen ground softened only during the warmest part of the day, and was then slick mud over ice, treacherous for horses, oxen, and walkers alike. The wind, still bitter and biting, froze her even in her woolens and furs, fierce enough to kill the unwary.

The winter had been a time of suspension. She suffered in the cold. Chilblains decked her fingertips and toes; they itched more than they hurt, and drove her to distraction when she needed to look imperturbable and imperial. For example, when she was sitting in court—if you could call a felt-walled tent and a pile of rugs and cushions "court."

The Qersnyk were kind enough about it. Paian and Esen in particular brought her coats and saw to it that the women of their households showed her how to grease herself and dress for warmth. Shahruz was scornful of her womanish weakness, though he condescended to help her when she practiced with the rifle al-Sepehr had given her. And al-Sepehr . . . barely came into her presence at all after their disagreement on the day of Tsaagan Buqa's birth.

And yet, already, the yak cows were calving; the mares were foaling their leggy, attenuated, alien-looking fillies and colts. The meals that had achieved a stultifying sameness in the dark of winter now included eye-watering wild onions no bigger than a chickpea and the roasted remains of stillborn lambs, buried in the embers overnight.

Tsaagan Buqa nursed and grew and learned to lift his head and gaze about himself—with dark mysterious eyes. Saadet very soon began wearing him in a sling, looking forward to the day when he would be strong enough for a cradleboard such as the Qersnyk women used. She brought him on horseback, and finally flew her great, nameless eagle at foxes, if not wolves. Her winter hood was lined with thick, breath-soft russet fur not long after.

And, like the Kyivvan cranes whose pale wings bleached the sky in spring and autumn until the White Sea took its name from them, the Qersnyk armies—and the armies of their allies—were on the move. Qersnyk clans trailed in as it became possible. Half a thousand new warriors arrived over the course of three weeks, and to Saadet's ongoing frustration, al-Sepehr dealt directly with their leaders and her generals and left instructions that she was not to be troubled on "matters of strategy."

She rose before sunrise to complete her own devotions and left her son with his nurse. Having finished before the usual hour, she snuck out early to al-Sepehr's chamber to find him at prayer one morning— the only time she could be sure of catching him alone. She waited— she guessed, in this clockless backwater—outside his door for a third of an hour before she heard him rise and set his pens aside. It was not becoming for the Khatun to wait upon anyone, even her father. But Saadet was not so much a barbarian yet that she would interrupt anyone, especially a man, at his prayers.

He looked up as she paused before him, and the expression on his face sent her reflexively groping for her veil. She drew it across her face, staring at the tips of his boots, the mud-stained hem of his over-robes. Rahazeen clothing was not ideal here on the steppe, but al-Sepehr would not abandon it.

She said, "Why was I not informed of the troop arrivals?"

"Shahruz," al-Sepehr said, "can you not control your sister?"

That brought her brother back, from whatever corner of Saadet's mind he sulked in. She felt him push her to step back, his disgust that she would leave her child and come, like this, to remonstrate with al-Sepehr as if she were a shrew and he a shopkeeper.

For the first time, she did not listen.

Her hands trembled with the effort, but if she could manage not to scratch between her toes in court, she could manage not to let Shahruz send her running in disgrace down the halls.

She drew herself upright, forced herself to look al-Sepehr in the face. His cheeks sucked in like a fish's, eyes widening.

"It is in my son's name they come," she said. She thought of Paian and Esen—would it have been better, or worse, if she had brought them with her?

Al-Sepehr's jaw tightened, and then relaxation smoothed the lines between his eyes. He said, "Of course this is true, Saadet. But they also come because I have arranged for them to come—"

"Are they not the allies of Qori Buqa?"

She startled herself by interrupting him. She reared back, what she had meant to say next stopping her mouth.

In the resulting silence, he inserted a smooth reply. "Qori Buqa's allies were sadly depleted by Qori Buqa's wars. You must understand, many of these come because Re Temur is linked to the blood ghosts, to the destruction of Qeshqer and the massacre here in Qarash."

"I see," said Saadet. Was she now intended to believe that al-Sepehr had planned that link from the first, rather than merely capitalizing upon it as a happy accident when he and Shahruz—and she, she must admit—had failed to kill that bastard slave-son Temur and his pack of whores? "I am not ignorant of strategy. You cannot hold Qarash without me and my son. In the future, I *will* be kept apprised of troop strength and logistics."

At that moment, she almost told him that she had spoken to Re Temur. She felt the words rise up in her on a bubble of wrath, and only bit them back with effort. *O perfidious daughter.* But she was too angry—that Temur had *used* Shahruz's stone! That he had dared!—and al-Sepehr was not angry enough.

Al-Sepehr would not meet her gaze. Politely, protecting her modesty, he stared over her head. "It will be as you say, Saadet."

Leaving, however, she did not feel as if she had won anything.

She resolved to speak to Esen, and have him in particular bring her all news of their readiness for war. And any news of Re Temur, styling himself Khagan, who would die by Saadet's hand alone.

THE KYIVVAN TROOPS ARRIVED BEFORE THE SNOW WAS PROPERLY MELTED. Even deep drifts were insignificant to their indrik-zver, and the immense beasts trampled a path that horses and infantry and even wagons had no trouble following. It was the Kyivvan caravans that kept commerce along the Celadon Highway flowing, albeit intermittently, through the brutal steppe winters and the searing desert summers. They were in company of a large contingent of Mehmed Caliph's troops, including the new caliph himself.

It was Esen who brought Saadet the news. She was in her steam bath—one luxury afforded by the lingering winter and, at least for the moment, bountiful water supplies—when a scratching at the hide door announced a visitor. Unthinking, she acknowledged it.

When the tall warrior strode in, bootless so as not to track in mud and animal droppings but otherwise fully clad, Saadet jumped up with a scream. She clapped her hand to her mouth and the other arm across her breasts and tottered there, dizzy from the heat, uncertain of where to turn.

"Khatun," Esen said uncomfortably. He turned away, sweat already shining on his balding pate, and shielded his eyes with a palm.

Of course nudity was nothing to the Qersnyk; they lived and bathed in their big felt tents and seemed to have no sense of separation of the sexes at all. Saadet forced her hands down and her back straight.

"You have an urgent message?"

"The Khatun had ordered me to report on further troop arrivals, movements, and departures," he said, more formally than he had ever spoken to her before. "This warrior brings the Khatun news that a foreign army is at the city gates, flying flags of treaty. This warrior must also inform his Khatun that her noble father has already ridden out to greet them—"

"Ysmat's *tears*," Saadet swore, already moving toward the doorway, heedless of her nakedness now.

"Khatun?"

She stalked out past attendants, who had yanked the hanging hide open at her cry and now stood befuddled. One of the guards had a sword drawn. Saadet shivered internally at the thought of how close she had come to getting poor loyal Esen gutted.

"Have my mare saddled," she called over her shoulder to Esen. And to the nearest attendant—by happenstance, the one with the naked blade—she snapped, "And get me a pair of pants!"

Ümmühan did not enjoy her journey across the White Sea to Asmaracanda by ship, closed into a tiny cabin and racked with seasickness. But it was privacy of a sort, and privacy she used to light a flame—a ship's lantern because she could not get a brazier—and, once her nausea permitted, to whisper the seventeen syllables comprising a djinn's name.

He appeared in a puff of brimstone reek, and she hastened to open the porthole before somebody could wonder why she was burning gunpowder. When some of the acrid smoke had wafted from the room, she turned on the djinn and whispered fiercely, "You will have me disemboweled for witchcraft!"

The djinn shrugged as if it were no concern of his. "Fire this time," he commented, as if only just noticing the lamp. "Do you mean to bargain with me, friend? Better you made me your ally, ally . . . or if you prefer, you can speak my name one more time to make thrice, and take three wishes of me."

"I do not wish your heathen sorcery," she said. "I'll not damn myself so easily."

His pointed eyebrows rose. His voice stayed soft. No one outside the cabin would hear him, and Ümmühan had wedged the door. "If you don't wish to take up my bargain, why call me back?"

She folded her arms and lounged against the edge of the small fixed table, trying to look insouciant. "I need to know how to protect the Hasitani."

"In the current political climate?" the djinn said. "You've got your work cut out for you. Get rid of Kara Mehmed. And don't let al-Sepehr or this Malului step into his shoes. Better yet, toss the whole caliphate and start over. Could your Hasitani do *worse,* running things?"

It was an impossible dream, but she took a moment to enjoy it. Then, with a frown, she forced herself back to reality. "Fourteen Falzeen princes, Djinn, and not one of them ever made a point of making life easy for the Hasitani."

"Alas," said the djinn. He rippled and faded, his voice crackling and seeming to grow dim. "But at least they didn't go out of their way to make it *hard,* now did they? Better answer the door, poetess. I think I hear your master coming."

He vanished, leaving Ümmühan to rush to do as he suggested—and then to light incense, quickly, to hide the lingering pall in the room. It helped only inasmuch as it was confusing: Mehmed told her specifically never to burn that joss again.

The barge up the Mother River through the Range of Ghosts had been a pleasant interlude, but it hadn't made up for the lurching and bone-jolting progress of the enclosed litter in which she had accompanied Mehmed Caliph's army—and Mehmed Caliph—overland to their rendezvous with the troops from Kyiv. She had not enjoyed sleeping rough—though she shared Mehmed Caliph's tent—camp food, or the unexpectedly brutal cold of the steppe.

She spent a good deal of that time—especially aboard ship—cursing herself for the pleading, pleasing, and gentle manipulation she had used to convince Kara Mehmed that her place was at his side—and that it was his idea to bring her. She was not any woman, after all, she reminded him. She was the Illiterate, and who better to write a sympathetic history of his triumph?

Men were vain, and Mehmed was no exception. He did not even consider that she might have a motive beyond wishing to be with him, wishing to glorify him with her art, and being eager to continue her role as his liaison with al-Sepehr. But even Ümmühan was forced to admit that her powers of persuasion might have availed her not if Mehmed's lieutenant Malului had not taken up *against* her inclusion.

Mehmed was not the sort of man to be dictated to—by underlings, or even by presumed superiors. Ümmühan was packed up like baggage in her sandalwood birdcage and brought along.

She *had* enjoyed the vast, changeless and yet changing panorama of the world beyond the porthole of the ship and the louvers of her litter—the tossed waves of the White Sea; the towering white and blue walls of Asmaracanda; the rolling, textured hills and flanking mountains of the Mother River and its pass; the snowy and endless expanse of the steppe. She had nearly died of envy at the Kyivvans who swarmed over the backs of their armor-laden indrik-zver like monkeys on elephants, discommoding their great mounts as little as those monkeys might have. Some of the indrik-zver hauled *cannon,* and the cannon crew to man them. The equivalent weight of a horse team and wagon seemed insignificant, matched against the strength of an indrik-bull.

As breathtaking as the expanse of the steppes was, and as fascinatingly alien as the Kyivvans were, by the time they reached Qarash, Ümmühan had written all the poems she ever intended to write about mud. Still, she reminded herself, this was a tremendous opportunity for a poet.

How many women actually got to ride out and experience war? Truth—and mud, and lice, and ruined food were certainly the truth—was the heart of poetry. The books she would write for her sisters! Some would not wish to hear it. Some would prefer their romances, with their dearth of dysentery and gangrene.

But some would hear it, and by the truth be remade. The world stood pinned on two thorns. One was ugliness. One was beauty. The truth did not lie in the middle or at either extreme.

The truth encompassed both.

ÜMMÜHAN'S BOREDOM CURRENTLY ENCOMPASSED BOTH AS WELL. Mehmed was meeting with al-Sepehr and a Kyivvan warlord named Pyotr, which seemed to be what *most* Kyivvans were named, except the ones named Taras. Pyotr had pale eyes, a color so light that Ümmühan had to remind herself constantly that he was not blind. Mehmed had called with them in his tent, which meant that she, Ümmühan, was bent under the weight of cloaks and veils, trying to keep her sleeves and gloves from catching fire as she boiled water for coffee and toasted little cakes.

It was dim in the tent, the only light coming through the smoke hole and from the low coals in the brazier—and from two lamps on the map table that gave plenty of light to the men and none at all to her. And Ümmühan was having enough trouble seeing through the netting of her veils that she wished she could just go and throw open the heavy oiled linen flap that served as a door.

The water boiled; the coffee steeped. She strained the grounds and added honey before decorating the cakes with goat cheese and slices of fig. Once it was assembled on a silver tray, she knelt under it and lifted carefully.

Like a ghost in her gray veiling, she slipped up to the table and served the men. They took no notice of her, as was proper. At least, al-Sepehr and Mehmed took no notice. Pyotr the Kyivvan mouthed a thanks, and seemed to want to catch her eye.

She kept her head turned, the better to eavesdrop. Al-Sepehr's voice, his erudition, the precision of his speech—they still made her shiver. But she called up images of Asitaneh burning, of the mingled craftiness and despair in the expression of the djinn as he bargained with her. Al-Sepehr might bring a quiver to her loins . . . but no one knew better than Ümmühan how such quivers could mislead one into tragic mistakes.

And she was no man, to be destroyed by her desires.

She would not allow him to degrade the Scholar-God's religion with his vile idolatry. She, Ümmühan, would put a stop to it.

Somehow.

As she was returning to the brazier, a commotion of footsteps outside sent her scurrying to the shadows at the edge of the tent. The men leaped up, not quite oversetting the table, though coffee splashed. Ümmühan put her back against the wall and let the tapestries that insulated it fall around her, hoping her gray cloak would help her vanish.

The flap twitched aside, letting in the light she had desired and now cringed from—an irony she would have to include in a poem someday—and revealing a tall Qersnyk man and a small woman costumed as a Nameless assassin, though of course such a thing was impossible. The woman's face was bare, her indigo veil dropped around her throat as a scarf, and she wore a Qersnyk shearling coat with a fox-fur-lined hood open over her Rahazeen trousers.

It took a moment, but Ümmühan had had plenty of time to eavesdrop on her journeys, and she knew the political situation they were entering well. *This is the Khatun, mother of the infant prince. The Rahazeen woman who became a barbarian queen.*

Ümmühan felt a pang of envy as Saadet and her companion strode into Mehmed's tent as if they owned it. *To move so freely. To seem so in command.* Three more good-sized Qersnyk warriors paused outside the tent, and a little one in a blue coat who must be one of their barbarian shamans of questionable gender.

Ümmühan crowded herself into the corner by her birdcage litter, mad with desire to hear what might follow. But Mehmed's eye caught her, and he jerked his chin to the door. "Outside, woman."

"Your slave, my Caliph," she murmured, and whisked through the still-open door—past the four frowning Qersnyk—to plaster herself against the tent wall just around the corner and out of their sight.

The argument that followed was exactly predictable in every detail, except that it was a Rahazeen woman dressing down three grown men. And the Kyivvan was taking her side—when he could get a word in edgewise, in his halting Uthman.

Ümmühan bit her gloved hand through her veil to stifle giggles. She had never dreamed to hear such a thing—and she had never dreamed how it would delight her. It took all her willpower not to stand so close she made a woman-shaped dent in the wall of the tent. Her feet ached with cold in their slippers, but the rest of her was warm enough—at least for a little while.

She was listening so hard that she almost fell *through* that tent wall when someone abruptly loomed up before her. Malului, Mehmed's lieutenant. The unbearable one.

He did not even trouble himself to frown. In a soft, singsong voice like a bullying child, he said, mockingly, "Did Mehmed's little pet piddle a carpet? Is that why she's exiled out in the cold? And what would her master say if he could see her leaning in to catch his every word when she has clearly been banished?"

Ümmühan straightened herself away from the tent. She let her chin drop demurely, hiding even a glimpse of her eyes behind the net of her veils. But a courtesan's ancient practice showed the outline of her breast and hip through the cloak, as if by accident.

"It is out of the wind," she said.

His hand darted out. Through the veils, he grabbed her chin and squeezed. Her jaw came open. She knew better than to lean away. She let a little gasp of pain come into her voice. He pulled her close; she could smell the coffee on his breath, and the stale garlic of his dinner. She turned her eyes aside, afraid he would catch their glitter through her veils, and be even more angry that she had the insolence to stare at him.

Whatever he might have hissed into her ear, she never knew. Because a sharp, feminine voice with a strong Rahazeen accent snapped, "Unhand that woman. Now."

Ümmühan opened her eyes. There was the glitter of a blade in sunlight, but it was not leveled at her. It hovered, instead, with its point lost in Malului's dense black beard.

Gently, his fingers opened. Slowly, his hand fell to his side.

Ümmühan stepped back, rubbing her jaw.

The argument within the tent had ended. The Rahazeen Khatun stood perpendicular to Ümmühan and Malului, and a naked scimitar hung in her hand.

"Step back," she told Malului, and he did. The point of the scimitar reappeared.

"Touch my sister again in this place," she said, "and you will face Qersnyk justice for it. Which will *not* be a simple requirement that you marry the woman wronged. I guarantee you that."

He stepped back again. Her sword did not droop. She smiled. Ümmühan did not see where Malului went, because she was staring at the Khatun when he vanished. A moment later, and the Khatun's sword vanished too.

Ümmühan knelt in the mud at her feet. With her left hand, reflexively, she made the sign of the Women's Rite. Her right, she pressed to her bowed forehead, palm facing her benefactress.

"Khatun," she said. "This unworthy one praises you."

"I believe I have heard of you, sister," the Khatun said. "I would consider myself rather most unworthy of your praise."

Ümmühan kept her head down, her spine bent. Only some of it was because now, suddenly, she was shaking.

"Stand," said the Khatun. "Face me."

Ümmühan did. The Khatun's eyes were beautiful, chipped amber and tiger-eye.

"I am Saadet ai-Mukhtar," the Khatun said. "Are you the poet Ümmühan?"

"I have that honor," said Ümmühan.

"Are you safe here, sister?"

"Kara Mehmed will keep me safe. He is my protector," said Ümmühan. The words grated at her for the first time. She did not wish to state so plainly to this woman—this unveiled queen!—that she was a slave, a courtesan. And then she realized that she had forgotten, and blurted: "Mehmed Caliph, I mean."

Saadet Khatun smiled wider. "I miss the society of pious women," she said. "I will send for you to visit me."

"Khatun?"

But the Khatun was already walking away, diminutive and queenly, light on her feet as any swordsman, dwarfed by the warriors who flocked around her like kittens following their dam.

SAADET KEPT HER BACK STRAIGHT AND DID NOT SPEAK. SHE LET HER WAR-riors and Paian follow her. They made no attempts at conversation, and she knew they assumed she was seething.

So she was, but not for the reasons they probably assumed.

Shahruz had chosen this moment to break his sulky silence, and now he raged at her. *How dare you defy al-Sepehr in front of strangers? How dare you defy al-Sepehr?!*

She did not answer.

You should grovel before him. You owe him all duty and piety! Where would we be without him? What of the future of the Nameless? What of our place in Heaven?

She remained silent.

And what of this slut you have befriended?

She is an artist, Saadet replied.

She is a courtesan. A whore.

She is a sister, sacred in the image of the Scholar-God!

Oh yes, I heard what you thought when she made her secret sign at you. She is a heretic, a chanter of blasphemy! You must grovel before our master and beg to be cleansed. If you tell him what the whore showed you, perhaps he will forgive us—

She is a priest of the Women's Rite, brother. Saadet bit her cheek, hoping he felt the pain as well. *And you will say nothing of her to al-Sepehr.*

24

TEMUR STOOD AT THE MOUTH OF THE CAVE AND LET ITS MOIST BREATH SPILL over him. In the spring chill, it seemed almost warm—but he would rather have felt the dragon's breath.

Soon enough, he told himself, *you will.*

The shards of the dream that had awakened him—and its urgency—seemed barbed under his skin. Trees rose on every side—he had approached the caverns not from the direction of the road, as Samarkar's party had, but via the route the dragon had shown her. Based on her descriptions, it seemed a more direct route—and he'd rather spend as little time underground as he could manage.

He was alone. His pack dug gouges in his shoulders, and the mud of his climb clung to his boots. It was Soft-twilight, and below, much of the camp slept still.

He should go if he was going. No point in sneaking off by himself if he was just going to stand around until somebody noticed he was missing and came looking—and with the demands on his time these days, somebody might notice he was missing pretty much any minute.

The mouth of the cave was muddy and shaped like a kohled eye, bordered above and below by the thick roots of the tree. The bark had been polished from the pale wood in places, worn smooth in others:

Temur was hardly the first person to consider sliding himself into the bowels of the earth this way.

He wondered if the palms of the others had chilled so at the thought. He wondered if they had been able to make their feet take the step forward.

No gut-worms here, he told himself. *And no one is going to wall you inside. And even if it collapses, which it hasn't in however many hundred years people have been bothering that dragon, there's another way out.*

That led him to wonder, then, if there wasn't a third exit. Because from Samarkar's description, a dragon could not fit through this one or the path she'd taken in. And yet, somehow, it had emerged to raid the library.

His heart beat so he barely heard the chirping of rousing songbirds, or their silence that followed. He forced one more step, shaking. Belatedly, he pulled the backpack off and held it against his chest, where it might snag less as he was sliding down.

It might be easier with someone watching. Then he'd be forced not to disgrace himself.

But for now, all he had was himself and a pack full of gold.

It would have to suffice.

He made himself sit down on the wet wood of the tree root, his legs dangling inside the cave. The sky above was brightening, the blue sun making radiant golden spearheads of incipient leaves.

He closed his eyes and took a breath. *Just slide down. There'll be stone under your feet.*

"I thought I'd find you here," said Hrahima.

Samarkar awakened at Soft-twilight to the sounds of Edene's distress.

She and Temur had grown accustomed to Edene's sleeplessness, her strangeness, the way the ghulim drifted in and out, and the way she vanished into their company for hours, sometimes days, at a time. But now, as Samarkar raised her head and blinked sleep-sticky eyes, she noticed two things: one, that Temur was missing and the blankets beside her were cold . . . and two, that Edene crouched beside the brazier with her fingers stuffed into her mouth, keening from the throat, rocking backward and forward on the balls of her feet until Samarkar feared she would fall into the brazier and—

—well, she was the Queen of Erem. She probably would not burn herself. But she might spill the coals.

Samarkar lurched up and found her feet, hopping across the little distance between herself and Edene when the bedclothes snatched at her ankles. She caught Edene's shoulders and pulled her up, back, away. Hugged her and held her close.

Samarkar expected Edene to struggle, but she was rigid as a plank. As an acolyte, Samarkar had once handled a frozen corpse, retrieved from the slopes of the Island-in-the-Mists, that had not been much stiffer. Carefully, Samarkar slid an arm around Edene's waist and lifted her, then laid her down in the bed Samarkar herself had just vacated.

In his corner, Ganjin rolled on his blankets and began to wail.

Edene's breathing was even, though strained. Her heart beat too quickly, but with a strong rhythm. Her jaw was locked, her eyes rolled back as if in some kind of a fit. There were guards outside. Samarkar needed to yell for Tsering-la or Hong; medicine was not her own specialty, and this fit was beyond her reckoning. But she couldn't get a breath herself with fear and her own exerted breathing.

She didn't need to. She had just begun to coach herself into getting a good lungful of air when Edene drew one deep breath and let it out slowly. Ganjin's screaming took on aspects of the wail of battle horns. Edene's eyes focused on Samarkar as she took another and Samarkar had the sharp, sick certainty that it was not *exactly* Edene that assessed her. A smile curved Edene's mouth cruelly—

Then Edene said sharply, "You shall *not!*" in her own voice, and the spell was broken.

"Edene—"

"The ring," Edene said, raising her voice over her son's. "Help me sit now."

"You should rest."

"I want to *sit*," Edene said sharply. "It's bad enough the voices in my head patronize me."

Stung, Samarkar pulled back. Edene rose on her elbows and shook her head, squinting, as Ganjin trailed off in sobs for a moment before commencing another shriek. "I'm sorry."

"I might have deserved it," said Samarkar. "This has been going on for a while, I take it?" *And you haven't mentioned anything?*

Edene sat, and swung her legs over the edge of the sleeping-bench. Lattice creaked under her as her weight shifted. Edene sighed and rose. Moving stiffly but with surety, she collected Ganjin and laid him on her shoulder. She jiggled him twice, and he promptly stopped howling.

Edene said, "And justly am I rebuked in my own turn. The ring wants what it wants. I do not choose to obey its blandishments."

"What did it want that time?"

Edene glanced up at Samarkar through her lashes and did not speak.

"I think," Samarkar said slowly, "that it would not hurt you to come and meditate with Hsiung and me. And Hrahima comes sometimes too. For all her arguements that there is no utility in religion, she likes her breathing exercises."

"I need to talk to the ghulim."

Neither of them pretended it had been an answer. Samarkar was still considering her next avenue of alliance when the door was drawn aside and Hong-la stooped to enter. As he straightened, he bowed to Edene, nodded to Samarkar, and said, "Where is the Khagan?"

Samarkar glanced at Edene. Edene shook her head. The Green Ring gleamed on her finger as she stroked Ganjin's cloud of ebony hair. "He was gone when I came in."

"He snuck out after I fell asleep," said Samarkar. Struck by a sudden supposition, she rose from her own place by the bed and crossed to a chest against the wall. "The key?"

One-handed, the other still full of infant, Edene bent down and unlocked it with the keys from her belt. Samarkar opened the lid and nodded. "He took the tithe."

"By himself!?" Edene asked sharply, apparently reaching the same conclusion Samarkar had. At the note in her voice, Ganjin took a breath to commence wailing again, and—hurriedly—she hushed him.

Hong-la would never be called slow. "He's gone to deal with the dragon. Curse it, why *now*?"

"Why alone?" Edene asked.

"No, why before I could give him the news I carry—" Hong stopped himself, made a snipping gesture, and recommenced. "I have news. A scout has returned with word that al-Sepehr's army is on the move. It is greater than we anticipated. And Jurchadai adds that al-Sepehr has troops from Kyiv, and now, it would seem, the caliphate. We are . . . vastly outnumbered, Khatun."

"Damn," said Edene. "We can hold this valley. But we cannot afford to be pinned in it."

"Just so."

Samarkar made a face. "Still, if we can use the Ways of Erem——"

"If we can get our hands on that map, and somehow read it, you mean?" Hong-la waved his own question away as an irrelevancy. "Actually, Zhang found something in the ledger that the Khagan should know before he treats with the Dragon. It might just solve that problem."

For a moment, Samarkar stood undecided, the weight of uncertainty becoming inevitability paralyzing her.

Still jiggling her son, Edene said, "How far is the army?"

"The scout says . . . less than a hand of days behind him, but not much less. He all but killed his horses on the ride, and they have wagons and materiel."

Samarkar recollected herself, though her pulse beat sharp in her ears. "Then that can wait a few moments before we begin to deploy for battle. The ledger?"

"One of the earliest entries lists a contract—a treaty—between the Sudden Emperor and Joyful Dawn Agate Slumbering."

Samarkar blinked at him. She glanced at Edene, hoping for clarification, but Edene was blinking too.

"What good is a fifteen-hundred-year-old treaty that we can't get our hands on to analyze?" Samarkar asked at last.

"Joyful Dawn Agate Slumbering," said the Wizard Hong, "is the name of a dragon."

TEMUR OPENED HIS EYES AND CRANED HIS HEAD BACK. AS HE HAD EXpected, the branches of the tree above him now framed a great Cho-tse silhouette against the bright sky. It must have been a prodigious leap. He had not even heard her land. "I was trying to be sneaky."

"You snuck," she agreed. She dropped to the earth beside him, mud smacking from between her toes. It splattered his trouser leg, but he was already muddy. He felt the thud more than heard it, and that only because she was close enough to touch. "You snuck so well you nearly went into the lair of a dragon without knowing his name. Or that he's bound by a formal treaty."

Of course they had sent Hrahima to catch him when they realized he was gone. She could cover the ground between here and the camp in . . . moments, not much more. Temur could save his breath for more immediately important questions.

"Where did you find a treaty?"

"Alas," said Hrahima. "It's probably in his lair. But Hong's lover, that monkey-lord's emissary Zhan Zhang, found the record of it in Samarkar's library catalogue. And *I'm* willing to bet there's some line item in it which would preclude swiping both the emperor's copy of it . . . and the rest of his library."

She held out a sheaf of papers covered in neat black calligraphy. The nail on her thumb carved a dent into the top sheet. "The catalogue of books. As translated by Zhan-zi. Of course, they've been in a dragon's lair for who knows how long now. They're steeped in slow poison."

Temur nodded, a thinking gesture. "Do you have an oilcloth I can wrap those in?"

With a flourish, she whipped one from a pouch that dangled from her harness. She shook it out like a Song gallant offering a marriageable young lady his silken handkerchief. "Hong-la thinks of everything. Also, I'm coming with you. I can see in the dark."

"There are magic lanterns. And I'm the Khagan," Temur said reasonably. "I say I go alone."

"Khagan of whom?" Hrahima replied, equally reasonably. "We could arm wrestle over it."

He contemplated that and sighed. "All right. But you carry the paperwork."

It vanished into another pouch, already folded and packaged securely in its attendant oilcloth.

"And the gold."

He held out the pack as best he could, though the weight made his arms tremble. Hrahima lifted it from his grip as if it weighed nothing. "I'd have it no other way. Khagan."

It was easy to tell when a tiger was laughing at you, Temur decided. Their whiskers fluffed forward, just like any cat's. He put his hands on the root before his face, and—gritting his teeth—slipped down into the tunnel.

It was easier with someone watching. The floating lanterns bobbed slightly in the updraft as he slithered down beside them, mud gritting between the polished stone of the tunnel and his coat. There was plenty of room, as he had known there must be: both Hong-la and Hrahima had squeezed through here, after all. That didn't stop Temur from feeling as if the opposite wall—or perhaps, given his angle, he should call it the ceiling—were about to scrape his nose. He tried to listen to the sound of his boots on stone as he wriggled down the shaft, because the accelerating rhythm of his breathing was too nauseating.

"It's easier on the way up," Hrahima promised. "Not too much farther now."

Still, the last drop caught him by surprise, and he found himself crouched on damp stone in a pile of half-rotted leaves before he'd quite accepted that he'd lost contact with the roof and was sliding.

He moved aside before he caught his breath, not wanting to find himself under more than three times his own mass of falling tiger. She dropped beside him a moment later, more gracefully than he'd managed. "How did you know?"

"Echoes," she said, tail flipping. Then her ears came up and she added, "And I did it before."

"Well, since you did it before, lead on, Lady Tiger."

Tail lashing—in amusement?—she did.

THE CAVE OF THE DRAGON WAS AS SAMARKAR AND THE OTHERS HAD DEscribed it, and yet infinitely more rich, wonderful, and strange. Their words had not prepared Temur for the sense of grandeur that attended it, as if this were a place of worship. The lanterns cast a jeweled light, broken into shafts by drips and columns of stone. Some of them, over time, had become entombed in translucent calcite, so some of the formations were illuminated—radiant—from within.

The flocks of books hovering among them imparted a strange ponderous sense of ceremony. The glitter of gold and jewels on every side seemed merely evidence of dignity.

Temur walked with a hushed step, the weight of silence and the weight of stone equal on his shoulders. A moment before he had been struggling against the sensation that the cavern walls were collapsing in against him. What he felt now was peace: not the lightness of relief, but the solemnity of awe.

Then he saw the dragon.

It was as perfectly at-home and camouflaged in its environment as a mantis invisible on stems of grass, and it fastened the same species of motionless predatory regard on Temur. Samarkar had said how it blended with the flowstone, and now Temur saw with his own eyes the drape of wet tendrils, the undulating horns, the folds of loose, scaled skin and the drooping frills like wrinkled draperies. The dragon was every shade of red and gold, russet and orange—and so was the stone around it, like an icy waterfall stained with earth and rust. Its long body wound back through the cavern until Temur lost track of where rocks ended and dragon began, lying slack through a crystalline lake that lapped gently against its scaled hide in rhythm with its breathing.

Temur fought the urge to bow. He was Khagan in title if barely a Khan, so far, in actuality; surely a dragon would expect an emperor to meet it on equal footing. He heard Hrahima come out of the tunnel behind him because she allowed him to hear her.

"Joyful Dawn Agate Slumbering," he said in his accented Song. "I am Re Temur, Khagan of the Qersnyk Steppe and Emperor of Northern Song. In accordance with the terms of treaty, I have come to meet with you."

"Re Temur," the dragon replied. Its voice shivered droplets from the tips of drooping stone teeth overhead, splashing Temur's forehead and hair. The words it spoke next were a dialect of Song he'd never heard before, but somehow the meanings came clear in his mind a moment after he heard the words, as if they echoed. "An emperor and his cat. Well-met. In accordance with the terms of my treaty with your ancestors, you have brought my tribute, then?"

"I have." Temur glanced at Hrahima. She patted the pack, which she wore slung over one arm like a shoulder bag.

Temur said, "First, we wish to negotiate the return of the emperor's library, which we understand you have taken for safekeeping in his absence."

The dragon drew his chin back slightly, so his beard dipped in the lake. The expression that followed could be called a smile. Temur wondered if it was one.

"I believe," said the dragon, "that if you examine our treaty, you will find that in the absence of suitable tribute for an extended period, I am entitled to seek my own."

Temur faltered. He would have to admit it later, too, because Hrahima stepped up beside him and asked, "Is there a copy of the treaty here? We could consult it."

"Somewhere," the dragon said negligently. "Perhaps if there were specific items of interest to you, we could bargain for them."

Temur made a show of stepping back. "Perhaps it's time to negotiate a new treaty," he said. "I'll send my diplomats along when they have time."

He was surprised when the dragon tilted its enormous head, lifted one bushy, scaled eyebrow, and sighed. "You have no sense of occasion, Khagan."

"You are not the first to feel that way," Temur agreed.

Joyful Dawn Agate Slumbering half-lidded his enormous carnelian eyes and laid his chin on his forepaws like a bored dog abandoning itself to enervation. His eyebrow was still higher than Temur's head. "What, in particular, are the items you most wish to reclaim?"

Temur glanced again at Hrahima. Hrahima nodded slightly. Temur said, "There is a map of the Ways of Reason."

"That is a vile old magic, mortal Emperor," the dragon said. "You would risk dragon poison *and* the taint of Erem? Find another way."

Temur had not heard her come. He had not heard her slither down the passage beneath the tree, and he had not heard her pick her way along the connecting tunnel, but suddenly Edene was beside him, dressed in a ghulish robe worn open over Qersnyk shirt and trousers. The first outline of her swelling belly just pushed out the blouse over the waistband of her pants; her shoulders seemed broad and powerful under the drape of red wool.

She laid a hand on his elbow, straightened her back, and said—in Quersnyk—"Are they different, then?"

The dragon jerked upright, all pretense of lassitude and indifference abandoned. It had obviously had no problems understanding what she said. Clouds boiled from its nostrils like steam from a kettle as it hissed. The reaches of the cavern were lost in mist. But Edene stepped forward, holding up her hand. A bitter light flared from it, burning the mist back so it unraveled like fog before the sun. The stark green blaze washed out the more welcoming glow of all those floating lanterns, rendering the dragon's faintly comical old-man face and the stone formations into a looming skull ringed by teeth of stone.

Temur half-expected the dragon to say something perfectly obvious and patent, like, *You wield the Green Ring!*

Instead, for a long moment he stared down at Edene, and Edene stared back at him. He neither bowed nor blustered, but when he spoke, he said simply, "So it is come to this."

"It does not have to," said Edene. "You too are a remnant of ancient Erem, are you not? And subject to this ring."

"All beasts with poison," said the dragon, "are subject to that ring."

Again, Temur heard the meaning of his words like an echo.

"In avoiding the question, you answer it," said Edene. "Can you fly beneath the suns of Erem and take no harm?"

The dragon's gaze did not shift from her face as he nodded. "Is that what you will of me? Or will you have me tear your enemies, as did Danupati? For I am at your command, Queen of the Broken Places."

His voice, so resonant and cat-satisfied a moment before, had fallen flat and rote. He mouthed the last sentence like a slave asking for his punishment when he knows it will go worse if he does not.

Temur saw Edene's face fall, and a moment after it her upraised fist. The harsh green light died, and the friendlier light of the wizardly Song lamps filled the cavern again.

Her hand twitched. She balled it up again and pressed it into the folds of her robe. "Am I al-Sepehr, or Sepehr al-Rachīd? Am I Danupati?"

"You are Edene," the dragon said. "You are the Empress of the Ruins of Erem."

"I am a free Qersnyk woman," she said. "And you are a dragon older than my world."

"That is so," the dragon said.

Temur could hear Hrahima breathing softly through her whiskers beside him, her stripes and shading rendering her—as should have been impossible, for all her size—nearly invisible in the striped and shadowy light. She did not move, and so neither did he, though his hands burned with the desire to lunge forward, clutch Edene, and shield her with his body.

She is a free Qersnyk woman, he told himself. *She will care for our babe and herself.*

Edene said, "I will not use you as this . . . *artifact* suggests. I will make my own decisions."

"You always have," the dragon said, with the same preternatural assurance in its tone that had led Hrahima to remark that it asked questions to which it knew the answers.

Regal, Edene said, "You will answer my questions."

The dragon bowed his head, touching his nose to the gold between his forelimbs. "My queen."

"Do you remember Erem?"

"I remember the world that became Erem, in your tongue," the dragon said. "I had little to do with those who wrote its grimoires and raised its cities and crafted your ghulim, then destroyed most of those cities along with themselves and left the ghulim all but orphaned, long before Danupati used me and my kind to raze their final failing strongholds. They were not my race. And I remember the coming of your race, and the bindings that knit my world to your soft, wet worlds with their tender climates and gentle suns."

Temur was transported by a sudden, vivid memory of a woman veiled in blackest indigo, the warmth of a running horse between his thighs, the thunder of hooves ringing on air. The curve of a wide world beneath him, revealed by impossible distance as a shape like an egg or a ball rather than a stretching plain. He thought of a woman's deft hand pinching an earring through a veil, and the great curved globe it became.

I dreamed this. I dreamed this in my first dream.

"Worlds?" he asked, befuddled.

The dragon smirked at him tolerantly. "Your great-grandchildren will understand. If any of your descendants survive so long."

"Do you know?" Edene asked. "The fate of our children?"

"Do *you* want to?" the dragon countered.

An avid moment—and Hrahima stepped close beside her and murmured, "There is only one fate for all things, Edene."

Edene drew a breath and dashed her eyes with her unringed hand. She shook her head. "I do not wish to know."

"Just as well," said the dragon. "No tiger ever learned to lie."

"Did a serpent speak the truth?" Hrahima said, but she smiled.

"When it serves one," the dragon answered. "Sometimes we do not speak. But no, dragons see patterns, not prophecies. I can speak to likelihoods, but not certainties. Are you done with questions, Queen of the Ruins? Shall we move on to commands?"

Edene snorted, and the chilly dignity fell away from her, leaving the brash girl Temur loved. "Samarkar would have deeper questions."

His heart aching with her loveliness, he said, "We could send for her—"

"She would have deeper questions. But for now, I have questions enough," Edene replied. "You will tell me the name of al-Sepehr's djinn, complete and in its entirety."

"I can guess," the dragon said. "I cannot be certain."

"Guess, then."

He slowly spoke the first half of a long and fluid name, then introduced the second half and spoke it, then repeated both again. Temur thought neither he nor Edene would ever manage to remember it, but when he looked over, Hrahima was scribbling on the back of a folded wad of paper with a charcoal-stick. She winked a slow cat-wink at him when she caught his eye.

Edene waited until she was sure Hrahima had captured it, then said, "And you will tell me the name of my son, complete and in its entirety."

The dragon's shrug of innocence was a little too self-pleased, like a Song bureaucrat saying *sorry, I can't help you with that, it's not my department.* "That is recorded in no book that I have read, and neither have I heard it spoken, O Queen. Nor has one who knows it come before me."

She nodded, but Temur saw the frustration with which she bit her lip. She tried again. "You will tell me the name of this man with me, Re Temur, complete and in its entirety."

The dragon's smile grew sardonic. "That is recorded in no book that I have read, and neither have I heard it spoken. Nor has one who knows it come before me . . . O Queen."

This time, she nodded as if she had been expecting it. Her hair was loose in its braid, fine strands around her face curly with the damp. "I will have, then, the treaty between you and the Sudden Emperor. And I will have the map of the Ways of Reason."

"O Queen. They are slow poison," the dragon said.

"Really?" Edene answered. "Do you suppose they will be poison to *me?*"

Tsering found Brother Hsiung among the ruins.

He moved with the aid of a stick, probing before him with each step, though the blue sun was high and the Hard-day bright. He was alone, walking what had once been a smooth garden path and was now a deer-trail through tumbled masonry overgrown by a profusion of vines and briars. In the summer it would be a riot of bloom and color such as you saw in Song silk-paintings. Tsering tried to imagine the oranges and golds, the lushness of the greens they would overlay. Would there be roses, peonies, chrysanthemums?

Would she live to see them?

She did not speak, but Hsiung must have heard her coming up behind him. He paused and turned, folding his hands over the knob on his staff. He smiled slightly, the expression both eerie and beneficent beneath his filmy eyes.

"It is Tsering-la," she said.

He bowed, and she remembered his vow of silence and almost lost her purpose. But perhaps she needed to be heard more than she needed to be answered.

She wrung her braid like a neck between her two hands and said, "Samarkar says you are a priest—"

He shook his head, but it was a temporizing sort of denial.

"A monk, then. Well, whatever you are, Brother Hsiung, I think I need one."

After a moment, he inclined his head in acceptance. Then cast around, gesturing finally to a sloping granite bench set in a bank. The bank faced south; the snow had melted; the soft earth was riotous with the summer-butter flowers of winter aconite.

Tsering sank to the stone gratefully. The chill snaked through her woolen trousers before Hsiung had even settled beside her, but the green fecund odor of spring was strong enough to compensate. She folded her hands on her lap and said, "No one becomes a Wizard of Tsarepheth because they have a happy family."

He had leaned his staff against his shoulder. Now he laced his hands over it again, hanging forward comfortably. It seemed encouragement to continue.

"I left my family," she said, "and my family is dead. In that order. My grandmother was . . . the only thing that kept me with them for as long as I stayed. My father—" she shook her head, feeling the words close up her throat. "There were bad harvests. There was debt. There was the threat of the Bstangpo's justice, which is not kind. Perhaps he thought his wife and children and his mother-in-law better served in the next life than on earth."

How had the palm of her hand come to be so firmly against her lips? She bit the flesh to make it move away, glad that Hsiung did not move to comfort her. She might have split like a tree in a storm if he had.

She continued. "But if he acted out of benevolence, it was the first time in his life. And he thought enough of his own life to join the bandits in the mountain passes, and Tsarepheth never saw him anymore."

She had been staring away from Hsiung. It was easier to say to a stranger, and easier to say to a stranger she was not looking upon.

"I was already in the Citadel, an acolyte.

"I was the last daughter; the last that could have carried forward my ancestors' line. The Citadel would have released me. I chose to become a wizard anyway."

Now she glanced at Hsiung. She did not know if he saw the movement, or if he saw well enough to see her expression, but he nodded once, as if to encourage her to continue.

She touched her warm figured-jade and pearl collar with her fingertips. It was a source of strength and a reminder of failure both at once.

"And having undergone the surgery . . . I failed in my vigil." She extended her hand, snapped her fingers, watched the spark of light that did not form and flare and die. Snapped them again, just to see the emptiness once more. "So I am a scholar, and no kind of wizard, and the end of my line. My ancestors will have no grandchildren to be re-born into. And I have no magic to show for it."

She tossed her braid behind her shoulder before she could begin twisting it again. She stared away again, out over the picked-over ruins, down the valley to the road and the camp and a small herd of horses and Qersnyk playing the bloody, violent game that involved dragging the carcass of a goat this way and that until somebody managed to carry it over a line. She could pick out the ethereal shimmer of the Khagan's near-white stud amid the crush, but could not see who rode him. Except for one bright chestnut, all the other mounts were too smeared with filth to seem anything but a muddy brown.

Now there was a hand on her forearm, gently, and Hsiung frowning at her when her attention came back to him. Somewhere in the briars a thrush sang, more evidence of spring.

"What?" Tsering said. "That's not enough?"

He smiled. She understood. *Enough. But not new.*

She closed her eyes. "It's Jurchadai. I don't know how . . . he is not like other men. And I have had lovers, of course—I am a wizard, and we entertain ourselves as we see fit. But he does not see me as *entertainment*. And I—" She shook her head.

When she stopped, and peeked, Hsiung was still watching her, blind eyes patient and face serene.

"I am my father's daughter," she said. "I do not know how to trust. I do not know how to be with someone in that way, and to be kind."

She lapsed into silence, shocked by the truth that had escaped her. It knocked the breath and words out of her, so she found herself staring into the yellow cup of an aconite blossom and sucking her lower lip. Hsiung sat beside her, his silence companionable now.

"I miss my grandmother," she managed finally. "And because of my decisions, she can never be reborn. And taking up with Jurchadai will not change that. Nothing I do can change that."

He looked at her. He nodded. He leaned his staff against his shoulder again, steepled his hands before his face, and without rising from his seat he bowed.

What might have happened next, Tsering never knew, because the moment was broken by the uneven patter of a child's feet running along the path, and the streaming black hair and open coat of Toragana's little cousin Sarangerel, healed now, hove into view. The little girl bounced up, all childish officiousness, and plunged to a halt before Hsiung.

"Brother Hsiung! Brother Hsiung! Elder Sister says come back to camp now! There is a map that you must read, please!"

THEY HAD LEFT THE TITHE WITH THE DRAGON—CAST TESEFAHUN'S GOLD bullion out around his taloned feet as if they were scattering corn for chickens—and come back to the surface carrying their spoils. Edene had handled both scrolls: the map, and the treaty. She would let no one else hold them.

Temur argued that they might be a threat to their babe; she had countered that Ganjin had been *born* in Erem, and he was fine, so obviously the ring protected her children as well as herself. But she was nevertheless incapable of getting him—and Hrahima, and Samarkar—to leave the white-house when she sent her sister for Brother Hsiung. Instead, Temur sent for a casket of lead and gold, into which he sealed the treaty for later examination. That accomplished, he insisted on having a table set up for Edene, with Samarkar's witch-lights hanging over it. Both of them refused to stay nearly far enough back as she unrolled the map.

It was parchment of some sort, and she expected it to be stiff and friable with age. Indeed, she half-expected it to crumble in her hands. Instead, it was flexible and soft as new leather, fine and well-preserved, scraped so thoroughly that she could not even pick out the pattern of the hairs that had once grown on it. Maps were not her expertise, but as she spread it, she recognized the outline of the steep valley inhabited by the city of Reason.

Whoever had drawn it had used a variety of inks and dyes in several colors—black, violet, green, blue—and had gilded it with illumina-tions. The hand was fair and even, it seemed to her, though what did she know of such things? Written words were a wizardry much wasted on Edene.

The others turned away and flinched at the sight of them, and so Edene draped a finely woven woolen banner over the surface, found her sister playing with puppies in the yard, and sent her after Hsiung.

When she came back inside, Samarkar frowned at her like a thunder-cloud. "I disagree with this."

Temur, behind her, nodded. Hrahima had vanished into the shad-ows in that way that she had.

Edene hooked her thumbs through her belt and answered, "I too. But what other choice do we have?" and stood back with them to wait for Hsiung.

He arrived before the sun had moved another finger's width across the sky, accompanied—led—by Tsering and a somewhat officious Sarangerel.

Samarkar explained the problem, and her objections to so using Hsiung. Hsiung seemed to listen, head turned toward her, and then made it plain by gestures that he could not proceed without Master War. This led to another delay, and another joyous opportunity for Sarangerel to feel like she was part of the proceedings, while Master War was located.

Edene retrieved Ganjin from his cradleboard—he had been sleeping, miraculously, through all of this, and remained asleep when she pulled him into her arms—and paced. She envied Sarangerel her freedom from responsibility and doubt. The child was still young enough that her pleasure was to be included—to be thought useful. The ethics of what transpired would not be her problem for another five years or more.

May we all live that long.

War-zi came, and with him Besha Ghul, following on like a shadow. It wore its deep hood up, hiding its expressive ears and its face except for the tip of the long muzzle, and Sarangerel watched it with the same adoring fascination she usually devoted to the mastiffs.

Perhaps Besha Ghul could read the map. The ring pricked Edene, but she fisted her hand around it and turned away. She was finished with its blandishments. Instead, she explained the problem quickly to Master War. He listened, then glanced at Hsiung. Hsiung nodded.

"This must be Novice Hsiung's choice," said Master War, as if the words pained him. He scratched the stump of his arm. "I will not forbid it."

Hsiung bowed very deeply and turned away. Two steps took him to the table, which Samarkar uncovered for him with a show of steely resolve. He bent over it, gesturing for more light as his nose nearly brushed the paper. Samarkar, scowling, hung more witchfires about his head, but still he waved impatiently. *More light.*

She brightened them, and Hsiung squinted down. Again he gestured, and now the witchlights glowed more white than green. They did not trouble Edene, but she saw Master War's eyes streaming. Sarangerel hid her face in the hem of her coat, and Samarkar and Temur both turned away. Besha Ghul stood unmoving, but perhaps the robe low across its eyes protected it.

Abruptly, Hsiung straightened. He pressed his hands to his back, and for a moment a grimace of irritation contorted his face. Then it was gone again, as he smoothed a hand over the soft-looking stubble on his skull. He waved the lights away, and Samarkar banished them.

He cast about for a moment until Samarkar, apparently sensing his need, placed paper and a charcoal stick in his hands. Then he went to the end of the table away from the map and wrote quickly.

Edene knotted her hands in frustration until Master War read aloud: *"Please send for the Wizard Hong."*

HONG-LA CAME AT A RUN—AN IMPRESSIVE SIGHT, ALL LONG LEGS AND COAT flapping—and Ato Tesefahun and Zhan Zhang were not far behind him. Of course, the wizards and bureaucrats were often found in one another's company. They had had time to begin discovering all they held in common. But by now Edene was wishing that her white-house, though the largest she had ever inhabited, were twice the size. She cuddled her son to her chest, put her back to the king pole, and waited. Hsiung and Hong-la were arguing—Hong-la in Song too fast for her to follow accurately, Hsiung in letters dashed on paper. She understood the gist of it: Hsiung was requesting something that Hong-la simply was not willing to provide. The look of dawning horror on Samarkar's face provided sufficient context, but Edene noticed that Master War stood back with Temur, arms folded inside his sleeves, and frowned behind his moustache.

It was Hrahima who broke the standoff, finally. Perhaps everyone in the room had forgotten her, her demeanor was so silent, her ability to melt into the shadows so profound. When she stepped forward, she reasserted herself as a massive presence, and gazes followed her.

"They are Hsiung's eyes," she said, a slow rumble. "Surely, it is his to decide the disposition of them."

"They are my hands," Hong-la replied. "Is it mine to decide to which work they shall be turned?"

"Wait," said Edene. "I have not understood the argument."

Tesefahun detached himself from his place by the door. "Brother Hsiung—"

"Novice," said Master War.

"*Novice* Hsiung has requested that the Wizard Hong perform a surgery on him, which has the potential to restore the sight to his eyes. He proposes that he then use this restored sight to read and transcribe the map into a form we can all use."

"There's a surgery to cure blindness?" Edene said.

"No," said Hong-la.

All eyes turned on him, even Hsiung's white ones. Even at the center of the white-house, beside the king pole, he stooped. When he drew himself up in outrage, as now, his head brushed the ceiling.

He said, "It does not cure anything. The surgeon punctures the front of the eye"—he gestured—"like so. And drains the clouded fluid away. It restores sight for a few days."

"And then the fluid returns?"

Hong-la huffed. "And then the eye collapses. Blindness is total from that point."

Edene glanced down at her hands. She thought of what the scouts had told them—of the size of al-Sepehr's forces. Of the allies joining him on the march. Of their own paltry resources, even including her own few thousand ghulim. She saw the anguish on Samarkar's face, the grim set of Temur's, and knew how her family felt about this monk, this Hsiung.

Still she steeled her own jaw and said, "If we *can* use the Ways to get behind al-Sepehr. To surprise him, catch him in disarray—"

"There's no guarantee," Temur said, "that the Way we want even ex—"

A voice Edene had never heard—male, unpracticed, sharp—broke across Temur's. "It is a risk I am prepared to assume. What is my sight to all those lives, my friends?"

It was, of course, Hsiung. To Edene's surprise, Tsering-la was the first to walk out of the crowd and stand beside him. Her hands shook; she hid them in her coat.

"I know a little something about losing gambles," she said, looking directly at Hong. He hadn't backed down from anyone else's gaze, but he ducked from hers. "They *are* Hsiung's eyes."

"What if we only did one?" Samarkar asked.

Edene said, "Looking at the map would blind the other one, anyway."

Master War nodded. "They are Novice Hsiung's eyes. And his errors are his to redeem." He glanced at Hsiung askance. "You'll never find your voice that way, however."

Hsiung shrugged, his chin almost down to his shoulder in embarrassment. "It didn't seem to be working out. And I fear other things more than that I might let slip the tongue of Erem."

Master War made a gesture of acceptance and dropped his hand on Hsiung's shoulder. "He has the permission of his order to attempt this thing."

Hong-la looked around helplessly. Edene saw Samarkar's fist clench, but her teeth also sank into her lip and she said nothing.

"Very well," Hong-la snarled.

Guiltily, Edene glanced down at her hand. At the ring. She had been tugging at it unconsciously, and Hong-la's attention followed her motion. He glanced back at her face; she shrugged, and held his gaze.

The anger in his face collapsed into resignation. "May I mutilate one friend at a time, if you please?"

. . . *Friend?*

The ring pricked at her. *We have no friends.*

My *friends are many!* she replied, as a familiar wave of nausea and resistance washed over her. She wobbled, but she thought she hid it well.

"Fear not, Wizard Hong," she said, formally. "I would not so discommode you without greater need than I now feel."

 25

SOMETIME LATER, WHEN EDENE'S WHITE-HOUSE WAS FINALLY CLEAR OF arguing monks and wizards, Temur lay down for a nap to repair his abandoned sleep, and Samarkar went for a walk. She wasn't entirely sure of her goal or her direction, but she had some idea of walking off nervous—to be honest, *wrathful*—energy, and some idea of refamiliarizing herself with the changing layout of the camp.

It was less improvisational than it had been—the organizational genius of Jurchadai, Hong-la, and Zhan Zhang, more than anything— and laid out neatly in sectors with an eye toward defense, if they should be surprised. Each group had its own camp or series of encampments, from the smallest—the former caliph and his half-a-dozen Dead Men—to the largest—Edene's ghulim. Before too long, Samarkar found herself leaning on a post that supported a corral constructed of rope line tied with scraps of cloth to ward the horses back. Two of Ato Tesefahun's curly-coated mounts played a kicking and pawing game. The horses were all improving in condition as fresh forage became available, and the better diet was evident in their better spirits.

Watching them improved Samarkar's disposition as well, to the point where she didn't even say anything rude when the former Uthman Caliph Fourteenth, now turned mercenary captain, wandered up on her left.

"Wizard Samarkar," he said.

"Captain Iskandar." She stretched her spine out, listening to one crack after another. It wasn't enough; the ache between her vertebrae seemed permanent, these days. She suffered a moment of bitter nostalgia for the volcanic hot springs and deep tubs of the Citadel. "How may I be of service?"

"Put me back on my dais?" he asked, with a sly grin. There was an edge behind it, of course. There always would be, with him.

"That should be a pleasant side effect," she said, making it sound like she was agreeing.

He rocked to one foot, hesitant and dog-eager, and she found that she pitied him. He had gone from caliph, monarch of all he surveyed, to a beggar at Temur's feast. And while he had not been gracious when their roles were reversed, Samarkar felt herself moved to further charity.

"The shaman-rememberers tell us that Kara Mehmed's troops have joined al-Sepehr's army, and that the man who styles himself Mehmed Caliph leads them in his own person."

"As befits a *martial* king."

"Or one who cannot trust his army."

His lips quirked. Her touch had not deserted her entirely. She looked down at the mud spattering her boots, the calves of her black trousers, and spared a moment to marvel at the pampered, silk-swaddled, litter-borne creature she had been, when last she came to Song.

As if her thought had been a summoning, she heard the squelch of pattens behind her. She turned to see lady Diao, improbably tall on the wooden platforms that kept her slippers from the mud, knees still hobbled by a tight court skirt. That she could walk at all so hindered, let alone with grace, was a mystery to Samarkar.

Instantly, Iskandar ducked around Samarkar, offering his hand to steady the lady. She accepted it, though Samarkar could see her veiled reluctance.

His Song was stilted, but improving. "My lady Diao, you should not be out unescorted. Let me assist you to your destination, and I will speak strongly to your attendants."

Her tone, by contrast, was musical and cultivated. "Thank you, Captain Iskandar. But this is my destination. You see, I have come to talk to Doctor Samarkar."

She shot Samarkar a pleading glance that Samarkar recognized too well. Her words allowed Samarkar to insinuate herself into the conversation. "Of course, my lady. I had not forgotten our appointment."

"I will be pleased to escort you—"

"It is a private matter between women," Samarkar said. "If you will excuse us, *Captain*?"

His look of bemusement followed them as they returned the way Lady Diao had come. Their pace, though constrained by Diao's garments, was as fast as they could manage. The pattens made Diao tower over Samarkar. When Samarkar stole a look at her, her jaw was set, her mouth firm beneath the cosmetics.

"You should use zinc white," Samarkar said, when they were out of earshot of the once-caliph. "Or chalk pounded in coconut oil. The lead is bad for your complexion and will eventually make you stupid. And use charcoal for your eyes instead of kohl."

Lady Diao blinked at her, then smiled with the lips behind her painted-on carmine rosebud. "I had a sister like you, Doctor Samarkar. She galloped horses and wore trousers, and if father would have permitted it, she would have practiced alchemy and worn a sword."

She used the male form for *doctor*; Song did not have a feminine equivalent. Samarkar made a note to herself to teach her the ungendered Rasan honorifics.

"What happened to her?" Samarkar asked, wishing she didn't have to.

"She married," the Lady Diao said, to which Samarkar had no answer.

They trudged in silence through the mud until they came to Lady Diao's pavilion. Two women and an armed guard clustered by the doorway looked up in relief and quickly veiled irritation as they entered. Lady Diao walked past them as if they were no more to her than the drape they drew aside for her. She stepped from her pattens onto the carpet and ushered Samarkar into her temporary home.

By the standards of a war camp, it was more than luxurious. The rich scent of aloes-wood incense permeated brocade hangings, and a frame of planks elevated the carpets off the muddy ground. There were low chairs designed like slings in a folding frame. Lady Diao waited until Samarkar—the guest—had left her muddy boots by the door and chosen a chair, then settled herself in the other.

She said, "Even the Scholar-God's dog treats you as a person."

Samarkar shrugged acknowledgment. The gesture moved her wizard's collar against her throat, and she realized with surprise that she barely felt it anymore. "Half a person, anyway," she said. "Maybe not the better half."

Lady Diao laughed, a tinkling, cultivated sound. Then her face stilled, and she said, "I throw myself upon your mercy as a woman, Doctor Samarkar."

"Then you believe we have some?"

"Well," said Lady Diao, "as you know, those who study the Sages disagree. . . . Yes. I believe you have some. My father had seventeen daughters, Doctor Samarkar. I am the youngest but one." She paused delicately. "All the possible alliances have been forged—or honored—you see."

Samarkar nodded. She saw indeed. If every available marriage for the Lady Diao had already been made by one of her sisters, this chance at dynastic marriage to a barbarian emperor and life as an exile in his court was truly the best *this* Lady Diao could hope for. To return home would mean some even more desperately undesirable alliance—young bride to a very old man, or to a man with a dozen wives already—as the best that she could hope for. The worst would be to become a spinster attaché to some brother's household, or—worse—as the personal servant of some sister's mother-in-law.

Lady Diao was pretty enough, and had a studied elegance . . . but she was not the sort of ravishing otherworldly beauty who might manage to thrive as a twenty-second wife. And Samarkar thought, looking at her, that she did not have the makings of a nun.

The lady glanced down at her hands, veiling her eyes behind her lashes. "I do not mean to play politics with you, or win away your man. I just—"

"You need to live," said Samarkar.

A tear shivered in the lady's lashes. With a fingertip, careful of her cosmetics, she dabbed it away. "I am at your mercy, Doctor Samarkar."

✳   ✳   ✳

THE WHORES FROM THE CALIPHATE CAME TO ÜMMÜHAN FOR BLESSINGS. Camp followers, professionals, slaves—word of who and what she was trickled between them, and soon some of them brought their heathen sisters as well. Ümmühan ministered to Kyivvan women—some of them warriors! Shield-maidens, though if one in five were a maiden in more than name she'd die of shock—and even one or two Qersnyks, though mostly there were enough heathen shaman-rememberers floating about that the steppe folk could get their spiritual needs seen to without going outside their religion.

For those seekers who did come to her, Kyivvan and Qersnyk both, Ümmühan tried to witness simply, quietly, as Ysmat of the Beads might have done.

And she gave them poems to whisper. Poems that seemed safe on the surface, little plaints of lovers and astronomy, of historical betrayals. Of old stories of how a trusted lieutenant had turned on his sworn captain, and how the displeasure of the Scholar-God and Her prophets had ensued.

In the hours she had remaining, she and Saadet Khatun became inseparable. They spent hours on horseback, guarded by the Khatun's Qersnyk guards, chaperoning each other.

Kara Mehmed took to encouraging her to go out more, for he commented more than once on the new enthusiasm and spontaneity she brought to his bed in the aftermath of those wild, joyous rides.

SAMARKAR RETURNED TO THE WHITE-HOUSE TO FIND EDENE AND GANJIN gone, along with Afrit—no surprise, as Edene had already begun tying her son into the mannerly young stallion's saddle—and Temur just awakening. He struggled up, eyes glossy and distant, and seemed relieved to see her brewing tea by the brazier.

"I know where to get the horses," he said.

Samarkar gave the tea a final stir and strained it into two bowls. She handed one to Temur and sat beside him in the rumpled bedclothes to drink the other. They leaned together, shoulder to shoulder, and she contemplated the coiling steam as she waited for him to continue.

"I dreamed once of the Ideal Land, where the mares of every color run like bright rivers across an endless steppe. I dreamed of it again just now, and of Mother Night, and that shaman-rememberer Tolui." He sipped tea, the expression on his face more concentration than dreaming. "There are horses there by the thousands. More than this little army could ever ride."

"How will you get there?" Samarkar asked, not sure if she should feel like a seek-sorrow or as if she were being the practical one.

Temur waggled his eyebrows at her. "Do you think for an instant that Bansh cannot get me there?"

"You're the Khagan. Shouldn't you delegate?"

He shrugged. "I'm the one with the prophetic dreams."

"Spoilsport," she said, and hid her smile behind her bowl. When she lowered it again, she said, "You need to deal with that Song princess, Temur. And if you send her home, her father will just dispose of her in some even more desperate manner."

"What am I supposed to do? Marry her? I have no *name*, Samarkar."

"Lord Diao is offering an alliance. He's taking a gamble that you will win. That is all this marriage is. Neither he nor she expects a Qersnyk marriage. You can marry her under the traditions of Song and . . . you know, if you had done it before now, you might have gotten troops out of it. Or saddles. Who knows?"

He blew a stray strand of hair from sleep-red eyes. "Curse you," he said. "I'll settle it after the war. After al-Sepehr."

The tea was Song style, a mellow red oolong sweetened with puffed rice. Samarkar sipped before she said, "I wish we could take the fight to him."

"Al-Sepehr? Better if *he's* worn out from the road, and risking the late storms. Our best hope is that nature will whittle him down for us, because we have nothing that can stand against a battalion of indrik-zver. Not to mention the Rukh."

"I thought our best hope was that Hsiung would find something in the map that we could use to rig an ambush."

"Assuming the surgery works, this Soft-dawn."

"Hong-la's are the best hands he could be in. He did my neutering"— Temur frowned but held his tongue—"and if it has a chance of working, Hong-la is the one who can make it work."

Temur grunted and changed the subject—or at least angled it differently. "If only the entrance to Edene's Grave Roads was in a better position for hitting their flank."

She smiled.

"You're the stateswoman," said Temur. "This is a war. I know how to handle *this*."

"I think Hong-la and I will have something to say to the Rukh, anyway." Samarkar balanced her bowl on her knees and stretched her fingers one against another. In a previous encounter, she'd managed to discomfit it badly by turning the wind against it. "Maybe . . . there is a way. To arrange an ambush. Even if Hsiung's search doesn't work."

Quickly, she outlined her idea. "We will need the gunpowder. Such as has not already been used for rockets and fire arrows."

He thought, and nodded. "You and Tsering see to it. In the meantime, I want to give you something."

"Temur—"

"Hush," he said, and kissed her mouth. He tasted of tea and sleep. She held her breath to keep the flavor when he leaned back again.

"I want you to have Afrit," he said.

"Edene—"

"Edene agrees."

She stared at him, but he looked away, into the brazier, and cuddled up to his tea. After a long time, he sighed and said, "No matter what happens to me—or to Edene—if the battle turns bad, you will take Ganjin and flee. Afrit will get you clear. Take him . . . take him to the Citadel. Take him somewhere where he might have a chance of surviving al-Sepehr."

"I can't take Edene's son and not Edene—"

"She will be in the fight, Samarkar."

"She's *bearing*."

"And she wears the Green Ring."

She opened her mouth. She closed it. She spat a curse and finished off her tea.

"I hate this."

Temur's hand was warm on her knee. "That's because you are wise, lovely Samarkar."

✳   ✳   ✳

EDENE RETURNED BEFORE TWILIGHT WITH GANJIN EXCITED AND BUBBLY and smelling of horse. She sat beside the brazier and slipped her son inside her blouse. Without asking, Temur came behind her. He brought a bone comb from his pocket, and strand by strand he unbound and oiled and combed out her hair.

Seeing this, Samarkar rose from the maps she was studying. She went to a trunk, and pulled out a book of Song epic poetry that she had borrowed from Zhan Zhang as an excuse to get to know him better. For on such things as friendships did empires rise or fall.

Beside the lamp, where the light was best, she settled herself and began to read aloud. She was halfway through the battles of the Conjured Emperor (who had apparently had rather a lot of them) when the door was pulled aside and Hsiung entered.

His face was serene, his eyes bright brown as Samarkar had never seen them. His new robes hung on a frame still unnaturally spare. He held a cloth in one hand, and Samarkar could see the watery red stains of bloody tears upon it.

He paused just inside the doorway and studied each of them in turn, then bowed and said, "It has been a privilege to know all of you. It is good to see you, finally."

Samarkar had started to her feet, the book dangling from her hand. Guiltily, she closed it on a ribbon and set it aside. "Brother Hsiung . . ."

Whatever she might have said, it died in helplessness. Temur and Edene sat mute as well.

The corner of Hsiung's mouth twitched up. "I know," he said. "Believe me. Now, show me this map I am meant to be working on?"

THEY LEFT AT SOFT-DUSK.

In the end it was as it had been in the beginning; Temur alone with his liver-bay mare. That she had ribbons braided into her sparse mane now, in promise of the jeweled chamfron yet to come; that he wore a coat unmarred by battle and unstreaked by blood; that she was groomed to a mirror finish in the dazzling light; these things were insignificant. It was he and it was she, and they were together at the end of winter once again.

This time, there was a crowd to see them off, however, and a shaman-rememberer to bless their journey. And two women who hid their faces, but not their eyes, behind martial helms—one in armor of black lacquer, and one in armor of red metal that flickered flame.

Jurchadai finished his brief invocation, shook a rattle, flicked the dust of the steppe on Bansh's hooves with a vulture's feather. He stepped back and stamped the butt of his rattle-tipped staff on the earth.

Temur touched the bow slung by his thigh, and nodded. Then he gave Bansh the reins, and her head.

Though they had left the road clear before her, she mounted the air with the first stride. Temur felt the bunch and push of her powerful haunches, heard her hooves ring with every stride as if they were glass bells. Silence attended her first leap and her second: at her third there rose a shriek. At her fourth, the sound of cheering, and then she galloped into the sky on a rising battlement of noise.

Temur did not look down.

He had done this before—had he done this before?—though the mare had been of the color called storm and he had ridden pillion behind a man in horse-hoof armor, or behind a woman veiled in clouds of silk. The wind rushed in his ears. The cold of altitude burned his nose and fingertips. He did not look down.

He leaned into the small lee of Bansh's surging neck as she romped joyously skyward. Surely they must strike the vast tent of the heavens soon, smell hair scorching in the fires of the—no, this was Song; there were no stars to burn them. But wait, the sky shivered, the violet-blue softness of dusk, yes, but without opposing sunrise and sunset burnishing the edges of the world. Instead, the eastern sky dimmed indigo, and the western breathed the last gasp of fading rose and gold.

A woman on a horse the streaked color of thunderclouds waited for him ahead, as if at the top of a hill.

She was hard to look at, her whole form lost in veils of indigo that bled off at the edges as if the night behind her had somehow gotten caught and wrapped about her. A plump brown hand held the reins. A curve of breast swelled the stretch of fabric. Stars gleamed in her hair, or perhaps her veil was spangled with diamonds and beaten mirrors, here and there.

He reined Bansh in before her—the mare sidled closer than he would have chosen—and found he had no words.

"Re Temur." Her voice was the sigh of night winds. "I was beginning to think you'd never come."

She lifted her right hand and folded down her veils. Temur found himself staring into the face of the shaman-rememberer Tolui, wearing a familiar smug-cat smile. Behind the veiled woman, as if Temur looked past her from the top of a cliff, a green and endless rolling landscape unfurled, grasslands waving to the horizon and beyond. Vast herds of horses roamed that landscape—mares in vivid mineral colors mortal steeds never approached: lavender, yellow, vermilion, crimson, and sky blue. Temur's eye was caught by a stallion the color of lapis lazuli, streaks of sparkling gold threading his haunches and withers like stars in a midnight sky, his mane and tail blown forward by a bitter wind.

Temur could see through the woman with Tolui's face, and through her storm-colored mare, as if they were sheerest silken veils. And it was a bright day beyond them, a bright and beautiful day, with all the steppe stretching out and the ragged mountains rising at the edge of the world to hold up a cerulean sky. The indigo stallion called; far away, another stallion answered him. *I am here with my mares, and a wise horse would avoid me.*

Perhaps both stallions were wise, because Temur saw no sign of another herd approaching. He opened his mouth and cupped his hands to his ears, hoping to hear the second one again and locate him, but there was only the rustle of the wind blowing through the long green stalks of new vegetation.

Bansh sidled again, nickering to the storm-colored mare as if they were old friends. The woman with Tolui's face raised her veils again. "You know this aid does not come without price, Temur Khagan."

"Oh," Temur said. "I understand."

26

Bansh climbed, and climbed, and her hoofbeats and silhouette dwindled at a rate far greater than even her great speed justified. It seemed as if she ran through mist, though the sky was cloudless. It was not long before the dusk enveloped her.

Edene watched with head craned back, feeling the gorget of her armor press into her neck below her hair, wishing she had the solid warmth of a good mare under her.

She stood motionless until the Hard-sun rose, and Samarkar stood beside her. They might, in truth, have waited longer—but the thunder of merely earthbound hooves announced one of the Qersnyk outriders, the corpse of a juvenile rukh he'd shot draped across the rump of his mare, blood dripping.

He whooped as he rode, waving a hand in a circle over his head. Edene didn't need to hear what he was shouting to know.

Here they come.

Armies have an inertia, a great, sliding, grinding weight like loaded wagons skidding. The deployment of Temur's raggle-taggle troops were already nearly complete—half of them arrayed holding the gorge and barricading the Dragon Road beyond the valley's mouth. The others—

mostly ghulim and the Qersnyk who remained unmounted—were held in reserve. The monks vanished among the trees and the mountainous limestone spires as if they were ghosts in yellow ochre robes.

Edene heard the messenger in her white-house without so much as loosening the collar on her blazing armor. Hsiung was still bent over the map and though he gave only evidence of absorption in his task, she actually would have preferred him to eavesdrop. Temur had regaled her with enough stories of the monk's courage and resourcefulness that she would not turn down any aid or perspective he might bring.

Edene finished listening to the scout's information, and that of the two more messengers who arrived while she was debriefing him. She guessed that Samarkar would still be busy managing the few remaining troop deployments. And once that was finished, there would be nothing to do but wait.

But as Edene showed the last messenger out—before she even reached to loosen the straps on her armor—a familiar shimmer of heat and intention burst into presence behind her. Hsiung's chair tumbled over with a crash, but she turned slowly. She would not show him startlement, weakness, or fear.

Only disdain.

"I was wondering when you'd show up," she said, when her eye settled on the outline of the djinn. He still blazed actinic blue-white, limned in cooler flames. Her eyebrows sizzled. As she watched, his radiance dimmed until the lines of his face, the curl of his hair became apparent.

He bowed. She wished she could detect mockery in the gesture, but it was spare and crisp, not overelaborate at all. He said, "Perhaps you wish to speak in private?"

Over his shoulder, she met the monk's gaze. He watched intently, with his newly bright eyes. "I have no secrets from Brother Hsiung."

"Really?" Now the djinn was mocking. "Not even Stechko?"

"Why are you here?"

"You know why," the djinn said, with another mercurial change of aspect. Now he was serious, stern. A disappointed parent. "I have come to tell your son his name."

"So a demon can learn it, and call him by it? Is that the threat you're too cowardly to speak?"

"A demon? Or a djinn?"

"He shall not hear the filthy name you've given him from you, or from any person."

"You *are* a great and terrible queen."

"Great and terrible enough that you mean to use me to defeat al-Sepehr—"

He scoffed. "To distract him, you mean."

"I'll kill you first," said Edene, aware though she was of the unwisdom of pricking a djinn's vanity.

The djinn laughed. "With your little ring? In the armor I made for you? I'm terrified."

"With your *name*, O Fy-m'shar-ala-easfh-ala-wtqe-shra-tw'qe-al-nar-ala-fasheer!"

The djinn stepped back. His eyes narrowed, the blue within them blazing so they seemed like slits exposing the heart of a kiln. "Or perhaps you will bargain," he said.

Hsiung had come up to flank him—completely out of his depth, and yet unwilling to let Edene face the djinn alone. Edene shook her head, the faintest movement. *Stand back. Have a care.* Whether Hsiung understood her gesture or not, he did not reach out for the djinn's arm. Which, considering the djinn's fury, might just have been wisdom. She would not have cared to see Hsiung's hand flash to ashes.

Edene crossed her arms. "Bargain?"

"Perhaps."

"For your son's name," the djinn said. "Use your ghulim against Re Temur. Turn upon him on the battlefield. Your son can be Khagan; marry him off to Qori Buqa's get—"

"A *boy?*"

"A shaman-rememberer," the djinn clarified. "They can be co-Khagans, and their children will unite both rival lines. And carry Tsareg blood. Al-Sepehr will be happy to allow his grandson to rule the steppe, with the proper treaties and alliances."

The whole sharp ugliness of it clicked into place for Edene at once, like a roused and ruffled bird when it shakes out its plumage and is sleek and well-designed once more. Her hand almost went to her belly, protectively. She closed it into a fist instead. The weight of the ring dragged sharply at her, made her stupid and sick.

She struggled, found her focus, found her words though the world swam.

"I don't think so," she said. "O Fy-m'shar-ala-easfh-ala-wtqe-shra-tw'qe-al-nar-ala-fasheer."

"That is my name," said the djinn. "Say it a third time, and I'll roast your sweetbreads and share them among the carrion birds."

"How will al-Sepehr hold his empire?" Hsiung asked.

The djinn's head turned. He regarded the monk with mild amazement, as one might a cat that walked on two legs as a trick, or a dancing bear. "It speaks?"

Edene ached as if with exhaustion or an ague. Her will was elaborately diffuse. Her head had sagged somehow; she forced it up. Hsiung's words pierced her daze. She echoed and expanded them.

"How many armies has al-Sepehr?" she asked. "How many of his own? How many not manipulated, blackmailed, bribed, or falsified to? How *will* he hold an empire, Djinn?"

"Need he hold one?" the djinn asked. "Does he make one?"

It struck Edene through and through, the confusion burning back before its sharp energy like mist in a mounting sun. But not enough—she faltered, and the fog rolled in again. Against its dullness, she said, "He doesn't *wish* to hold it. He has no reason to. He really *is* going to try to call the Joy-of-Ravens from the grave."

"I am forbidden to answer that question," the djinn said carefully. A slow and toothy grin split his drowned blue lips, pulled down the hook of his nose. "Queen Edene."

The ghulim, she thought. *What I do to them is what al-Sepehr does to this creature. I am a free Qersnyk woman. Shall I take slaves?*

She staggered. There was Hsiung beside her, silent and sturdy, supporting half her weight.

"Where is Besha Ghul?" she said. She turned from side to side. Her eyes felt dazzled. "Where is Ka-asha?"

All she ever needed to do was speak their names to find them there. She reached out a hand and felt twig-velvet ghul fingers close on hers. Besha Ghul's whirring voice: "We are here."

"Hold me up," she said.

Ghul claws caught her under the arms, supported her waist. Edene let her body sag as it would. She had no strength to stand, now, against the lassitude that suffused her, against the impossible weight of the ring.

She had asked the djinn once if he could take the ring from her, and he had suggested that, perhaps, he could. What would al-Sepehr, power-mad, collector of indentures, never expect her to do?

"O Fy-m'shar-ala-easfh-ala-wtqe-shra-tw'qe-al-nar-ala-fasheer," she said—and then, as he snarled and raised a hand flaring blue as light-ning to her, a wavering flare against a whirling background as her head spun—she added: "Remove this ring. And leave it on the table there."

Something tugged her hand. Hsiung cried out in betrayal, and he might have hurled himself against the djinn again except Edene—head now clear, vision sharp—saw him moving and lashed out to grab his arm. She wrapped her hands around his bicep, dragging him around in an arc, and saw the smooth stump of her ring finger, the unbroken flesh where it had been.

She hung on, panting, until Hsiung lurched to a stop. She had to step out of the rucked-up tangle of carpeting to catch her balance, and almost fell against him.

The djinn said, "By my name you bind me, Tsareg Edene. You have two wishes more."

His eyes sparkled—literally sparkled, like water faceted in the sun, like floating embers blown from a fire. He smiled—not the cruel delighted grin of a moment before, but honest pleasure, sweet and sincere.

"Wishes?" she said, steadying herself against Hsiung's stolid arm. She half-wished the monk would put a hand around her shoulders, but that would make her feel even weaker. She pushed herself upright and drew herself straight. "What about my guts? Sweetbreads, rather?"

"I'll do you the courtesy of waiting until your eventual and due demise," he allowed.

"That seems a decent compromise." She tugged her collar. Despite the armor, her chest felt loose, her lungs free, for the first time she could remember. "A decent burial, even."

"You have said my name three times, and claimed one wish. What are your other two?"

The armor was heavy, that had not been heavy before. Nausea

flirted in her stomach. The ghulim withdrew from her slowly, heads ducked into cowls.

Edene asked, "Can they contradict the orders of al-Sepehr?"

The djinn smiled. "He made a younger bargain with me, and tricked me into serving him. Wishes are more limited in some ways, but stronger in others. Be careful what you wish for, though; I do hold the power of a . . . free . . . interpretation."

She bit her lip. She glanced at Hsiung. He met her gaze but offered nothing. When she looked for the ghulim, they hid their heads and huddled beside the door.

"I wish you would tell me—whisper to me secretly—the full and complete name of my son."

If possible, the djinn's smile widened.

"It is my pleasure," he said, "Tsareg Edene." He leaned close, and breathed against her ear, "Re Sepehr Rakasa al-Kara ai-Erem ai-Nar ai-Edene Stoneborn."

Then he leaned back. "Third wish?"

"Must I use it now?"

"No," he said, and frowned. "But I may not feel so moved to humane charity tomorrow."

Hsiung swayed sideways, close enough to let her feel his warmth. She breathed deep.

She looked down at her boots. *I could ask for Temur's name as well. I could ask for horses for the battle. Cannon—*

When she raised her eyes, the djinn still regarded her.

"I wish you were free of al-Sepehr," she said.

"Keep the armor, Edene Khatun," he said. "A freely offered gift."

And vanished in a whorl of azure fire.

Edene stood, for a moment, watching the smoke rise from a scorched place on the carpet. Her nostrils stung with the scent of burning wool. She glanced over at the table. There, beside the dragon's map and Hsiung's, the Green Ring lay—a plain band, gleaming innocently.

Edene walked the two steps to it, wrapped her hand in her cloak, and lifted it. The balance was wrong; there was no pain, but it almost dropped through the gap where her finger was missing.

"Besha Ghul," she said.

She turned, and found the ghul before her, head twisted aside as if to show its throat, though the drape of its robes covered everything. Ka-asha still huddled by the door, as if the ring on Edene's hand were the only thing that had given them courage.

Edene thrust her hand out. "This is yours now."

The ghul made no move to take it.

"Besha," Edene said. "You must take the ring. You must be the ghulim's leader."

"Some will not fight," Besha Ghul said.

"That must be their choice," said Edene.

"This is not for me," Besha Ghul said.

"Besha," Edene said. "My friend—"

"I," said Ka-asha suddenly. It straightened. Its royal-blue hood slid down its long gray velvet neck. Edene, Hsiung, and Besha all turned as one.

Ka-asha choked softly, swallowed with a toss of its head. "I will take the ring."

Edene glanced at Besha Ghul. It said, "Ka-asha should take the ring."

"It's yours." Edene extended her hand again. "I will not make you fight. I am not al-Sepehr."

Ka-asha's hand came to hers as slowly as drifting smoke. Long black nails plucked the ring from the folds of Edene's cloak as delicately as a berry.

"Some will not fight," Ka-asha said. "I will."

THE EVE OF BATTLE WAS A POOR CHOICE ON WHICH TO ACQUAINT ONE'S SELF with a new mount—especially an at-least-slightly supernatural one. But the battle proper would be a worse choice, and the potential advantage of an at-least-slightly supernatural mount was too much to ignore.

Samarkar had been minded to bridle the dun Jerboa anyway, and take her chances with a horse with no smack of godhood about her. But when she had gone out into the paddock with the rope, Afrit had herded the mares away from her with stallion nips and squeals, then trotted up with his sparse forelock blowing across eyes the china color of a Rahazeen sky and thrust his head into her hands. He'd given a jump and two midair kicks as he did it, showing off his mother's trick of running on air.

Edene, waiting by the gate for her turn to come catch Buldshak, had laughed. She did not seem to mind her missing finger, and something about her—some ice that Samarkar had presumed intrinsic—had melted into vivacity. Which did not remove the air of sorrow, still.

"He knows Temur gave you to him. Besides, we can loan Jerboa to anybody. Nobody but you or me is going to ride the Ghost."

His muzzle was soft pink, so pale Samarkar wondered how he would ever be able to endure the steppe sun. His hide, shed out of baby softness and winter shag, was the most incredible color that she had ever seen.

The steppe horses had a look to them—their summer coats caught light like lacquered metal no matter what shade they were. But Afrit's creamy white-gold coat had the luster of pearls from the coast of the Lotus Kingdoms, a depth and gloss that Samarkar would not have thought possible even after long exposure to Bansh, Buldshak, and Jerboa. Silk might have that sheen, or certain minerals. Nothing living should. And no living horse should have those bones, that spare structure. Those pale, eerie eyes and that skeletal body.

A chill chased through her as his warm head leaned into her chest. Automatically, her hand came up to scratch the soft place under his mane; she breathed deep of the warm smell of horse. He lipped her armor, ears lazy, but she could not shake the searing cold that ran like molten lead down her bones.

He is the pale horse of the soul, she thought, aware that she was giving her own religion's imprint to Qersnyk superstition. *This is my death asking me to ride.*

It wasn't as if Afrit were a stranger to Samarkar. She had watched him slide into Temur's hands, after all—a short half-year before, even if she now had to stand on tiptoe to see over his withers, and his neck was developing the elegant muscle and crest of a mature steppe stallion. If this were her death, it was one she knew, had watched grow. One she could sit comfortably astride.

So be it.

She pulled a handful of grain from her pocket, and while he nibbled it she slid the rope around his neck.

Edene had done a fine job breaking him. He bore the cracked old salvaged saddle, the only one she had found to fit him, like a falconer bore a glove. Sitting astride him made Samarkar feel like a Qersnyk herself. He was so responsive to her weight and leg that he might have been an extension of her own body—except he was smarter about his balance than she had ever been, and had a better sense of footing. It was more a matter of breaking herself in to the colt than breaking the colt in to her.

Edene soon kicked them out of the paddock—some time before Samarkar would have deemed them ready—and set them to roam. "Show him some magic," she told Samarkar. "He needs to smell magic and know it won't hurt him before you ride him into battle."

"He's seen magic since he was a baby," Samarkar argued.

"Not from his back, he hasn't."

I'm letting you win, Samarkar thought, and did not point out that magic very well *could* hurt him. Him, and Samarkar, and Edene too. Instead, she bowed low in the saddle—Afrit bowed as well, surprising a laugh from both Samarkar and Edene—and reined him at the fence.

It wasn't much of a fence. Just as well, because the colt had three strides going at it, and then he gathered himself up and hurtled over it without doing more than extending his stride. Jerboa could have made that jump, true to her name. And Bansh, but Bansh was more than just-slightly supernatural.

Afrit drew up on the other side, kicking out with glee and spirits, and came around almost before Samarkar reined him. Edene sat Buldshak beyond the fence, grinning.

"Go get used to each other," she called. "Don't come back until you've stopped looking shocked at what he can jump."

Not just what he could jump; how far, and how fast, he could run.

Samarkar brought him around the lake on a grand loop, reining him back and keeping him off the hills to save his strength. He took her breath away nonetheless: a comet of pale silk, a meteor of flesh and blood and bone, kicking and playing the whole way.

To her relief and disappointment, at no point did his light strides ring on air instead of thudding ground.

When she brought him back to the camp at a high-footed canter, Iskandar on a curly bay fell in beside them. Five strides, ten—just long enough for Samarkar to hope it might prove companionable. And then he heaved a sigh at her and said, "What happens if Re Temur does not return before the battle?"

There was the faintest of hesitations before *before*. Samarkar rode on over it, and let the beat of Afrit's hooves dismantle Iskandar's implication of doubt. "I have his plan of battle."

"And when the tide of battle changes?"

"I have a plan for that as well." Samarkar let her gaze flick sideways. After the stare and the pause, she said, "In almost any circumstance."

Iskandar's lip dented when he bit it. Was that new since he'd been Uthman Caliph? Or was Samarkar only noting it now? A pity if so—it might have been previously useful.

"I can advise you," he said.

"I could advise *you*," she answered. For a moment, hope lit his face— *she will tell the troops to follow me.* She had to remind herself not to take too much pleasure in dashing it. "But I will advise myself, and Edene, instead."

"Samarkar-la—"

"No," she said. "It is decided, Iskandar. You are better down in the battle, where your strong arm and sense of tactics can be played to our advantage. And your courage. Do not underestimate the power of a wizard—or three—to turn a display of heroism to your advantage, once-caliph."

He frowned at her, lips oddly red against that beard dyed blue. "Heroism."

"Do you suppose," she asked, "that every man in Kara Mehmed's army actually *prefers* Mehmed Caliph to you? Especially in the teeth of a winter march from Asmaracanda all the way to the outskirts of Song?"

He tapped his fingers on the pommel of his saddle and frowned deeper, as if not quite certain how he might have just been outmaneuvered.

"Some of them might once," he admitted. "Some of those might have changed their minds by now."

"And so you fight," said Samarkar.

"Find red coats for my men," was all he answered.

TEMUR WAS NOT BACK BY SUNSET, NOR BY THE SUNSET AFTER. NOW GRAY birds scattered the skies at such distances that they could not be easily thinned by arrows. Scouts returned with estimates of al-Sepehr's numbers; perhaps twice what Temur's patchwork army mustered.

Their preparations were complete, their troops in place. All they had left was the waiting.

And the muttering—that Temur had abandoned them with his unlucky stud, that he had left his women to fight in his place, that he had slipped away and saved himself after his own brother's death, so why not now?

Samarkar knew that some of the new arrivals among the Qersnyk would use Temur's presumed desertion to justify their own, if they could. And she and Edene had nothing to fight it with except Tsareg loyalty and Qersnyk pride. What warrior could face himself if he left two women, one of them gravid, to stand against a conquering enemy?

AL-SEPEHR'S RAGE AS THE SOFT-DAY PASSED AND THERE WAS NO SIGN OF the djinn should have been terrible to behold. Saadet remembered being frightened of him, but it was like something that had happened to someone else. In the Hard-dawn, as they broke camp, she found reasons to busy herself elsewhere, such as with her horses: her own Khongordzol and her dead husband's prize mare Syr, the blood-shouldered gray. But it wasn't out of fear of her father, she realized, too tired to be surprised at herself.

It was out of boredom.

Shahruz, at least, had a use for her again, though half of it seemed to be haranguing her for protecting Ümmühan. The other half was using her to study Mehmed and Pyotr's battle plans, which at least meant she got them explained to her. Often condescendingly, but Saadet had learned through all the years of her life to swallow her temper and learn anyway.

She'd been teaching Ümmühan to ride. First they would review the troops, and she would speak to them for morale's sake. She'd hoped al-Sepehr would allow her to remain with the commanders, but he had told her that he would ride the wind throughout the battle, and he did not require the assistance of a woman. So Ümmühan had secured permission from Mehmed to join Saadet on the stony crest above the battlefield to observe their victory despite the spring storm threatening. Paian would accompany them, with Esen and two other warriors as a guard. Saadet caused both mares to be saddled, putting the Padparadscha Seat on Syr. With Tsaagan Buqa in his cradleboard, she was entitled to his grandfather's saddle—and since this battle was about who would sit in it tomorrow, she would not leave it in a pavilion or a tent.

Inside the pavilion Saadet shared with al-Sepehr, he sat before a table stewing, poring over maps, caressing a yellowed skull of all-but-toothless antiquity, and ignoring her. It was only by fortune that she had ducked back in to stomp into her riding boots, Tsaagan's cradle-board in her left hand, when a sparkling whorl of azure light shimmered into existence before the undraped door. Al-Sepehr was on his feet then, fast enough to give the lie to his previous apparent absorption.

Saadet jumped back from the door, one foot booted and one just socked, swinging the cradleboard over one shoulder. She put her baby and her back to the pavilion's woolen wall and forced herself not to grope after the pistol in her sash. Powder and shot would do no good against a djinn.

The djinn, anyway, took no notice of her at all. Instead he pranced up to al-Sepehr, swinging his feet like a cocky boy, and tipped his head to one side fetchingly as he looked up at the tall man. The form the djinn wore was wiry, a grown boy, not tall. His blue skin was smooth with youth, his waist trim where he'd cinched it into billowing white pantaloons. His feet were bare, the toenails gilded.

He hooked a thumb into his sash. "I've come to bid you farewell, Mukhtar ai-Idoj. And to have one final look at your face as you realize what a damned fool you've been."

If al-Sepehr had seemed wreathed in thunderclouds previously, now lightning sparked in his visage. Low and dangerous, he said, "Did you not bring me a message from Re Temur's whore?"

The djinn smiled and sidestepped, so al-Sepehr had to wheel in a circle to follow him. Saadet almost missed what he said next, al-Sepehr's words were such a punch to her. *Re Temur's whore.* As Saadet had been Qori Buqa's?

"Her message is not fit for tender ears," the djinn said, mockingly. "Nor, it happens is mine."

"Did you not offer her the name of her child for her obedience?"

"In accordance with your orders, so I did." The djinn shrugged. "And as I served you, in accordance with the bond established when you tricked me, now I have tricked you back and do not serve."

Saadet had never seen al-Sepehr at a loss for words before. His mouth worked like a fish's. His cheeks grew dark with rage.

"I bade you name him," snarled al-Sepehr. "I bade you name him Sepehr al-Kara ai-Erem ai-Nar. How then have you *tricked* me in return?"

"So you did," said the djinn, inclining his head while the flames slid in his hair like an unruly crown. "But you did not bid me name him that *only*. And if that were not enough to break your hold, a lady just wished me free—on my name. So that trick won't work on me either, should you have a mind to try. Good day, Mukhtar! Enjoy your little war."

He vanished in a silent flash, leaving al-Sepehr and Saadet gaping after. Then, as if Saadet were not there at all, al-Sepehr whirled and strode out of the pavilion, the chains decorating his sword-sheath clattering.

By Hard-dawn, Samarkar had polished Afrit from head to hooves until he seemed to glow not just with captured light but from within. She'd even oiled his cracked old second-hand furniture, comically incongruous though age-worn leather was on such a glorious young beast. Now she stood hugging his head as he lipped in her pockets for mutton-fat and grain sweets.

It kept her from staring off at the louring sky above, where a steppe vulture stitched the clouds, harried by five or six of the juvenile rukhs, but from which no trace of a bay mare or rider descended. It kept her from staring off at the curve of the mountain beyond which al-Sepehr's army would be beginning to form up, even now. *Twice our numbers.*

She hugged the stallion closer and told herself, *We will win because we have no choice but to win.*

Her anxious misery was interrupted as Hsiung all but danced out of the pavilion that served as their forward command, a roll of rag paper clutched in his hand. His smile grew broad as their gazes met. He lifted up the scroll and waved it triumphantly.

"Where's your ghul general?" he said. "I've found its way around behind."

"I'll open the gates," she said. "How far?"

"There's one in the cave of the lanterns. The other will bring them out along the Dragon Road, twenty *li* further on. They can double back and fall on al-Sepehr's flank once he's fully engaged with our lines." He put the paper in her hand.

She held it as tenderly as if he had given her a fragile, thorny flower. His face seemed sunken. Transparent red crusts lurked in the corners of his too-bright eyes. "You should rest."

"Rest in war?" He smiled. "I have a request, Wizard Samarkar."

Because she could not bring herself to nod, she waited.

He said, "I would like to join King Tzitzik for the battle. We have discussed it, and we would like to volunteer to take the left flank, the forward position."

Horror sparked with irritation. "Hsiung, that's in the teeth of the trap!"

He bowed. "King Tzitzik will make her case to you as well, I am certain. She feels responsible, for was not the barrow of Danupati in her care when it was disturbed? But as for me, who better? You will need someone to act as a lure, and while my sight and strength remain to me, it is I who will do this thing."

She swallowed her first, angry retort, and thought of something better to say. "I can't argue you out of this."

"You could assign me elsewhere."

"And send someone else in your place. You're right; we need a lure. This is a gift you give, Hsiung."

He smiled crookedly. "Tell Hong-la I'll see him in Hell."

WHEN SAMARKAR ENTERED THE PAVILION, SHE WAS UNSURPRISED TO SEE Edene pinning her braid around her head, her armor flickering at every gesture with cold flames. Ganjin was not in evidence. Perhaps one of the ghulim had him somewhere in safekeeping.

Whatever Samarkar meant to say in greeting, it was diverted by Edene's question—directed at her small bronze mirror, but intended for Samarkar. "Has Temur returned?"

Samarkar shook her head. "What if he doesn't?"

"Then we fight without him."

"If the Nameless win this battle, they will be seen as unstoppable throughout every land between the Pillars of Heaven. Who then would deny the return of the Sorcerer-Prince?"

Edene looked at her. "Did you see Hsiung's map?"

Samarkar held up her armored right hand, with the scroll of paper in it. "He's determined to kill himself."

"It is his life to give," Edene said callously. No, not callously. But with Qersnyk fatalism, here on the brink of war. "Unroll the map and tell me what you read."

"Did Hsiung not?"

"Hsiung did," said Edene. "I wish to be shown it again."

Samarkar slipped the ribbon that bound the scroll. Crisp paper crinkling, she spread it on the table. Her eye scanned—yes, there the door that could take the ghulim to Reason. And there the door that could bring them out behind al-Sepehr. Her eye caught on something else, though, and a blaze of hope sprang up in her as if someone had poked the coals.

"Tsarepheth," she said. "He thinks this one would lead us to the Cold Fire?"

"Do you mean to bring us more wizards?" Edene said. "I would not complain."

"I hadn't thought of that," Samarkar said, delighted. "We can only ask!"

"What was *your* plan?"

"The Cold Fire is supposed to have been raised where the Sorcerer-Prince took his final fall. Just let me send for Hong-la, and Tsering. What would happen to faith in his resurrection, do you suppose, if we brought back his bones?"

Edene grinned. She leaned over Samarkar's shoulder and pointed and said, "Hsiung says there is a path there that will bring us near Ala-Din."

"And so?" Samarkar asked. "We take his citadel and let him have the steppe, and Rasa, and Asmaracanda, and Asitaneh, and Song? Tempting, but a last resort, I'd say."

"I was thinking," Edene said, "that Hrahima, Besha Ghul, and I could go and break loose the male Rukh, actually. Losing the services of his mate would probably put a cramp in al-Sepehr's plans, don't you think?"

Samarkar shook her head in delight. "Six Thousand keep you."

✳   ✳   ✳

"I will go," Tsering said. "But Hong-la should remain here. I am better for the errand; he is better for the battle."

So it was Samarkar on Afrit, Edene and Tsering and Hrahima unmounted, and Besha and Ka-asha and the remaining willing ghulim who returned to Dragon Lake and descended by floating lantern-light into the caverns. Jurchadai came to see them off, and Samarkar pretended not to see his and Tsering's tearful farewell.

Behind them, the first drops of rain began to fall on the warriors who took up arms and found their places with those who would lead the battle until Samarkar's return. Under Re Chagatai, the captains of the field would be Master War, Tzitzik, Nilufer, Toragana, Iskandar, Oljei, Hong-la, and Zhan Zhang.

Afrit seemed not to mind the cave at all. His pale form slid through the gloom like the opposite of a shadow. It was Ka-asha who found the doorway, once it knew what to look for. There were two slabs of stone three times a man's height, leaned together in a triangle like propped cards. These were not fallen so by chance. Rather they had been set there, and the ghul noticed the toolmarks where they had been carved to interlock.

Samarkar pressed her boot into the stirrup, leaned over Afrit's shoulder, and laid her palm against the stone. She felt no eldritch energy in it, but neither had she in the closed doors in Reason.

She did not give herself time to grit her teeth, or even think about what she was doing. She said the words, and took the pain, and clung to Afrit's saddle as he danced aside. Then she collected herself, collected him, and reined him through the door.

It seemed a calm spring morning in Reason, and it took a moment before Samarkar realized what had changed. On every tree, on every vine, the leaves were open and in flower, lush and green despite the warmth of the sun. She shoved a fist against her stomach, keeping the nausea in, and glanced around startled as the rest of the party followed her. Even three or four abreast, it took quite a while to bring the ghulim through.

By the time Ka-asha came up to let Edene and Besha know the army was assembled, Samarkar was feeling less like vomiting. She tried not to think that she had three doors yet to open. Perhaps she should have let one of the other wizards who had accompanied the Tsareg caravan out of Rasa help . . . but though one or two had offered, she had convinced herself that Hong-la needed all the help he could get.

THE RUKH FLEW LOW AND HEAVY, CLOUDS AND RAIN SOAKING HER WINGS. Al-Sepehr bent low to her feathers, his wet veil plastered to his neck, sharply miserable in a bullying wind. He wondered if Temur's pet warlocks and witches had some weather-sorcery behind them, or if this was just ill luck for everyone.

Lightning searched the distant sky, and al-Sepehr kept one eye on it—but as long as the thunder remained distant, he would accept the risk. The tactical advantage of the Rukh's-eye view was too great to sacrifice easily.

Below him, the forces of the enemy spread out like a map. There was the long curve of Qersnyk cavalry—fewer than he'd feared, and there were steppe men behind them on foot. He realized that they did not have enough horses to mount all their archers, and some would be fighting from the ground. And there, on the left bank of the river, a little group seemed out of place—too far in advance of the others. This led to a weakness in the line behind them, and al-Sepehr determined to send the indrik-zver there.

The enemy had some advantages, however. They'd be fools if they had not held the high ground on either side, and there was no way to attack without getting caught between their pincers. Fortunately, once they committed, he had the cure for that.

He bit his lip against a surge of glee. This would not be *easy*. But he also did not think it would exactly be hard. And once it was accomplished, no one under the sky would doubt that Sepehr al-Rachīd was a great God indeed, to so bestride the world again.

WATER DRIPPED DOWN HSIUNG'S COLLAR AS HE MOVED UP BESIDE THE Woman-King Tzitzik and her hoof-armored warriors. They were strange in the rain, the horses head-bowed and seeming half-melted, the banners like swags of hardened candle dripping on their lance poles. For a moment, Hsiung wished he were hidden among the trees with Master War—and then, for a longer moment, he wished Hrahima were at his side.

The distant sound of drums and trumpets cut the rattle of the rain. The jade of the Dragon Road jumped, then began to tremble under his feet. Hsiung heard shouts, orders, the bugled challenge of a horse. Out of the misty distance, between the sculptured limestone pillars of the mountains, the great bobbing heads of charging indrik-zver loomed.

King Tzitzik lifted her lance. What she shouted, Hsiung did not know. But he added his voice to the tumult that came after, and when she charged, his feet pounded after.

HONG-LA HAD CHOSEN HIS AND ZHANG'S VANTAGE WITH AN EYE TOWARD the sweep and scope of the battlefield—but that was before the rain began to cut sideways, and the clouds lopped the tops off the mountains. Now they peered through mist and relied on runners, even the flag signals vanishing in the gloom. Horses slid in mud; screams and the crash of weapons told him battle had been joined.

Zhang gave the order to fire the rocket arrow batteries, and torches were applied to fuses. The launch was erratic. Five hundred shrieking missiles whistled from their tubes, spitting and sizzling, but it should have been twice that many. All the fuses and all the powder had not stayed dry.

"Maybe we should send the reserves in on foot," Zhang said.

"Give Re Temur a little longer," Hong-la said. "If they have to fight on foot, we'll let them fall back closer to the ruin, and see if they can hold the pass."

Hong-la reached out *otherwise*, thinking he could dry and spark them by manipulating the process of fire. But somewhere up there in the mist was Samarkar's trap, and he—Hong-la—was the one among them delegated to trigger it. And he must trigger it at the right moment, or Tzitzik and Hsiung would suffer the results, rather than the intended victims.

He strained his ears, listening for the timbre of a Lizard-Folk bugle. A great shadow swept over—the Rukh!—and a volley of arrows pursued it even as he pulled Zhang down and ducked. The unmistakable, terrible trumpeting of the indrik-zver rang out over every other sound of battle, and the earth trembled with their thundering feet. Had he missed—no, there! There, the sound of the Woman-King's bugler, and there, the dip of a yellow signal flag, and another, and another as the sign was relayed. Hong-la summoned heat, awakened the process of fire. Not near at hand, but halfway up the valley and underground.

The cavern along the river that Samarkar had caused to be mined with the balance of the gunpowder exploded under the feet of the charging beasts, and the bellowed challenges of the first rank of the monsters turned to bellowed cries of pain and fear. They thrashed and slid into the suddenly open sinkhole, mud and water swirling around them, the second rank crashing into those of the first who had managed to avoid falling and plowing some of those into the pit.

Hong-la caught a breath, but only one. He straightened up, and reached out again, this time for the rest of the rocket arrows. The enemy might be too close now, too mixed up with his own people—but it would do no harm to churn up the earth behind them, and he might catch a few stragglers, he supposed.

QERSNYK GENERALS LED FROM THE FRONT, AND NO GRANDSON OF TEMU-san's would fight differently. Re Chagatai saw the streaks of fire pass overhead, the rocket arrows sizzling in the rain. They plunged to earth ahead, and some of the enemy fell screaming before the Re and Tsareg vanguard even reached them. He heard the shuddering boom of the mines detonating beyond the river, and the hiss and whistle of the enemy's shot piercing his own lines. Curse the Nameless guns! Curse the Kyivvan artillery! A horse on his left stumbled and rolled, fountaining blood as a bouncing cannonball severed its legs.

Its rider went down under the hooves of his own clansmen. Chagatai loosed, loosed again. He did not see what happened to the fallen rider then, but another roar ahead told him of the explosion of that artillery emplacement, or one like it. One of Temur Khagan's foreign wizards, or the Kyivvan's own miscalculated load? It didn't matter. One less cannon to worry him.

There were brothers—tribesmen—on the other side of that charge, and Chagatai felt a familiar pang as he drew his bow back to his ear.

The Qersnyk had been fighting each other for too long. If he survived this, it would be good to get back to fighting outlanders again.

They struck the enemy vanguard. Screams—men and horses—and the thunder of metal on metal, shattering. Another, belated, streak of rocket arrows overhead, one leaving a smoking line of pain on Chagatai's arm before plunging into the throat of the man he ducked away from. He dropped his bow on its lanyard, feeling it bump his thigh. His long knife came out with a hiss as he hauled hard on the third rein. His black mare Cinder wheeled, kicking out, and Chagatai's blade whipped a shining arc in the air. Its second arc shone wet. The shock of a parry rang up the blade, numbed his arm.

Cinder slipped in mud, caught herself, skidded back as a big Kyivvan warhorse pounded into her, chest to chest. The mounts squealed and snapped. Chagatai dropped the knotted reins and snatched his left-hand dagger from the saddle sheath. He left it in the hinge of the big chestnut's throat as the horse fell, gurgling.

A moment's respite. He stood in the saddle, turning Cinder with his weight. The Kyivvan cavalry and the other Qersnyk were pushing his warriors back; the line was behind him. He dropped into the saddle and kicked Cinder back the way they'd come, long knife leveled at the back of a man wearing the three horsehair falls of Qori Buqa—now of the infant Tsaagan Buqa—who crossed blades with a Tsareg man old enough that by rights he should have been back with the wagons and women.

Except this time, half the Tsareg women were fighting as well.

Chagatai plunged his blade into the back of a Re clan brother, the shock knocking his body back against his armored coat and the high cantle of the saddle. This was no ordinary war. And yet, it was no different from every other.

THE FEET OF THE CITADEL OF TSAREPHETH WERE BURIED IN MASSES OF wildflowers. Tsering stumbled down the rocky lower slope of the Island-in-the-Mists, running flatly toward the guarded stair. A thousand steps led up the face of the great white stone bulwark that spanned the pass between mountains and she hurtled toward them without hesitation, trusting that the guards would know her.

The guards did know her; they drew together at first, but when she ran up they lowered their spears and stepped aside. What they thought of a wizard last seen heading for the northern mountains sprinting up shouting, she did not ask. She suspected the Citadel staff in general had a lot of opinions about wizards she was better off not knowing.

Travel and life in the camp had hardened her, but the stairs were not easy to manage at the breakneck pace she took them at. By the time she reached the battlement, Yongten-la awaited her, his arms folded and his hands tucked inside his black cotton sleeves.

She doubled over, dropped to her knees. When she tried to speak, someone held a cup of millet beer to her lips and she was forced to drink three swallows before they would take it away again.

"Wizard Tsering," said Yongten-la. "Why such haste?"

More evenly, now, between heavy breaths, she told him.

IT SEEMED THAT EDENE WAS NEVER GOING TO RUN OUT OF NEW REASONS to feel gratitude to Hrahima. The most recent was the ease with which Hrahima and Besha Ghul brought her through the tunnels below Ala-Din. Edene more than once found herself rubbing at the empty place where her finger had been, longing for the smooth courageous certainty that had come with the Green Ring. She wished it even more so when the last great stone door—after the straight stair and the winding stair—opened to Besha Ghul, and not to her. She had been a goddess, she realized now. And she had given it up to be a girl.

I will regret it all my life, she thought. And then she thought, *And if I had not, I would have regretted that as well.*

Once they were inside the compound, however, it was she who led them. She who knew the way to the Rukh's perch, and she who had cleaned and cared for him when she, too, was caged in this aerie. They met only one guard—an old man—and Hrahima smashed his head into a wall before he could gurgle. The Cho-tse bowed to the corpse and apologized. Edene simply stepped over the blood.

And then they were in the tunnel that led out to the Rukh's perch, and Edene realized that this was for her, her only—and that the others would have to stay behind. She felt herself trembling and wondered, *is this what it is to be human? To know fear? Or is it merely cowardice?*

She set her foot in the passageway and walked on.

The Rukh was waiting for her.

It knew her step, it knew her scent. She had served as its handmaiden once, and here she was again. It stared at her, crimson crest fluffed, first out of one vast gold-gray eye and then out of the other.

She wondered how long it had been abandoned here. Someone had been feeding it—that was plain—but the nest was filthy, caked with guano and redolent with carcasses, and its long primaries had gone unclipped through the last molt. The shackle on its leg had galled it viciously. It stood with that foot drawn up, the talon balled tight in a fist. Edene wondered if it could even open it.

"Hello, handsome," she told it. Then, when it cocked its head and cheeped at her—a cheep the size of a mountain range, but somehow encouraging nonetheless—she added, "If you promise not to eat me, I brought a chisel."

SHAHRUZ SEEMED TO THINK THEY WERE WINNING, THOUGH EVEN FROM the height and with a spyglass, it was hard to see what was going on. The first fury of the storm had broken, the clouds now lifting and giving the twins a better view of the battlefield—but everyone below was black with Song mud now, and the valley they fought in had become a bloody mire. On the far side of the river, one vast flagstone of the Dragon Road hung mostly unsupported over a smoking crater, and the screams of an injured indrik-zver dominated even the frightful sounds of the rest of the battle. Two more had been killed in the explosion, and a third lay broken-spined on this side of the river, forelegs scrabbling intermittently. The cannon mounted to its howdah had exploded.

The three remaining indrik-zver spread terrible carnage among a company of Song monks, trampling everything that did not run from their paths, even though the hide of all three bristled with Qersnyk arrows. One suddenly shrieked and went down, thrashing; Saadet managed to trace the flight of the arrow that had felled it to a woman using a Western-style longbow, well-back from the line of battle, who stood in the stirrups of an Asitaneh horse.

Tsaagan Buqa hung in his cradleboard beside her knee. Saadet stroked her son's soft head and ignored Shahruz's sharp disdain for her *unnatural* child. She wished she could un-hear her brother's opinion that perhaps, if she were not an *unnatural* woman, her child might have been born whole, and not some Qersnyk half-thing, an abomination against the Scholar-God.

Ümmühan, shrouded in veils on the gray mare beside Saadet, touched her knee and said, "Can you see Mehmed Caliph's troops from here?"

"There," Saadet said, pointing. "They're pushing the enemy center back. Do you see the blue banners?" She handed Ümmühan the spyglass and watched as the poetess rearranged her veils to use it. She managed the telescope like an expert, and Saadet quickly shifted her attention back to the battle. *Where is Re Temur?*

The shadow of the Rukh passed overhead, a hurtling blur. Saadet could just make out the streaming pale robes of al-Sepehr on its back as it rocked sharply, as if a strong wind had struck it broadside and then battered it again from the opposite side. The damned wizards.

Saadet slipped the rifle al-Sepehr had given her from the saddle sheath. The rain had tapered off to a fine mist, now. She cast her eye over the churned mire below.

"Ümmühan," she said. "Paian, Esen, you too. Look for wizards. And their barbarian princeling, too, if you spot him. Unless he's too much a coward to come out and fight for his own empire."

Iskandar had held his Dead Men back, awaiting the moment when Kara Mehmed committed his troops. In the chaos, he missed it, realizing that the caliph's forces had charged only as they crushed into Temur's lines like a boulder bouncing downhill. The blue banners were sodden with rain and smeared with mud; the colors of the cloth-draped helms muted in gray light. But he heard the shouting, the familiar lilt of Uthman battle-commands, and drew his own paltry force of half-a-dozen warriors around him.

Their red uniforms were makeshift, more patchwork tabards than proper coats, and none of them matched the others. The cloth had been scavenged from all over the camp—including one of the lady Diao's silk dresses—and not a rag of it was the proper shade of crimson.

It mustn't matter.

The moment came. The Dead Man on Iskandar's left unfurled the personal banner of the Uthman Caliphs: blue, for the caliphate and the Scholar-God, and charged with a golden lion. As one, seven men on seven horses shouted; seven men and seven horses charged. Iskandar found the voice of an old warrior deep within himself, and knowing that Hong-la would be catching his words, amplifying them, sending them ringing around the battlefield, he shouted, "Loyal men of the caliphate! You were told my own Dead Men turned against me and slew me in my bed. That is a lie. Loyal men of the caliphate! Kara Mehmed is an usurper and a traitor! Loyal men of the caliphate, TO ME!"

AL-SEPEHR HAD THE PERFECT VANTAGE POINT WHEN UTHMAN CALIPH'S booming, amplified voice blasted across the valley, and Mehmed Caliph's men began to turn on one another. He could watch the wave of chaos spread from the front, where only a moment before they had been beating back Temur's pathetic excuse for an army. Al-Sepehr's forces were superior, not just in numbers and in armaments, but in communication. He had the Rukh's offspring to carry messages and do his bidding, and the Rukh herself as a great, mobile platform from which he could see the entire battle and relay his commands.

He was crushing the enemy. They were being beaten back. And even this brawl among the factions for two caliphs couldn't derail his eventual victory. All it would do was leave the caliphate in even further disarray; easier pickings for al-Sepehr. He had other weapons in reserve; perhaps they could stay there.

Al-Sepehr was still thinking that when the third army appeared at the back of the valley and fell on his own rearguard with the ferocity of steppe wolves tearing prey down in the hungry teeth of winter.

THE GHULIM WERE MORE EFFECTIVE THAN HONG-LA HAD IMAGINED, sowing chaos and confusion all out of proportion to their numbers—and raising the morale of their allies with the proof that even if there was no sign of Temur, the young Khagan's plan was working. Down the valley below, Temur's troops rallied against what had pushed them back, and pushed forward again. Al-Sepehr's line wavered; the troops from the caliphate had dissolved into a whirl of undisciplined self-slaughter; the Kyivvans alone seemed to be regrouping.

The mountains rang, suddenly, with the echoes of distant thunder—no, not thunder. Hoofbeats, rolling the length and breadth of the valley. A sound like a cavalry charge that was also like a mad carillon of more bells than Hong-la had ever imagined.

He whipped his head around in time to see the clouds split wide, roll back like snapped canvas. The blue sky above them blazed fierce and hot, and from it pounded a stream of horses, mares in impossible bright colors, led by a man hunched low and clinging like a burr in the mane of a shining liver bay.

The Tsareg and other Qersnyk reserves at the bottom of the height Hong-la and Zhang commanded began to make their own noise, whooping and screaming, as the mares ran in among them, slowing only long enough for a rider to swing up onto each back and find his seat before they lengthened stride again.

"KILL THEM," AL-SEPEHR SAID TO THE RUKH. HE POINTED TO THE GRAY, toothy monsters falling upon his army's flank. "Kill them now."

THE RUKH FOLDED ITS WINGS AND STOOPED LIKE A HAWK, BEAK EXTENDED like an arrow toward the ghulim company. Hong-la had seen this before. His hand moved, fingers clutching, calling up the shield—

A cream-and-emerald blur from the right of his field of vision hurtled across the sky and slammed against the Rukh, knocking her spiraling. Afrit! And on his back, wielding the wall of her wards like a battering ram, all in black armor—rode the Wizard Samarkar.

YONGTEN-LA LED TSERING DOWN TUNNELS SHE KNEW EXISTED, BUT WHICH she had never explored. Past the dark chambers where new wizards sat their vigils, into the warm bowels of the earth. He brought her through the sulfur-reeking caverns where the hot springs boiled up in the heart of the Cold Fire; the steam rising from the swift river they trotted alongside made her feel dizzy and sick.

Soon enough, they left the water behind. Now they must skirt great orange pools of molten sulfur, and sulfur-falls that burned with a shining blue flame. Yongten-la wrapped them in the cool silver light of his wards, filtering the air they breathed so they were not overcome by heat or fumes. The floor underfoot, the walls of the cavern, were melted-and-puddled fantasias of crumbly yellow stone, as if they navigated the remains of an enormous candle.

"What if the body's under all this mess?" Tsering asked.

Yongten-la said, "We're going to ask directions. Here."

A face loomed out of the mist, and smoke—tendrils and jaws that Tsering knew, attached as they were to a translucent gray-white shape with bright blue eyes blinking along its length on either side. The mist dragon Great Compassion Turquoise Stone laced one set of talons through the other and said, "Have you found the dragon in you yet, Tsering-la?"

She stopped in her tracks, uncomfortable heat filtering up through the sulfur underfoot. She wasn't sure where she found the courage to speak, let alone to speak insolence. But she raised her voice anyway and answered, "I'm not looking for a dragon today. We have come here for the body of a man."

IT WAS HARDER TO HAMMER THE RUKH LOOSE THAN EDENE HAD EXPECTED, and the noise attracted a crowd. Besha Ghul and Hrahima were kept busy guarding the tunnel, and they were all lucky that the warriors among the Nameless were either scattered around the civilized world making skinned bodies appear in marketplaces, or had gone to fight Temur's army in Song.

"We're not getting out of here through this route," Hrahima called, after a particularly vicious series of thuds and cries. "I don't suppose you have another idea?"

"Jump?" Edene called back, and kept chiseling.

At least the Rukh's nest shielded them from arrow and gunfire from below, and the Rukh itself sheltered Edene with broad wings while she worked, so no projectiles fell on her from above. She worked in a ring of its curious offspring, ranging in size from eagle to heron, jostling shoulder-to-shoulder among the limbs of the enormous nest.

At last, she pounded the bolt free, and the shackle fell from the bird's thick ankle. She tossed the chain away—or dragged and swung it, rather; it was too heavy to *toss*.

The bird was staring down at her when she raised her eyes again.

"Go on," she said. "Get out of here."

The bird reached for her, its long neck bending double as if it groomed its breast, or turned an egg. Edene half-flinched, expecting a sharp bite to snap her in half—but the wickedly curved beak only nudged her.

The Ruhk, still balanced on one leg, pushed its shackle-galled foot toward her.

Hesitantly, she reached and touched it. Warm; scaly. It did not pull away.

"Oh," she said. Then she called to Hrahima and Besha: "Fall back! We have a ride!"

They clutched the Rukh's legs—Edene and Besha on one side to counterbalance Hrahima on the other—and Edene shrieked aloud when the bird fell into flight. She held on to the tree-trunk–like limb with all her strength, feeling the rush and swoop of the wind as the Rukh dove, without ceremony, earthward—and then the pull as it leveled off more gently than she would have expected. Which was good, that gentleness, or she would have wound up bouncing, smeared, across the desert ground.

It seemed to know where it was taking them, and set down not far from the door into Reason's Ways. Hrahima, Besha, and Edene tumbled away from it, massaging cramped limbs, and collapsed briefly to the ground in the shadow of its wings.

"I wonder if that's the first time a cat has gotten a ride from a bird," Hrahima said. She shook and fluffed herself, and added, "There's no way we're getting a Rukh back through that door."

"Not a grown one," Edene said. "But will this one not lend us one of his chicks as a messenger and emissary?"

THE RUKH ROLLED, BRINGING HER TALONS UP, FLAPPING CONVULSIVELY. Her head snaked sideways and her massive beak snapped—but Afrit was no longer where she struck. He leaped aside, snorting, as Samarkar slapped the great bird sideways with a sharp buffet of wind. She reoriented and beat hard to get above them; Afrit spun and sprinted, zigzagging, while Samarkar whirled a ward of green light over their heads. Still the great bird's strike missed them by less than the length of Samarkar's arm. Pinions slapped Afrit's shoulder and Samarkar's thigh, knocking the young stallion sideways.

He staggered on air, limping, and turned to face the Rukh as she climbed again, her wings pounding the air with a sound like heavy drums. Across the space between them, Samarkar saw al-Sepehr's scowl, the trailing streamer of his veil knocked askew and blowing back, slipping from about his neck in a coil. He raised a hand, a dagger in it, and Samarkar sent a wand of light darting out to knock the blade aside.

The Rukh snapped, a blow solid enough to crack Samarkar's ward and leave her sagging in the saddle. Afrit sprawled back, climbed to his feet again.

Suddenly, Hong-la rose beside Samarkar, his petaled skirts blowing wide in the wind that lifted him. One big hand slapped, as if he issued a challenge—and a buffet of wind hurled the Rukh back, wings trailing, as if a giant had punched her in the breast.

SAADET LAID HER CHEEK AGAINST THE RIFLE, FEELING THE METAL COOL AND bright in the sudden return of the sun. Somehow, it had become evening; twilight would be upon them soon. Hard-sunset, and Soft-dawn.

Had the battle really raged all day? Here in Song, there was nothing to stop it from raging through the night as well. Nothing but exhaustion. Which army would falter first?

The wizards rose to meet al-Sepehr; the male wizard knocked the Rukh aside. Saadet did not know she smiled. A clear shot, with no danger of striking al-Sepehr. Her finger found the trigger. First, the bitch Samarkar. And then this other wizard.

Ümmühan shouted, "I see Re Temur! I think I do!" and Saadet's shot went wide.

TEMUR RODE AMIDST TUMULT, AMIDST THE GLEE OF MOUNTED WARRIORS who had been held back from battle and now felt they had some slaughter to make up for. He heard their shouting, their cries of delight and bloodlust, the bugling challenges of the Ideal Mares. On every side, war horses and warriors threw themselves at the enemy with wild abandon.

He should have felt the lust of battle himself. But all he felt was the peace of the bargain he had made, and a sort of worried sorrow, even as his arrows flew, his long-knife carved flesh and chopped bone.

He still had things he wanted to say to Edene, and to Samarkar.

But they were reclaiming the valley, carving their way through al-Sepehr's troops toward the pincer of their own ghulim allies. Bansh was a demon beneath him, and his heart was empty of battle-song.

Perhaps that was why he was the first to see and hear the chiming demon-things descending from the torn clouds that still flocked the sky. They fell upon the battlefield, and with shrieks and the sound of struck crystal, ripped into the fray without regard for banners.

EDENE PLUNGED THROUGH THE DOOR FROM REASON INTO THE LANTERN-light of the great cavern, her arms full of struggling raptor. She opened them wide, cast the young Rukh toward the gloaming far above. Blood ran freely from her scratched hands and cheeks; the djinn's armor had protected her chest and arms.

Behind her, Hrahima and Besha Ghul each in turn released their feathery cargos.

They did not stand to watch the long-necked birds beat skyward, but set out up the trail to the road at a run.

Behind them, more running feet belonged to the first of a group of black-coat wizards charging out of the Way from Reason, none of whom Edene had ever seen before.

AS TWILIGHT FELL, THE GLASS DEMONS CAME, AND AL-SEPEHR GLORIED. Their razored claws flashed. Their obsidian wings sliced. Here; here was the sacrifice. Here was the power. Here was the control and the understanding he had sought, the effortless puissance, the world held in the palm of his hand. Though the Rasan Wizards—one on her pale horse, one kicked forward by winds of his own summoning—chased and harried him, he waved them aside as the insignificant creatures they were. A gnat might trouble him more.

Gnats could carry disease.

He had studied. He had prayed. He had worked his benedictions. Here was the chance to win a godhead so long denied his worthy an-cestor. Here he was: al-Sepehr no longer, but the Sorcerer-Prince incar-nate. Not just a subject and worshiper to the Scholar-God, but Her equal, Her superior, Her fit master and lord.

The Rasan Wizard's trick of an amplified voice was a good one. He understood it, recognized its mechanism—a forced vibration of what they limitedly considered the process of air—and took it for his own. On his first attempt to speak, even without sorcery, the voice was wrong—but he had worn many skins in his time, and spoken in many voices.

He tried again, and this time the voice that rolled from his lips was his own familiar resonance and timbre. As the Rukh's scions flocked around her, he severed the straps that his past self had used to bind himself to the saddle. He stood in the stirrups, summoned up the resonant power of his mimicked spell, and in his own true voice declaimed, "I am Sepehr al-Rachīd, called the Sorcerer-Prince, called the Joy-of-Ravens! You believed in me, and I have come!"

Below him, the fighting stuttered, broke apart, did not stop entirely because still the glass demons struck and slashed and tried to slay. But men and women, where they could, turned their faces up to the sky and stared, dumbstruck.

The Rukh twisted away under him. The air caught him, bore him up as the great bird turned to snap, beak wide. With a negligent gesture he struck her from the sky.

As Soft-dawn broke, he called the blood ghosts. And they came.

27

Great Compassion Turquoise Stone winked—or blinked—the lucent blue eyes all along its nearer side closing and opening in a wave. Did dragons smile?

The dragon reached out with one moonstone-scaled, translucent forelimb—neither quite a leg, nor an arm. The taloned appendage it crooked beneath Tsering's chin, however, was definitely a hand.

Tsering held herself perfectly still, except in allowing the dragon to lift her face for inspection. The dragon was as chill as the mist from which it took its name. Its breath wrapped Tsering as if she had climbed into clouds, and she found herself cool, soothed, swept clean of pains and stiffnesses that had grown so customary she only noticed them in the absence. After the stench of the brimstone caverns, the relief of it came as a blessing.

The coolness, the moisture came with a memory. She had sat alone in darkness, clad only in her loincloth and halter, her flesh prickled up in cold. Water dripped somewhere in the black basalt chamber, inciting thirst. She was dry and she could drink, if she groped through the dark to find it.

Looking into the dragon's eyes, Tsering recollected her vigil. She found the place in her center where she had gone, where she had tried to remain throughout that long cold failure, and she fell into the silence there. Something in the dragon's gaze questioned her, held her accountable—even as something else forgave.

Failure, little wizard?

As if in a dream—as if she shouted orders to herself from a great height and a great distance, Tsering lifted up her fingers and snapped. No light sparked from them.

You failed to find your power. Does that mean you failed in your vigil?

Tsering realized her mouth had dropped open. She shut it slowly, considering.

She had not made her own way out of the chamber. After five days, they had come to find her. And they had carried her. She knew this because Yongten-la had told her, later. She had been in no state to recall.

Some things are beyond strength, Tsering-la. For humans, and for dragons.

Distantly, she was aware of Yongten-la taking her elbow, but all she could see was the thousand eyes along the length of Great Compassion Turquoise Stone, and every one focused on her.

Then we die.

The dragon bowed. *That is indeed what happens.*

As if a dream had shattered, Tsering-la found herself snapped back into herself. The dragon turned away, reached out, and dragged its half-material talons through the molten sulfur. They came out tangled in a mess of semi-articulated human bones, a heap of ribs and long bones, a sulfur-encrusted skull lolling on an accreted length of spine.

What the dragon said next, it said aloud. "Here is the corpse of your enemy. What will you have me do now?"

Tsering looked at the bones. They could be anything. But dragons did not lie.

She thought of the Rukh. She wasn't sure after that what she thought anymore.

"Here is the dragon in me, Great Compassion Turquoise Stone," she said. "You must come with us to Lung Ching, and bring those bones."

The dragon tilted its head like a cat examining prey, so that its beard swept from side to side. "Then you must ride."

"Ride?!"

But Yongten-la still cupped Tsering's elbow in his hand, and now he steered her forward. She found herself *climbing* the dragon, one boot on its elbow, its scaled flesh cool and half-unreal beneath her hands. A long scramble across its shoulder, Yongten-la behind her, and then she slung a leg over the ridge of its neck and settled between the fluffed spines. The eyes beneath her knees lidded themselves, sealed in the dragon's hide as Yongten-la slid into place behind her.

"Here is the dragon in you," he whispered in her ear.

Shocked, she laughed. And clutched the spines before her as, with a rush she had not expected and should have—with a whistle like winter winds—the mist-dragon in all its endless sinuous length began to fly back out along the caverns from which they had come, and then through caverns Tsering had never seen before.

They burst out over Tsarepheth, wreathed in mists and vapors. Great Compassion Turquoise Stone did not so much arc across the sky as writhe and coil against it, like a swimming snake. Below, Tsering could see the lines of wizards and imperial guards filing up the slope of the Island In The Mists, heading for the Way into Reason and thence to Dragon Lake.

She prayed they were in time. And then she thought of the size of the doorway, and the size of the dragon—but before she could mention anything, she realized that the world around them was getting larger—no. The dragon was shrinking, and they were shrinking with him.

Of course, that made sense. Dragons could be any size at all.

"Tsering!"

Yongten-la's urgency snapped her head around. She stared at him, then followed where he was pointing.

Above them, against a sky stained gray and bright with the last glow of the sun, loomed the ash and smoke cloud from the Cold Fire. And within it, twisting and coiling just as did Great Compassion Turquoise Stone, hung the form of an enormous dragon. Lightning flashed in her eyes; a glow of embers flared behind the fangs of her open maw. The smoke tore behind her, a full moon gleaming beside her head like a smooth, incomprehensible pearl.

"Mother Dragon!" Tsering whispered, her chest aching as if someone had punched her in the heart.

Great Compassion Turquoise Stone's sides fluttered between her legs as he chuckled. He shifted his grip on the bones dripping between his claws and said, "We are all the Mother Dragon, Tsering-la."

As Sepehr raised his palm beside his cheek and with the back of his hand struck the Rukh streaking like a meteor, wings trailing, from the sky, Samarkar felt her courage fail. It skipped in her chest, kicked like a caged bird in her belly, cringed and crumpled. Afrit pawed clouds, shaking out his reins. She knew he felt her distress. But she was watching Sepehr borrow her own spells, just from observation, and those of Hong-la.

How did you fight a sorcerer so powerful, so learned he could copy anything you did, just by watching it? Below, the noise of combat changed. Samarkar had lost sight of Hong-la. She heard shrieking, screams.

She was alone in the sky with Sepehr.

Then Sepehr cackled like an old woman cheating at cards, and Samarkar found a shred of herself again.

"Come and get me, you nothing!" she shouted, using the amplification trick herself this time. "I am the Wizard Samarkar!"

His hand came up, fingers bent to his thumb as if he meant to burst the clock of an invisible dandelion. He flicked them open and blew across, and a streak of bruised light leapt from his fingertips toward Samarkar.

A purple-black explosion blossomed beside her with the dull whump of concussed air. Her wards were back up already. Reflexively, she slammed the entirety of her will behind them, and still felt them flex and bow under the force. Afrit staggered a step—

—his ears went back, and he charged.

Samarkar's courage might have failed her; Afrit's flagged not once. He was a cataract; a winter storm; a thunderhead sunlicked and towering, lashed in the rain-veils of his mane and tail. As if he were cast of the shining impervious metal he resembled, he raced at the would-be godling with no hesitation at all.

He was everything his name promised and more. And Samarkar could not bear to disappoint him by being less herself, no matter what transpired. That explosion—how had al-Sepehr done that? Was it something she could manage herself?

No, she thought. Now is not the time for experiment.

She focused her wards, hardened them. Slammed them before her into a moving wall with all of Afrit's unearthly momentum behind it. Sepehr raised a hand, palm flat this time—just as negligent a gesture as before.

Samarkar braced herself against the saddle. The force when her wards struck Sepehr shattered them into spinning plates of blue-green light, like shattered glass, like shattered jade. She felt as if she, too, had ridden into a wall. Air punched from her. Afrit staggered, missed Sepehr.

As he ran past, out of the corner of her eye Samarkar saw Sepehr raise his hand in the flicking gesture again. She threw her weight against Afrit, curving him; there was no time to collect her wards again. The explosion streaked the sky like one of Hong-la's celebratory fire-chrysanthemums. The explosion scorched and deafened her. But they were on their feet still and moving, Afrit zigging and zagging across the sky as if they were engaged in a game of buzkashi.

Assembling her wards again, Samarkar glanced back over her shoulder to see Sepehr streaking after.

TEMUR HAD SEEN THE DAWN MISTS BOIL AND TEAR THAT WAY BEFORE. HE'D seen the vapory shapes detach themselves and drift earthward, their eyes as white as their wounds. He witnessed it now and—ducking the whistling pass of a glass demon—he reached for his riding crop with the whistle carved in the butt end, and for the bag of salt he'd kept in his sash ever since the morning when Edene had been stolen.

Tsareg Oljei had established a system of warning signals, should the encampment be attacked. Temur blew the one for blood ghosts now, and salted his knife as he heard it spread. Bansh's hooves sucked in mud, thumped wetly on a body in the mire. An Ideal Mare as red as heart's-blood raced past, a whooping warrior standing in her saddle. He glimpsed Afrit above, heard the unmistakable ring of hooves on clear sky, and knew that he—and Samarkar on his back—meant to charge the transfigured al-Sepehr. Where was Hong-la?

Where was Hong! Temur reined Bansh around, intent to follow, and realized—

Men were not fighting men any longer, nor were men fighting

ghulim. Temur saw an unhorsed Qersnyk wearing the three falls of Tsaagan Buqa back to back with Master War; he saw a Kyivvan lean from a ladder on the shoulder of an indrik-zver at the lumbering gallop to scoop one of Nilufer's men-at-arms from the path of a glass demon's stoop. Swords, arrows, talons turned now to fighting the horrors from the sky.

But command and discipline had evaporated, and half the armies were in rout.

"Hold out," Temur shouted. "The ghosts flee with full sun! To me, to me! To me!"

Did the rout turn? He could not tell. The flight of those closest to him checked.

He heard a voice take up his name. Another.

Temur! Re Temur! To Re Temur!

The sky behind Temur flared with light, so sharp and thousand-colored it cast his and Bansh's shadow before them as heavy and dark as a stair. He shaded his eyes and turned—

—to see black coats by the dozens, and the army parting before them as they advanced. Each one shone like a lantern, like a baby sun, like a star as Mother Night hung it in her veils. The tallest among them, hatless, crop-headed even in silhouette, raising his hands—a savage glare—a patchwork wave of brilliance sliding across the battlefield just above head-height to a man on horseback, as if somebody were closing a box with a lid.

The Wizards of Tsarepheth were there, and the Imperial Guards surrounded them. They were warding the entire battlefield. The knot of grim sorrow and ferocity in Temur's belly broke, unfolded, blossomed into unexpected hope. *Mother Night, how did I misunderstand you?*

Temur heard Sepehr laughing, heard Afrit's stallion scream. He reined Bansh around; they must outrun the wards to help Samarkar. But if ever a mare could outrace light itself, this was her.

Just before the light would have passed over Temur, something punched him sharp between the shoulders. The impact knocked him sideways and Bansh staggered too. Then he was on his side, in the mud, seeing a glimpse of her mud-sheathed legs straddling him through the slit in his helmet knocked askew.

From very far away, someone was screaming his name.

✳   ✳   ✳

TEMUR WAS ALREADY GONE WHEN EDENE REACHED HIM. SHE KNEW BEFORE
she fell to her knees in the bloody mire of the battlefield, before she
tried to lift his helm and felt the spill of all his blood hot as boiling
water across her hands. There was a hole in the center of his armor-
coat she could have put her thumb into; he was limp and stank of piss.
Besha Ghul crouched beside her but did not touch. Hrahima had
caught the reins of Temur's mare.

"Edene—" the tiger said.

The reins slipped from Hrahima's fingers when Edene snatched
them. Bansh was moving before Edene got a leg over her, but this was
not her first time vaulting into the saddle of a running mare. Three
strides, five: she was settled. Five strides, seven: they spurted ahead of
the wards. Eight, and Bansh's hooves rang crystalline on air.

There was Samarkar wreathed in emerald flames, black-armored on
the back of her cream-gold steed. There was Sepehr rising before her,
his hands spread wide, a shifting blackness outlining his form like the
opposite of flames. But Edene had her own flames, her own armor, that
the djinn had given her. They whipped high with the speed of Bansh's
hoofbeats, and Edene did not guide the mare toward Sepehr or even
Samarkar.

No; there, on a hilltop opposite, she marked her target. Some horses
and some mounted people, and one of those people raising the long
barrel of a rifle shining in the sun that—just now—touched the peak
of the rise.

Bansh's hooves licked sparks from the sky. Glass demons and a few
dissolving blood ghosts grasped after them. Bansh shouldered them
aside, ran over them. Kicked them to pieces with her flaming feet. They
dragged at her, and somehow, she ran even faster.

Edene leaned close, the mare's sparse mane slapping the side of her
helm. She had no bow, no arrows. Temur's long knife was fallen in the
mud by his hand. She had her dagger. That was all.

The woman on the blood-shouldered gray wore an indigo veil
about her neck. She lowered her eye to the rifle sight. Edene knew her.
Across the closing distance between them, she could see that Saadet
also knew Edene.

The woman beside her, swaddled in veils, clutched her gray mare's mane as the horse skittered away from Bansh's charge. One of the men caught the second gray's reins. The blood-shouldered mare stood like a statue, ears pricked, waiting on this horse that ran at her from the sky. The other man bent his bow back to his ear.

Something struck Edene's shoulder and twisted her in the saddle. Bruised pain numbed her arm, but the djinn's armor held, and an arrow bounced away. She lost the reins. Bansh never hesitated. A bright line of blood creased the side of Bansh's neck, and a moment later the sound of the gunshot rattled Edene's ears. And then she was there, the bay mare piling into the gray, teeth and hooves striking, the thud of flesh on flesh as the gray reared to take the charge.

Edene lunged from the stirrups, that dagger in her fist, and struck Saadet in the chest.

They tumbled to the hard earth, Edene on top. She outweighed Saadet; her armor took what must have been another blow from the man on horseback. Saadet's dagger found a joint in the armor, and new bright pain blossomed, but it was in the shoulder of Edene's already numbed and useless arm. Mares were screaming, and a woman.

Edene thrust, felt her knife scrape, bounce. Raised her hand, dove forward. Plunged the blade again.

Saadet kicked once under her and fell still.

And there was nothing. Edene expected the next blow, could not even find the strength to cower from it. Nothing fell. She put a hand under her knee and yanked her leg up so her foot was flat. Pushed down on it with both hands, abandoning her dagger. Blood all over her hands, blood smearing her armor. The bruises ached now.

Her breasts ached too, and slicked the inside of her armor with oozing milk. A baby was wailing.

She stood.

Bansh loomed behind her, head snake-low, teeth bared, holding the blood-shouldered gray at a distance. The wailing baby was in a cradleboard strapped to the mare's shoulder. The warrior was frozen on the back of his mare, his knife still lifted. The other man— wearing the blue knots of a shaman-rememberer—held him back with an outstretched arm, and still clutched the Uthman woman's mare's reins in his other hand.

The baby wailed still.

The veiled woman slid from the back of her horse and walked up to Edene. She paused before her, head bent, eyes down, as if waiting for a blow. When Edene offered nothing but the acknowledgment of her eyes, the woman said, "I will give the death rite to my friend."

She slipped past Edene to kneel in the blood beside the dead woman, and Edene barely found the strength to turn her head. She raised her eyes to the shaman-rememberer, noticing absently that the light had barely moved, that there was still shadow in the valley.

"I am Tsareg Edene Khatun," she said, reaching to open the breastplate on her armor. Anything to stop the wailing, and the ache in her breasts. "This is Bansh, first of her line. Will you *please* give me that child?"

HRAHIMA COULD HAVE STOPPED EDENE. SHE EVEN THOUGHT OF IT IN time. But she could not make herself feel any desire to, and so she stood aside and watched Bansh's heels flash away through the muck until she climbed into the sky. Then the tiger knelt beside Temur in the mud.

She pulled his helm off and—casting about for a cloak or some other scrap of cloth—made him peaceful on a bloody banner. Besha Ghul helped straighten his limbs and pull his bloody queue across his shoulder. It only took a few moments. All around them, the fighting was over, and the wizards' ward kept the blood ghosts and the glass demons at bay.

Through the ward, Hrahima could see Samarkar's duel with the Sorcerer-Prince, her and Afrit's increasingly desperate evasions. Shields of other colors flew up around her and were shattered as the wizards on the ground tried to help. But that, like Edene, had gone beyond Hrahima's power.

That's not precisely true, my warm one, is it?

You are dead, Hrahima said. *You have left me.* Then she snapped at and bit her wrist savagely, until the blood flowed rich and meaty over her own tongue. She would not hear his voice! She would not respond as if she heard it.

She wasn't sure if it *was* his voice, or her own, that answered, *She has lost her warm one too, and yet she fights on.*

She doesn't know yet—

Oh. The voice had tricked her.

Besha Ghul was beside her, Hrahima only half-aware of the ghul's touch as it tugged at her arm. It could not have moved her unless she allowed it, so in the end it kept her from further savaging herself by shielding her wrist with its own body.

She did not know yet. And Hrahima had the power to tell her.

She crouched beside the monkey-king's body again, laid her blood-streaked paw on his mud-streaked brow. He was warm still, and she knew ... Hrahima knew ... that there was no one to speak his true name and set him free.

He was still in there, or nearby, and it was his doom to become a ghost—eternally and eventually.

But for now, he could help her.

This doesn't mean I forgive you for leaving me, she told the Feroushi in her head.

I forgive you, he answered, and she wished she had not heard him.

The wizards were gathering around her now, and some of the Tsareg—still on horseback—and was that Master War? She did not look up, but by his scent she knew the rustle of black fabric beside her was Hong-la—crouching, and reaching for Temur's pulse before wincing and shaking his head.

Hrahima opened herself, the pain unfathomable, the howling loss, stealing the breath from her lungs and the blood from her veins until she was cold, cold, cold. She felt the emptiness, the place where Feroushi and her Khraveh had been and were no more. And through that emptiness she felt Temur—what was left of Temur—confused and startled, disorganized in his transition between states, just like any being. Trying, like a new foal, to find his limbs and move them with his will. But he had no limbs, and his will was a shattered, drifting thing.

Carefully, Hrahima gathered him up. All the shards and wisps and fragments. She gathered him into her arms, the arms of her imagination, and she turned him so he would not see the empty, despairing place where her mate and cub were not. She showed him Samarkar.

Your monkey-wizard needs you, little king. She needs your strength right now.

She felt him understand.

"Hong-la," she gasped, opening her eyes. "Drop the wards. *Drop the wards right now.*"

*   *   *

Samarkar felt the other wizards loose their wards in unison, in a manner that could only be an intentional response. She whipped her head around to see what was happening, and might have died in a shower of bruised-black fire if Afrit—already staggering with tiredness—had not still danced aside and saved them both. He dodged behind one of the limestone pinnacles, found his footing on its stone, and charged up to the top of it. She thought he might have leapt back into the fray, even, one last doomed charge—but she reined him in. She'd dismount here. She'd save the colt at least, and fight the end on her own two feet.

But before she could swing out of the saddle, there—something—a pale streak blurred from the earth in the center of a ring of black coats. A lance of corpse-light whipped past her, though Afrit snapped at it and screamed—and blazed right into the face of the pursuing Sepehr.

She could not see, not clearly, but she had a glimpse of . . . a blood ghost? And its clawed hands plunged in Sepehr's face? Sepehr scream-ing, taken by surprise—

Hong-la tugged at her power, a polite request, and she gave it up to him freely. Feeding him, pushing hard, willing to trust whatever he might do.

The spear of rainbow light that sprang from the earth below to transfix the distracted Sepehr had a brilliant lance of blue-green like the finest jade laced through all its other colors. Hong-la gave it the force and the guidance, but it was Samarkar's magic that bound it together.

Sepehr screamed. Convulsed. And then choked softly like a man run through and sagged there, pinned on the lance Hong-la had forged from his companions' wards.

All around the battlefield, eyes turned skyward. Sepehr hung like a puppet, arms akimbo, head twisted. The blood ghost offered one last slash to his motionless face and then, touched by the rays of the Soft-dawn, blew away as if it were a mist.

Samarkar let out a breath—

And Sepehr lifted up his head. The skin of al-Sepehr's face was split, brow to chin, and sagging back from a skeleton grin. Blood dripped, thick and black, down his chest. He reached up and grasped the impal-ing energy in one fist, and though his palm smoked, began to squeeze.

The pain of his strength split Samarkar's head like an axe. She gagged, and suddenly glad of the suffering she'd endured from the Ways of Reason, she focused her concentration anyway. The impaling beam thinned. Flickered. Brightened again. She heard a gasp from be-low as one of the wizards assisting Hong went to her knees.

Sepehr cast his shining eyes across them all. Then he looked at her, in particular, and smiled. "Little wizard, they believe in me more than they do you. I'll wear your skin tomorrow."

She sat. She could do nothing more. All her strength was Hong-la's, and Afrit heaved with exhaustion between her legs. His head hung. She rather thought hers did too.

"Sepehr is *dead*, Mukhtar ai-Idoj!" another voice boomed, amplified until it shook Afrit's ribs between her knees. He picked his head up, ears pricked, tracking. Samarkar turned to follow.

And there was Yongten, and there was Tsering. On the back of a dragon wrought of mist and moonstones, with a sulfur-encrusted mess of bones dripping from its claws.

"Sepehr is dead!" Tsering shouted again, while Yongten beside her made the passes to raise her voice to the heavens. "This is his *corpse*! You are a caricature, a travesty! A swindler! You are not even the force Sepehr al-Rachīd was, that took a god to throw him down. For we are only mortals, and look what we have done!"

He struggled. He was no coward; Samarkar must grant him that. He struggled, and it availed him not. The glass demons shivered into nothing—into blowing black ash and the dust of obsidian. The sun-light blew the last of the blood ghosts away.

And past al-Sepehr's pinioned, failing body—only mortal, all too mortal, just mortal enough in the end—the black wings of a steppe vulture spiraled.

AFRIT LIMPED DOWN THE SKY LIKE AN OLD WARHORSE RETURNING TO THE paddock, and if it had not been air under his hooves, Samarkar would have dismounted to give him ease. As it was, they came to ground not far from Hrahima and the circle of wizards surrounding the im-promptu pallet which supported what remained of Temur.

Afrit still limped. She meant to dismount. But she had no strength in her, and sat slumped in the saddle until Hrahima came to lift her down like a child from its pony.

"Water," Samarkar said. When someone offered her a skin she waved it away. "For the horse." And then she saw. "Oh, stand aside, stand aside—"

She pulled from Hrahima's grasp and ran to him. He seemed uninjured, except the blood that soaked the cloth upon which he lay. A horse huffed the back of Samarkar's neck as she kneeled down in the mud, her armor cutting her thighs. "How?"

"A rifle bullet," said Edene, who was there suddenly, holding Bansh's reins, a baby on her back as if it were the sort of thing anybody might slide on over her armor. "I avenged him."

Samarkar nodded. She lifted off her own helm. The tears dripped down her nose and fell unchecked. *You were a Princess of Rasa. Will you weep where all can see?*

Yes. It seemed she would.

"That was his shade," Hrahima said. "His ghost that saved us at the end." Her tone suggested there was more to the story, and suggested also that it would be useless to ask.

Samarkar heard the beat of wings. She could not open her eyes. She reached out and laid her fingertips on Temur's cool hand as Edene knelt beside her, graceful under the weight of her armor and the child.

The child who was not Ganjin. "Who—"

"Tsaagan Buqa. I killed his mother." Edene shrugged. "He will be a shaman-rememberer when he is grown." She laid a gauntlet flat against the armor over her womb. "It seems I will raise three children, not . . . oh, look, Samarkar."

A steppe vulture hovered over them, over Temur. Its sooty body seemed to bob up and down between undulating wings. Its head—red, warty, featherless—was drawn back into a collar of pale feathers. It had a strange look of wisdom, like an ugly old man.

It settled on Temur's chest and flipped closed its wings. The primary feathers crossed over its back like a pair of swords. Samarkar knew to lean close: there was no doubt in her heart that this was the vulture that had followed them from one end of the world to the other, beneath every conceivable sky.

Edene leaned close with her.

The vulture thrust its head between theirs, and in the human voice of an old man—an old, arrogant, Qersnyk man—it whispered: *Re Temur Qutlugh.*

Twice it whispered, as if to be sure they had heard. It fixed them each with a rheumy, withering gaze. Then it pulled its head back, flipped its wings again to settle them, and waddled off toward the field of corpses as if it had important business there.

"Thank you, Grandfather!" Edene called after it, her gaze unwavering. Samarkar realized she herself had one hand outstretched as if requesting some benediction.

Edene leaned down to Temur to whisper his true name just once into each ear. Samarkar watched, fascinated. When Edene sat back up, she knuckled a tearless eye and said, "Now his ghost can rest, and he can tell his name to the other vultures when they carry him back to the Eternal Sky."

"That bird followed us from Tsarepheth to Ala-Din and back again."

Edene's smile was thin. "Do you think the spirit of Re Temusan Khagan would let so little a thing as death keep him from his family duties?"

Samarkar could easily imagine the spirit of the Great Khagan carried heavenward on such wings, and refusing to move on until the question of his succession was settled to his liking. "If he was anything like Temur," she said, "no."

It was Hrahima who found Hsiung, crumpled among the Kyivvan dead on the Dragon Road, at the edge of Samarkar's crater. The mud had turned his robe the color of the earth, and one hand was cast across his face in a pose of abject surrender. But he did not smell dead, and when Hrahima crouched next to him he moaned softly.

She had a skin of rice wine and trickled some into his mouth. His hand dropped, caught her wrist, and he smiled. Blood crusted his eyelids shut, but the sockets were sunken behind them, and she did not think it would be any use to soak them clean.

"Master War?" he asked, after she fed him a few more spoonfuls of wine.

"Alive," she answered. "You won't be quit of your obligations that easily, old friend."

✸   ✸   ✸

E̲D̲E̲N̲E̲—O̲N̲E̲ C̲R̲A̲D̲L̲E̲B̲O̲A̲R̲D̲ S̲L̲U̲N̲G̲ O̲N̲ E̲I̲T̲H̲E̲R̲ S̲I̲D̲E̲ O̲F̲ T̲H̲E̲ P̲A̲D̲P̲A̲R̲A̲D̲-scha Seat, which fitted Bansh as if she had been born to wear that saddle—found the female Rukh among the rice fields of the Dragon Lake Valley, soaked in mud, surrounded by unhappy villagers, and stunningly alive. She had a broken leg, a wrenched wing, and seemed dazed and disoriented—but the flocks of her younglings surrounded her, and they seemed to be feeding her—and neither she nor they would let anyone approach her.

She drank the muddy water in which she sat, and eventually recovered herself enough to hop and flap to the verge of the lake and bathe in its clearer waters.

On the third day, her mate spiraled out of the translucent sky of Song, and everybody in the vicinity decided they were better off sightseeing from a distance until the Rukhs felt well enough to leave.

O̲T̲H̲E̲R̲ W̲I̲Z̲A̲R̲D̲S̲, N̲I̲L̲U̲F̲E̲R̲'S̲ W̲I̲T̲C̲H̲, A̲N̲D̲ T̲H̲O̲S̲E̲ W̲I̲T̲H̲ S̲O̲M̲E̲ S̲K̲I̲L̲L̲ F̲O̲R̲ I̲T̲ tended the wounded. The Ideal Mares had vanished with the deaths of al-Sepehr and Temur, which was one less problem and one more. To Samarkar fell the administration of the camp and the disposition of the survivors. She was not without help: she had Hong-la, Zhan Zhang, and Jurchadai . . . and Temur's grandfather, who accepted the death of his grandson with a brutal kind of stoicism that worried Samarkar even as she understood it. It was the same look he'd worn when Temur informed him of the death of his daughter. Samarkar hadn't liked it then, either.

But there was not much she could do, other than let him work. Tesefahun buried himself in helping to organize the cleanup efforts. "What about the prisoners?" he asked.

"There are no prisoners. Send them home, or let them stay. I care not; the war is over."

"Kara Mehmed?"

She lifted her eyes at that. "He lives?"

Tesefahun nodded.

"Does Captain Iskandar?"

"He's wounded. But Hong-la thinks he'll make it."

"Then Mehmed is his problem."

"And Mehmed's woman?" Tesefahun paused. "A slave. A poetess. You heard her sing."

"Does she wish to stay with Mehmed?"

"She begs an audience."

"Fine," said Samarkar. "Whatever. She can stay if she wants, and I'll talk to her after the funeral. Oh. Before Tzitzik goes—"

He nodded. "We're already searching the other camp for the skull of Danupati."

"Good," said Samarkar. "She really ought to take that with her, and put it back where it belongs."

Tsareg Sarangerel was serving as Samarkar's runner—her page, in Rasan terms. As Tesefahun was leaving, she poked her head in through the door-hide and said, "Samarkar, there is a smith to see you."

"Send him in."

He was a Qersnyk, and she found she preferred their straightforward approach to all the scraping and cringing. She straightened up on her bolsters and heaped rugs and cushions, wincing when she heard her back crack. "Tea?" she offered.

"No, Doctor," he said, using the Song word. "Thank you." He dipped his head and held a flat cloth packet out to her. "The Khagan ordered this. Before."

She gestured him to lay it down. "I will see that you are paid."

"I was paid," he said, and bowed once quickly—awkwardly—before showing himself out again.

Curiously, she picked it up. It was hard, convex, slightly bumpy within the wrappings. She peeled them back, and found herself holding an ornate chamfron—a horse's face-armor—in beaten gold, studded with cabochon rubies.

"Oh, Temur," Samarkar said. She laid it before her on the carpet and dropped her head into her hands. "I'll see she gets it from you, love."

THERE WERE ENOUGH WOUNDED FOR EVERYONE TO PRACTICE ON A SHARE. Tsering and Hong-la found themselves side by side in the medical pavilions quite often, and Tsering took comfort in his skill, his power, his calm professionalism as she had so often before. She was not prepared, as they scrubbed their hands between patients, for him to treat her with awe.

When she complained, he gave her a sideways look and said, "You will be numbered in the histories of our order, as one of the wizards whose work is to be studied."

"Oh, I'm a regular Tsechen of the Five Eyes," she replied.

"He had power," said Hong-la. "Power is useless without the work of the scholar. And he never rode a dragon, Tsering-la."

She wound a bandage tighter, had to go back and loosen it again. She shrugged. "We are who we pretend to be, they say. And when we stop pretending?"

"Then we're nothing at all." The smile in his voice reminded her that they were wizards, and some of their power grew from that nothingness, and being able to hold its peace and certainty within.

Her face hot, Tsering glanced away. "I'm going to check the amputations for wound fever," she said, and told herself she could not sense the weight of his attention on her shoulders as she ducked and walked away.

ÜMMÜHAN COULD NOT BEAR TO FACE THE WOMAN WHO HAD KILLED SAAdet ai-Mukhtar. But she thought—just barely—that she could stand to talk to the Wizard Samarkar. After all, it was not as if Samarkar were a complete stranger. From within the safety of her scented cage, Ümmühan had watched her and her allies fence verbally with the old caliph. It was better than facing Edene, or—worse—begging asylum from the newly reinstated Uthman Fourteenth. Idly, Ümmühan wondered if history would remember him as Uthman Fourteenth *and* Fifteenth.

It didn't matter, she supposed. One king was as bad as another, unless he was the sort of king who taxed and harassed someone other than you. Or other than the Hasitani.

Still, when Ümmühan was led by her guards into the white-house and before Samarkar, her ostentatious courtesy and self-prostration concealed no little actual awe. The woman wore black, a worn coat and boots and trousers, frayed leather gloves, a thick braid no paler in color. The only brightness on her was the collar of carved jade panels and river pearls at her throat.

Ümmühan snuck another glance between genuflections—and stopped her elaborate self-abasement at once when she caught the exasperated look on Samarkar's face. Ümmühan knelt, finally, her veils in some disarray, and waited.

"Leave us," Samarkar said to unseen guards and attendants.

There was a rustle as they did. When it ended, Samarkar continued. Her Uthman was very good. "Speak, Ümmühan. What do you require of me?"

"I beg my freedom," Ümmühan said. "My master is defeated. I am a spoil of war. I beg of you release me."

"If you are not a slave, poetess, how will you live?"

Ümmühan dared to raise her face. Samarkar was leaning forward, elbows on her knees.

Ümmühan read the expression of honest interest that the wizard wore and said, "I am no mere poetess, Wizard, if you will forgive my impertinence. I am a historian and a scholar. I could be of use to your court."

The wizard sat back, face suddenly a porcelain mask. "You don't want to go back to the caliphate?"

"I would ask a boon of Uthman Caliph," she admitted. "I do think my poetry had some little effect on the troops that turned back to his service. I had been sowing my vipers among their ranks all the long march here. I have . . . some little influence."

"I have heard you sing," said Samarkar. "I do not think you over-brag. I cannot promise on the caliph's behalf, of course, but I can give him your request. What is it?"

"I wish him to protect the temples of the Hasitani," Ümmühan said. "That is all. And perhaps make it easier for young women who wish to study rather than to marry to enter their ranks."

"Huh," said Samarkar. "Well, I'll ask. But elaborate: you wish to stay here? Among barbarians?"

Ümmühan bowed her head. She folded her hands in her kneeling lap and tried to look demure. "There is history here to be written," she said. "There are poems such as have never been heard—in dragon-scale, in stallion's mane, in the actions of God through the hands of men."

"Gods," Samarkar corrected.

Ümmühan let herself smile behind her veil. "We may debate that as much as you wish."

It startled Samarkar into a laugh. "You're a missionary."

"And a historian," Ümmühan agreed. She meant *poet* as part of *historian*, but she imagined the Wizard Samarkar probably understood it.

Samarkar said, "I'll want your oath not to seek vengeance here."

"You have it."

"I'll want your oath you are no agent of a foreign power."

Ümmühan laid herself almost flat on the rugs again. "You have it."

"Oh, sit up," said Samarkar. "We're all spoiled by Qersnyk informality around here. If you keep crawling to people, someone will trip over you."

Silently, Ümmühan obeyed. She sat very still while the wizard studied her.

Abruptly, Samarkar seemed to come to a decision. She said, "I will put you in the charge of the Wizard Tesefahun. His magic is good Falzeen stuff, not my heathen witchery. I'll want to read your poems."

"To censor them," Ümmühan said, understanding.

"Because poetry is a sort of comfort," said the Wizard Samarkar.

THE FIRST TIME BANSH WORE THE RUBY GILT CHAMFRON WAS AT TEMUR'S funeral. He would be exposed to the sky on a platform, left for the carrion birds to bring home to the Eternal Sky, as was the way of his people. But first he would be fixed in a saddle in his armor so he could ride to that final destination as befitted a Khagan.

It had to be Bansh that bore him home, because Saadet's curse was not broken with her death or his, and still no other horse would bear him.

Samarkar found this all a little horrific and macabre. But no one was asking her opinion, just that she ride and observe. That, she could do. And even carry one of Edene's children, slung in a cradleboard on Afrit's withers. Hsiung sat beside them, supported in a sedan-chair for now, until his strength returned. Hrahima draped an arm over Afrit's withers before the saddlebow. She leaned on the colt and the colt leaned on her, just as if they were not prey and predator. Across the open space, Samarkar could see the Dowager Yangchen's set face among the red coats of her guards. Though their eyes met, though perhaps a debt of gratitude was owed for Yangchen's assistance in the final battle, Samarkar had nothing to say to her brother's widow.

The funeral began at Soft-dawn, with all imperial, barbaric pomp and circumstance. Drums were beaten, swords heaped up like jackstraws around the scaffolding. Bansh paced regally along an avenue lined with mounted mourners despite the deadweight on her back—until she came even with Afrit, Edene, Hsiung, Hrahima, and Samarkar. Then she turned and bowed—a horsy scrape, one leg tucked, nose bent to earth in a delicate bend—and reared up, dragging her rein from the hand of the young man leading her.

She crouched back and dug in as if faced with a steep hill. Then she hurled herself up and forward: at a gallop, snorting, she leaped into the sky. Her hooves rang on the air, that familiar crystalline, carrying tone. She whinnied, and Afrit whinnied after her—but she did not turn, and he did not follow.

Buldshak bumped Samarkar's knee. Samarkar felt a pain in her hand and looked down to see Edene clutching it, squeezing her fingers. She glanced over, and Edene's cheeks were glossy-wet, her lashes spiked and shining over her dark, dark eyes.

The sky dimmed swiftly, as if the sun were eclipsed—as if a veil were thrown across it. The bay mare seemed to shimmer as she climbed, her white foot flashing like a star with every stride. The night sky prickled out over them—over a land in Song, guarded by a dragon, which had never before seen a night—and this was a steppe night, thick with stars and moons.

She searched for Temur's moon, reflexively. But of course it was not there. Not at first, and not as the mare and her grisly rider faded from view, as they had once before.

The sky broke black, it was so indigo. The stars in it burned with a hurtful beauty. A light . . . flared.

Flared and shattered, scattered. Samarkar thought of a dropped ember splashing sparks. They blazed brighter, though, rather than dimming, seeming to settle into the darkness and there make nests.

The dozen bright stars and two dozen less bright twinkled mostly in shades of gold and orange, but three near the leading edge of the pattern were ruby-red, and one near the bottom was sharply white.

They flared once more and made an outline, if Samarkar squinted right: a man, on a racing mare, head turned and arms raised to bend a bow. Then they faded and were just bright stars once more.

A bell tolled that none had rung. Hsiung startled in his chair. The indigo night shivered and blew away like a veil stripped by a breeze. One vulture spiraled on an updraft, wings gleaming like beaten bronze in the strong, red, rising sun.